D0879793

LITTLE FORTRESS

Also by Laisha Rosnau

Fiction
The Sudden Weight of Snow

Poetry
Lousy Explorers
Notes on Leaving
Our Familiar Hunger
Pluck

LITTLE FORTRESS

LAISHA ROSNAU

a novel

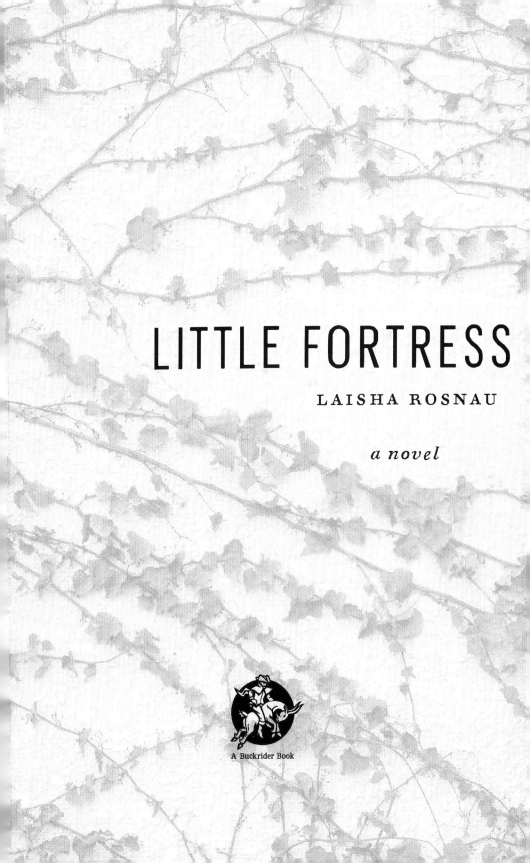

A Buckrider Book

Buckrider Books is an imprint of Wolsak and Wynn Publishers.

Cover image: voyata/iStock
Cover design by: Peter Cocking
Interior design by: Jennifer Rawlinson
Author photograph: Renee Leveille Biebly
Typeset in Adobe Devanagari and Garamond
Printed by Ball Media, Brantford, Canada

10 9 8 7 6 5 4 3 2 1

The publisher gratefully acknowledges the support of the Canada Council for the Arts, the Ontario Arts Council and the Government of Canada.

Buckrider Books
280 James Street North
Hamilton, ON
Canada L8R 2L3

Library and Archives Canada Cataloguing in Publication

Title: Little fortress / Laisha Rosnau
Names: Rosnau, Laisha, 1972- author.
Identifiers: Canadiana 20190159901 | ISBN 9781928088998 (softcover)
Classification: LCC PS8585.O8336 L58 2019 | DDC C813/.6—dc23

For Sveva Caetani, Ofelia Fabiani and Inger-Marie Jüül

Canada, 1945

Could you call that singing? I suppose, though that might be overstatement. Ofelia has tried her voice at opera, to varying success. Once her voice was said to be lovely, but this sound is more like squalling. I try to ignore it, go about my morning. I am in the kitchen, rewashing china and silver, my hands pink and raw in scalding water. The window faces east and a blurred hem of sunlight has begun to saturate the top of the hills along the back of the property.

Ofelia asks that we do this – wash everything after it's been used and once more before we drink or eat from it again. I suppose she wouldn't know if we didn't do so every time, yet I feel as though I should. There are larger things I keep from her. I can be truthful about fulfilling her smaller wishes. When she woke, she sounded so strange. I mean no disrespect to Ofelia. She's still every part a lady, but grief moves through her as feral as a cat. Every few minutes, she lets out a yowl, just as I do when Sveva startles me, suddenly at my shoulder. "Can you not hear that, Miss Jüül?"

I turn from the sink and take a step to the side to give myself some space. I clutch silverware wrapped in a towel between us, the warmth dissolving in the cool morning air.

"Can you not hear her?" Sveva's hair is loose, a mess, her eyes circled in a faint burgundy as though bruised. It is early for her; she was probably still awake until only a few hours ago. Ofelia likes her daughter to sleep beside her each night, but lately Sveva has been staying up well into the night to read, likely to avoid this. She's twenty-seven years old, after all, and her mother is not a sound sleeper.

"I can." I unwrap the spoons, place one on the tray with the teapot and cups. "I hear her." From the clock in the hall, six round chimes. When I was first up, I let the dogs out of their kennels and I can hear them circling the house, barking. "Be thankful it's not earlier."

Sveva blinks, runs her palms over her hair, then reaches for me. "Oh, my Miss Jüüly-Jüül." She pushes me into her chest as though I am the child. She is so tall and I so small that there I am, against the buttons of her gown. "I'm sorry. When she started I was in the middle of a dream, all these garish spirals and spikes folding in on me. I woke up panicked." Sveva lets me go. "I've been up reading physics again. I know, I know. I shouldn't. I should read dear Austen before I sleep – she leaves me with better dreams."

Upstairs, her mother is still keening, although what began as a howl has lessened to moaning. I pick up the tray. "We should go to her."

"Yes, of course."

By the time we reach the top of the stairs, Ofelia's sounds are more like a kitten's mews, and when I knock on her door, it's silent except for her faint, "Yes, come in," in Italian, always Italian. In my lifetime, I've taught myself English, French, Italian, even a little Arabic. We've lived in Canada for over two decades and Ofelia still will not speak much English.

She sits up in bed, pillows behind her, palms smoothing the white bedding. "Oh, look, you're both here!" I see a slight jump in her hands from her lap. "You are both here," she says again with less enthusiasm.

"Of course we are, Mau." Sveva moves around the room, swaying slightly as though she may begin dancing. I wait with the tray; I don't want to be intercepted by her. Ofelia's head is high on the pillows, her lips a slack line.

Sveva drops her shoulders, rolls her neck slightly. She shivers once, rubs her arms. "And I, for one, do not want to be awake this early – let me into bed!" Sveva leaps onto the bed, a six-foot girl in a too-small gown.

Ofelia puts her hand on Sveva's head. "Oh, my Beo."

"My Mau-Mau." Their terms of endearment have no translation, but they've been calling each other these names for years so it doesn't matter.

Sveva closes her eyes, her head large against her mother's slim shoulder. I stand beside the bed without pouring tea. I don't want it to cool too soon, though it is already losing some heat.

Sveva opens her eyes, tips back her head and lets out one sharp laugh. "Oh, Jüül! How ridiculous we are! Two crazy old ladies and yet you stay with us – she stays with us, Mau! Where did you find her, our blessed Scandinavian Virgin?" This is one of their nicknames for me, as inappropriate as it may be.

Ofelia reaches for her daughter. "You are not old, darling. Don't say or believe that for a moment." She lays her hand on Sveva's forehead as though conferring a blessing.

Sveva stretches her arms, twists her wrists. "I may not be old, not technically, but I can feel old, can't I, Mother?"

I've poured the tea now, hand them each a cup. Sveva looks at it as though it's foreign to her. She isn't old, the age that I was before I left for Egypt. At that time, though, I was already considered in danger of becoming an old maid.

"Is it your joints again, Beo?" Ofelia asks.

"No, no." Sveva sits up in the bed, holding her cup and saucer in front of her like a ballast. "Well, it is – it's always my joints to a certain extent – but more than that, it's my mind, Mau, my blasted mind!"

"You and your father and your minds."

"Indeed." It's the first thing I've said in minutes. I open the window. With the rub of window against frame, the dogs start up. "I'll go see to Baby and Onyx. They probably need a good long run today. I may even go out with them."

"A run?" Ofelia asks. "You won't let them out of the gate, will you?"

"Oh no," I say. "No." I shouldn't have said anything. I forget myself sometimes. I've spent years trying to forget myself and at times, it works. "I'll just take them round the property while you two get some more rest."

Ofelia's eyes are already closed. "You're too good to us, Miss Jüül." Perhaps I am. I bend to pick up their teacups, mostly full. Sveva is still lying beside her mother. She looks directly at me, half of her face visible on the other side of Ofelia, and holds her stare for a moment before blinking in rapid succession, as though to communicate something to me. What, I don't know – and I could be imagining things. I often am. I turn and carry the tea service out of the room.

When I open the back door, both dogs are there, panting. They are tall and slim, these hounds. They each reach my waist, but then, I am a small person. Their narrow haunches sway from side to side as their tails wag and they circle me, eager to go. When I let them out of the kennel earlier, it was completely dark, stars sharp against the sky. Now, it's beginning to flush with light, though it's still so cold. It's as though winter is hanging on. Spring would be too much to take now, a reminder of how the war goes on regardless of seasons, years. I walk down the drive, the dogs looping around me. First, I will check the mailbox, then I will decide whether or not I will leave the property. I could skirt the trees and then slip out, hoping my movements would be obscured by foliage, although I'm not sure that there's enough this time of year, the branches skeletal and grey.

We planted more trees nearly a decade ago – and by *we* I mean I told the cook, George, by then the only one in our employ, where to plant them. He muttered the entire time, cursing me in Cantonese, I'm sure, but I didn't leave his side, telling him that it was as the ladies wished. Imagine, staff! They once seemed so plentiful. Now even George is gone, though the trees he planted have taken root. They are lovely little things, but not yet big enough to conceal the house entirely. I know that Ofelia wishes they would grow taller faster. Sveva likes the trees as they are; from the house, she can still see to the street.

A large fence with a gate is our concession for gaps in the trees. Near the end of the drive, I see something move between the slats of wood. The dogs are in a different part of the yard. Between their barking, I hear crunching footsteps on the other side of the fence. I whistle for Baby and Onyx, wait for them to circle back before I open the gate. As I wait, I listen. I don't hear the scuff of gravel as I would if someone was walking away. When the dogs are by my side, I ask them to heel and they do their best, though both are unable to do so in any conventional way. Then I open the gate. A man is there, standing beside the mailbox. A soldier, in uniform. He backs away when I come out with the dogs.

"Officer." I nod my chin toward him.

"Ma'am." It shouldn't surprise me anymore, this term, but it does. To those closest to me, I am forever *Miss*. I suppose I am to myself, as well.

An officer at the end of the drive during wartime can't be bearing good news, though there aren't any men in our household to lose.

"Is there anything wrong, Officer?" The dogs are twitching, shifting on their haunches, readying to bolt, it seems, but they don't. I put a hand on each of their heads. They pant, lick and snap their mouths.

"I have a piece of personal correspondence for a Miss Sveva Caetani." I wonder why an officer would be delivering her mail, but I don't say anything, wait for him to continue. "I am an old friend of hers from school – well, an acquaintance, really, a school chum – this is the last address I have for her."

In the first couple of years, people stopped by, but it was easy enough to let them know that the ladies were resting or otherwise occupied. Sometimes, a visitor would jot down a note. More often, they would leave their names and best wishes and carry on. Now, here is a man in uniform with a sealed envelope.

"Do I have the correct address?" he asks. "Does Miss Caetani still reside here?"

I am an honest person. I would prefer to say nothing than to speak a mistruth, but I have figured out how to do both, how to say just enough that I am not lying. "A school chum?"

"Yes, well, not exactly. She was at Crofton House – all young ladies, as you may know." He pauses here as though to gauge my reaction. "I was at the brother school, Saint George's. We had the same circle of friends. I –" he stops himself here. "Is she at this address?"

"The girl you knew doesn't live here anymore." This answer isn't completely untrue. "Baby!" I snap at one of the dogs, hold her collar. "Heel." She does.

The man looks at me then away, runs his fingers up the buttons on his coat, adjusts his collar and clears his throat, all as though he is biding time. "Oh, I see." He looks back to me. "Do you know her?"

This isn't as easy a question to answer. "I did."

"Do you have a forwarding address for Miss Caetani?"

"No."

The officer moves the letter from hand to hand, looks toward the dogs, which are still at my side as though they recognize a uniform and have decided to behave. "Well." He turns and looks down the street, as though he'll discover where she is. "I've nowhere else to send this."

I wait.

"This may be an imposition, ma'am, but perhaps I could leave this with you. Perhaps Miss Caetani will be back through the area and may stop by." When he says this, I don't know whether he is hopeful or whether he has seen through my charade. I'm a terrible liar, I know. H once told me.

"Yes, I can do that." The officer looks beyond me, toward the house, then hands me the envelope.

"Thank you, ma'am. I appreciate it."

As though the dogs know that some sort of transaction has taken place, Baby takes off after something down the road, and Onyx follows, barking.

The officer tips his cap, takes a couple of steps then turns around. "I was here for training camp in '41. I thought I should look up Miss Caetani then, but there wasn't time. We were deployed so quickly. I rarely left the front – a medic – I was discharged early for service.

"It's a different world over there." He pauses. "I am trying to find those I knew before. I know it won't make a difference, not really, but I am trying."

I hear the sound of the dogs running back and then they are circling me. *I know*, I think. I want to tell him that I understand what he is talking about – about war and dislocation and trying to find those you used to know – but all I say is, "Good luck."

The officer smiles weakly, doesn't tip his hat again, turns and walks away. It isn't until then that I notice that Baby has a squirrel between her teeth. Onyx pants and jumps a quick little dance around us. The sun has broken over the trees. "Let that go," I scold. "Come, you two."

You may think me complicit in our situation, and perhaps I am. After all, what happened to us can't have been from one person's will alone.

"You are so good," a man once told me. "Better than me, stronger."

When I wrote to him about my body wracked with pain, my mind muddied with grief, he repeated: "Be good. Be strong." The words were clear on the page, between those that had been censored by authorities during the war. Soon, more phrases, then entire sentences were blacked out, until one day the letters stopped. When they did, I lay on a terrace in the lovely sunshine and thought of how easy it would be to die. It was cowardly to think like that. To die is easy; to have the courage to keep living is what is difficult. I promised myself then that I would become good at living.

How good have I been? I'll tell you the story and let you decide. It begins in so many places, at so many times, loops back, repeats itself in infinite patterns. I'll choose a place to begin, yet again.

ONE
Precinct of False Gods

each instant we stand on the
edge of the
edge of event's
undecidable future

– Daphne Marlatt, "harbouring"

ONE

Canada, 1921

In the last days before we reached America, the air was biting with cold. Some nights, after the ladies were asleep, I would put on a coat, hat, scarf and gloves over my evening attire and go out on the deck. The ship's staff told me not to, warned the cold was too much, it was dangerous. I ignored them, minced along the deck. A sharp chill wrapped around the ship, twisted around my ankles, legs, waist. The cold was pocketed in clouds of air I would walk into, a casing covering me until I blundered through to the other side. Eventually, we were so high in the Atlantic that I would watch icebergs calf and moan, float by as if apparitions. The slow movement of the liner against the steady drift of the bergs made it seem everything – water, land, sky, stars – was moving around and against each other, like parts in a clock. I would never last long, the cold slicing into me as mountains of ice lumbered by in dark water.

We'd left England shrouded in fog that obscured the coastline, and Italy's coast burned gold in my mind, blurred with sunlight. On the morning we approached the Atlantic coast of Canada, the light was so clear in the cold air that everything seemed sharply focused – each shadow etched on the rocky coast, every tree against every other tree. That was all I could see – rock and tree, light and shadow stark against each other. The ship steered out of the Atlantic into the Saint Lawrence, the rock gave way and then, aside from an occasional lighthouse and small croppings of tiny wooden houses perched on uncertain shores, there were only trees.

We didn't know for how long we'd be exiled in this country. I travelled as staff of the family – Duke Leone Caetani di Sermoneta, Ofelia and their four-year-old daughter, Sveva. It was she, not her mother, who watched with me as we passed into our new country. "Where are the people, Miss Jüül?" she asked.

"I'm sure they're in the cities, Sveva. We'll meet them soon."

"Will we like them will they like us what will it all be like?" She spoke in one continual stream, a hybrid between Italian, French and English. I'd become accustomed to the mixed singsong of her speech.

"I'm sure it will all be wonderful," I told her, though, of course, I was not sure at all.

Did I long for my own home? I thought often of my own family, people I had once known so well that I could recognize the cadence of footsteps, a cleared throat. Now they'd become more of a concept to me, like figures in a photograph, locked in time, fading. I had left them behind so long ago. Since then, I'd become separated from other people who felt more real to me, my desire for them keening just below the surface of my skin. One person in particular, though I would not name him. I had little idea of what my role would be in this new world, but I had grown accustomed to uncertainty, the spaces between, the ways I could slip into them.

"Oh, this is just awful," Ofelia leaned into me and whispered. We had disembarked in Montreal and were checking into a hotel.

"The hotel?"

"No, everything – this cold air, their accents, even the calls of the birds. It's all so strange, so shrill somehow." She spoke to me in Italian. Ofelia did not like the sound of the English language. She had told me this every time we'd visited London, alternating her own speech between Italian and French. Around us in the lobby, we heard more French than English, but both languages seemed flatter, more nasal, coarser. Later, in the hotel restaurant, I overheard a Danish waiter serve a businessman from Copenhagen. It gave me some comfort, hearing my own language so far from home. I could hear in them my brothers, though I knew that I didn't, not really. Our northern dialect was a blunter, lower Danish.

We were in Montreal for three days to get our official papers sorted before we boarded a train. I didn't sleep much, watched the country outside the window instead. Rock on rock, dense forest, huge stretches of lakes and long tracts that seemed locked in winter, the only variations in the way the cold covered the land – frosted over rock, stunting trees, textured in ice on lakes, flattened by wind or squalls of snow twisting upward before falling like curtains. Then, one day, the skies were saturated with blue pressing down on the pale prairie. Occasionally, a town or village with dirt streets, wooden sidewalks, tiny wooden churches, wooden houses with smoke rising out of thin stone chimneys and settling on the landscape. The cities – Winnipeg, Regina – were unlike those we were used to. There were paved roads and streetcars and buildings made of brick and stone, but on the outskirts of these, more wooden houses, more smoke. Once, I saw what looked like Native Indians – men, women and children – outside a train station, dressed like Europeans but without shoes, pulling wagons and wagons of what appeared to be hay.

While I watched, Ofelia slept, or tried to sleep. I don't know how much she saw from her berth. And I don't know for what I hoped more – for her to see as little as possible, to minimize the shock, or for her to witness some of where we now were so that she could begin to familiarize herself with this place. I had spent my childhood on a farm in northern Denmark, so while Canada looked more vast, rougher, I could comprehend parts of it. For her, it would be completely foreign.

The duke sat down across from me. "The Wild West, would you say?" He raised his eyebrow, looked amused. "Well, it will be an adventure." He turned his face to the window for a moment, his expression more serious. "I'm not sure how Ofelia will adapt."

"No, neither am I."

He opened his cigarette case, slid one out, tapped the tip on his palm. "You'll try to help her adjust?"

"I will do my best." I always did.

"I'm thankful for that, you do know."

I nodded.

"It will be an adjustment for all of us, but you and she will have each other."

Sveva came running down the aisle. "Daddy!" She'd been napping alongside Ofelia. I looked down the train to see if her mother was behind her.

"Wurr-Burr!" He put his unlit cigarette back in his case and picked up Sveva as he stood. "Isn't it a grand adventure, my girl?"

"Yes!" She squirmed to get out of his hold and stood in front of me, took both of my hands and leaned across my lap, grin stretched as she strained her neck to bring her face close to mine. "A grand adventure, yes, Miss Jüül?"

"Of course it is, sweetheart." I rarely called her endearments. I was not Sveva's nanny, though I would often be mistaken as such. I adored her, but she was her parents' little girl, and I their employee. If nothing else, I had learned to know my place.

"Do you think Mau-Mau is going to like it?" She pushed off from my lap and rebounded against the bench opposite me. "She's been sleeping the whole time!" Sveva held her arms wide. "The whole time!"

The duke reached for his daughter, one palm on her head, the other on her shoulder to calm her. He laughed. "Slow down, little one. Come." He guided her into the aisle. "Let's go see how your mother is doing, shall we?"

She turned to me with her chin raised, a closed-lip smile broad across her face. Sveva looked proud in a way that only a four-year-old can, delighted with herself and her place in the world, secure with her father's hand around hers.

As we moved west, the snow disappeared from the prairie and I saw instead fields of brown, flattened by weather, pocked with patches of new green. It seemed we had already moved through a continent of climate. We reached the Rocky Mountains, hulks of stone pushing up the sky high above us. We'd been on the train four days. "In that time, we could have crossed the farthest reaches of Russia," said Ofelia. She was out of the sleeping cabin for the first time since we'd boarded, wearing a watered silk dress, black pearls set against the collar, gloves on as though we were about to disembark to a formal dinner.

"Inspiring, isn't it?" said the duke. "This much land, this much potential." He lifted his chest as though he, or those like him, were in some way responsible for the size of this country. Ofelia looked toward me and rolled her eyes, her fingers tracing each pearl around her neck as she looked out the window.

We stayed for a month at the Banff Springs Hotel, where we watched from the windows as bears tracked dark shapes across the exposed slopes of mountains. One of the animals shambled into the village and was shot and removed quickly by men in hotel uniforms. It was the Wild West, complete with real redskins. We saw them in a performance put on by the hotel – *The Noble Savage*. Indian men with feathered headdresses rode bareback on horses that reared on their hind legs and thrashed their necks as though they might break. Those wild-eyed beasts were as much a part of the show as were the buckskinned, painted men who beat drums and mumbled guttural ditties. I watched the sinewed horses, felt the drums pounding up through my legs. I had become separated from the family during the performance. I saw them across the circle that the guests had formed. The duke had one arm around Ofelia's waist and she leaned into him. In his other arm, he held Sveva. They were closer together as a family than I'd ever seen them in Europe.

When the performance was over, Ofelia clapped politely, but the duke raised his long arms, applauded loudly, said, "Bravo, bravo!" I watched as Ofelia stepped away from him and reached for Sveva, who was beaming at her father, jumping from foot to foot, joining him in saying, "Bravo, bravo!" No one else did, the other patrons' applause more subdued. I backed away from the crowd and made my way back to our rooms.

That night in the dining room, I heard the duke talking to other guests. "I commend them. A country really must celebrate its natives. I think of parts of India – Benares, Kashmir – as well as Egypt, Turkey, Syria. Those places where the ancient and the modern meet and are celebrated, I find them to be the most fascinating, enlivening places in the world."

As he talked, Ofelia leaned toward me. "It's grown tiresome, all this talk about the fascinating New World. Can we not be enlivened at home, in Italy, where we belong?"

It wasn't my place to say, either way.

After a month, we came down from the mountains, the train travelling along rivers, a thick white muscle of water below us, sending spray up to mist the windows. The water slowed to languid creeks and eventually the land smoothed into green valleys and what looked like the hills of Italy. We were told that the lakes here were aquamarine jewels between golden slopes, but what we saw as the train pulled into Vernon was one small, swampy lake rimmed with cattails and some sort of camp on the outskirts of town, high wooden fences and smoke rising from the other side.

"This cannot be where we're stopping." Ofelia's voice was sharp and desperate against my ear.

It was.

The duke and Ofelia believed that they were travelling lightly – and, for them, they were. I'd already become accustomed to what they carried with them, but no one in the tiny Western Canadian town could fathom the number of things we had. When all thirty large steamer trunks were set out on the platform, a crowd gathered around us. A young man pushed through it with a camera, a flashbulb going off, each of us wiping at our eyes as we looked around the tiny station. "Well, I hope that doesn't end up in the daily," the duke joked with the estate agent who was there to meet us.

"Oh no, sir – I mean, Duke, Your Highness." Leone waved his hand to indicate that formality wasn't necessary. "The *Vernon Daily News* respects our citizens' privacy. Of course, your arrival is news, but we wouldn't print photographs of your possessions." He didn't understand that the duke was joking.

"Good to know." The duke nodded to him.

A small crowd looked from the luggage to us, staring quite openly, as though we couldn't see them watching us. I don't know who was more stunned, the locals who had gathered to view our small group or Ofelia, who stood perfectly still on the platform. I sensed I was not noticed, not really, certainly not as much as the duke, Ofelia and even Sveva, who laughed as she spun circles around us. The man ensured that most of our belongings would be stored at the station, found a porter for our remaining luggage and ushered us to a waiting Ford. The duke took Sveva's hand and I held my arm out to Ofelia like a thin ballast. She placed her fingers along my forearm, nothing more, though if she needed to steady herself it would be easy enough to wrap her hand into a grip.

The man opened the door to the car with an almost exaggerated movement. "You have many of these in Europe yet?"

"Automobiles? Oh yes, we're not that far behind the times!" The duke lifted Sveva into the car, then helped Ofelia. I kept my hands at my side, nodded at him and got myself into the car before he closed the door. He sat in the front beside the man, who drove us two blocks over pitted dirt roads to a three-storey wooden structure on the main street of town. It was so close to the station that the porter had simply walked from there and was now ready to take our bags to our rooms. "I'm sure you'll be comfortable here."

We looked up at the building, *Royal Hotel* looped in fading paint. Ofelia leaned into me. "He's sure, is he? He's the only one then, I'm afraid."

Sveva ran up and down the boardwalk, delighted at the sound of her boots on the wood. Leone took Ofelia around the waist, smiled up at the building, squinted. When their daughter ran by the next time, I put out my arm to stop her, then knelt to her. "Go to your parents now. Tell them how happy you are to be here." Someone should be. The duke was probably delighted, Ofelia horrified. I convinced myself I was used to being an afterthought, my reactions not entirely worth noting. If they had been, I would claim the territory between optimistic and noncommittal. I tried to convince myself I was still open to new experiences, though that word – *open* – hardly seemed to apply anymore, each move and change blocking off different parts of me, my mind a series of closed doors, storage trunks overfull, locked.

The next day, the estate agent came to pick up the duke to show him some houses for sale. Leone thought we might prefer to stay at the hotel. "Or go for a walk along Main Street, perhaps?"

Ofelia stared at him, tilted her head – and did her eyes narrow, just a bit? "Oh no, we're coming with you, darling. Who knows what you'll purchase at this point – a teepee?"

The duke rubbed his chin, looked above our heads as he said, "The Indians of this valley don't live in teepees but in structures built into hills and mounds of earth. They're called, depending on the area, *quichis* or *kekulis.*" When he looked back at us, his expression was earnest, as though he were quoting from an anthropological text, which he may well have been.

"Fine, I also do not want to live in a mound of earth. Come, Sveva, Miss Jüül, we're all going."

The man drove us around what there was of a town. We passed a large structure – an open-air factory, it seemed – stacked with large wooden crates. "The fruit-packing plant," he explained.

The duke turned to us and smiled. He put his hand on Ofelia's. "See, darling – it really is warm enough here to grow fruit." Ofelia nodded, something like a smile pulled tight across her mouth.

"Oh yes, all sorts of fruit in this valley – perfect conditions, they say. We even have a fruit growers' association now, a kind of union." He let out a ragged laugh then cleared his throat. "Though I suppose you wouldn't know much about unions, sir."

"Here you're mistaken. I actually consider myself a union man."

"Oh?"

"Being born a duke held me back in Italy, but I did help those on our family's holdings to form union-like groups, to take more ownership of the land." He looked from Ofelia to me, nodding, as though looking for our confirmation. "It's one of the reasons I've moved my family to Canada, a free country as they say, one in which we can be free of the narrow strictures of a culture based on blood, not merit."

Leone said all this in English and the man nodded along, though it seemed heavy conversation for a morning drive.

We were passing the high wooden fencing we'd seen as we'd entered Vernon. "What is that?" asked Ofelia, also in English, perhaps the first I'd heard her speak the language since we arrived.

"An internment camp left over from the war. Enemy aliens, Ukrainians and other Slavs – a precautionary measure, I'm afraid."

"Well, let's hope we stay on the right side of the good Canadians!" Leone turned to us and laughed, though neither Ofelia nor I smiled in response. "Of course, I have a fair amount of Slavic blood myself. As does my daughter – you be careful, Sveva!" he called back to her.

Sveva smiled as though she understood the joke, looked wide-eyed and blinking first toward her mother, then me. I reached out for her hand, gave it a squeeze and winked at her as though she and I were in on the same joke. Sveva beamed back at me.

"But the war is over," Ofelia said to me quietly in Italian.

The war was over, and I knew we should all be relieved. It wasn't right that I pined for the first years of war, when my role within a household had become as indispensable as sleep. But I'd been wrong about that. I was sent away before peace was declared and now, here I was with another family, touring a tiny town in Western Canada.

As if in answer to Ofelia's Italian, the man said, "The camp is officially closed. It's been standing vacant for two years. We do need to dismantle it – it's getting taken over by vagrants and Indians. They go and set up their own tents in there, build fires. It's a public danger, I keep telling council."

Leone turned to the estate agent, then away, clearing his throat. "The Indians, I'm given to understand, don't live in teepees here."

The man laughed. "No, not teepees, exactly! Canvas tents or, mostly, shacks. There aren't many in town, though. They aren't really supposed to leave the reserve out on Okanagan Lake, need a pass to do so – though some always find a way. Occasionally, their fires get out of control on the hillside by Long Lake, but don't worry, they won't bother you. You'll be living in town."

"The lakes!" Leone clapped his hands together and rubbed them. "I've heard so much about these lakes!" He looked over the seat toward us, raised his eyebrows.

Ofelia and I sat in silence as the men talked. I pictured roaming Indians, the abandoned imprisonment camp, fires out of control. I couldn't imagine who would choose to live in such a place.

The house the duke and Ofelia chose was a three-storey wooden home on Pleasant Valley Road. "Quite spacious. Stately," the estate agent said when we first saw it.

I nearly sputtered a laugh.

"You all right then, Miss Jüül?" Leone winked at me.

I looked toward Ofelia, who was using her cane to walk that day. She held her small frame completely straight, as though she didn't need assistance, but I saw how her thin hand was clenched around the cane, tendons tight against her skin.

Sveva ran circles in the parlour, leaping around the edge of the room through dust motes lit in lines of diluted sunlight. "Second owner was a dance instructor," the agent said. "He built the addition so that this room could be used for dancing."

Later, Ofelia said to me, "Imagine, holding a dance in that tiny parlour! This is what they believe is a grand home, Miss Jüül."

It was much bigger than the one in which I'd grown up on the farm, and that one had been considered a big home in our district. "Think of it as your country retreat." I repeated what I'd heard the duke say.

"I don't want a country retreat." Neither did I, really.

Two

Four years earlier, when I'd first been in the Caetani's employ in Rome, I'd rarely left the walls and courtyards of Villa Miraggio. The duke was having it built for Ofelia and it wasn't yet finished when I arrived, weeks before baby Sveva's birth. Laddered in scaffolding, partially draped in canvas, the villa rose like a large, tiered cake from the highest hill in the city. "Windows on every level, every side. When it's complete, no view of Rome will be obscured," the duke had told me. This was their first home as a couple, away from the official palace residence where the duke's parents, his siblings and their spouses all occupied different wings. The staff in Villa Miraggio, of which I was one, seemed modest to them in comparison, plentiful to me.

Ofelia wasn't well after Sveva's birth, but when she was healthy enough to join the duke's family at Palazzo Caetani, she invited me along. "Oh, I'll stay here," I told her. "I'm used to dining on my own." Not that I would be. I'd likely be joined by any number of the senior staff at the villa.

"Well, stop being used to it! I won't always be an invalid, and if you are to be my companion, you are to be treated like one, not like one of the house girls. Come on then, let's get dressed for dinner." She took my hands and opened my arms, as though we might start waltzing. "Though Duchess Ada is as likely to turn up at the table in her pajamas as she is to get dressed for dinner, we should dress in semi-formal wear. Do you have something, Miss Jüül? If not, I can –"

"Oh yes, certainly, I do." I must have seemed so provincial standing in Ofelia's drawing room, wearing one of the plain, dark dresses I wore daily. There had been a time, not that long before, when I'd chosen my clothes for dinner carefully each evening, dressed with only my body and pleasure in mind. Time could shift in a moment, become a scent both smoky and sweet, a jump in my rib cage, a turn in my stomach, then be gone again.

We entered the walls of the palazzo, which didn't open into courtyards or gardens but dark passageways climbing with as much scaffolding as did the villa. The duke led us down halls lined with stacks of paint cans, hammers and tools leaning against stone walls. I whispered to Ofelia, "Is the palazzo under construction, as well?"

The duke heard. "When isn't the palazzo under construction?" He turned and winked. "It's perpetual, has been since I was a child – one wing is finished and then another begins to crumble, but none has ever actually been completed to my knowledge!" He laughed at this. "Designed by one of Michelangelo's pupils. It's too bad we didn't have the master himself, as it will always be a work in progress, never a masterpiece." The duke seemed genuinely amused rather than bothered by this. I'd assumed that the villa would be completed soon, but now I wasn't as sure.

Ofelia had told me that there was no set hour for dinner and that we would be expected to remain at the table until the last of the family had eaten. We were among the first to arrive, though a brother sat at one end of the long table, a newspaper open and obscuring his face like a screen. "Miche, show some manners," the duke said. "Say a proper hello to the ladies."

The man folded one side of the paper and peered over it. "A proper hello to you both." He snapped the newspaper up around him again. As he did, an enormous man appeared in a coat decorated with medals of some sort.

I nearly stood in respect, but Ofelia held onto my arm and leaned to me, whispered, "The old footman." I noticed then that his arm was cocked, a cloth draped over it, a bottle of wine in one hand. The man said something, but even though it must have been in Italian, I didn't understand him. Ofelia simply smiled at him in response.

The duke said, "Yes, please, Pagolo," and the man poured us wine.

When the man left the room, the brother put down his paper. "Poor Pag's got such a speech impediment that only a Caetani can understand him, and then only half the time, yes, Leone?"

"Half at best, I'd say."

The brother stood up and rounded the table. "Excuse my rudeness, ladies. Caught up in war propaganda, I'm afraid." We both stood as he made his way toward us. He bowed to Ofelia, kissed her hand and then turned to me. "Another young thing you're keeping in the villa, Leo?" More than ten years older than Ofelia, I was hardly young.

"Please excuse his utter deficiency of civility, Miss Jüül. This is my brother, Michelangelo, the youngest as I'm afraid you can tell." Indeed, he looked younger than me. "Michelangelo, this is Miss Jüül, Ofelia's companion."

His brother flicked his eyes up and down my body, then turned and began circling the table, hands slapping against the tops of each chair as he went by. "This war, it's interminable."

"Most seem as though they are." The duke leaned against the high-backed chair, took a sip of wine. "Let's not get into this with the ladies here."

Michelangelo was pacing, making rounds of the table. "I suppose you still think we would have been best to abstain, remain neutral, as though such a thing were possible, Leo?" He clutched the top of a chair opposite us.

Leone put down his wineglass and adjusted his collar. "I'll remind you that I fought on the front last year."

His brother pulled out a chair, slumped into it. "I thought we weren't getting into this with the ladies here." He raised an eyebrow.

"We're not."

Two more family members came into the room – a brother, Roffredo, and his wife, Marguerite – nodding through brief introductions as they sat down. Around each family member's setting were varying arrays of small pots of pickles and spices, as well as vials and jars of what appeared to be medication around some. When his wine came, Roffredo opened a narrow jar and threw a pill into his mouth before taking a drink.

Marguerite leaned forward. "Miss Jüül, is it?" She spoke to me in English.

I was surprised to be spoken to directly, felt my neck and chest spark with the quick heat of nerves. "Yes."

"Not Italian." This was neither a question nor quite a statement. Her voice had the round lilt of an American.

"No." Few would mistake me for being Italian. My hair was a dull brown, and though I'd seen several fair-skinned and light-eyed Italians since I'd been in the country, my skin was what betrayed me, never burnishing, going from white to pink to red under a dusting of freckles that might spread if exposed to direct sunlight too long. "I'm Danish."

"Oh yes." She turned to the duke. "Is this –"

He interrupted her, switching to English as well. "Miss Jüül's joined us from a household in Cairo." He looked pointedly at his sister-in-law.

"Yes, of course." Marguerite nodded.

The patriarch, Duke Onorato, came to dinner an hour or more after we'd arrived. He was bent over a cane, but even then, I could tell that at one point he would have been taller than the duke, himself well over six feet tall. Everyone stood and said, "Father," then resumed what they'd been doing. Ofelia had told me that the senior duke had once challenged Buffalo Bill to a horse-wrangling contest when the American cowboy had a show in Rome – and that he had won. I looked at the old, stooped man. With his height, his long, white beard and his cane, he looked like a prophet.

Leone's mother, Duchess Ada, arrived a few minutes after her husband. Her hair was set with a wave and held up with jewelled pins, and she had emerald drop earrings, but she was dressed in a violet dressing gown. "Oh, look at you all!" She came first to Leone, who stood and then bent so his mother could put her hands on his face to kiss his cheeks. She then held Ofelia's hand in both of hers. "You look so well, dear – you're better?" When Ofelia said she was, the duchess asked, "And Sveva? How is that little beauty? Where is my darling little granddaughter?"

"We hope she's sleeping," the duke said and raised a wineglass at this thought. "If not, God bless those who are tasked with caring for her – the girl has quite the lungs. We can hear her clear across the villa from the nurse-maid's quarters."

"Oh, you should have brought her! None of us mind a little noise, and you know how I adore babies." She turned, looked directly at me. "And who's this?"

"Mother, this is Ofelia's companion, Miss Jüül."

The duchess took my hand as she had Ofelia's. "Lovely to meet you. I do hope that you enjoy your time with my family." The duchess spoke in English the entire time, her accent the king's own, Received Pronunciation. I knew already that she was English aristocracy, her marriage one of both political union and what anyone who spoke of it agreed was genuine love between her and Duke Onorato. He didn't speak at all that evening and, at one point, appeared to be asleep. The duchess and her sons joked and sparred, moving between English, Italian and, at times, French. The meal, if one could call it that, was random dishes set down now and again by the incomprehensible giant footman, and the food, too, seemed to alternate between English, Italian and French.

"You know Gelasio has plans to blow up a mountain on the northern front, don't you, Leone?" their mother asked at one point, as though this were the stuff of chit-chat.

"He mentioned something about that when we spoke, yes. If anyone has the bombast, it's him, isn't that right, Roff?"

Instead of answering his brother, Roffredo asked the duke, "Are you finding you have any time for your research these days?"

"Oh, it's coming along. The war has slowed things down, certainly."

Ofelia turned to me. "Leone is compiling a multi-volume account of Islamic history and culture."

I looked at her for a moment in response, blinked. I wasn't always sure I'd understood what she'd said – both my English and French were stronger than my Italian then. "He is?"

Marguerite laughed. "That was exactly my response! It does make perfect sense, really, but what these Caetani men will take on – while Roff composes his symphonies, Leone compiles a history of one of the world's great religions."

"Great?" Michelangelo said from the other end of the table. "Some would beg to differ. Regardless, the entire Western world is at war and my big brother is writing about the Middle East, which, after this war, will no longer exist."

"Oh, it won't, will it?" Leone took a drink, then seemed to study the liquid in his glass before putting it down.

As though to change the subject, Margeurite turned to me, "Are you familiar with the work of Marie Bregendahl? If you've not yet read *A Night of Death*, you must."

"*A Night of Death*? Why that sounds cheery." Her husband was spooning various condiments onto his plate, dragging shapes through them with his spoon as though he were a child.

"Roff!" She batted at him. Her husband recoiled in mock alarm, shrugged dramatically toward Ofelia and me.

"I do adore literature." My voice sounded stiff and put-on, like a precocious child, even to me. "But I've not lived in Denmark for some time, so I'm a bit out of step with the current authors."

"This came out – when? – maybe 1912, 1913? I'd say probably no more than four or five years ago."

Roffredo said, "I'm surprised you don't know the exact publication date." He looked toward me. "Marguerite has a mind for not only books but publishing – hopes to go into it herself one day."

I smiled and nodded at some comments to seem both amiable and intelligent. The Caetanis were generous to me, treating me as though I belonged at the table with them. In my time away from Denmark, my language skills had improved – French, English and then Italian. By the time we left Italy, I felt as though I could move fluidly between both languages and worlds alike, but I wondered how much slipped between gaps as my mind shifted between them. I couldn't know how much of my experience would be locked in memory to be shaken loose years later.

THREE

When the first correspondence arrived in the box on Pleasant Valley Road, it wasn't from any of the duke's family. Rather, it was from Ofelia's sister, Emerika, addressed to me. She had come to stay with Ofelia in the months after Sveva was born and had quickly assumed a friendship and familiarity with me. She wrote that she wanted to scold me for having forgotten so soon about her – a distant flirt, she called either herself or me, I wasn't sure. She imagined my Canadian attire was a short pleated dress with high boots like the girls of the Wild West. "Please say it's so!" I could practically hear the delight in her voice, see her swinging her full skirts, winking, doing all those very animated things she had done at Ofelia and the duke's residence in Rome.

Emerika asked after Sveva and implored me to distract her niece and make her happy. Even if that had been my role in this family, it wasn't something that I was sure I could do. It was Ofelia whom I was trying to distract and keep happy, not an easy task. She refused to speak English, and I knew the chances were slim of finding anyone who spoke Italian in this small Western Canadian town. Instead, I was able to find two French-speaking ladies in the area. Though we hosted them for tea, and were invited into their homes in turn, I can't say much friendship resulted.

"I have so little in common with those women." Ofelia leaned against a hall table when we arrived home from one of the teas. She hadn't used her cane that day and was likely tired from the strain of socializing with strangers. It was true, of course; she was quite different from the Canadian women we'd met. The duke felt she should try harder, but I thought this unfair. She was exhausted by the toll of travel, and there was little of comfort to Ofelia in Canada. The country was as unfamiliar to me as it was her, but I'd convinced myself I was adaptable. Being a buffer between Ofelia and our new world became a distraction for me, a way to keep my mind away from the edges that dropped into memory. I was stronger than that.

When we first arrived, the days seemed modulated – warm sunshine during the day, cool breeze through the trees in the evening, nights smattered with stars. Then it began to rain and it continued, alternating between pounding downpour and dull cloud, for more than a month. When the rain cleared, the sun bore down day after day, baking the ground. Even in the early mornings when the cook, George, and I went out – he to collect the milk and egg deliveries, I to collect the mail – I could feel the heat loosened from the gravel drive with each of my steps. By afternoon, the pine trees would drop their needles and I could smell the bark of ponderosas like vanilla through any open window.

In the distilled light of early morning or evening, white-tailed deer would walk through the property, hooves high and ears twitching. They moved at such a languid pace that even when they were spooked and jumped in response, they would turn toward us and stare, their eyes large and dark, regarding us with incomprehension, a kind of blinking curiosity as to why we were there, looking at them. Their confusion at our presence seemed right, natural. I wasn't sure what we were doing there, either.

The first fall we were in Canada, Sveva called from the top balcony, "Come, come, come! Look!" We followed to where she pointed and saw a sow bear on a thick tree branch, her back arched and fur standing on end like a frightened cat. The sow made a huffing noise as the four of us backed off the balcony, Ofelia holding Sveva by the shoulders.

"She's more scared of us," the duke whispered. "Look," he pointed higher up into the tree, to dark spots in the turning leaves. "Her cubs."

When we were back inside, in the hall, Ofelia knelt in front of Sveva, told her, "You're not to go out, darling." She looked up at the duke and me. "None of us should. It's too dangerous. We don't know what the bear will do."

"The bear will sleep and protect her young, I suspect. And when they've figured out that this isn't the best place for them, they'll move on." The duke looked amused.

"You're an expert on Canadian fauna now, are you?" Ofelia stood with her hands on her hips, head tilted, her mouth wavering as she tried not to smile. She looked toward Sveva and me. "In the meantime, we will stay inside. I will not risk anything."

The duke had been right. The bear and her cubs were on the property for two days, and by the third, they were gone. The deer always returned. Some evenings, after the family had retired, I would go onto a porch or veranda, stand in the dark and listen. Most nights, I could hear something – tree trunks moaning when they were hit with wind, our dogs turning circles in their kennel, other sounds for which I had no reference – a thin screeching sound that I assumed was a kind of bird, footfalls of animals big and small snapping branches in the understorey. Even inside, the wood walls of the house seemed thin, and I sensed animals all around us. As I listened for them, I knew the animals were concerned only with food and mating and sleep, and not with us at all.

One morning, more than a year after we'd first arrived, the pots in the kitchen began to sway against each other like crude chimes. Rumbling shook the house, and I followed the play of silver rattling in the dining room, the sound of shivering china. From outside, the clang of metal joined a rhythmic pounding on the road. Sveva came running down the front stairs in her nightclothes. "What is it, Miss Jüül?" She must have been five or six years old by then.

I opened the door to elephants stepping in unison down Pleasant Valley Road, as improbable as that seemed, each holding the tail of the one in front with its trunk, metal harnesses swaying. We watched ten or more go by. On the back of the last elephant was a monkey, dressed in a vest and cap. It looked toward us and yelped. Following the elephants were horses pulling carts loaded with caged animals. A leopard circled her cage. A lion opened her mouth but let out more of a yawn than a roar, and the wolf did not howl. She stared at us, her eyes so icy that even at a distance, I shivered.

After the procession passed, I brought Sveva back into the house and up the stairs to get dressed for the day. When I went into the kitchen, I could hear her father's low voice, and I knew when they were hinging open the front closet to get their coats and boots. The cook came in from his cabin at the back of the property, bowed slightly and went toward the pantry. "George?" He turned to me. "I need to go to town. The duke and Sveva are out for a morning walk. If the duchess wakes, you'll tell her that I'll be back soon?"

I followed the tracks of the circus along Pleasant Valley Road and then up the hill past the Campbell house. I skirted the edge of the road, stayed close to the trees, hoping that I wouldn't be seen. On a flat field, one of three red-striped tents was already unfurled, elephants ringing it, their trunks wrapped around poles. The animals rose from their knees and took measured steps backward, the voice of a man heard above the lumbering of their feet, until the tent was upright. They held the posts perfectly rigid in their trunks as the men secured them with thick ropes and enormous stakes. The men stood in a circle, each stripped to the waist, black skin gleaming. They swung sledgehammers over their heads, then drove the stakes into the ground. While they worked, they sang, the hammers pounding, again and again, in unison. I could see Sveva and the duke on the other side of the field. The sun had cracked over the hill behind me and shone into their faces, which I knew left them partly blinded to the other side.

A low mist clung to the ground and steam rose off the workingmen's backs. It was late summer, the grass brown after a season of heat. The perimeter was thick with trees beginning to speckle with orange and yellow. The light at that time of day was perfect, eerie. The men's skin was so dark it looked nearly purple. Their dungarees may have once been blue, but they were grey then, leached of colour. The vapour off their bodies as they sang was another paler shade of grey, almost white, as if the group of men were superimposed against the rich red of the tent's stripes; the green, yellow and orange of the foliage; the blue of the sky. And then sunlight reached the valley and everything was washed with light.

FOUR

Denmark, 1906

The fire was out. I wanted to remain in bed but I'd always been the one to get up to stoke it, so I rolled from under the weight of bedding, then prodded at embers still winking in the ash, sprinkled wood shavings and blew them into licks of flame before I added more kindling. My sister, Johanna, shifted in her sleep, moaned a long, slow sigh. "Poor darling, cozied while I rebuild the fire." She kept sleeping.

I was outside before most of the household was awake. I liked it that way. The dim and cold lent an edge to everything, made it otherworldly. In an hour, sunlight would blur the horizon, the air would warm and it would be just another day. I knew the farmhands were still eating breakfast, and by the time they came to feed and water the animals, I had already slipped the horses some oats and apples, taken one of them out for a ride. I was out for an hour. When I got back, steam lifted off the horse's sides and haunches when I jumped down. "Inger-Marie!" my mother called from across the gravel yard. "Come!" There was someone standing with her. I tied the horse and walked toward them, squinting at the form of another woman, her skirts to the ground, coat nearly as long, a broad hat hiding her face.

"An early morning ride?" The woman lifted her hat as she came toward me. My cousin Kristine, wink of her blue eye, twist of a grin on her lips. "Are you vying to take over the role of one of the farm boys then, Marie?"

My mother had us each by the elbow. "Come, come in! We're just sitting down to breakfast." She let go of my arm and pushed slightly. "Go get cleaned up, darling, won't you?"

"Of course."

Later, in my bedroom, boots off, stockings unrolled, Kristine and I lay on the bed, faces turned toward the wood beams crossing the ceiling. She was travelling from the south, where she'd been working as a governess, to a city in the north where she would be a lady's personal secretary. "She interviewed me in Esbjerg. I honestly had no idea how I did – I fumbled horribly, Marie – but now she's sent for me. I'll need to be in Aalborg by the morning after next to begin."

"What will you do?"

"I'll take care of the lady while her husband is away – at sea." She said this last bit in English, swung both arms in arcs. As she flung her hands back down, she hit my elbow and I made a show of rubbing it. It hadn't hurt, but I smarted from being nicked by her drama. "I suppose it will be somewhat like being a governess – without the children, thank God! I've about had enough of children for now."

"I just can't imagine what you'll actually do – will you dress her?"

"Good Lord, I hope not. I'm not a lady-in-waiting." Kristine sat up from the bed, went toward the fireplace. "And while I'm no longer a governess, this position is just the next as I work my way up."

I spoke toward the ceiling. "Up to what?"

"I'm not sure, really. I haven't quite figured out that part. Not a wife, though – that much I know." She ran a hand along the mantle. I saw the ring she wore, a thin slip of gold around her smallest finger. I knew that my mother and the aunts disapproved – the ring was from a former employer, a woman, and this did not seem right to them.

"You should hear Mother – you probably will, in fact. Every dinner it seems she brings up another candidate for a husband. All farm boys, of course, and there are so few that she brings the same ones up again and again."

"No interest then?" Kristine sat back down at the end of the bed.

"Not in marriage, not to them. If I could tumble around with one or two, maybe, but there's no anonymity here, only expectations."

"Is that why you like the horses so much, Inger-Marie? If not a man clenched between your thighs, at least another muscled beast?"

I shook my hair, made the sound of a horse exhaling, and I kicked at her hip with my stocking foot until Kristine lunged, held me by the waist. She pushed her thumbs into my bottom ribs and I spat out a laugh, then could not stop, my ribs aching with it.

The next morning, I crossed the yard, apples in my palms, and went into the stable, the musk of horses heavy in the dark. They juddered greetings with their quavering lips, the light stomp of hooves. Once they quieted, there was another sound – laboured breathing, a sick colt. I went toward the stall and stopped, saw the pale clenched buttocks of a man, pants pushed to his shins, knee bent at an awkward angle. In the curve of his ear, corner of his jaw, I recognized him as one does family – at a glance, even in such an ugly position. It was my younger brother, Soren, and around him, a woman's bare legs, her nightgown pushed up, his hand against her breast. He ground into her again and again and she moaned. All I could think of was how uncomfortable her bare skin must be against the hay. I felt bile in my throat, a thrum of itchy heat catch between my legs. I wanted to turn and go but kept watching long enough that I recognized Kristine's nightgown, her hand on his back. Did I imagine the flash of her thin gold ring?

I was surprised, yes. But it was something more than that – I felt embarrassed, not only for the two of them in their contorted and grasping positions, but also for my own naïveté. Kristine had convinced me she was about to become independent, a woman who earned her own way in the world, and yet she knew how to fulfill the role of a country cousin, pinned beneath a rutting farm boy, pressed against a pile of prickly hay. Was one a betrayal of the other? Where was my role between suffrage and the sweet stench of common farm animals?

I left the stable as I'd come in, without being heard, apples still in my hands. The horses murmured and snorted their mild protest at me leaving with their treats. In the yard, the sun wasn't up but light was beginning to stain bushes and buildings. I stood for a moment, then returned to the stables, this time whistling and singing so I'd be heard. I saddled and led a horse out. Fog clung to the ground, hummocked with mounds of earth turned over last fall. The remnants of hay that hadn't been cleared were flattened and grey. I could feel the give of thawing ground as I rode.

When I returned, my stomach was hollow with hunger, my skin burning with the sting of riding against the wind. I had missed Kristine's departure. "She waited as long as she could," my mother told me. She hadn't, though, had she? I judged her for giving in, not waiting for a future in which her desire would take her beyond a stable, a farm boy. I decided then that I would go farther away than Kristine ever had. More importantly, I wouldn't return to be held down in a bed of hay like a common farmer's daughter. Kristine was more than that. If she didn't know, I did. I wouldn't let that happen to me.

The next week when Soren went to town, I said I'd ride with him. I wore my riding pants and when Mother gave me a list of things to purchase, she protested. "Inger-Marie, pants are only appropriate for the farm. You can't wear them to town."

"Of course I can." I took the list from her. "Look, I've got a change of clothes." I held up a bag to her, then kissed her on both cheeks. "Don't worry, Mother, I won't always be an embarrassment to you." My mother swatted gently at me, but I'd already slipped out of her range. She didn't know that I had shown her part of my departure plan, as scant and hasty as it was. In town, I ran the last errand, bought the tea, sugar, peppercorns and bolt of fabric my mother had requested. I could've left without doing so, and I suppose I would've if the train had been due to arrive sooner. I tied them in a parcel, along with a letter to my family, to the place on the saddle where my bag had been, pushed my forehead into the soft heat of my horse's neck, then boarded a train and left.

FIVE

I stood on a platform in Copenhagen as the train sucked the steam of humidity after it, leaving a vacuum of cool air. I arrived in the city with no experience and no one to provide me passage into their world, yet I hoped that things would become clear once I got there, somehow. That I would know what to do. Was it God who was supposed to provide these signs? If so, was I supposed to know how to read them?

I stood and nothing came to me – no signs or at least not the ability to discern them – so I approached the ticket counter. "To where?" the man asked me.

"A place to stay?"

"I meant, a ticket to where?"

"Oh, I'm sorry. Could you direct me toward a place to stay?"

The man looked from my hat down toward my chest and then to the air beside me, without ever looking at my face. "On your own?"

"Yes."

"This isn't a visitors' office. You'll have to move along." I stammered that I was sorry, my heel catching as I backed up. I teetered into the man behind me and his hand caught my shoulder for a moment as I steadied myself. I began walking away from the line, cheeks stung with heat, and someone called out, "Miss!" I turned, scanned the line until I saw a woman looking at me, brow pinched. "You're on your own?" I answered yes. "Mrs. Stemme's pension, near the port, admits single women. Go out front and ask one of the hackneys to take you there."

Gulls wheeled and screeched in the air above me, though we weren't near the water. The air was laced with dust, weighted with the sour smell of garbage. Men leaned against carriages, some smoking, some staring at me, it seemed. I approached one of the hackneys and he stood up straight, ground a cigarette under his foot and thrust his chin at me. "Miss?"

"Could you take me to Mrs. Stemme's pension, please? By the port?"

He looked to either side of me. "Travelling alone?" When I answered yes, he picked up my bags, said, "Get in then," and didn't speak to me for the rest of the ride.

At the pension, I was assigned a room with a girl named Lovise. We were two girls in a boarding house full of men. The only other woman worked at the front desk, her skin cracked and teeth greying. She averted her eyes and spoke to the wall beside her rather than to our faces. I knew that she considered neither of us ladies, even though it was she who often had a yellowing line of dried spittle along her lip, her mouth gummy with it.

At twenty, Lovise seemed like an older woman. She was only a year older than I was, but she'd been in the city since she was seventeen. She would corset, stitch and hook herself into dresses so that her breasts were two tight, smooth mounds just below her collarbone, freckles like fallen leaves on a hill. She returned each night late, between eleven and midnight, rarely later, and she still smelled fresh. My mother had told me that you could tell much of what you need to know about a woman by how she smelled. Lovise smelled lovely, despite the cigarettes she smoked. She would open the window, push away the drapes and smoke a cigarette so slowly and methodically that the rhythm of her inhalations and exhalations was like an incantation. After this, she would leave the room with the water basin, return with it filled and wash her face. As she applied cold cream, she would talk, but not too much. Once she'd returned from emptying the basin, she would kneel by her slim bed in silent prayer, then sit on the bed and beam at me. "So, my little Inger-Marie, tell me about your day!" she would say, as though we were sisters or cousins, not two women who had met each other earlier that week in a questionable rooming house.

I spent my first week going into shops to ask if they might need an employee. None did. Lovise suggested I might find a gentleman to go with me when I inquired about work. "But where will I find this gentleman, and why would he want to spend an afternoon with me going in and out of shops?"

"Men like being seen with beautiful women."

"Perhaps, but not poorly dressed farm girls."

She made a motion over me with her palm. "You are not poorly dressed, my dear." Then she stepped toward me, traced ribs to waist with her index finger. "And this is where you are wrong. They especially like being seen with girls – not too young that it would cause a scandal, of course, but young enough that other men wonder how on earth they enchanted that little bright-eyed sprite."

"And I am the little bright-eyed sprite?" I pushed her hand away, gripped my side.

"Of course you are, spritely Inger-Marie!" Lovise backed away from me, hands up and eyebrows raised. "The clothes are good. Your boots, however, could use some work." She gestured to them, tucked under the lip of my bed. I hadn't thought much about them. "Nearly any outfit can be saved with the proper hat and, especially, footwear." I looked to her side of the room where there was a row of boots, each with buttons so numerous they seemed to be vying for space. Lovise had evening shoes as well, and these were bowed, beaded, feathered. Each pair looked tiny and I'd seen her struggle in and out of them several times, wondered why she didn't own any that were the size of her feet.

"But they're hardly even visible beneath my skirts."

"Yes, and like any part of a woman that is hardly visible, every glimpse must be worth it. Your boots should be as soft and clean as skin and should have as many buttons as a corset has hooks and eyes."

"Oh." I'd never considered any of this, had not thought much of the appearance of my boots beyond special occasions, of which daily life was not one. My greatest concern had been that my boots be comfortable enough to walk in all day. They were clean and polished and I'd congratulated myself on their practicality. Lovise may have congratulated herself on other things – delicacy and extravagance. Perhaps I could temper my dependability with a bit of both.

"Once you secure a position, one of your first purchases should be a good pair of boots. Until then, don't worry, I'll lend you one of mine."

"All right." I was skeptical. "And how will I find this mysterious gentleman who is going to accompany me from shop to shop?"

"I can lend you one of those as well." Lovise winked.

Six

Though his manners were probably fine, and he was very well dressed, the man who Lovise arranged to accompany me around to the shops seemed a little rough, unfinished. His face was heavy, the skin thick on his cheeks, sagging at his chin. He had the teeth of someone who wasn't from the city. Even I could see this, though he tried to hide his mouth with a thick moustache. I looked at his boots. They were so polished that they looked wet, laces thick enough to seem to cast a small shadow over the gleaming leather. He bowed slightly toward me, one eyebrow cocked, mouth clamped over those teeth, so all seemed a mockery of proper manners.

We went into only the most high-end shops, none of which I'd been in yet as they'd seemed too exclusive to me. The man spoke, introduced me as Miss Inger-Marie Jüül of Gudumlund estate and asked if my assistance might be needed in any way. The shop ladies looked at him as though he was suggesting something scandalous and regarded me as though I was either to be pitied or reviled. I looked down at Lovise's boots on my feet and concentrated on the pain radiating from my cramped toes, aching heels. When we left the shops, I would give the slightest, most discreet nod and almost a curtsy, as though to convey that they were wrong. I was not the girl they thought me to be; this man had no purchase over me. I owed him nothing. I didn't believe I did. By the end of the afternoon, the man seemed more hindrance than help, and I thought of the grasping quality of both him and Lovise, how they pretended at wealth and class. How thin their veneers. How cheap Lovise now seemed after a day spent not with her but with the man she'd sent me out with as though it were a favour.

As with most things that set our fate, it only takes one – in this case, one shop, one shop matron to ask me some questions about my experience and the position I sought. I was honest about my limited experience, equally so about the position. "Whatever you see fit for me to do."

"Well, as it happens, one of my dressers left unexpectedly this week. I can only imagine why." She directed this to the man. "I wouldn't usually hire anyone off the street, but I am in an awkward position with her departure. Can you begin tomorrow?"

I felt such relief when we left the shop. We walked a few steps away from the storefront and I turned to the man, smiled at him for the first time that afternoon. He suggested we have supper together. "We'll celebrate. It makes me feel good to be able to help a young lady out. It's as much my celebration as yours."

I felt like I'd been too hard on him in my mind, had judged Lovise harshly in her absence. Who was I to pass such judgment? Both had helped me.

I went into the supper club through the ladies' door and met him in the dining room. As we ate together, I attempted to make conversation, but I wasn't sure what was proper in this situation. I praised the food in the club, but I kept my comments brief. I didn't want to come across as effusive. The man didn't seem to mind. He smiled and nodded and ordered several drinks. I declined and he seemed happy to drink without me. When I suggested that I was fine to walk back to the pension on my own, he swallowed hard, wiped his mouth with the back of his hand, his palm splayed toward me, and waved his arm for a waiter. "Absolutely not," he said, spitting a bit as he did. "I will escort you home."

We were a block away from the pension, nearly there. "Come." His voice gravelled in his throat. I followed him into a lane, and it wasn't until we were shadowed from the street lamps that I questioned why I had. When he turned to me, I thought he might give me an explanation or pay me a compliment, but instead he pushed me up against a building so forcefully my hat fell off. I bent to try to reach it, and the man slammed me against the wall by my shoulders again. "Got you a nice little job, didn't I?" His lips strained against his awful teeth, eyes glazed in a way I'd seen with animals in distress. "A nice little job for a nice little girl." He took my hair in his fist and pulled my head back. Shock of cold air against my neck, my hair strained against my scalp. When his hold on my hair loosened, I thought, *that's it, that's done*, but it wasn't. His hand became a clamp on my skull, and he slammed my mouth up against his, his tongue forcing open my lips. He smelled of smoke and sour alcohol and some deeper, base, more disgusting smell, not unlike that of a dead stag that my brothers brought home from the northern woods after hunting season. He jerked his head back. "Oh, you're going to hold that little mouth of yours tight, are you? I like a tight mouth." He pushed me down onto my knees in front of him.

The man hooked my mouth with his thumb and pulled it open as he unbuttoned his pants. He pushed himself at me, his wretched smell, the wire of his hair. He shoved himself against my nose, my chin, sloppy in his need. I tried to close my mouth against his thumb, against the sour smell, against him, but he wrenched it open and forced himself in. I could feel how he hardened, and I gagged so much that I thought my throat would seize. I couldn't breathe, concentrated on how my vision was going black. I would see nothing, smell nothing, feel nothing but that black. I stayed in the blackness until my head slammed back and stars spilled across my closed vision. I rolled to my side, then went forward onto my hands, a line of spit coming out of my mouth until I was able to vomit. I emptied my mouth of him, my stomach spasming.

"Stop that!" he yelled. "Get up. Get up now." He pulled me up by the back of my dress, as though I were a kitten. Once I was standing, he handed me his handkerchief. I wiped my mouth, smelling him on the fabric, felt the saliva build in my mouth again. He cleared his throat, once, twice, then said, "You all right, miss?" his voice softer than it had been all day. I nodded. "Here, look at me." I did. I let him straighten out my clothing, allowed his hands to push the hair off my face. When he was finished, he smiled, looked proud, congratulatory. It seemed he might reach over and pat my head as though I were a child. He walked me the remaining block back to the pension, bowed slightly and took my hand at the door, pushed coins into my palm and tipped his hat.

One might think that I would refuse the money, throw it at his feet as I spat into his face. I wonder if that would've been the larger thing to do, but I was so small. I clutched them like a child, felt the coins' heat in my hold. In my room, I spilled them onto my bed, brought my palms to my face, smelled the tang of metal. I returned the boots to Lovise's side of the room and sat staring at her as she slept, then lay on the bed on top of the bedclothes. Every time I felt as though I wanted to clutch my knees to my chest and sob, I lay straight and still, told myself that I was stronger than that, that I cared less. A shudder crawled along my skin, burrowed in, and I got out of bed, gave up on sleep.

I made my way to where I'd seen Lovise take a bottle from out of the narrow chest at the foot of her bed, heard the tight gulps of her throat as she swallowed, the quiet smack of her lips. Blood banged in my ears, my palms itchy with sweat as I tried to ease the cork out quietly. When it left the bottle, the noise inflated in the room, but Lovise didn't stir. I waited a minute, a minute more, then brought the bottle to my mouth. What was it? Brandy or moonshine, I didn't know. It seared against my lips, marked a flame down my throat, burst into heat in my stomach.

As tense as I'd been earlier, I lay as loose, cushioned by warmth and then buffeted by cold as dawn blanched the room. I got up and went down the hall to wash myself with water that had been sitting in a pot on the radiator all night. I dressed in my cleanest, plainest, most humble clothes and boots and went to work.

The shop lady outfitted me again from undergarments to satin-laced shoes as she showed me how I would dress the ladies who shopped at the store. "This is the proper way to roll a silk stocking. This is how you arrange the stays." And finally, "This is the last time I will show you any of this; I expect you to do this as gently and as perfectly as I have shown you from now on."

"Of course," I answered. I had followed her fingers across my skin, her palms smoothing fabric as she charted out not only the right way to dress a lady, but a new map of my body. The gentle neutrality of her hands absolved me as much as the night before had stained me. Tarnish and absolution, I could carry both. I considered what to do with the money all day. It was a small amount but enough to buy a ticket home to visit my family. Instead, I went in and out of banks until I found one that would allow me to open my own account without it being countersigned by a man. "My father is dead," I told them. "I have no brothers." Both lies.

"Perhaps you should wait until you get married," one banker suggested.

"I don't believe I will be marrying any time soon."

Who's to know if, in that moment, I thought this to be true? It hardly matters anymore.

Seven

I moved into a thin building cramped between two others on a narrow street behind the Royal Theatre. I lived there with three floors of young women, each of us in simply appointed rooms, only those facing the road with windows. Originally for actresses, it also housed those like me, who worked in high-end shops, and a couple of girls who modelled clothing. The girls who had been there longest had the front rooms, if they wanted them, with the understanding that the rest of us would crowd toward the windows, jostle to feel the sun on our skin through glass. In warm weather, we would push panes open, dangle things out the window – scarves, garters, even our hair, loosed from pins, as we leaned into the street – until we were reprimanded as though we were children. No men were permitted in the residence and there was a small staff – a cleaning girl, a cook who provided breakfasts and light dinners. There was an older woman, a spinster and patroness of the arts, who ensured the household was kept in a way fitting for the young ladies who lodged there.

My employer had recommended me to the residence. "We've a certain standard to uphold in this shop – each of us do, and that extends beyond our working hours." She looked at me closely, as though to gauge whether I understood. "The residence is held in high esteem. It's an appropriate place for a single young lady like yourself to live."

"I understand."

I woke early, breakfasted, walked to work and back. Some days I would stop at the library, others I would sit on a park bench and read. I had learned French in school and was teaching myself English. I began work at ten in the morning, finished at six each evening, an hour on either end of opening hours to arrange and steam the clothes, unpack any new shipments, lay out and later lock away the jewellery. When I returned to the residence, I would peel away the garments that kept me so tightly presented each workday, work my fingers into points of pain and pressure in my feet, circle my ankles, stretch my arms overhead and feel the slip of my undergarments ride along my skin.

I knew my place in our residence. There were young women who were more attractive, some who were better bred. Some were more adventurous; others took their roles as ladies very seriously. I was one of the good ones – quiet, kind, petite. In a word, *unintimidating*. I was one of the women who the others would come to saying, "Oh, Marie, what am I going to do?" faces sloppy with tears, or dry-eyed, mouths in slack lines set by exhaustion. Most, if not all, of the time, the problem was men. Men pushing their hands under skirts, between stays. Men getting in or being kept out. Men moving on or wanting more or marrying other women. What did I know of men? Very little, but I suspect this is why the other women came to me – they told me things for which I had little context to get an honest opinion, to titillate, to make their own lives seem more meaningful, perhaps, in the drama they created. I didn't know why they came to me, but I listened and offered little advice. I hardly felt qualified.

Nearly a year after moving into the residence, I returned from work and found a man standing on the top step. I cleared my throat as I approached the stairs. He turned and smiled as though he were expecting me, then leaned against the ledge, arms folded in front of him, and blocked the door. I stopped before the last two stairs. "Can I help you?"

"Perhaps." He didn't say anything else, held his mouth as though his bottom lip were pushed up against his teeth, top lip plumped out. A smirk or a suppressed laugh. I looked to his eyes for a cue. He raised an eyebrow, his eyes directly on mine when I met his.

I tried to keep my own expression neutral. My mouth was tight and heat gathered under my clothes, pressed into my ribs, as if with the effort.

His eyebrow dropped and he nodded toward the residence. "Do you live here?"

I cleared my throat and kept my eyes on his. "Yes." If this was a test or a joke, I wouldn't stand down.

He pushed off the ledge and fiddled with his collar as he looked down the street. "So does my cousin."

"Oh?" His cousin could've been any one of a dozen other girls.

"Anita." He looked back at me. "Do you know her?"

"Yes, of course." She was one of the actresses. It wasn't unusual for men to come around for them, even pretend to be family to gain entry.

"I'm visiting from Zealand and would like to call on her." He'd taken a step down toward me, top lip parting into a smile over teeth perfect but for one rogue incisor. "You can let me in?"

"No, I can't." My voice sounded flat, tired. Did he really think this appeal would work? "No gentlemen are permitted in our residence. You'll have to make other arrangements." I spoke as though I was reading from a posted page of rules.

"No gentlemen permitted?" He raised his hands, palms toward me, and then dropped them. "What about a simple workingman?"

He didn't look simple, or much like a workingman, his pants pleated, jacket too long. I suspected he wore suspenders rather than a belt. More like the men in the theatre district than my brothers back home. I didn't answer and the man sighed, ran a hand through his hair. "Yes, that's what the woman who answered the door told me."

I had a hard time not looking at one errant curl, held upright as if by its own will. "And you hoped someone else would come along and give you a different answer?"

His laugh was soft, kind. "That, and I was considering what to do next." He looked at me directly again, and I could see a scar nicked into the top of one of his cheeks. The man reached out his hand. "You can come up, you know. I don't want to keep you from your own door."

I took his hand and walked past him to the landing above. "It's hardly my own."

"No, I suppose not, if you have to adhere to someone else's rules."

"Only those I would apply myself."

"Well, can you pass on a message to my cousin – or, can you ask her to come to the door?"

"Oh, you weren't told? Anita will be at the theatre tonight."

"The theatre? What will she be doing there?"

Perhaps he wasn't a suitor, but he certainly didn't seem to know his cousin well. "She'll be on stage."

"Oh, of course she will be." He looked out to the street, hand against his mouth, then he dropped it, looked back at me. "Well, then, I guess I should see her perform. Would you like to accompany me?"

"I beg your pardon?"

"To the play. What time will it start?"

"It must be starting soon." I reached for the door. "I'm sorry, I can't come."

"You've a prior engagement? Or perhaps I've not been enough of a gentleman?" He winked, then began stepping down the stairs. "I'm sorry, miss," he said. "I've been a bother, I can tell." He turned and took another step or two, then stopped to face me again. "Unlike Anita, I'm never sure how to act, especially when in front of a young lady as beautiful as you are." He put his fingers to his forehead and bowed slightly, a kind of salute.

I stood with my hand on the door handle, watched him go. It had been a year, I reminded myself. Nearly a year since I'd moved to the city, found good employment, a respectable place to live. A year of vigilance at our barred doorway, turning away the men who came for my flatmates. This man had come for someone else, as well, but it had been I who was there – why shouldn't I go with him?

I called, "Wait!" Something held in my throat, tight and round, like a small plum lodged there. The man turned, slowly, as though I was going to say something to further disappoint him. "I'll come with you." He smiled and folded his hands, stood up straight, stiff, as though he were a porter or wait staff, playing a part.

The play was Ibsen's *A Doll's House*, which, I knew from my flatmates, played every couple of years between premieres. "You've seen this before?"

I hadn't. "I've not yet seen Anita in this role. I've heard she plays it very well." I was inventing myself as I went along.

I'd found out that the man was Mr. Bertram Bruun, visiting from the seaside village of Tisvilde. "She's not playing Nora, is she?" he asked.

"No, not Nora." I strained out a tight little laugh, as though I knew what was funny. "The maid, perhaps? Or the governess." The girls had been talking about the parts over dinner for several nights. I wished I'd paid closer attention.

"Well, there's certainly a difference. I suppose we'll soon find out!"

Anita played the maid and her role was smaller than I'd expected. Perhaps it was because the other characters played through so many variations of sacrifice, lies and deceit. They snuck about and drank and stormed at each other. Oh, and Nora's awful dance! Such melodrama, yes, but by the third act, I was hardly aware of Mr. Bruun at my side. When the maid delivered the fated letter on stage, I sensed him beside me again. I'd moved forward in my seat and when I sat back again, his arm pressed up against mine. The play of fabric on my arm, the heat of him. I didn't move away.

After the final curtain, I suggested that we say hello to Anita. "You've been backstage before?" Mr. Bruun was still seated, leaning back. As I watched others leaving, I could sense him in my periphery, watching me. I turned back to him and he looked like he was swallowing a smile.

"No." Nor had I been to the theatre with a man, only with other girls from the residence. "It's worth a try, yes?" I could be whomever I wanted that night.

We made our way against the crowd, down one narrow, dark hall, then another. Mr. Bruun followed me closely, his hands reaching out, touching my waist as we rounded corners. We came up against dead ends, doubled back on ourselves, stumbled and tripped on ropes, laughing as we did. "Good Lord, you've led us into quite a labyrinth, haven't you? Okay, one last try and then we admit defeat. Deal?"

"It can't be this hard to find! Let's listen." I thought we might hear voices that would lead us to where the actors and actresses were.

"Here, a door." Bertram pushed against it and took my hand. We emerged into a lane behind the theatre, a slap of cool air and the fetid smell of garbage, both of us laughing. "Well, this is certainly not backstage!"

"Certainly not."

Bertram put his hands on my shoulders and gently steered me out of the lane. I liked the weight of his hands there, the warmth. When we were almost at the street, a woman pushed up away from a shadowed wall of the building and came toward us. I turned away without seeing her, not wanting to stop.

"Inger-Marie?" My name, a voice I recognized.

I took another step toward the street and the lights there.

"It is!" she said. "You must recognize me, too, Marie. It's not been that long, has it?" I turned to face her, Mr. Bruun close behind me. Her makeup was more garish than it had been – rouge visible even in the low light, kohl heavy around her eyes – and her hair in a different style, a fringe hanging over her face, the rest piled like a nest, spilling over the top of her head.

"Lovise?"

"It is you!" She lunged at me in a hug. I held myself stiffly, patted her back. She smelled slightly of vinegar under a cloyingly sweet smell – sugar, jasmine. She backed away, held my hands in hers and swung our arms back and forth together, giggling, as though we were sisters, children. She dropped my hands and took a step toward Bertram, then stood posing, hand on hip, bottom lip jutted out. She motioned toward him with her chin, "And who's this?" Voice an octave lower.

"Lovise, I –" I wanted to get away, to turn from her.

"Yes? You?" She looked from me to Bertram, both hands on her hips now, a frown before her face split into a laugh and she threw her head back, then leaned toward us, voice a whisper. "You'd like a deal for the two of you? I can do that, you know. Two are better than one, three's a treat." She winked at Bertram, made a little kiss-kiss motion toward me in a way that seemed guileless, childlike.

"Oh no, Lovise. I can't, we –"

"We have to go, miss." Mr. Bruun took my elbow and we turned away from her, walked briskly away. When we were around the corner, I pulled my arm away from his. "An old friend?"

"Not a friend, exactly. I didn't know her long." We were on the street of my residence. It seemed so dim, darkness sporing the edges as it narrowed. "Are the lights low on gas?" I walked a few steps before I realized that Mr. Bruun had stopped. I turned back to him.

"Are you okay?" he asked.

"I'm fine." The person I'd been trying to be at the theatre – the one who made suggestions, laughed at being lost backstage – was gone.

"You seem – was it seeing your friend?"

"I told you, she isn't my friend."

"Friend or not, did seeing her upset you?"

"Not exactly." I kept walking and he joined me. I remembered the man whom Lovise had found to take me to the shops. My body slammed against stones, his terrible smell. Lovise's scent, both syrup and curdle at once. I stopped, put a palm to my forehead to stop the tilt of the ground, spin of my head. When I looked up, we were at the bottom of the stairs to the residence and I stared at the stone cut of the steps, as though studying them. At the top, the doors framed two rectangles of hazy light.

Mr. Bruun held my hand as he walked me up. "You're sure you're all right?" I nodded. "I suppose I can't see you in, make sure you're well?"

"Of course not. It's policy."

"Yes, policy. You've mentioned."

"Yes." The smell of Lovise was still in my nose. I resisted raising a sleeve to see if her scent was on the fabric. "I'm not to feel sorry for you, am I?"

"Of course not! And I won't feel sorry for you, either, Miss Jüül." I'd seen the lick of discomfort pass over Mr. Bruun's face before he snapped it into a quick smile. "I mean, I am sorry that you're upset about something."

"I'm fine."

"Of course."

We stood facing each other, the air cool, damp where it met my skin. Laughter came from the other side of the door. I wanted to go in.

"You'll let Anita know that I'll be by tomorrow morning?"

"I will." I watched Mr. Bruun go down the steps. He turned at the bottom, raised his hand to his temple, his chin low. His stride was quick and steady as he walked away. The evening hadn't gone as I had planned, but then I'd planned none of it, had I?

Eight

.

The next morning when I left to go to work, Mr. Bruun and Anita were on the front steps. They stood when I came out. Anita's face was blurred as she turned away from me, wiped at her eyes. Her voice cracked as she went back in. "I'll see you tonight, Marie."

When the door closed, I turned to Mr. Bruun. "Is your cousin all right?"

"She will be. She's had some trouble. I know she'll be fine, though." He reached toward my shoulder, then dropped his hands to his sides. "Can I walk you to work?"

Mr. Bruun accompanied me to and from the shop for the next three days. On the third evening, we were at the front door of my building, standing on the steps as we had each time, when he said, "I leave tomorrow to go home." He moved toward me and I wondered if this was it, a proper first kiss, but he leaned down and whispered, "Come with me."

"I can't." I fancied myself an adult by then. Someone who performed her job well. Someone who aspired to more but hadn't figured out what that might be. "I couldn't."

Mr. Bruun backed away from me, leaned against the stone ledge and crossed his arms over his chest. "I've spent three days with you. Enough time to know that each morning you walk the same way to work, stop in the same places along the way. And every evening, you've let me walk you home, made small talk, then said a polite goodbye. How long do you want to live your life like this?"

"You don't know me, Mr. Bruun. You don't know what I do or don't want for myself."

"Well, answer me this: Are you living the life you want to be living?"

"I believe I'm living a good life for a young woman of my social standing."

"So, no."

"What would you suggest – that I leave my position and my residence without notice, leave the shop without an employee and the ladies short a flatmate? How will this make my life more fulfilling?" Before he could answer, I added, "I don't believe our lives should be guided by whims."

"Of course you don't. And you'll never know, will you, what might happen if you were to leave this dull, ordered world?" He looked at me briefly and then seemed to study something over my head. "My sister and brother-in-law have a tea shop where I'm sure you could work. You could leave a month's rent when you go or send it from there," he said, as though he'd already given it some thought. "Neither the shop nor the ladies here will be without a replacement for you for long – and what is that saying?"

"You're trying to convince me that I'm replaceable? That this is a good enough reason to leave?"

"I suppose I am."

I was on the platform minutes before the train was to depart, wearing my best wool coat and hat, my finest stockings, my boots well polished. I looked every part a young lady of a certain class, not the farm girl that I'd been when I'd arrived in Copenhagen. I could've been going on a weekend junket, as I'd wanted to do with my fine luggage ever since I'd bought it at cost from the shop. A lovers' weekend, though I was giving up a lot for something that was more than a weekend, following someone who was less than a lover. I stood, a suitcase in both hands, and looked straight ahead at the space above the tracks where the train would appear, where the conductor would step down and hold out his hand for tickets. I had one. I was ready. I just needed to keep looking straight ahead.

When Mr. Bruun yelled, "Miss Jüül!" I saw him in my periphery, but I wouldn't turn. He took the luggage out of my hands and spun me to face him, the smile too big, sloppy on his face. "You're here!"

I pulled my hands from his and lowered them. I knew that people were watching, expecting something from us – something sweet and uplifting, perhaps, or brooding and dramatic, but something nonetheless. "I'm here."

Mr. Bruun said quietly into my ear, "I'm so happy." I wondered if he was happy for me or for himself. What we had seemed superficial, based on banter and a kind of bravado on both our parts, and Mr. Bruun's reaction to me seemed overblown, misplaced. I felt like someone in a role in which she had no idea how to behave or react. I wasn't an actress like his cousin, but I could learn what was expected of me.

The train moved north into lowlands snaked with waterways and pools, the land vibrant green puzzle pieces, the sky a smear of grey. I sat by the window and watched. Mr. Bruun cleared his throat a few times as though he might speak, but he didn't say anything. Several minutes into the trip, he said, "You'll like it there," and I jumped. I turned from the window and looked at him. "North, in Zealand."

"You're sure, then?" I meant to tease him, to sound carefree, but I heard the anxious edge in my voice.

"Yes," he said, and I saw something in the way he tilted his head, softened his eyes. In Copenhagen, we had been a kind of equals. Now, I would be under his care in a way. As though to confirm this, he reached over, took my hand. I didn't move it from off my own lap. It was all I could do to not pull away. In that moment, I wanted to be able to stand up and get off the train. I wanted to go back. I leaned against the seat and fell asleep.

"Miss Jüül?" I heard my name a few times before I saw Mr. Bruun, his face so close I could see the scar chipped out of his cheekbone, the deep brown of his eyes. He moved away a bit, a hand on each knee, still leaning toward me. "You're awake."

"I suppose." I watched him, a stranger again. If anything, a feeling of reserve had grown between us, those four days together in the city now a spot in the distance from which we were moving away.

"Can I call you by your first name? I'd like it if you called me Bertram."

"All right." I tried out the sound of his first name, "Bertram."

"There's something I need to tell you, Marie." Of course there was. I waited for what it would be. "My sister's tea and sweets shop, it's not – it's not in Tisvilde, where I live."

I blinked, then rubbed my palm against one eye, then the other. "Oh?"

"Tisvilde is so small. I didn't know of any work there. But you won't be far, and I know you'll like my sister."

I didn't know what to say in response, so I said nothing.

"I'll visit."

We disembarked at a flat, wet town, and Bertram led me along a canal cut through the centre, linking a large lake to the fjord, binding moisture into the air. Willows sprinkled water on us as we entered Soeberg's Bakery and Confectionery on a street across from the canal. We went through the shop to the bakery in the back. Two people looked up: a man who tucked his long blond hair behind his ears and a woman, her hair braided loosely and looped around her head. "Oh, Bertram!" She moved around a table toward us, wiping flour against her apron. "Who have you brought us? She looks so lovely, like a northern milkmaid! Are you from the north, darling?"

"We met in Copenhagen," I answered.

"Yes, of course, but where are you from?"

"My family has a holding in Gudum, in Jutland."

"Anna, this is Inger-Marie Jüül."

She took a cigarette from the pocket of her apron and lit it as she looked at me, touched it to her mouth for just a moment, seemed to kiss the end of it, then held it like a tiny wand between her fingers.

"Miss Jüül, this is my sister, Anna."

The man came around me, hand on my back for a moment, held out a pastry on a plate. "Taste this." I took a bite of the pastry, folded with layers of jellied fruit. He watched me. "Well, what do you think?"

I swallowed, licked the icing sugar from my lips. "It's delicious."

He looked from Bertram to Anna, grinning, then asked, "Are you an early morning person?"

"I can be."

They all laughed at this, as though I were being clever, and Bertram said, "And this is my brother-in-law, Diderik Soeberg."

"So formal! My God. Call me Dirk, Inger-Marie, is it? You're hired. And we've a lovely little flat for you upstairs."

I accepted the job, said goodbye to Bertram in front of his sister and brother-in-law with no more affection than pressed cheeks, lips in the air beside our faces. I'd misunderstood something, possibly a whole series of things. I'd assumed we were engaged in a kind of courtship. I liked the way Bertram's mouth pressed upward into a smile, caught on one sharp tooth. I liked the sheen in his eyes when he joked, chiding me, as he had the day we met on the steps. Now, it seemed I'd misread something. I had no friend like I'd been to so many women at our shared residence, waiting for me to come home, to parse the events of the past week and figure out what had been misinterpreted, and by whom.

NINE

I worked in the bakery alongside Dirk, beginning at four in the morning and finishing at noon. Anna would arrive mid-morning with three children, each of them under four. They had blond hair that rose from their round heads like dandelion fluff. Anna's hair was a colour between blond and a red so pale that it looked pink. Her face was pushed into a heart shape by cheekbones that were dotted with freckles. The most striking thing about Anna, though, was that she wore men's apparel. Rarely, if ever, did I see her in a skirt or dress. I was never sure if she and Dirk shared clothes or if they each had their own men's wardrobes. Her pants hung loosely from fine leather belts, and she didn't wear a vest or tie with her shirts. Nor did she wear a brassiere. She would undo a few buttons on her shirt and nurse one child or another, sometimes two at once, while sitting in the back of the shop, talking with us while we rolled or pounded dough, cut shapes, folded pastries.

I'm not sure whom I found more distracting as I worked – the children, who were generally well-behaved, as well as they could be for infants and toddlers, or Anna, her skin covered by the loose cotton of a man's shirt and nothing else, or exposed as those shirts slipped from her shoulder.

Anna never asked me if I minded or begged pardon or anything beyond carrying on as though it were the most natural thing to do to nurse her children in the bakery. She and Dirk showed each other affection in the same way Anna dressed – loose, open, presumptuous. He would cup and squeeze her behind; Anna would pull Dirk toward her. Their kisses were frequent and relaxed. The fair-haired brood played with dough or blocks or dolls around our feet, often barefoot themselves and smattered with flour. I wondered if it was appropriate for me, never mind their children, to see the couple that way. They may have been playing it up for me a bit. They thought me naive. I suppose I was. I'd not met people like the Soebergs before. In Copenhagen, there were the girls who tenaciously guarded their honour even as they continued to blunder, led astray by their own desire or the honeyed words of handsome men. And there were women like Lovise, propped along alleys, reminders that decorum didn't pull everyone with equal strength.

When I first arrived, there was another girl who worked in the front in the confectionery and tea shop. She and I rarely spoke and when she left, she did so abruptly, coming into the back where Dirk and I were baking and Anna was singing as she rolled dough with the children. The girl interrupted. "I am going now. God no longer wants me to work here." She took off her apron and left. We all watched her leave, then stared at the closed door. When we finally looked at each other, Anna began laughing first, followed by Dirk. "Well, I guess you've a new position." I didn't understand. "I know you've got a chest full of nice clothes up there. Bertram has told me as much." I wondered how and when that had ever come up. "You'd best get changed and out front before we lose some customers."

So, I began working in the front of the shop. I would have preferred to have stayed in the bakery, hands kneading warm dough, heat swelling out of ovens. The tea shop's clientele were ladies of a class able to buy baked goods rather than make their own. They were familiar to me, much like the ladies who had come into the boutique in Copenhagen. Friendlier, perhaps. They would praise my appearance and manners and tease that they would marry me to their sons. I wondered what they thought of Dirk and Anna, though I suppose they didn't see them much. This was a different place than my home. In Gudum, businesses run by eccentrics would not last.

Because I was no longer in the bakery, Dirk hired someone else, a young man named Knud who may have been my age, perhaps a year or two older or younger. He looked ageless. His brown hair was glassy, his eyes layers of colour – a dark outer rim, then brown, hazel, green and blue rings all blending together. He adored Anna. I would hear their laughter barking out of the bakery. Knud had convinced Anna that they shouldn't smoke in the bakery, and she happily complied, followed him outside. I would see them leaning into each other, all giggles and whispers, smoking behind the shop. I wondered why Dirk didn't seem to mind.

Knud moved into the other room in the flat above the bakery. Since I wasn't asked, I wasn't able to speak to Anna until he was already there. I told her that I wasn't sure it was right, living in such proximity as an unmarried man and woman. "Not right? What's not right about it, Marie?"

"Well, you know, it's –"

"Yes?"

"I don't know – improper."

When she laughed it didn't seem mean-spirited, not completely. "Oh, darling, Knud's not going to bother you, I promise. He can be a friend to you, if you'll let him. We're not bound by dated rules like those in Jutland, or even the nonsense about society and propriety in Copenhagen – and you don't have to be bound by them either!"

I wasn't comfortable and showed this with how little I spoke to Knud, how I would straighten my back and leave the room when he entered. I would've liked to have addressed him properly, by his last name, but when I asked, he said, "Well, why would I tell you that? You'll want to call me Mister Something." He assumed a familiarity I didn't feel we had. "If I tell you anything, it is this: I am no mister." I must have looked uneasy at this statement. He took both of my hands in his. "Don't worry, Miss Jüül. Not everything needs to be proper. And besides, why waste such a gloriously strong fist of a name like Knud?" He winked and laughed at this, and I couldn't help but sputter a laugh back.

TEN

One afternoon, nearly two months after I'd arrived in Frederiksvaerk, Anna
came into the shop smelling of smoke, her hair loose, shirt held together by
two buttons near her sternum. She turned over the sign on the door. "We're
closing a couple of hours early today. We've an event of sorts tonight. You best
go rest up. We'll want you there tonight and it will go late."

"An event of sorts?"

"A salon." She came toward me, touched the hairs at my temples as if
to push them out of my face, though it was her hair that was loose, frowzy.
"You'll see." I was going to ask her if Bertram was coming but thought better
of it. I'd received a couple of polite cards from him since I'd arrived. He hoped
I was enjoying my work. He would visit soon. His words were as flat and dull
as the paper on which he wrote. He certainly hadn't suggested a longing to
see me again. I wouldn't show interest to see him, either, even with a simple
question to his sister.

Knud and I kept different hours, and he was often asleep when I finished
my shift. That day was no different, though he had left a piece of meat pie and
a bowl of onion soup on the table with a note that said: *Eat up, my dear, and
have a rest. It will be a late night tonight.* We'd not shared food before, nor
had Knud displayed any kind of paternal behaviour toward me. No one had,
really. Here, it was assumed that I was able to look after myself. Someone – a
man – leaving me food and a note seemed both a sweet gesture and an odd

one. I ate and I napped, as instructed. I woke to Knud crouched beside my bed, touching my arm. I pushed myself up. "What are you doing in here?"

Knud dropped his hand, stood and laughed. "It's time to get ready for the salon, beautiful." He extended an arm as though to help me out of bed. Aside from my brothers, I'd never had a man so close to my bed before. I was thankful that I was wearing my day clothes. I stood up without his help, tried to smooth my skirts out. "You'll have to change, of course," Knud said.

"I won't." I didn't like having anyone tell me what I would wear, especially a man I hardly knew, standing beside my bed.

He pursed his lips and put a hand on his hip like a prude, a school marm. "You will. Wear black if you've got some. Or a dark colour. You'll want to look like an intellectual."

"And you assume I'm not?"

Knud dropped his pose and laughed. "No, I assume you are. Your garments will only accentuate that." When he left the room, I did as Knud said and buttoned myself into a navy-blue dress, then took that off and pulled on a white blouse with a high lace collar and a blue skirt. I wouldn't be told what to wear – at least, not all of me would. Partial compliance could hardly be called submission.

When I came out of my room, Knud was still there. He stood and extended his arm, as though he were my date, to escort me to the narrow stairs that led into the shop. He let go of my hand when we got to the stairwell. It was too narrow for two.

Here I was. I had come to this place when I thought I was going to another. I was just a girl, working in a tea shop, with the hand of a man named Knud on the curve of my back as we entered a room.

Soeberg's Bakery and Confectionery was cloying with warmth, and a layer of smoke hovered like a garland around those standing. As I looked around for a place to sit, Anna came toward us. "There you are!" She kissed first Knud on both cheeks, then me. I stared at her, dressed in skirts for the first time since we'd met, a man's shirt tied above her waist with a strip of skin showing, a belt of nothing. "We wondered when you two would finally emerge." She winked at me, as though we were in on some amusing conspiracy together, and turned, put her hand on a man's back. "Didn't we, Bertram?" I felt my throat clench.

Bertram turned to face us, slowly, and glanced first at Knud, his eyes a quick wash of appraisal, then at me. He moved toward me and I took a step back. Bertram put his hand to his forehead, then brought it to his chest before reaching it out to take my hand. "Miss Jüül."

"We're back to that, then, are we?"

Bertram let out a sound between a laugh and a cough and looked toward Knud. "To what?"

"Our formal names, Mr. Bruun."

"Not if you wish otherwise, Miss Jüül."

"Marie," I said, and looked past him into the crush of people in the tea shop. Men and women drank wine from small juice glasses, smoked, tipped their heads back in exaggerated laughter. Knud touched my elbow lightly and then moved away from us.

"Marie," Bertram said quietly, leaning toward me while still facing the room. "Are you enjoying it here?"

"Well, I'm not sure what to expect from a salon, but it looks like the harvest gatherings I used to sneak into as a girl."

Bertram laughed. "I meant in Frederiksvaerk – but I suppose it does look much like a common gathering." He shifted and I could feel the fabric of his jacket against my blouse, a feeling that both tickled and nearly soothed me. "Don't worry, Dirk and Anna will raise the atmosphere, intellectually, or at least, they will try. They'll either have someone speak about some obscure subject, or they'll begin a formal debate. In the meantime, I'll get us something to drink. Wait here."

Bertram brought back a tray of tiny glasses, each full of wine. I drank one, the taste dense and bitter in my mouth. I wasn't used to drinking wine, but I followed with another. Bertram did the same – we stood side by side, staring into our glasses instead of talking. I looked around. "Where's Knud?" I hardly knew my new roommate and yet I not only wanted to see him then, I wanted him by my side.

Bertram glanced around, though it was clear he didn't want to find anyone. "So, you're permitted to reside with a man now. How do you like it?"

Before I could answer, Anna was standing on a table and clapping. "Hello! Hello!" she called. "Welcome, everyone! The more formal part of the evening will commence shortly." When she said the word *formal*, she raised her skirts and showed us her legs, pointed a bare foot. "Please gather round."

She jumped down and I looked where she had been, wondered how the owner of a business could stand, barefoot, on a table. I found another little glass and drank what was in it in a few swallows.

Bertram took the empty glass, his hand on mine for a moment as he did, cleared his throat. "What have you read recently?" I began to answer and then stopped, began again but couldn't finish because I was laughing. "What is it?" Bertram's grin seemed hopeful but forced.

"Nothing," I managed to get out through a laugh. "I've read nothing!" I continued to giggle and Bertram watched me. "I've read nothing since I arrived!" I leaned up against the wall, dug at my eyes with the heel of my hand so I could pretend that was why they were red, watery.

Bertram moved closer, put himself between the room and me. "Are you okay, Marie?"

I pushed myself away from the wall. "Was this a joke?"

"Pardon?"

"Was this some sort of joke? Pick up a naive girl, convince her to leave Copenhagen – where she had good employment and a respectable place to live – and suggest she move somewhere, I don't know, freer, more unconventional? Some place I could expand my mind, I suppose. Is this what this supposed salon is going to do?"

"Marie, I –"

"You left me at a tea shop!"

Bertram was so close that he nearly obscured my view of the rest of the room, but I could see Dirk moving toward us.

I lowered my voice to a tense whisper. "I could've had a job in a tea shop at home in Gudum!"

"Is everything okay here?" Dirk was beside Bertram, who had backed away from me a bit.

Knud appeared on Bertram's other side. I looked from one man to the other. They each watched me. "Are you all here to see if I'm all right? If little Jüül is all right?" Three juice glasses of wine and I was dizzy, the words thick on my tongue.

"I think she needs some fresh air," Dirk said to Bertram, as though I were out of earshot.

Bertram nodded, but it was Knud who moved forward, took my arm. "I'll take her outside for a bit."

I pulled my arm out of his hand. "I can make my own way outside, thank you." I pushed past them. When I got outside, I didn't stop walking, headed toward the canal. I wanted to be near water, away from Soeberg's Bakery and Confectionery and Dirk and Anna's pseudo-intellectual salon. I don't know how far I'd walked before Bertram caught up with me. The air was humid and warm. "Marie!"

I kept walking without looking at him.

"Marie." He turned around me so that he was walking backward at almost a jog. "Inger-Marie, Miss Jüül, what do you want me to say?" He stopped in front of me and took both my arms. I tried to find a way around him but he held me tightly, blocked my way. Unlike in Copenhagen, with this man there was no stone wall behind me. Just air and water. "Stop struggling." I tore my arms out of his hold but didn't move, stood looking at him until he said, "I'm sorry."

"For what, exactly?"

"For bringing you here. For dropping you off and not visiting until now."

"And what is there to be sorry for? You told me you could get me work and you did."

"I know. But I know this isn't what you expected."

"And what is it you think I expected?"

"More than this. And you're worth more than this, Marie." Each time he called me by my first name, it hit like a tiny fist in my chest. "I didn't think you'd come. I wasn't sure what to do."

"It was a game, then? A joke?"

"No! No, it wasn't. I wanted nothing more than you – a smart, beautiful girl from Copenhagen – to come with me."

"I'm not from Copenhagen."

"But I had no plans of what to do if you did. What was I supposed to do, ask you to marry me?"

"No! You think that's what this is about? That I wanted to marry you? I barely know you, and so far, you don't seem like the best candidate for marriage."

Bertram dropped his head and pulled at the hair that fell over his face. We were beside the water, beyond a strip of trees that separated the street from the canal. The darkness seemed complete there, long grass licking at my ankles.

"I did what I could," he said quietly. His voice was low and level. "But, I led you to believe –"

"Believe what?"

"Something other than what was true. I'm back, though. I returned. We can make this –"

"Make it what? Am I supposed to be grateful for your return?" I meant this to come out harder than it did. I felt close to tears, though I told myself I wasn't upset. I was angry, but not upset. "Are you trying to be noble by just turning up at your sister's party?"

"Inger-Marie." He came toward me. I stiffened my body, held it tight. "Miss Jüül." Somehow this was better. My shoulders dropped. He had moved so close that I could feel his breath on my face. He touched my cheek. I didn't move. "I'm sorry." And then his other hand was on my face, the roughness of the skin on his fingers giving way to the smoothness of his palm. He pushed his hand into my hair, catching on strands. As he did, the humidity broke and became drizzle, pocked the mist that blanketed the canal.

I closed my eyes and imagined water rising, spilling its banks until there was no delineation between canal and shore. My body slipping in, weightless, hair streaming away from my face toward the surface, strands twisting like weeds. Bertram kept his mouth close to mine, without kissing, waiting. I fell back, my hands on his jacket. "Whoa." His arm gripped me, broke my fall. Then we were on the ground, him over me, his hand up under my skirts, pressing heat into my skin. I pulled at his collar, wanted the weight of his warmth. Legs around him, I dug my boots into the back of his legs and tried to find his mouth. Our teeth knocked against each other and I licked a small sting of blood from my lips. When we tried again, both of our mouths felt dry, and I could smell the sour of wine on our breath. An ache began behind my eyes and stars appeared, the ones that came before blackness. The drizzle of rain misted my skin, my clothes damp under me. Bertram moved over me and my body responded as though it weren't quite my own, pushing up against him with a desperate kind of thirst, despite all the water.

We became only loose mouths, clumsy hands, hip bones knocking against each other. Through the drizzle, the damp, my spinning head, I felt a tear of pain. I called out, pressed my eyes closed, clamped my mouth, then rocked against Bertram as though I were angry, defiant. I did so until we created a sharp, clenching heat. A flare followed by release as warm and soft as firelight. Afterward, I stood, twisted my wet clothes back in place around me, my mouth dry, a throb clenched around my head. My legs were liquid and muscle at once, and I was shivering. The shower had stopped, clouds pushed aside with one quick blast of air from the coast, and the canal filled up with the reflection of stars.

Eleven

More than a month passed and I had not seen Bertram since the night of the salon. If I'd still been living in the residence, I could have sobbed about it, chided myself for being so foolish. Several girls could have tried to convince me it wasn't my fault, that I'd been charmed, deluded, cajoled. They would have gathered in my room to discuss what had gone wrong, what I could or should do next, whether there was anything to be done. But I was not in Copenhagen at a ladies' residence; I was in a cramped flat above a confectionery with a single man. Knud, too, was missing someone he'd last seen that night – a tall, taut Dutch poet named Ruben, he revealed a few days after the salon. "A man?" I asked.

"A man." He winked. "I think we can agree they're as delicious as Soeberg's baked goods, yes, Little Tree?" That was his nickname for me.

I laughed but felt little levity in it. Perhaps I would have concentrated more on the supposed scandal of what Knud had revealed, the incongruity with the world I once knew, if I'd not been so focused on my self-inflicted drama. On what was and was not happening with my body. It was in tears that I went to Knud weeks later. "I haven't had my monthly since my night with Bertram."

"Oh, Little Tree. When should it have been?"

"Two weeks ago."

He crossed the room, knelt in front of the chair where I sat and held my hands. "We'll make this all right." He smelled like cinnamon and sugar. Knud told me to wait, that he would figure out what to do. In the meantime, as expected, the pregnancy progressed. This is how I thought of it: *the pregnancy*, rather than *the baby* or *the child*. It was a condition, something physical, something going awry in my body. I knew of the pregnancies and births of farm animals, of how carrying and birthing multiple lambs could endanger, even kill, the ewe. Of calves being born breach while the cows bellowed in pain. I knew this had very little to do with Bertram and me, but so much with my body and how it would adjust.

Knud thought I should tell Bertram, that it was only fair. "Fair to whom?" I asked. What had I expected after our night together – flowers sent, a long letter expressing more than the flat pleasantries of the postcards he'd sent before? Bertram hadn't visited since the night of the salon, nor had he written. I couldn't remember the end of the evening, true, didn't know if any claims or promises had been made, but I was certain none had been fulfilled.

Six weeks after the night of the salon, the room spun in the morning when I woke and the floor lurched under me as I hung my legs off the bed and found the floor. I would spend the first few minutes of each morning with my head between my legs, waiting for the nausea to pass. It didn't, though it would settle a bit when I ate Dirk's fresh pastries. I ate those in the morning, large doughy pretzels in the afternoon and, if I could stomach it, a roll with a slice of the whitest, mildest Havarti for dinner. My body pale, I craved bland food, salt and ice.

"Is this normal?" asked Knud. "You're not even two months along yet."

"This is not normal. It is not normal that I, an unmarried woman, am alone and pregnant in godforsaken northern Zealand."

"Little Tree, it's hardly godforsaken, and you're hardly alone."

"Don't ask me about normal. I can tell you about the gestation of a sheep, if you like, but I know no more about that of a woman than you do."

"You should see a doctor."

"I won't – but even if I were to, who would I see?"

"I'm sure Dirk and Anna can recommend someone. We have to tell them."

"We? I don't, actually." I was surly and sarcastic, not at all the bright, witty young thing who should've been a companion for a dandy like Knud. Why he was hidden away with me in a bakery in northern Zealand was beyond my comprehension. I imagined there would be more men like him in Copenhagen.

One morning before my shift, there was a knock at the door of my room. It wasn't Knud – his was a jaunty rap. This was slower, more cautious. I was sitting on my bed, head heavy in my cupped palms against my knees. I lifted my head and walked to the door. Though I was sure I didn't yet look pregnant, I felt a new weight and heft in my body. My breasts were already fuller and sore – even the brush of heavy fabric caused them discomfort. There was a new heat between my legs, a tingling sensation that would have been pleasant if it had been caused by something else. I walked gingerly and took some time to open the door. Anna stepped in, put both hands on my face as though I were her lover or her child, then moved around me into the room.

"Knud told you." I closed the door.

"He did, but even before then, I suspected. I can sense these things. And I noticed your diet – you've been eating like I did with two of my pregnancies. The girls." This was more information than I wanted. I didn't want to hear the word *girl* – or *boy*. Anna looked at me, her face a wash of earnest concern. When I didn't say anything, she looked toward the window, then asked, "Is it Bertram's?"

A sadness that was both sharp and slack filled my cheeks. My voice was rough with choked tears. "Of course it's Bertram's." I brushed by her as I made my way back to the bed. I sat on the edge, head between my legs again.

She sat down beside me. "That was a silly question. I'm sorry."

"It –" I started, and my body involuntarily heaved out a sputtering sob. "It is a baby, I suppose, and I suppose it's mine." Anna put her hand on my back and I shook, though I didn't make any more sounds.

She waited until I stopped shaking, then asked, "Would you like to keep –" here Anna paused, "– the baby?"

I looked at my hands moving against the thin white fabric of my nightgown over my legs. "No." I wasn't completely foolish. "I will find someone to take it. I know that there are homes for women like me, ways to find the baby a family."

"That isn't the only option."

"I am not going to keep the baby."

"I meant there are other options if you don't want to keep the child."

"No." I shook my head while still looking at my own lap, then looked up and kept shaking it.

"You don't want to go to a home, that I know. And, though you've likely heard stories, there are good, respected surgeons who perform the operation in Copenhagen."

"Respected by whom?"

"If you like, our cousin Anita can meet you in Copenhagen and –"

"No!" I said again. I barely knew Anita then, and now here I was, pregnant with her cousin's child. I did not want to see her, nor did I want her to accompany me to a surgeon's backdoor practice. "I can make my own arrangements."

"Are you sure?" Anna clutched her wrist in a tight grasp, seemed older and more earnest than I was used to her looking. "I want to help."

"I'm sure."

I did want help, just not from Anna. I would find a place to follow through with the pregnancy, and I would find a good family to take the child. All I needed was someone to help me figure out how this could be possible. I would do it all on my own, if I needed to, but I was just so very, very tired. I wrote to my cousin Kristine and explained that I had got into some trouble. I asked her to please not mention the letter or my situation to any of my family. Kristine wrote back and gave me a date and the address of an apartment in Frederikshavn. She had sent me a train ticket and told me to meet her there, that she knew what we could do.

Twelve

When I got off the train in Frederikshavn, my abdomen throbbed not with the froth of anticipation I'd once felt when arriving in a new place, but with a dull ball of weight, like uncooked dough. I went to the address Kristine had sent. She opened the door, saying, "It's only me," and I dropped my bags, hugged her. When we let go, she rubbed my arms. "It's okay." I believed her. "I'll help you settle in. We're the only people here."

"Whose home is this?"

"My employers in Aalborg. This is one of their residences. I told them that I had a family matter, and they offered me the use of the apartment while I'm here."

"They just let you leave, on such short notice?"

"They're good employers – and I'm the best personal secretary my lady is likely to ever hire. Besides, everyone understands family matters – we've all got them."

"I suppose, though I never thought I would become a family matter."

"Well, you won't then, not in our family –" Kristine stopped there, though it seemed she had more to tell me. "Come, sit! How are you feeling?" She led me by the arm to one of the brocade chairs in the sitting room.

I perched on the edge. "I'm not an invalid!" Though only a week before I'd often felt too nauseated to stand. "Much of the queasiness seems to have passed, thankfully."

Kristine looked at me, blinking, her lips in a tight, straight smile, then said, "Tea! Would you like some tea?" She sounded uncertain, nervous.

"No, no, I just want to sit."

"Sit back then, pet."

I was still balanced on the front edge of the chair.

"I'll get you some water and put on some tea for myself. You might change your mind."

I leaned back, though the chair was uncomfortable. The entire room seemed stiff, cool, the drapes and upholstery patterned in shiny shades of pastels, a wealthy Danish couple's idea of cosmopolitan. My mind ranged backward to the simple wood furniture and warm textures of my apartment above the bakery, further back to the airy heft of our duvets and the smell of the fireplace lit in the bedroom I shared with my sister on the farm. After that, there was nowhere for my mind to go.

Kristine came back in the room carrying a tea service and a glass of water on a tray. I got up to help her. When we were both seated, on matching chairs, likely equally uncomfortable, she watched me as I drank most of the water. "You asked me not to tell your family."

I stopped drinking, put the glass down, held it on my lap.

"And I haven't, but I have spoken to someone."

"Who?"

"Do you remember our mothers' cousin, Agnete?"

"Only vaguely."

"Her daughter, Elisabeth – she's a few years older than us, remember? She's here, in Frederikshavn, and she and her husband haven't been able to have a child. My mother keeps telling me how heartbroken they are – I think she means me to take this as a cautionary tale, that I'd better find a suitable husband soon because, even then, children aren't guaranteed." She paused. "I've spoken to her, Elisabeth – I know she won't tell anyone –"

"How? When?"

"My employers often come here for business. I come along and they give me some time off in the evenings to visit Elisabeth. She told me about her, well, her problem. She's devastated."

We both faced forward then, rather than toward each other, a teacup balanced in her hand, a glass of water in mine. It seemed strange. I listened as Kristine kept speaking, not turning to her, and it seemed we were both addressing an empty couch. I saw sitting there a man and a woman, only a few years older than me, attractive and smartly dressed. I saw how they leaned forward slightly, yearning coiled in their bodies. I kept listening to Kristine.

"Elisabeth remembers you from when we were girls. She would never say anything. She wants you to know that if you want to find a home for the baby, a good home with someone you know, she and her husband will raise it as their own."

I nodded slowly, still looking at the empty couch. I should have felt relief – I did not want a baby, not now, not his. My family would turn away. They might speak to me again but the child would never be considered their relation. Already I did not consider the baby my own. It should be Elisabeth's. She and her unnamed husband's baby. It was theirs already. I stopped nodding and turned to Kristine, an itch and heat behind my eyes that I willed not to water.

I could stay in the Frederikshavn apartment when Kristine's employers weren't there, but I could not leave a trace of my presence. She would let me know in advance each time they were coming to town, which seemed quite often. During those times, I stayed at an inn, enduring the glances of reproach I received when I registered alone. I hid the pregnancy as long as I could, but I am a small woman and growth became hard to conceal. Once I began to show, I slipped a cheap ring on my finger each time I went to the markets for food, spoke as little as possible. I knew no one in Frederikshavn but my second cousin Elisabeth, and I didn't seek her out. I didn't want to see her, to watch her mouth moving in conversation, imagine her cooing to a child. Watch her hands adjust her hat, imagine her tying a bonnet under a chin. I didn't want those things myself – cooing and bonnets – but I didn't want the temptation to stitch stories from gestures. So, I kept to myself, stayed in the apartment as much as I could. Time seemed slow, an awkward, halting thing, but I reminded myself that the baby would arrive soon and then be gone. The rest of my life was waiting for me.

Kristine alerted me of her employers' impending arrivals through postcards. She'd given me a key to the apartment mailbox and I checked it daily. She disguised her handwriting and used a code to let me know the dates her employers would be there. I often had a week's notice before they arrived, plenty of time to erase any evidence of my habitation from the apartment. Despite my increasing girth, I lived lightly in the flat.

We had a plan. When the baby was about to arrive, I would go to Elisabeth's house. It would be the first time I would meet and see the man who was to become the baby's father. He would take me to the hospital and admit me under Elisabeth's name. All the official documents would be in his and Elisabeth's names, and after we left the hospital together, he would take the baby home. Kristine believed that she had found me a place where I could go afterward. "You can rest there at first, and then there will be employment for you," she told me in a letter. "I won't tell you anything else until I know more."

The plan, while not impervious, seemed like a good one, though it was almost entirely dependent on timing. I know now that timing cannot be relied on. Every opportunity for time and place and coincidence to slip and twist and contort must be considered. One cannot anticipate the unknown; we may not even recognize it when we stumble into it, disoriented. One must acknowledge that every plan is porous, the ways the unexpected can flood in.

THIRTEEN

It was early evening. I was washing a dish at the sink when the crashing began. My abdomen tightened into a knot, and I felt a sharp kick of pain downward between my legs. I gripped the counter and thought, *No*. It was too early. I wasn't ready. The apartment was not clean. I had to leave it immaculate. I began to tidy, thinking of what I had to do before leaving for the hospital. I was sure I'd be able to get it all done except the laundering of the bedding. I was sure they would smell me – the heat of my small yet burgeoning body imprinting the linens. I hoped that I would be able to return to the apartment. Sheets must always be left clean.

I didn't have much time to contemplate. The next wave crashed into me, knocked me to the ground. The tightness began at my back and wrapped around my abdomen, gripped my belly and then tore through my legs. I stayed on my hands and knees until it passed. *No*, I thought again. *This is too fast, too fast.* I had to get to the hospital. First, I had to find a way to get to the hospital. No, first, I had to get out of the apartment and down the stairs. No, no. First, I had to get my bag, my things – what was I supposed to take with me, everything? I had to get everything together, I had to – and then it came again. I gripped the doorway to the bedroom before falling to the ground. I squeezed my eyes closed and bore it, mouth open, panting. The feeling (such a gentle word – *feeling*!) climbed, peaked and fell away, leaving me clenched and trembling.

I needed to forget my bag. I needed to forget everything beyond getting down the stairs and to the street. There wasn't much time. There wasn't enough time. How would I make it from the sixth floor to the street without collapsing? After this, how would I wait until a hackney appeared? There wasn't enough time. I didn't even think of the baby's arrival. It still seemed to be somewhere else, submerged in a distant world. It was the pain, the way it demanded I drop to the ground to bear it out. How could I possibly make it down the stairs and to the street before it hit again? My mind shifted from saying *No, no, no* to *How, how, how.*

I made it to the landing outside the apartment. The stairwell was narrow, with one sharp turn in direction for every floor. I told myself that I only had to make it halfway down each flight before there would be a place to pause when the steps turned. I could make it. *I can make it*, I told myself, but as I did the sensation built again, hitting me in the middle of my back, pushing me face down onto my hands and knees. This is the position I was in when the woman across the hall opened her door. "Oh, sweet Mary," she said.

I wanted to tell her that I needed help getting down the stairs, that I needed to hail a hackney and driver, but I believe that all I could say was, "Help," if anything at all.

Once I could stand again, the woman took my arm and led me back toward the apartment. I pulled away from her. "No, I have to get to the hospital."

"You don't have time, dear. I'm going to try to find someone."

"No, no." I shook my head, resisting her, then I dropped to the ground again, endured another wave.

The woman helped me up. When she led me back to the apartment, I didn't protest again. "Where is your husband?" I shook my head. This was not the way it was supposed be. The woman got me to the bed and waited as I knelt against it until another contraction passed, then she said, "I need to find a midwife."

"Don't go!" The pitch and force of my voice surprised me.

"I'll be back, dear. I'll be back soon."

She left the room, and though I believed she would be back, I knew that

I was completely alone. A baby was pushing its way out of me and not even my body was my own. "I can't, I can't, I can't," I repeated as the next wave rose and the force plowed into me. When it passed, I was still alone. I had made it to the other side, as I had with each of the contractions. I would continue to get through this, each wave that dragged me under, gasping for air, left me panting and prone when it retreated. I could, I would.

I did. The woman returned to the apartment. Later, another woman was there. They each sat in the room with me as though keeping vigil while the raging sensations brought my body closer and closer to shore. In the moments that I was conscious of anything, I saw the night as a storm at sea.

The baby arrived before the light. One of the women put her to my breast. The baby's suckle was weak and clumsy at first, as though she had just woken, which I suppose she had. When she found the latch and clamped to my nipple, a different kind of pain than the one I'd just endured shot through me. I cried out, once, briefly, made a mewing sound much like the baby, then we must have both fallen asleep, the baby still on my breast. I surfaced out of sleep a couple of times and heard voices of women around me, once when they removed and replaced the sheets from under me while the baby and I still slept. I could feel their hands on my hips, the gentle yet heavy roll of my body from side to side, the baby tucked into me as though part of my skin. The apartment seemed damp, overly warm.

I woke to light leaking into the room and voices raised enough that they cut through my sleep, wouldn't let me plunge back. I heard the loud voice of a man against that of the woman from across the hall, her timbre familiar after a night in which she spoke little that I could remember. And I heard Kristine imploring, "It's all right. I know her. She is family. I can explain this."

Wouldn't it be wonderful if we truly could explain things, the big things – birth and life and family and timing and why we are where we are and when? As it was, Kristine set her mouth and held back tears as she packed my things. I sat on the bed, trying to nurse the baby, who seemed to have forgotten how after that first night together. I told myself it didn't matter, that she would soon be with someone else. We left together, Kristine with my bags, me with the baby, swaddled in an old, soft nightgown of mine. I had wanted to say thank you to the woman from across the hall, but I didn't.

When we got to Elisabeth's house, Kristine took the baby from me and I stayed seated in the carriage. "Kristine."

She turned to me, the baby held against her chest, her face not visible. I reached out and touched the baby's back lightly with my fingers, then folded my hands on my lap. "Tell them that she will probably be hungry." It seemed like the baby had nursed all night but it had been hours since then, or had it? How much time had passed? I remembered how small and warm she was against me, how good she smelled, though I could not compare it to anything at that moment. I remembered how strong her mouth was when she latched onto my breast, how her suckling sent shoots of pain through my chest and abdomen. I remembered how tired and sore I was and then, sitting in the back of the carriage alone, I felt so small. Kristine came back to the coach and gave the driver an address. The baby was gone. Rather, the baby was home and soon we would be gone.

Kristine gave the hackney driver instructions to take us to the wharf. A lighthouse keeper, Mr. Marsden, met us there and we got into his boat. I didn't ask questions. I was so tired. My breasts ached and I could feel the heat of milk gathering in them. Pain throbbed in me, from my hard breasts to the space the baby had left in me to the raw pain between my legs. I felt ravaged, sore and so very, very tired. In the boat, I dropped my head into my hands, elbows propped on my knees, and tried to hold steady, to shut out all else. When we arrived on the island, Mr. Marsden took my bags, and Kristine and I followed him up a narrow stone path to the lighthouse. With each step, pain bloomed in a different part of my body. I walked stiffly, cautiously, as though I'd been injured. Partway up the path, I stopped. Kristine stood beside me, waiting, while Mr. Marsden carried on.

"Where are we going?" My voice was nearly a whisper. I had been silent, simply following before then.

Kristine licked her lips and cleared her throat. "Here."

"Where?"

"To this lighthouse. You can rest here."

"Rest?"

"Mr. Marsden has two children. He's been recently widowed. He's able to care for them now and will allow you time to rest. When you've recovered, you can help with the children and the household. He's agreed to begin paying you a little now, regardless of when you're able to start work."

Mr. Marsden had walked on ahead of us. I put my hands against my breasts to try to stem the ache, but it didn't work. I clutched my waist and bent forward.

"They're hurting?"

I didn't answer, straightened myself, winced as I did.

"Mother says boiled cabbage leaves help – right on the skin – and that you can express some of the milk with your hands to relieve the pressure."

"You've talked to your mother?"

"No. Well, yes, but she doesn't know it's you. She told me that Mr. Marsden needed help. His wife has passed away. She was distant family, another cousin of ours, thrice-removed or some such thing. We were talking, I mentioned a friend, not you by name."

"Is this supposed to reassure me?"

"Marie! I found a home for your baby and now a safe place for you to stay, a job."

I should've been thankful, of course. I kept wondering how this had happened. The baby was no longer mine, and I was being brought back to Jutland, taken further north and left on an island in a cold sea with strangers who were meant to be family. And yet, yes, I should've been thankful. I knew this.

"I know, Kristine." I reached for her arm, squeezed her elbow, then brought my hand back to my own waist. "Thank you." I looked up at the lighthouse, a column of granite topped by a lantern, its red paint chipped and fading, the sky a flat, leaden grey behind it, and promised myself that I would find a way to leave again.

Fourteen

The constant throb of waves hitting the island was only masked when the wind built enough that it moaned and howled around the building, blocking out every other sound. The house was one storey, attached to the lighthouse by a wide, curved corridor. There, in a room on the far end of the house, the wind banging into it, I was supposed to rest. Mr. Marsden's wife had died of pneumonia four months earlier and he had two children, a boy and a girl, ages six and eight, who watched me whenever I emerged, silent in their own grief.

I feigned rest for three days and then decided it was time to get to work. I woke early, padded my undergarments and wrapped fabric around my abdomen in an attempt to stem the discomfort, then went to the kitchen. Mr. Marsden was sitting at the table with his hands wrapped around a mug. I cleared my throat and he faced me with a faint smile, then averted his eyes. I saw a line of tension stitch his brow. I spoke first. "Good morning."

He looked toward the table, said, "Morning," then stood up. "Coffee?"

I said yes, though I'd rarely drunk it before, and moved toward the stove before he did. Once I'd poured myself a cup, I remained standing. "I am ready to begin work." I hadn't yet sat at the table with him when the children weren't there.

Mr. Marsden nodded and looked away, as though down the hall, then said, "Please, have a seat." When I did, he took a moment before speaking. "You sure, then?"

I wasn't sure. Wasn't sure what I was doing there, on an island in northern Jutland, less sure that I would be capable of caring for two motherless children and a man who seemed unmoored. "Yes."

"You've run a household before?"

"Of course." I believed myself for a moment, yet I hadn't.

"How should we go about this?" Mr. Marsden rubbed at his jaw and I could hear the faint rasp of stubble. He hadn't shaved yet that morning.

"Why don't I just begin? I'll make breakfast. After that, I'll get the kids settled with some books –" I looked around, knowing I'd seen books somewhere, hoping some were suitable for children. "Then I'll take stock and make a list of staples that may have run low." Mr. Marsden nodded along to all this. Perhaps I was on the right track. "Where do you get supplies?"

"Once every month I go to the mainland – this month I made an extra trip to pick you up."

"Of course." I felt as though I was being reminded of something.

"And, the children." It was still so early and they weren't yet up. "Do they go away to school?"

"Well, no." Mr. Marsden shifted in his chair. The wood creaked. He looked toward the bottom of his cup. "Their mother was schooling them."

"Since then?"

"Jeppe is still quite young. Frieda does a lot of reading on her own."

"That's good," I said. "Were you considering school for them at any point?"

"I was hoping that you could school them here." He had put down his mug, but he picked it up and looked again toward the bottom, as though hoping to find something. "In the short term, at least. I will look into a school on the mainland eventually. I'm not sure it's necessary yet." He looked up at me, a twitch in his mouth as though he were challenging me – or perhaps he was nervous. I began to realize what was expected of me. Not only would I be running a household, I would be responsible for raising and educating two children. Days before, I had given up one small infant. Now, two children had been given into my care.

Mr. Marsden got up from the table and came to the sink to wash his cup. Our proximity seemed too close, this sudden domesticity. "My name is Carl."

"Yes." I knew that he knew my first and last name. "I'll call you Mr. Marsden, of course."

"Yes, of course. And I will call you Miss Jüül." My name, up until that day, had seemed like something simple – a straightforward part of me. In that moment, it seemed both part of me and something separate – a title, a position.

The phantom pains of childbirth had subsided within a couple of weeks on the island. My milk dried up and I began to feel myself again, at least physically. There were only two children to care for, a relatively modest house to keep, but there were several things I was not accustomed to doing. It was April when I arrived and, beyond showing me where the garden was and what seeds Mrs. Marsden had saved from the previous season, Mr. Marsden left it up to me to figure out what to do. I'd grown up on a farm, but we had a cook and one girl year-round, two or three in the summer. It was they who planted and cultivated the kitchen garden, ran the kitchen and cooked the food. Laundry had to be scrubbed in a steel basin and hung to dry, whipped by wind yet always slightly damp from sea air. There was no running water, so I carried buckets from the pump and heated water on the wood stove. In our house in Gudum, it had also been the help that brought the water in and heated it for us. Now, I was the help.

Mr. Marsden's oldest child, Frieda, remembered enough of what her mother had taught her that, between us, we figured things out. Frieda had seemed to delight in my floundering at first, and little Jeppe was oblivious. I told myself she wasn't malicious and he wasn't ignorant, they were simply children. By summer, I was used to the amount of work that had to be done. My body was trim and strong. On the days that we could spare an hour or two, the children and I would trace the island's ragged edge, collecting shells, pebbles, bits of glass worn by the sea. Sometimes we would take the skiff out, never rowing far from shore, the three of us laughing when the boat slapped against the waves and soaked us with spray.

Fifteen

The first months that I was on the island were clear in many ways – the changing quality of light, salt tang of sea air, grasses flattened by wind, then bending in summer heat. The children went barefoot, Frieda herding her little pack of sheep, Jeppe always with a stick in his hand, hacking away at the brush, rocks, anything he could, really. Even things I tried to ignore – the way the hairs on Carl's forearm lightened over the course of the summer, their glint when they caught light, the sinew of his muscles moving beneath his skin. *Don't look*, I told myself, and convinced myself that I had hardly glanced. Then, autumn set in.

How could the disappearing light be a surprise every year? Each morning, I woke to less light until there was none and I felt shocked, slighted by the darkness. It blanketed so many hours of the day, but it was no comfort, as oblivious to me as I was consumed by it. Carl had to maintain the light longer each night, and fog obscured the island often during the day, so he would be up then as well, sounding the foghorn in a series of precisely timed patterns. His skin was still stained by the hours of light in the summer, but I could see how, underneath, that pallor was waiting to emerge. By winter, he would be pale with both exhaustion and lack of light.

"Can I help?" I asked one morning.

"How?"

"If you show me what to do, I can operate the light for a couple of hours at night, allow you more time to sleep."

"No, no. You need your sleep as well. The children –"

"There's less for me to do now. The garden is all in, the canning done. Frieda may be able to care for Jeppe for an hour or two in the afternoon while I rest – she can do school work with him. She's a smart girl."

"I've always done it on my own, as is expected of me to do, with good reason. It's my job."

"I'm only suggesting an hour or two."

Carl didn't say anything more.

"Will you consider it?" I asked.

"I will."

He was a quiet man, calm, closed. I had never seen Carl angry. Nor had I seen him particularly happy, frustrated, overjoyed or annoyed. Emotion registered so lightly on his surface that it was barely discernible, if at all. Because I knew how unflappable he was, I asked him about my proposition nearly daily. "Have you considered my suggestion?" I would ask him as we both drank coffee in the near dark.

"Yes, I have," is all that he said for days until one morning. "We can try it."

"Pardon?" It was though I had forgotten what we were speaking about beyond our daily back and forth.

"Tonight, I'll show you how to operate the light. After a few nights of instruction, you may be able to try on your own." I felt like squealing and clapping like a girl, though I did not. The prospect of being in a tower at night, shining light out to sea, was a signal that there was something more out there. That there was so much beyond what I could see.

My few hours in the tower each night were a series of small chores – polishing the lenses, keeping the wick trim and neat so the flame wouldn't smoke and obscure a clean signal, updating the logbook. Carl would crank the mechanism that kept the light turning before he left the tower. I would make note of this, mark the times I trimmed the wick, record anything unusual. Carl had not wanted me to enter anything in the logbook, but I insisted. It was a way to stay awake.

Once he'd allowed me to spend two hours a night in the light tower, it seemed as though he wasn't able to forbid me anything. I made entries, a few each night, my handwriting delicate and finely looped between the rough block letters of his printing. I realized that this was, perhaps, why he didn't want me to log my records. If anything amiss were to happen at the lighthouse, the maritime guard would go over the logbook. Each night that winter, they would see the curves of a woman's handwriting in the book. Even that cursive evidence of me in the tower each night might embarrass Carl. It was a man's job, after all – one his wife had never done.

Books, Carl had told me, were what kept lighthouse keepers sane. I was reading one night, the words rearranging themselves, sliding off the page in the weak light, when Carl held me by my shoulders, gently shook me. "Inger-Marie," he said, "Marie, Marie," until I opened my eyes. I looked at him, confused. Why was his face so close? I started to sit up, reached for my book. I must have fallen asleep; the first time I had done so while on duty. I felt relief that the light was still bright, spinning. As it moved, it illuminated different parts of Carl's face. He kept his hands on my shoulders. I wanted to sit up straight but I also didn't want him to let go of me. His hold was warm.

The light traced one half of his face before it fell into shadow, then the other, then darkness again. Neither of us moved except to blink as we went in and out of faint light. Then, he leaned forward. Somehow, I knew he would. Without intimation of anything between us before, I had already seen his face moving toward mine. And I knew I wouldn't move until he touched me. Then, I would respond and he would pick me up from the chair, place me on the floor beneath him.

There was nothing soft or comfortable in the light tower, nothing that encouraged sleep. I felt the floor, hard and cold under me, knew we didn't have anywhere else to go. Not his marriage bed. Not the single bed in my narrow room at the end of the house. He put his hand under my head as though to provide a kind of pillow. With the other hand, he swiftly opened his pants as I lifted my skirts, pushed my undergarments aside. One hand remained under my head, the other on one buttock as we rocked together, the wood planks rough against my back, singing as they creaked. We breathed along with them, the tempo quickening, the skin along the knolls of my spine worn raw. It didn't matter. This wasn't about comfort but a kind of desperate companionship. Heat and skin and moving together – it may have been some kind of consolation, but it wasn't about ease.

SIXTEEN

After that first time in the light tower, I went back to my room and fell asleep quickly, heavily. When I woke, I did not remember what happened for a moment. It wasn't until I swung my legs off the bed that I felt the sensation between my legs, not quite a pain but a warmth and the kind of tightness I felt when I'd done a lot of walking. *Oh*, I thought, then I remembered. I reached around and felt the spot on my back where my skin had been scraped by the wood beneath me.

I didn't see Carl that day. That night, I went to the light tower and he was there, writing in the logbook. I stood and waited. When he looked up, Carl seemed to wince slightly, as though the sight of me caused him some discomfort, and then he smiled, a small, sad smile.

"Good evening," I said.

"Marie."

"Yes?"

"That can't happen again."

"Of course it can't." I believed this – not that it couldn't happen again but that it shouldn't. And it didn't, at least not for the first couple of weeks. I suppose it was naive of both of us to believe that it wouldn't happen again – the two of us alone with the children, playing family on an island, a man and a woman, both young and healthy. I was amazed that we made it as long as we did. I don't remember the second time as clearly as the first. The first time that we were together was followed by nothing but the waver of tension between us each day, each trying to forget that night, neither of us wanting to – and then there were all the times that we were together after that, a blanket beneath us to protect our knees, our backs. What we had between us was physical, separate from the day when I cared for Carl's children and took care of his household. At night, our bodies together were a form of physicality, release.

With the light diminishing each day, I was rarely out in the garden, no longer pulling at the oars as I rowed the skiff around the edges of the island. Aside from the times when I was on my hands and knees, washing the floor or moving against Carl in the light tower, I felt like my body could disappear and, with it, my mind. Now mostly indoors, the children were moody, resistant to what I asked of them; chores, school work and meal preparation were all a struggle. Confined to the small, low-ceilinged rooms during the day, the light tower gave me a feeling of space around me, not expansive but hollow. I couldn't see much beyond the fallout of the tower's bulb throwing light on one part of the island, then another and another, before stretching out into water.

One night, Carl's face moving in and out of illumination as the light pulsed around us, I felt revulsion so strong that it rose up in my throat, seized there. For a moment, I felt like I would cry – not out of sadness or pain but out of the frustration of my body betraying me, reacting with disgust when I should have felt pleasure. I prevented tears by stopping all sensation, not willfully but instinctively. Skin exposed, my torso against Carl's, limbs wrapped around him, my mind, once nestled so comfortably within me, had split off. It hovered above, numb and cold. I resisted pushing Carl away. Instead, I closed my eyes and left my body until he was finished.

After that happened once, it happened several times. Not every time, but enough that I began to dread, rather than anticipate, our time together. I wondered if it was like this for all women. Some nights, I wanted Carl like food on an empty stomach, wanted to take him in, to lick and suck and bite, the need was so great. Others, the thought of him near me twisted in my stomach, emptied my mouth so that all I felt was how hollow it was, tongue and teeth obstructing the emptiness. On the island, I had no other woman to ask about these feelings, this ricochet between desire and disgust. If I had, what would I have said, how would I have asked? Likely, had there been another there, even a confidant, I would not have said anything.

"The children need a mother." Carl sat up, rubbed his hands along his arms as though cold but didn't put a shirt on. He tucked his hands under his arms. I knew the salt-musk smell of his skin along his chest.

I pulled a sweater around me. "Frieda seems to be getting over the loss of her mother." We rarely spoke of the children in the light tower and had never spoken of his former wife. "And Jeppe is not nearly as wild anymore." I had been thinking that the children didn't really need a mother – that I could be enough.

"You've cared for them very well, as you have me."

It sounded like a compliment but I steeled myself for what might come next. I thought of the possibility of dismissal. I had behaved with impropriety, after all, had become almost cavalier with it.

"I think we should make our relationship more formal."

"Pardon?" I moved from the blanket on the floor to the stiff-backed chair.

Carl stood, then – I won't say *knelt* – bent into an awkward squat in front of me. "I know that this isn't a very romantic proposal, but ours has been a relationship that's evolved in a different way than most."

"A proposal of what?"

"Marie. The children need a mother. I need a wife. You've been so good to us, to me." He reached out as though to touch my knee.

I stood up. "Yes, I have – and I have done so as your household help. I had no expectation of anything beyond that."

"Of course you didn't, but that's what I'm offering you. You're so – you're so good, Marie."

"I'm not good," I said. Carl looked to the side, his jaw tight. "I am not good," I repeated. Then I told him, "I can't stay here."

"Don't say that." We were standing close together again. His mouth was set, eyes unblinking.

"Which part?"

"Neither. Neither is true, Marie." I could see how exhaustion settled along Carl's face, loosened his jaw.

I ran my hands along my arms. My eyes burned, so did my throat.

"Is it about your family?" He looked at me. "I know they miss you."

"Who tells you these things?"

Carl closed his eyes, rubbed his brow for a moment before opening them again. "Jutland's not a big place. News travels."

"Do they know I'm here, with you?"

He reached for his shirt, hung over the back of a chair, and pulled it on. "If they do, they don't know through me. I haven't told anyone. I thought you should be the one to do so."

"And do you think I will?"

Carl looked out the window of the tower as he buttoned his shirt. "I suppose you will when you're ready. Perhaps when you're ready to stay." He turned toward me. "You know that your options are few, Miss Jüül."

"I'm sorry?"

"I've accepted you here, and I certainly haven't said anything to anyone else, but you are, well, a disgraced woman. Other people do talk. There aren't many options for you. You might consider that more carefully."

I didn't say anything. Carl looked at me, and I held my eyes on his, watched him blink, the slight movements of his skin. I don't know if my expression told him anything. His seemed wiped clean. I suppose that he'd already lost enough that he could go numb at will – living on the island seemed a primer for that. He turned and left the room, and my mind sealed up against sound. I saw myself leaving the light tower, rounding down the stairs, walking the narrow hall to my quarters at the end of the house. Everything was silent. I lay down on the bed and the sound started again. Wind hit the window like a blow.

Seventeen

I'd kept track of my monthlies, counted days and, for one week a month, knelt by my narrow bed and prayed. I didn't know if it was God, luck or my monthly planning, but I left the island carrying only two small suitcases. I found work in Copenhagen again, this time with the British ambassador and his wife. They had no children, and I was considered an ideal employee because I had none either. Now in my mid-twenties with no husband and no suitor, none were expected, and I could devote myself to their household. I worked for them for more than two years, and during that time, I tried not to think of the baby, to convince myself that my life was simple, calm, but I could feel my youth draining away, puddled around my feet, standing water.

The ambassador was rarely home and his wife tried to keep herself busy. "I get quite restless if I don't have a schedule laid out." I organized her calendar of tennis matches, dress shopping, afternoon teas and charity work, and occasionally accompanied her. One afternoon, I sat with other staff on the side of a tennis lawn, watched ladies lob balls over the nets, their white skirts twisting and catching on their legs as they leaped across the courts. They fell into each other, giggling, while we pinned polite smiles to our faces. After a round of matches, the ladies came toward us, dabbing their cheeks and necks with cloths, reaching out for lemon water.

"Inger-Marie?"

I turned to the voice. One of the women, her face flushed, hair loosening out of her hat, smiled at me.

I stood. "Anita?"

"Yes!" She took my hands in hers and opened our arms wide together. "It's so good to see you! What are you doing here?"

"I'm working for the British ambassador now."

"Oh, Margaret is such a beautiful tennis player – as I suppose you know. Do you play at all?"

"No. Though it does look like good sport."

"You should try! I'll convince Margaret that she needs a training partner." She lowered her voice. "Of course, she hardly does – I'll see what I can do." Anita had poured a glass of water. She handed it to me, then got one for herself. "Come, let's go for a little walk."

I looked for the ambassador's wife, though it wasn't necessary to ask her permission. Not really. She was in a circle of ladies, chatting. She looked at me briefly, gave a small smile and nod, and I did the same, turned away with Anita.

We walked across the lawn. "I'm married now."

I knew this. She had a ring on her finger and I doubted that she'd be able to play tennis with these ladies if she'd been single.

"A government man, but don't hold that against him." Anita laughed as though she'd told that joke before, then stopped and turned to me. "Are you, as well? Married, I mean."

She must have known I wasn't. "Oh no, no."

Anita looked toward the house. "I hope you don't mind me saying – I heard about the trouble you had." She looked from the house to my face, seemed to study me, as though looking for signs of something. "I heard from Anna, no one else."

"You don't have to explain."

"It's just that – no one else has to know. Anna helped find me a good surgeon. You as well?"

"No."

Anita stared as though confused.

"The child is being raised by family."

"Oh, well that might complicate things, I suppose."

I was about to answer that it didn't, not really, but ladies called to Anita from the other end of the lawn – "Yoo-hoo!" – waving their rackets.

"Well, I guess I'm up for the next match." Anita started back toward the nets, then slowed her pace as I caught up. "It was good to see you, Marie." She brought a hand to my face, a maternal gesture for someone who was my contemporary – in age, at least. "There's hope yet, you'll see!" She ran back to the women, slid her arm around the slim waist of one of them, laughing as they headed back to the courts.

When the ambassador was given a new post in America, his wife introduced me to Mrs. Ingeborg Brandt. "Her husband is not a government man, you understand," the ambassador's wife droned to me in her low, British accent. "But he is a businessman of some renown. It's her family's business, but he's highly regarded in his own right. They are a good family and they will treat you well. More importantly, I've assured her that you will be more than capable of running her household, both here and abroad."

I met Mrs. Brandt for the first time at the home of the Egyptian ambassador to Denmark. It seemed strange to me that we do so, but I was beginning to become accustomed to the oddities of the upper classes. Mrs. Brandt was tall and athletic-looking, dressed almost entirely in white, as though to match her colouring. Her hair was so blond it was nearly colourless, her flushed cheeks the only spots of pigment on her pale face. She looked like more of a farm girl than I did, but I felt like a child beside her, though she must have been my junior by five or six years. She seemed so, what would the word be? So *strapping*. Her height and her fairness seemed to give her confidence, as though she knew she was striking and that others would always look at her. Had she been a farm girl, she had the kind of skin which, though fair, would tan easily and quickly while her hair would go even lighter, until her brown skin and white hair would make her look odd, unsophisticated.

We met in the dining room of the Egyptian ambassador's residence. Danish boys in Egyptian garb served us thick tea in tiny ceramic cups with no handles. It was both bitingly bitter and so sweet that it coated my tongue. I struggled to maintain a pleasant expression as my throat gripped around it. After we'd each taken a couple of drinks, Mrs. Brandt set down her cup. "You're aware of what this posting will entail?" she asked.

I wasn't aware of anything other than a businessman's wife's need to hire help. "Perhaps you can tell me more about the position."

"Of course. We will need to leave sooner than I initially anticipated."

Leave?

"I had thought that you, or whomever we hire, could help with some of the travel arrangements, but it seems those have already been made. We'll be setting sail for Egypt on October ninth. If I do hire you, you will have to be prepared to leave with us. I'll need assistance on board with our son and the other staff we may be bringing."

"Of course." Egypt! That was why Danish boys in Egyptian garb served us tea.

"Once in Cairo, I don't imagine it will be easy. We may be bringing a nanny from here, but we'll obviously have to hire more domestic staff."

"Obviously."

"The blacks, the locals, aren't always the easiest to deal with. Not always reliable either." She turned her head and sighed, then looked back at me with a slight smile, the first she'd directed toward me. "Isn't that always the case?"

"I would not know, ma'am."

"No." A slight laugh, a lilt and hitch, at this. "Of course not." She studied my face for a moment, then said, "You come highly recommended." Mrs. Brandt seemed to be watching for my reaction. "There's a certain amount of discretion expected in this posting. My family's business is one of imports and exports. There are people both here and in Egypt who don't approve of goods moving over borders."

I nodded. "I understand," though I understood nothing.

"I'm sure this arrangement will work out well for both of us – for all of us, really."

She referred, I supposed, to her son and husband. Mrs. Brandt looked at me for a moment without any expression beyond what seemed like the smallest of smirks and then got up to show me out. I was about to leave, one of the boys already holding my hat and coat. "It's a strange place, Egypt."

I turned to her and for the first time, we each looked directly into the other's eyes. "I hope you'll be coming with me. And I hope you will adjust."

Eighteen

Canada, 1928

If a woman worked for a household in Europe, especially for a lady, few expected that she would form her own relationship beyond the family that employed her. It wasn't considered proper that she might meet or marry anyone outside their world and leave. There were men who tried, of course. Those of us who were staff to the nobles knew we could only fancy those at a similar station. By the time I'd been with the Caetanis for a decade, I was familiar with the play and pull of staff along narrow halls, up back stairs and in the attic quarters of manors, villas and palaces around Europe. The families knew as well, especially the ladies. Better to have us find romance within the household than to lose good staff.

I spent several months of the year abroad with the Caetanis, a few weeks in America – Los Angeles, New York, Palm Beach – followed by several months in Europe. Monaco in the winter, Paris for the spring fashion season, perhaps a stop in London or Cheshire to visit Leone's family, though Ofelia hadn't grown a new fondness for England. When we travelled, there were still men who caught the hem of my skirts, slipped hands around my waist, pressed them lower. Most, I pushed off me and carried on. For a couple, I relented, let them hold me, after our working hours, in a fumbling embrace in the belly of an ocean liner as we bucked and swayed across the Atlantic. Some wrote postcards after we reached port and continued travelling with our separate parties. One even kept writing after I'd returned to Vernon. He was surprisingly persistent following a connection that, while little more than physical, had never been consummated. I wouldn't be that foolish again. I thought I had learned the limits to my folly.

When we returned to Canada in the spring of 1928, Ofelia's health had declined further, though no one was certain from what, exactly, she suffered. It was hard to discern how much was physical discomfort, how much was emotional strain. Doctors came and went, held stethoscopes to her chest, shined light into her eyes, her ears, had her open her pale mouth to them, and none could give us a specific diagnosis. We were told her heart was weak. "There's a tremor, some irregularity," one told us.

"Mild benign hypertension," reported another. "There isn't much we can do, unfortunately, as treatment may actually exacerbate it."

"I suspect a convergence of symptoms," another said. "A heart condition, certainly, perhaps some hypertension, both aggravated by melancholy."

"Melancholy?" the duke asked. We were in his library, the doctor, the duke and I.

"The duchess, is she prone to bouts of crying for little discerned reason, excessive sleep or insomnia? Does she ever describe feeling numb?"

The duke answered, "At times, yes."

At times? This described every day in Canada for Ofelia. Did the duke know her so little, or was he convincing himself that she was healthier, more well-adjusted, than she was? I'd realized sometime before that I was her main support within the household, the person who knew her best. Knowing this, I felt neither pride nor burden, but perhaps something so stuck between the two that each teetered then flattened into neutrality.

In Vernon, there were few households like ours, and unlike Europe, I didn't have a coterie of other women passing slips of gossip, quick winks, the pursed lips of held laughter. Our staff in Canada was mostly Asian men – our cook,

George; Leone's manservant, Chu; a Japanese man named Odo – and local teenage girls. We had few people in to visit, even fewer once Ofelia's health began to slip again. Mr. Earl H. Fumer was an exception. He was what they called in America a self-made man. A lumber baron, Mr. Fumer was in the Okanagan Valley to visit some of his mills when the duke asked him to advise on his own woodlot. He was invited to the house for a late dinner. The girls had already gone home, so it was the young men who served us the meal, then stood in their white shirts behind us. I was seated at the table like family, as I had been since we arrived in Canada. Ofelia was in one of her moods, nearly silent, looking at her hands twisting in her lap. Sveva did much of the speaking, telling Mr. Fumer about the plays she adored staging, detailed plot outlines for each, then switching to rapid questions – had he climbed any mountains? Which ones? Was it hard? Could she, perhaps, ever dream to climb one?

The duke didn't look concerned at either how silent Ofelia was or how much Sveva was going on, so I interjected. When Sveva stopped talking to take a bite, I asked, "Tell us, Mr. Fumer, what is the north of the province like?"

Mr. Fumer looked at me. A glance, really, but long enough that I saw how one of his eyebrows raised slightly. "Please, please call me Earl." A provocation before he looked away? I felt heat rise on my neck and dug my nails into my hands under the table in an attempt to stop the flush. There was no reason to feel either complimented or flustered. "The north is beautiful, really. Cold, of course, and it's a rougher beauty than I'm sure you're accustomed to – coarser, perhaps. You should all come visit. I would love to host you."

At this, Ofelia looked up, eyes wide, blinking, as though she were panicked. I looked at her until she turned to me, and I nodded slightly toward her plate to indicate she should eat.

"We should! We should, shouldn't we, Daddy?" said Sveva. The rest of us said nothing, the duke and I both focused on Ofelia and getting her through the meal.

Mr. Fumer gestured to his plate with his knife. "This is wonderful," he said of the roast beef and Yorkshire pudding, something the duke liked to serve to guests, as though it was only proper to serve when dining in the colonies. "And you say the cook is Chinese? They must be a different breed down here. Up north the Chinamen can cook only rice or noodles. I've got an old Polish lady to do my cooking, but I must say, this is better than anything she could make. And I thought she was quite good!"

"I'm part Polish!" Sveva stopped eating, held her hands around her face, framing herself with her fingers. "Aren't I, Daddy? Daddy's mother, Duchess Ada, was half-English and half-Polish –"

"Well, not quite half, Sveva." The duke's smile was kind, but there was a tightness in his eyes, as though he were preoccupied.

"Just enough to give us some fire and spirit then, right, Daddy?" Sveva was eleven and trying so hard to make conversation, to be as witty and delightful as her mother was sullen.

Mr. Fumer turned to us. "Ladies, the duke tells me that you are each avid readers and accomplished in the arts." What should we say in response to this? We said nothing, and Mr. Fumer carried on. "How fortunate you are, Duke, to live with such refined company. Beautiful as well." I was sure that his eyes were directly on me, a gesture that seemed blatant and inappropriate given our company. When I met his gaze, he turned and I saw the angle of his jaw, sharp and firm. I looked long enough at his lips to see that the top one was slightly plumper than the bottom. Soon enough, the boys were clearing our plates, bringing out a dessert of apple cake served with dollops of cream. The cake was sodden with some kind of liquor and I flicked my tongue quickly over my lips and rubbed them together to taste the heat and cream there.

In the parlour later that evening, Ofelia excused herself. When she did, the duke nodded once to Sveva and she got up. "I should be going to sleep too, of course. We need our beauty sleep, don't we, Mother?" She took her mother's elbow and led her out of the room.

When they'd left, the duke said, "You'll understand, my wife hasn't been feeling well."

"Oh, of course. No need to explain. I hope she didn't feel as though she needed to be at dinner because I was here?"

"No, no."

I was about to rise and excuse myself but Mr. Fumer turned to me. "Miss Jüül, I understand you're from Denmark. Tell me about it."

"Yes, do," said the duke. "I'll call Chu for some refreshments."

Ofelia could excuse herself from the superficial chit-chat, but I was expected to keep it up for a bit. I would try to sound both interested and interesting. "What would you like to know, sir?"

"Anything you would like to tell me – I've always wanted to visit those Nordic countries. It seems as though there is something so bracing and, I don't know, clean about them – am I right?"

"Clean?" Was this man speaking metaphorically?

"I'm not sure – pure, bright. Something truly northern about them."

"Canada is northern as well."

"Of course it is! Canada is just still so, I don't know, so raw, so dirty – *rugged*! That's the word I'm looking for. Is Denmark as rugged?"

"I wouldn't say so of Copenhagen, but the coastline can be very rugged. I spent some time in a lighthouse on the northwest coast –" I started, then stopped. The duke was looking at me intently. I knew that he wasn't upset – the duke was rarely upset – but what was it I saw there? Fascination, perhaps. I'd spoken so little about my past to the family and now I was telling this stranger, Mr. Fumer, something that the duke himself may not have known about me.

When I didn't say anything more for a moment, Mr. Fumer said, "A lighthouse? On the mainland or an island?"

"An island."

"Isolated?"

"Yes, quite."

"You must be adventurous, Miss Jüül!" He said this with a bit too much enthusiasm. "Of course, you are." I wasn't sure what he meant by this. "I admire you."

I began to stammer a response, but Mr. Fumer had turned and I realized he was speaking to the duke. "Leaving Europe, setting out for an entirely new continent and way of life."

"Well, I've been doing so since I was barely more than a boy. I want my daughter to see as much as she can, too. And this part of the world – a place where one can become what one makes of oneself – as you exemplify, Mr. Fumer."

I stood and waited. The men's conversation, which had turned to a sharing of mutual admiration, happened around me. I hadn't been in a room alone with two men for years by then and I wanted to leave. When the men stopped talking for a moment, I said, "You'll excuse me."

They both rose, and Mr. Fumer turned to the duke. "I'd best be going, as well."

The duke shook his hand, then held it with the other. What was it that endeared these men to each other?

"You'll see Mr. Fumer out, Miss Jüül?"

"Of course." It wasn't unusual that I would do this, but there seemed to be an air of complicity between them. Mr. Fumer and I went into the front foyer and I stood while he gathered his hat and coat, then I opened the door for him. Instead of stepping out the door, he moved forward so he was only a breath in front of me. The heat of his body, the cold air from outside. Mr. Fumer took my hand off the door handle and held it in one of his while the other ran down the side of my body. He leaned toward my ear and whispered, "You're lovely," brought one hand up to my cheek, my chin, and then he stepped away. "Please thank the duke and duchess for the delicious meal and fine company." His voice was louder than it had been a moment ago. As he tipped his hat, he winked at me, the conspiracy in it seeming more sweet than sinister. I closed the door behind him.

It felt good to be desired so openly, as though it might be an option for me to respond to this man. I tried not to think ahead, and yet I imagined where a response could lead. I could think of three possibilities – he and I would form a genuine connection and I would secure Mr. Fumer work with the family so that we could be together. That seemed very unlikely. Option two was that he and I would form a genuine connection and I would leave the family to marry him. That seemed impossible. Or, he and I would have an illicit affair that would be carried on when he came to visit. The latter seemed the most plausible, but, while not the least desirable, there wouldn't be much reward to it beyond the physical, would there? I went to the third floor of the house where my quarters were perched under slanted ceilings that harboured heat in summer, trapped cold in winter. I traced the compact contours of my own body, imagined my hands were someone else's.

Nineteen

After he'd been in Vancouver for business, Mr. Fumer stopped in Vernon on his way home to Prince George, though we were in no way directly on the route, and rang our bell. When I answered, he said, "Miss Jüül! You are a sight for sore eyes, indeed." I wished he had thought of something more original to say. He asked if the duke and I could come to the driveway, he had something to show us. Light gleamed off the curved hood of a new automobile and the duke recognized Mr. Fumer's car as a 1923 Earl Roadster.

Mr. Fumer was delighted by the duke's recognition. "Yes, an Earl! Named rather well, wouldn't you say?" He looked at me. "I'm no duke, of course, but I'm happy to have a car I can pretend to be named in my honour."

The duke rounded the car, stood with his hands on his hips, nodding, a smile playing the corners of his mouth. After considering the vehicle for a few minutes, his eyes over every part of it, the duke ran his long hand over the hood. "It's a fine vehicle, Mr. Fumer, a fine vehicle. You'll drive it north then?"

"Good Lord, no. The roads are terrible – horrible, really – and the cold, gravel and salt would all be too much for this beauty. I'm going to find a garage in Kamloops where I can store her for the winter."

The duke looked at the car once more and then back toward our simple garage, a converted stable. "Would you consider keeping the roadster here?"

"Consider it? If you're sure you've got the room – I'd pay a storage fee, of course."

The duke turned his head away and held up his hand. He was uncomfortable with talk of fees.

After a few words between them, it was settled. They shook hands and then Mr. Fumer rubbed his together, blew into his palms as though cold. "It may be bold of me to ask," he started, "but can I borrow your Miss Jüül as I sort out the insurance and papers for storage? I don't know Vernon well. It would be good to have someone accompany me who does."

"Not too bold, at all. You'll be happy to go, yes, Miss Jüül?"

It was expected that I'd consent, and truth was, I wanted to go with Mr. Fumer. My opportunities to be out with anyone other than the family were so few. "Yes, of course."

Once we'd got all the papers signed for his new automobile, Mr. Fumer sat, hands on the wheel without starting the car, as though considering something. "Before I put the Earl into storage, this Earl would like to take you for a drive in the country as a thank you."

"The country?" We were always in the country here.

"Yes. Name a direction, I'll drive you there."

"Southeast." I pointed the way, the road that led out to Coldstream Ranch. I hoped for the rangeland between mountains, the hillside thick green with trees on one side, gold grassland on the other. I hoped for horses running in unison, a sky doused deep blue. The roadster spit up gravel as we went and I laughed at the speed, the motion. We stopped at a rise in the road where we could look one direction and see the valley taper then rise into the Monashee Mountains, the other where it pooled into the jade of Long Lake. Mr. Fumer wanted to talk. He told me about his childhood and early years, how he had become the lumber baron that he was now known as, and then he asked about me. I skirted questions with slips of answers, shifted in the seat, the leather upholstery hot against the back of my legs.

Mr. Fumer stopped whatever he was saying, mid-sentence. "I'm sorry, Miss Jüül. You're uncomfortable."

I had slipped my hands, palms down, between my thighs and the seat. "Perhaps I'm no longer used to sitting still for so long."

Mr. Fumer looked at me for a moment, as if perplexed, then said, "Come, let's stretch our legs," and got out, rounded the car, opened my door.

I stayed seated, blinking against sunlight. Mr. Fumer stood with his hand open to me, smiling. When I shifted my legs out of the car, I knew what I did – I paused for the briefest time with my legs the slightest bit apart, felt air between my skirts as I held out my hand. Mr. Fumer lifted me from the car swiftly, had me standing too close to him, palm on the base of my spine, pressing. The proper thing to do would have been to push back, to express mortification. I put my hands against Mr. Earl Fumer's chest and it was hard and warm. I left them there. To his credit, Earl didn't move until I did. To my credit, we never got into the back of the car. Instead, we were up against it, pulsing like a couple of commoners. I kept all my clothes on and felt proud of this. I wasn't that wayward young woman anymore. I was so far from that young, reckless girl, yet we rocked against each other and caused enough friction between our clothes and bodies that we were both shuddering. I gasped and Mr. Fumer called out, once.

When we separated, catching our breath, Mr. Fumer wiped a piece of hair from his forehead. "It's as though we're young virgins again." He winked at me, and I smiled, then spent the drive back twisting my garments back into place, smoothing them out.

Twenty

Earl Fumer wrote to me all fall and winter from the north. He told me how new and rough the towns were – the roads recently cut, lumber stacked along roadsides, the smell of salt and boatloads of fish on the coast, of slash piles and smoke in the interior. He drew arrows to the smudges of sap that marked the paper and asked me if I would holiday with him in Jasper, in the northern Rocky Mountains. Instead, I left with the family – by train to Los Angeles, then by ship to Havana. We were there two weeks, during which Ofelia's health improved enough that she could sit poolside, shaded, and instruct Sveva on how to swim. Afternoons, the duke would take Sveva on tours of the city – art galleries, a sugar factory – and I stayed behind as Ofelia rested. More of Earl Fumer's letters were waiting for me in New York, where we stopped, rented a floor of the Ritz Carlton and spent each night at Broadway shows before sailing to Europe.

My first days in Paris in 1929 were spent writing – not responses to Mr. Fumer, but back and forth to Chanel's staff to attempt to find enough bookings. Ofelia had been going to see Coco Chanel since before we left Rome, and I knew from experience that more than one fitting would be necessary. I knew, as well, that Miss Chanel would make time for her, though that year it seemed more difficult to get appointments confirmed. When I told Ofelia, she said, "Well, it seems she has been admitted into wider circles than our own," with a bit of a flip in her voice.

Wider? That would not be difficult. My circle was tiny; Ofelia's not much larger. I asked, "Oh, who?"

"The Brits, I'm afraid." She lowered her voice as though the woman had contracted something. "She's rumoured to have been with the Duke of Westminster, and she seems to be chums with Prince Edward, those types. Leone doesn't agree with their politics, such as they are, but they hold so much sway these days. I'm not sure how much longer I'll see Coco, to be honest."

Before we left for a fitting one morning, she asked, "What do you think, Miss Jüül, the Schiaparelli?" She rotated and twisted in front of the mirror in a pleated skirt and a jumper with the pattern of a bow knit into the design. "There is just something about Italian design, don't you think?"

When we arrived at her studio, Miss Chanel ran her hands down Ofelia's arms and along her face for a moment, as though she were a dear child. I could see how tightly Ofelia held herself, a stature of both pride and protection. I knew how taxing simply standing for a period of time could be for her.

"Oh, I am so glad you came!" Coco said. "I'm playing with this design, toying with it, really, and you would be the perfect model – I must see you in it!" We both knew Chanel had in-house models by then, so this seemed like a ploy or an appeasement. One of the shopgirls took off Ofelia's coat and Coco narrowed her eyes. "My God, what on earth are you wearing?"

"Oh, a dear new Italian girl, Schiaparelli." Ofelia put her hands on her hips, raised her chest a bit as if to show off the patterned bow.

"It's awful. Take it off," Coco demanded. Ofelia looked toward me and shrugged, stripped down to her tailored undergarments. She was so thin, so pale.

Coco tried to convince her to doff those as well. "Oh, off with those! I design clothes in which women can move freely. They will only look perfect over nothing but your body." Ofelia refused to take off her undergarments, and for this I was relieved.

Each visit to Coco Chanel's shop was followed by Ofelia dictating notes to me on the precise tilt of the hat or fall of the seam of the garments that were being made for her. When they were delivered to the hotel and didn't fit as she'd envisioned, I wrote notes back to Miss Chanel on how these could be improved, my name signed at the bottom of each slip of criticism, "on behalf of Ofelia Caetani di Sermoneta." Back and forth we went, in letters and in person, until Ofelia had garments – two dresses, a suit, three hats and a short coat – that fit her exactly as she wished.

When I went to deliver the final payment, I expected only shopgirls in the studio, but Coco was there, dressed in wide pants and a striped shirt, like a sailor. She turned to me, a curled lock of her dark hair falling over her forehead. She looked at me, brow furrowed, eyes unusually bright, jaw jutted out slightly, as though she were a small bull about to charge. After a moment, her face relaxed, she pushed the hair off her forehead and laughed, I wasn't sure at what. "Oh, Miss Jüül, you little darling!" She was only a few years older than me. "How is our Ofelia? Our poor duchess in exile." Her laugh wasn't a kind one.

I watched the shopgirls for clues, but each averted her eyes. It was early evening, a time when the studio might have been closed, the girls gone home. Instead, Miss Chanel said to one of them, "Let's get Miss Jüül a glass of wine, shall we!" Her voice was loud, the cheer forced. Coco did not entertain Ofelia beyond her dress fittings. It was not right that she would socialize with me.

"Oh, thank you but no, I mustn't. The duchess is waiting for me." In our time away from Rome, I too had taken to calling Ofelia "the duchess." This was how the duke referred to her, how most knew her now, though in Vernon they were as often referred to as the count and countess. Small-town confusion, I supposed.

"Oh yes, yes, of course, you must get back to your duchess." Coco had turned away from me and was looking at a design spread out on a table. When the shopgirl brought two glasses of wine, Coco held one out to me, then took the other and drank it in two or three swift gulps.

I held the glass without drinking.

"You know, the first – some might say the real – Duchess Caetani di Sermoneta still comes to visit me, as well. Doesn't purchase any of my designs, as though they're beneath her – she is a bit dowdy, quite horsey really, so I'm not sure they would suit her. But do you know why she comes?"

"No."

"She comes to attempt to track the duke and his new family's whereabouts." I had nothing to say to this. "You do know that the duke won't be able to return to Italy, don't you?"

Again, I stayed quiet. It didn't seem as though Coco needed any input from me in any case.

"The real duchess is quite loyal to Mussolini, as is most of Italy. It seems Italy, and all of Europe, really, is moving beyond the duke's outmoded ideas of nobility as gentle benefactor. Following Russia's lead, perhaps, now everyone is talking about *the people*." Coco tossed back her head and scraped the hair away from her face with her red nails. "The people, Miss Jüül! I dare say, you too are one of the people!" She took another drink of her wine, this one slower, then wiped her mouth in a way that seemed crude. The entire evening was off-kilter, not right. "Does Ofelia's duke honestly believe that he can live as common folk in America? One amongst the corrupt Jews and savage Indians, I suppose."

A man emerged from somewhere in the studio, a dapper young thing wearing nearly the same outfit as Miss Chanel, his trousers slimmer, his hair long and floppy, quite like hers as well. "Coco!" he said. "Come, come!" He put his arm around her waist and seemed to dance her out of the room.

I let out a long exhalation when they left, not aware that I'd been holding my breath.

"I am so sorry," one of the shopgirls said as she showed me out. "Please, don't mention anything to the duchess."

"No, no, of course not." I wouldn't say anything to Ofelia. The whole incident had been so odd to me.

After Paris, we went to London, where we stayed in Mayfair with relatives on the duke's mother's side. Ofelia, Sveva and I were left to drink milky tea and eat crumbling biscuits with Duchess Ada's cousins while the duke went to visit his colleagues at the universities. It was October 1929 and the days were grey, grainy with heavy fog and lowered voices. Ofelia and I understood that something had gone wrong with the stock market. Women made references to men speaking about it. Though we tried not to worry, the men's mouths were tight, their hands balled in fists and then released, clenched and released. Men rubbed their foreheads and their eyes, and they looked so tired. One late-night conversation between Ofelia and the duke slipped under a door as I walked down a hall. "No one knows for sure, of course, but word is it's all going to come down."

I stopped, held my body still, breath shallow, and heard Ofelia ask, "What will this mean?"

"We don't yet know, but it probably won't be good."

"Leone, we can't lose any more."

There was a pause and some movement, then the duke: "We may not have a choice." It sounded as though he was moving closer to the door, so I stepped away as lightly as I could.

We were in England long enough for the market to react. The initial hit in London reverberated to Wall Street and back. It was no longer conjecture between men but known by everyone – the entire market was felled. The duke had left most of his wealth in Italy. There hadn't been much option; most of it was the kind that can't be carried – land and property and family – though he insisted none but the latter meant anything to him.

Ofelia and I kept to ourselves in our rooms. One evening, she called me to her. A girl stoked the fire as I came in, and Ofelia was lying in bed. I nodded at the girl and she left. At Ofelia's bedside, despite the sound of crackling wood from across the room, heat was more of an idea than a sensation. Cold and damp crept through the walls as the fire roared. Ofelia didn't rouse or turn to me. "Miss Jüül, I want to go –" *home*, I heard in my mind, although we had no home, as she knew "– back."

"I know." I sat on the bed, considered reaching out to her but didn't.

She turned toward me, her eyes closed. "We could make our way back into Italy." Her eyes opened, looked from one side of my face to the other. "We can live quietly and simply at one of the Caetani properties and wait out Mussolini." She pushed herself up onto her elbows, settled back onto the pillows in a seated position and looked toward the fire. "It could be Ninfa or any one of the country properties. You know me, I don't need to go out much, certainly don't need to be at any society functions. Back in Italy with Leone and Sveva – all we would need would be a small staff, including you, of course." She livened at the prospect, her face softening.

I didn't want to break the spell. It would be easier, even for a couple of days, to have Ofelia believing that we could return to Italy, imagining herself hidden in the fortress above the family gardens in Ninfa, but after that, it would be so much more difficult to pull her back. "We can't, Ofelia. You know that we can't."

Her eyes snapped back to me, her mouth firming into a tight line. "I don't know this, and neither do you."

"The duke's opposition to Mussolini has been too vocal, too documented. He'll be targeted, Ofelia – you and Sveva might be in danger. We can't go back."

Something flashed across Ofelia's face then, a flare of anger that I thought might rupture, and just as quickly both of her hands were on my arms, her grip stronger than I thought possible.

My arms burned under her hold. "Ofelia, that hurts."

She let go, pushed the pillows away and fell back onto the bed, face to the ceiling. "Oh, I know it hurts, it hurts, it hurts." She tossed her head from side to side, clamped her fists against the bones of her hips. I sat beside her and watched as her whole body tensed and pushed up from the mattress, tendons ridged against her neck, chest flushed, face pale, mouth clenched. I wanted to reach out to comfort her, but her body was coiled and I knew she might strike back in misaimed defense.

I stood from the bed, said in a low, steady voice, "It's all right, Ofelia, it's all right. I'll go get Leone, I'll go get him." As I left the room, I heard a suppressed scream pushed against her throat, the choke of a sob breaking at the end of it.

TWENTY-ONE

We returned to Vernon the following February. Clouds smothered the valley and the snow melted a little each day until any brightness was gone and all we were left with was grey and brown. We attempted to cheer Ofelia, Sveva with her plays and theatrics, piano and voice recitals, but it was the duke who succeeded most often in bolstering her. Sometimes he would sit her on his lap like a girl while they played cards. Other times, he would stroke her hair while she sat in front of the fire. Once, when we were all in the parlour, he pretended that his large hand was a kitten; he raised his voice into a feminine mew and moved his hand in quick, skittish movements, alighting on Ofelia and leaping off again and again until she collapsed into giggles, her mouth arced open, body shaking. Sveva stood up, panicked. "Daddy, stop it!"

"Oh, Sveva, darling donetta." The duke held out his arms as though to encompass Sveva as well, but she moved away from him. "Let your dear Mau have some fun!"

I overheard some of the other ways the duke comforted Ofelia, a different kind of mewing and caterwauling. I would feel myself blushing on my own on a landing, and then I would carry on. We would meet for dinner that night or breakfast the next day, Sveva and I both pretending we'd heard nothing at all. Ofelia's eyes would be cloudy, empty again, and the duke so awkward and formal with both of us. At times when they thought they were alone, I would see him reach for Ofelia, how he held her while she cried.

During this time, Earl Fumer kept writing to me. I responded to his letters but was careful to write nothing about going to Jasper, heading off into the mountains with him. When he came back that spring to collect his car on his way to Vancouver, his eyes lit with expectation, his hands kept rising from his sides as though he wanted to hold something, which I imagine he did. He had dinner with the family, as he had each time he'd come through Vernon, but this time the mood was less jovial. "I suppose we've all taken quite a hit," he started. Talking about money at dinner had been considered impolite – talking about money at all had been – but now it seemed it had become appropriate for conversation, the crash pulling down previous mores as well as everything else.

"Yes, I suppose we have," the duke responded. He would know better than most. "You'll be able to keep the roadster, though?"

"I need it for business, really. I don't know about Europe, but rail travel isn't what it used to be here – trains are becoming overrun by vagrants, riff-raff jumping on and off boxcars like vermin. Travelling by car sends the right message. Sometimes we have to make it look as though business is doing fine, even if it's not quite, just now, isn't that right?"

"Certainly is."

I wondered what the duke knew of business.

Ofelia excused herself early from dinner and looked at me long enough that I did as well. We rose from the table and she paused before we left the room. "Sveva, come up soon, please."

"Yes, Mother, just a few more minutes." As we left, I saw how Sveva leaned toward the conversation at the table. I knew that she would find a way to speak more once we'd left the room. While Ofelia insisted on decorum, especially with company, the duke indulged her. He would let Sveva go on about world politics as though she were well informed, and I suppose she was in comparison to most girls her age.

As I looked at Sveva, I felt Earl watching me. I turned to say good evening. "You'll join us later, won't you, Miss Jüül?"

Ofelia cleared her throat in the landing. Instead of implicating myself either way, I nodded. I met his eyes once, briefly, before turning.

When we were in her room, Ofelia said, "If she's not up soon, you'll go get her, Miss Jüül. It's not right for a young girl to be up late on her own with adults."

I was glad to hear the stairs a few minutes later. Sveva came slouching into the room with a pout. "Daddy sent me up."

"Good, it's time to get ready for bed."

"Why? It's not like we have a busy day tomorrow, Mau. It's not like we ever have a busy day here. We could sleep all day and no one would even notice."

"That doesn't matter. We've no reason to sleep all day if we get a good night's rest."

"A good night's rest, a good night's rest – as though it's a virtue!"

"Rest is a virtue, especially for a growing girl."

"Conversation, discourse, knowledge – those are also virtues!"

"Knowledge, perhaps, but I wouldn't put too much store into conversation. As often as not, it devolves into rumour and conjecture."

"Not with Daddy! It's not fair. Mr. Fumer wants Miss Jüül to come back down to talk with him and Daddy – and it's not even like Miss Jüül knows any more about world finances than I do. Much less, I'd imagine!"

She spoke as though I wasn't there. I'd been with Sveva her entire life, increasingly more like a family member than staff, and yet I knew she saw me as something other, something less than herself and the parents she idolized. I reminded myself she was still a child in many ways, to be easy on her.

"Sveva, that's enough. Miss Jüül is a grown woman, and a lady. I'm sure she's not going to talk about finances." Ofelia turned to me. "And I'm sure she won't be downstairs long at all, will you, Miss Jüül?"

I understood that Ofelia was instructing me, rather than asking. "No, of course not."

The men were smoking cigars when I came back down. They both put them out and stood when I came in the room. "No, no." I gave a slight wave of my hand as if to say *don't mind me. Pretend that I'm not even here.*

When Earl sat back down, the duke remained standing and turned to me. "Miss Jüül, I'll need some help finding the Armagnac that we brought back. You don't mind, do you, Mr. Fumer?"

"No, not at all. Take your time." It seemed a shame that he'd put out his cigar. He could have continued to smoke while the duke and I went looking for the brandy, which I suspected was a bit of a ruse.

In the dining room, after I'd located the liquor easily, the duke stopped me. "I suspect I know what Mr. Fumer may ask of you." His voice was kind, not accusatory. "I know he'd like some time alone with you."

I didn't respond.

"And I think it would be fine, I really do, but with Sveva – and Ofelia's condition –" Here he paused. "It may be hard for her if you're not here. She's come to depend on you."

"Yes, she has."

"As I said, I think we'd be fine – especially for a week or two – Ofelia seems a little better these days, and I'm here to take care of my family!" He laughed at this, as though it were a joke or a novelty. He was quiet for a moment, hand across his chin. When he looked at me, he stretched a forced smile across his face. "It may do us all some good, to be on our own. It may. Please, make your own decision. Don't let thoughts of Ofelia influence you either way."

After thinking of his family's needs for years, did he really believe I could set those aside and decide something based solely on my own desires? Ofelia always told me that the duke was childlike in his ideals. I'd protested this – he was such a learned man, a scholar of languages and religions; certainly he wasn't naive. Now, I knew what she meant.

We went back into the parlour, and the men raised glasses to good health and renewed fortune. It wasn't long until the duke excused himself.

"Now I can pour you a splash, yes, Miss Jüül?" Earl winked at me.

I didn't say yes or no and he poured me a drink. I held it in my hand and looked at the liquid, as round and gold as a large coin in the glass.

"Come, sit with me." He sat back down, motioned beside him. "Have you given it some thought? To Jasper?"

I took a drink. To be away from here, from Vernon and the house on Pleasant Valley Road, the family. To be on my own in the world as I had once been. To be with a man again. It would be absurd to push away from the advances of one man in favour of someone who had sent me away more than a decade ago. My thoughts weren't long with men, however. They doubled back to Ofelia, sobbing at night, raking at her neck and chest as though she couldn't breathe. I thought of Sveva, and how someone would need to ensure that she would go to school now that it was unlikely the family could afford private tutors. "I couldn't – the time it would take to travel there and back. I couldn't."

Perhaps he could convince me.

"I see how hard you work. A good holiday, two or three weeks away entirely, would make a new woman of you."

"Two or three weeks?" I had been thinking of a week, ten days at the very most. How did he think that the family could get on without me, one of the only staff members left, for that long? I had wanted him to convince me with reasonable means, not pipe dreams.

"Yes, a complete rest and change – it would do you a world of good."

"Do I seem as though I need rest?" I raised an eyebrow and took another drink, looked at Earl over the rim of the glass.

"No, you seem the very picture of good health, Miss Jüül – glowing with it, if you don't mind me saying – but surely you've got some time off? You can't always be working."

"Of course not. But my time off is spent – here. The Caetanis give me plenty of my own time throughout the week. I just, it wouldn't be right – Ofelia, her health. I couldn't just go for that length of time." As I spoke, it seemed even more absurd to me. Imagine, me packing my luggage and donning a travelling suit, then waving to the family as I was spirited out the door by Mr. Fumer. "Toodle-oo!" I'd toss over my shoulder. I nearly laughed at the thought. "If there was a way that I could accompany you for a shorter junket?"

"A junket, that's all you want with me?" He pulled me to him, took the glass from my hand and set it down. "You worry too much, I can tell. The Caetanis are so fortunate to have you, but you needn't worry about them so much. They are adults. Why shouldn't you have some time off? Why won't you let me take you away?" He tilted his chin, raised his eyebrows in question. "I'll bring you back, I promise." He placed a finger on his lips.

When I didn't answer, he put the same finger on my mouth and traced it. As he did, I felt a shot of desire rend through me. He took me by the waist and pulled me close. I wanted to be with him then, I did, but we were in the wrong place, the family somewhere in the house around us. I pushed thoughts of them away from me as Earl Fumer pressed up against me. Then I heard the bell, faint at first and then more insistent.

I put my hands on Earl Fumer's chest and pushed away from him. "I have to go to her." The bell rang on from Ofelia's room. "I have to – you'll excuse me. I'm sorry." The yearning that I'd felt for him, the heat that had wrapped both my body and his together as I tried to cocoon myself away from the household, lifted as soon as I stood. All the drafts of the house slipped in, a shiver of cold rather than desire charged my skin, and I straightened and tucked in my clothes, rubbed at my arms to warm them. I turned back to Earl at the library door. "I may be able to slip back down in a few minutes." I didn't look at him, spoke quickly and quietly as I left the room.

Ofelia's small glass bell continued to ring as I took the stairs. I passed Leone on the landing. "I'm sorry," he said. "I tried, but she's asking for you." His eyes, large and brown with a slight downward slope, could be comforting, warm, but just then they seemed emptied of that warmth, simply sad, tired. We were all tired.

When I got to her room, Ofelia looked asleep, but as I walked closer to her bed, she pushed herself up and announced in a loud whisper, "I cannot fall asleep."

"Why not?"

"Why not, why not. How am I to know, Miss Jüül?" Her voice sounded both angry and close to tears, and I knew how thin the edge was between the two. "I just want to get some rest!" She lowered her voice to a whisper. "I need some rest."

"The duke couldn't comfort you?"

"Leone – he thinks it's all in my mind. That man and *his* mind. I try to tell him there is more – that our bodies have their own language and sometimes they scream within us, *screech*, frustrated because we don't know what they are trying to say."

"Ofelia, darling." She calmed a bit when I called her this endearment. "There are times when, loud as they are, we need to tell our bodies to hush."

"If it were only that easy, Marie. You know I want to, don't you?"

I nodded, rubbed her arm. She was cold – as was I, all the warmth I'd felt from Earl Fumer gone.

"Leone says that I shouldn't take anything to help me sleep, that I've been doing that too often." Ofelia clutched my wrist and pulled me closer, her grip surprisingly strong. "My body, my mind, they're like Babel, all the chattering, so much I can't understand. I just need some sleep, Miss Jüül." She let go of my arm, fell back to the bed. "You'll get me a Veronal, yes? So I can stop the clamour of my blasted nerves and fall asleep?"

"Of course." It seemed unreasonable that the duke refused Ofelia medication that had been prescribed by her doctor.

I brought the prescription to Ofelia, placed two on her palm, poured her a glass of water from the jug beside the bed.

After she swallowed, she held one of my hands in both of hers. "Stay with me."

"Of course." My answer was a reflex before I thought of Earl Fumer somewhere in the house – would he still be in the parlour, staring into the fire? If he took the back stairs to the guest quarters, would I hear the house shift and creak from where I was?

Before slipping into sleep, Ofelia said, "Be careful, Miss Jüül."

"Of what?"

"Your reputation, your heart. In equal measure."

I left her room quietly, stood on the landing and listened, as though this would tell me if Earl Fumer was still in the parlour, waiting for me. The only sound I heard was from outside, the rounded hoots of an owl before it settled on the last long O of its call. It sounded again, once, twice, and I wasn't sure if it was one bird repeating or two, a call-and-response. I went back to the parlour so quietly that Earl didn't hear me when I entered. He was looking into his glass, empty of liquor. I whispered, "Not here," and startled him.

"Pardon?" he whispered as he stood.

I held a finger to my lips and motioned with my hand for him to follow. I took him to the three-season room off the kitchen, the place where we kept the icebox. There was a small seating arrangement in the room, a place to view the back garden. Most importantly, it was off the back of the house, with no rooms above it. I closed and locked the door to the kitchen behind us, led Earl to a chair and then stood in front of him. He wasn't the man I wanted him to be – nearly two decades already separated me from that man – but I unbuttoned my dress and let it fall as though he were. When Earl Fumer lifted my slip and pulled me to straddle his lap, I closed my eyes and moved against him as I once had the man I still wanted. Too much time had passed, that man was gone, yet I tried to bring him back. These weren't his hands, this wasn't his smell. I felt a pleasure so sharp it was painful and called out in a kind of yelp, thankful I'd chosen a room from which it would be unlikely I'd be heard. I kept my eyes closed a few moments more. When I opened them, I could see Earl Fumer's face in the low light, his expression so benign and thankful it made me sad.

He continued to write all through the next winter. He sent pamphlets for Jasper Park Lodge, newspaper clippings praising its luxury, and suggested that if I couldn't come on my own, that the whole family should come, assured me that even my lady would enjoy it there. I chuckled at this suggestion. Imagine, Ofelia and me in Jasper with our lovers. The men could hunt grizzlies in the craggy mountains while we went to therapeutic spas, water springing hot from stones, steam and the smell of sulphur cloaking us. Ofelia and I could consult each other on our gowns before we met for dinner in the dining room, the four of us debating politics over aperitifs. The more I imagined scenarios, the more absurd they seemed. I might be Earl Fumer's equal, but I was in an entirely different class than the duke and Ofelia. If we were to go together, would I be staff or contemporary? What use in questioning this when it seemed all but impossible?

Eventually, we stopped writing to each other. I can no longer remember who wrote last. I imagined that Mr. Fumer eventually found a lady who would accompany him to Jasper Park Lodge. That they breathed in the high mountain air together and felt reinvigorated, so very alive.

TWO

We All Found Small Kingdoms

So much has changed. And still, you are fortunate:
the ideal burns in you like a fever.
Or not like a fever, like a second heart.

– Louise Glück, "October"

Twenty-Two

Canada, 1931

The duke and Ofelia could no longer afford private tutors and governesses, so each night after Sveva went to bed, they considered schools in England and France, discussed the size and state of the residence and grounds of various boarding schools, whether or not their daughter would be able to have a private room and bath as she was accustomed. It was always the duke looking for the best opportunity for their brilliant daughter and Ofelia saying, "It's too far, Leone. You can't take her so far from me, from us."

In the end, Sveva went no farther than Vancouver to Crofton House School for girls. I knew the decision must have been based partly on cost. Despite this, there were several letters from the headmistress imploring the Caetanis to stop sending so much to her for allowance. I collected these, as well as letter after letter from Sveva imploring her parents to visit more often. *There are girls whose parents come every weekend!* she wrote. *If you're not going to permit me to leave the school grounds on weekends, at least come visit me! I miss you both so much, my dearest most darling Daddy, my beloved Mau-Mau!* They developed a new routine while their daughter was gone, one in which the duke convinced Ofelia to come to the woodlot each day. They, the dogs and sometimes even I would all pile into the duke's Ford Model A to drive there. I didn't go often. Because the two-seater was so small, I would offer to sit in the back with the dogs. "You can't be serious, Miss Jüül," Ofelia would protest each time I did.

"Do you know me to be a joker?" At this, the duke laughed. Ofelia thought it was absurd that I should ride in the back like one of the Japanese or Ukrainian labourers who worked in the orchards. She didn't believe me when I told her I thought it good fun – which I did. I knew we made the people of Vernon talk; we always had. Why not give them one more thing to mutter about? They already didn't know what to make of us. I was often assumed to be either a nanny or a housekeeper, though of course I was neither. What would they make of me riding along with the dogs? It mattered more what I made of it myself, which was an opportunity for fresh air, being separate from expectations.

Once at the woodlot, Ofelia would sit and read on a chair that the duke had fashioned for her from a stump. She would turn her face toward the sun. The duke would throw an axe over his shoulders and into the newly felled lumber over and over again until it became firewood. He was never shirtless in our presence, though he would remind us nearly every morning that if we weren't there with him, he would be. "Not that it's anything you haven't seen before, Miss Jüül, I'm sure," Leone once said. "Of good Viking farm stock, our Scandinavian Virgin!"

He laughed and Ofelia looked at him as though he were a small child, said, "Really," but it stuck, both the name and the use of it in my presence, though never often. When Sveva was home for Christmas that year, I heard her say, "So, where is our Scandinavian Virgin?" I was between the dining room and the kitchen. She had a lilt in her voice, a hitch of glee. Later, I would hear him and Ofelia refer to me as this when they thought I was out of earshot.

The winter of her second year away at school, shortly after Christmas, we got word from the headmistress that Sveva had the measles. We were told that her fever had risen considerably and that she was sequestered in the nurse's quarters of the school. As soon as we found out, Ofelia and I boarded a train to the coast. We went first to Sveva in seclusion, next to the headmistress's office, where Ofelia yelled, "Why weren't we called earlier? This is unacceptable!"

"You were called as soon as diagnosis was certain, Duchess," said the headmistress, standing stiffly beside her desk. I wished that the duke had been there. He had a way of being both imposing and charming. Ofelia, I feared, was being imperious.

We moved Sveva to a room in a private clinic on Georgia Street. Beside her daughter's bed, Ofelia lodged a ragged vigil. I felt like she cried too much, that it wasn't good for her daughter. While Sveva seemed as comfortable as she could be in her condition, it was Ofelia that I found myself trying to console with handkerchiefs and warm cloths. "Ofelia, she's sure to recover."

"How can you know this, Miss Jüül? Everyone seems so certain, and yet we cannot know what will happen. I've told you of the curse, haven't I?"

"Yes, you have." The Caetani curse. Like Leone, his father was a parliamentarian as well. After a national referendum, he was the minster tasked with telling Pope Pius that Italy would be a republic, no longer a papal state. Legend was that in response, Pope Pius cursed the Caetani family line to die out within two generations. "But the family seems to be doing fine in Italy, don't they?"

"For now, yes, but as each generation passes, there are fewer carrying on the line. All those children and only three grandchildren so far, two of them girls. And we can never know what will happen, can we, Miss Jüül? It's up to me to keep Sveva safe."

One evening, I came into the room to wake Ofelia so that we could make our way back to our hotel. She was slumped over, asleep across the bottom of Sveva's bed, a letter open in her hand. I shook her awake, gently. The first thing she said was, "I knew that he would be upset about the cost. We've got to get her back to Vernon."

I booked a sleeping berth for Sveva and we left the next day, each of us sitting beside her as she slept, neither of us speaking much. When we disembarked in Vernon, the duke was there with the car. He'd made the back-seat into a bed even though we had such a short drive home. I sat cramped between Ofelia and the duke in the front while Sveva lay out in the back. When we got home, her father helped Sveva upstairs. "Only a few weeks, my donetta," I heard him tell her. "You'll be well soon and then you'll be back at school. It will take you no time to catch up, you'll see." I felt like we would all need to catch up, eventually. Yet, with what? The shape and topography of both our inner and outer worlds had shifted so many times already. There was nothing constant to either catch up with or run from. We imagined our possible futures as foreign countries we would one day visit, but as we struggled with language and climate, the future became the present. What had once been familiar was now gone, replaced with the reality of our lives.

Twenty-Three

The summer of 1934, windows closed against the heat that pushed in through the drapes, the duke began to complain about his aching throat, the pain radiating from his neck. They were small complaints – "Oh, just a bit of discomfort here," his hand on his chest – but the way he rubbed at his neck, his strained expression as he swallowed when eating, suggested something more.

In September, days were edged with a hem of cold and the first leaves had begun to turn. It was quiet in the middle of the day. Children had returned to school. The summer people were gone. The duke began to miss meals, and without him at the table, the three of us sat stiffly and said little. In the evenings, Ofelia and the duke began to retreat to their quarters without Sveva, and she was left moving from room to room, sighing and looking out windows. I didn't think she should still be there, with us. She should've been with her contemporaries, back at school – even a parochial school.

I heard calls being made, words between Leone and Ofelia. Sveva and I cast about the house, each alone. I felt as though I should tell her to go outside, get some fresh air, but I didn't. Sveva was sixteen, no longer a little girl. Gone were her insistent cheer and theatrics, replaced with earnestness marked either by despondency or what she called "great intellectual fervour" when she spoke about the books she read or artists she studied.

One afternoon, the duke called us both into the parlour. "We've found out some unfortunate news."

"Unfortunate? What does *unfortunate* mean?" asked Sveva. We each looked toward Ofelia, sitting on the couch, twisting a kerchief, her hands trembling.

"I'm afraid I've been diagnosed –" The duke stopped.

"Diagnosed with what?" Sveva looked from parent to parent.

"It's a cancer of the throat."

Sveva circled the outer edge of the furniture. "What does that mean?" Her voice was raised, thin and crackling. Ofelia remained seated, her hands stilled, a muffled choke catching, a match on rough paper, lighting into sobs.

"We have a plan." The duke held out his hand to stop Sveva's pacing. "I'll be able to travel to the Mayo Clinic in Rochester, Minnesota – world-class cancer treatment. The best there is."

"The best there is." Ofelia nodded.

"Of course!" Sveva hugged her father, clung to him like a little girl, though she was nearly as tall as he was by then. "We can leave right away. We can be ready by tomorrow – can't we, Mau-Mau?"

Leone gently loosened her hold. "You'll stay here with your mother, Sveva. I'll need you to be here with her."

Ofelia looked up, dabbed her eyes with her kerchief, then held it up to her nose as she sniffled once, quietly. "Miss Jüül will accompany your father to the clinic."

It was the first I was told of it.

"What?" Sveva yelled. "She is going with him and we are staying behind? I don't want to be left here! I want to go with you, Daddy. Miss Jüül can stay."

"I can stay," I agreed, though I understood that, of the three of us, I was likely the most fit to accompany the duke, the least at the mercy of emotional fragility or unchecked zeal. Is this why was I being dispatched without a preliminary request?

"No, your mother and I have decided that this is what is best. We don't all need to go – I'll be back soon. It won't be long. I'll be back soon," Leone said, as though saying it more than once would make this certain.

In the months at the Mayo Clinic, the duke's pain seemed like something other than his own, a spectre that had taken him over. He slept, or tried to sleep, propped up by pillows. If he was prone, the pain in his throat increased and he would pull at it, try to call out. Upright, he was more stoic, though the pain passed over his face even as he slept or lay drugged. When he could write, he scribbled notes to the medical staff to ask for whatever he thought could ease the agony – water, drugs – again and again, though nothing seemed to help.

I sat beside the duke as he grasped at his throat and struggled. I delivered his notes to the medical staff, brought him water, tried to help him drink. I piled letters neatly on a table beside him, sorted and stacked them. Most were from Ofelia and Sveva. They arrived daily for a while. If a day went by without one, the next day two or three would arrive. They implored Leone to write back. They begged me to write to tell them how he was. I could tell from their letters, though they were desperate, almost hysterical, that each woman expected Leone would eventually return to them, healthy. And I knew, there in the clinic in Rochester, that he wouldn't, so I stared at the stationery poised on my lap until I wrote letters to my siblings, my cousin Kristine, eventually to my former lover, though the latter I never sent. For a time, the letters from Sveva and Ofelia stopped, and then the telegrams began to arrive, each more desperate than the last. *Please send word full stop. We are going mad with not knowing full stop.*

Though the pain the duke was in was constant, his ability to speak came and went. One afternoon, when his throat was too sore to speak, he wrote on a piece of paper – *tell me your story* – and held it out to me.

"About what?"

Before – Denmark – Egypt –

So, I did. It took me days. Leone passed in and out of wakefulness, and doctors and nurses came to check on him and administer medications. He slept and woke fitfully, the pain lurching through him. Some days he could speak, others he could not. Whenever he had moments of both wakefulness and lucidity, he would look toward me, and I knew this meant *carry on*. I told him about leaving the farm and the men I didn't love. About carrying, birthing and giving away a child. About the man who would have made me his wife if I could have resigned myself to a life with him and his children on a wind-battered island in a northern sea. I told him about my first trip overseas, through the Mediterranean and down the Suez Canal. About Egypt before the war, and how the war changed the shape of our household and our villa, nearly abandoned but for a very small staff.

On one of the afternoons when Leone could speak again, he turned his face to me, his eyelids heavy. "I'm leaving too soon, leaving them. This wasn't meant to happen." He tried to cough but only sputtered. "I was so certain for so long that it was the right thing to do, leaving Italy, coming here. It was the only way I could stay with Sveva and her mother. I'm not so certain anymore." He faltered, his voice strained. "They're not ready for this."

"No one can be ready for the loss of –" I stopped myself. "There's still a chance –"

"There's no chance, Marie. You know this as well as I do." There was an intimacy not only in him using my first name, but in this knowledge he and I now shared. He closed his eyes and pain passed across his face like lightning across the sky. Leone took a shallow, scraping breath. "Please, help Ofelia – and help Sveva. Ofelia won't be able to and I am leaving them so little."

"No, sir, you have given them so much."

When Leone laughed at this, it looked as though he was about to cry. "Everything you've given us." He said this as a statement. I wasn't used to the duke speaking to me this way. The medication usually made him quiet. I began to respond but he lifted his hand, then dropped it heavily. He closed his eyes and rolled his head to the side. "I know it is so unfair to ask this of you. You should be able to go now, to lead your own life – but I worry about what will happen to them if you do." Each word was carved out of his throat. "I worry that without anyone, Ofelia will go under and –" He stopped here, then rasped, "I worry she may take Sveva with her."

Given the variance and extremes of Ofelia's emotional states, it was a valid concern.

"I can't ask you to do this, I know that I can't ask you this now, but –"

I waited.

His words were hoarse, nearly a whisper. "Will you stay with them?"

This didn't seem like too much to ask. I'd stayed with them for seventeen years already. "Of course I will."

Once the duke fell asleep again, I left for the hotel where I slept nights. When we'd arrived it was still mild, but the weather had turned. As I rounded the street outside the clinic, the wind slapped me, tore the hat from my head. I pushed against it for two flat blocks to the hotel, watched the last of the fall leaves stripped from branches, shot down the middle of the street. There was little traffic, few people out. At the hotel, the awning was snapping in the wind, and moments later, as I crossed the lobby, there was a loud crack, then rumbling that could be felt through the thick carpet. By the time I reached my room, hail was coming down. I opened the window and listened to it clatter and ping off everything it could hit – posts, cars, street, awnings. A glorious racket, dissolving into the steady *shh, shh* of ordinary rain.

Twenty-Four

The duke was transferred back to Canada, but not Vernon. Lying in a hospital room in Vancouver, dull with weak light strained through clouds, windows streaked with rain, his bones, which had always been prominent, were now the most substantial part of him. His skin draped over his figure, seeming as thin as the hospital sheets. "Because of his condition, Duke Caetani is being fed intravenously," a doctor told us as we sat beside the outline of him on the bed.

It was December, and someone had hung strings of cranberries and popped corn over the railings around the mint-green halls. Near the nurse's station there was a spindly little tree with shining jewel-toned decorations that I imagined must have been castoffs from a hospital patron's household. Everything seemed strange – the glittering ornaments on the pathetic tree, the strings of cranberries and corn as though we were in someone's country home, the long halls an artificial green – as incongruous as the person the duke had once been.

On Christmas Eve, the archbishop of Sacred Heart Roman Catholic Church swung his robes down the halls toward the duke, trailing the smell of incense with him. The archbishop paid no attention to Sveva or me but turned to Ofelia, bowed and crossed the air in front of her before he began to chant and pray and intone over the duke. When he left the room, Sveva did as well, and I followed. "I can't go back in there yet, Jüül."

The lights crackled overhead, our skin mottled with a weak, cold hue. "Would you like to go back to the hotel? To Mass?"

"No, no, I can't be that far from him. I just can't go back in yet."

We both fell asleep in the waiting area on chairs sticky with cold vinyl. A nurse woke us. "Your father." She looked at Sveva and, instead of finishing her thought, turned to me. "The duchess." She left this incomplete as well.

Sveva pushed herself to standing, swayed slightly and steadied herself. "What?" she yelled. "My father what?" She ran down the hall to her father's room.

Ofelia was too weak to wail. What few tears she had left drained her until she was wrung dry, her eyes rimmed with red, nose raw. Her mouth so pale. Later, there were huge, hacking dry sobs. Ofelia's face contorted, her mouth gaping, body prone on the hotel bed. Sveva and I sat in armchairs, the drapes drawn, the sound of rain against the window, and watched over her. At some point, we all slept. I woke to a wet pillow, whether from tears or sweat I didn't know. The room was dark and I had no idea if it was day or night. Ofelia was lying beside me, her eyes open. "We need to get the death mask done." She startled me, her voice thin, words slow. "We need to get the death mask done and the body prepared to be sent back home."

In the next couple of days, I found a sculptor on Granville Street who had made death masks before. "The man was noble, a prince, a duke," I told him. "His mask will be on display in Rome." The sculptor assured me everything would be done perfectly.

I returned to Ofelia and Sveva in the hotel, the curtains still closed, neither talking. "The masks will be done soon – the face and the right hand. And then he'll be able to be transported."

"He needs to go back to Italy, Marie. He needs to go home." It was one of the only things Ofelia said in those days.

"I know, Ofelia. I know."

Over the next week in Vancouver, I researched the costs of embalming the body and preparing the casket for travel. There were fees for storage before a sailing could be secured, and for the packaging for the crossing, then transport and delivery once in Italy. I ran my fingers up and down rows of numbers and calculations. Eventually, it was up to me to tell the ladies, "I'm afraid our financial situation will not allow it."

Ofelia seemed resigned by then. Sveva was indignant, furious. "Our financial situation will not allow it!" she hollered. "Our financial situation! You insult my father when you speak about him like that. Of course, people will help us – our family will help us. He's Duke Caetani di Sermoneta!"

"Yes, yes, of course he is." I suspected she knew as well that there was something more in not sending the body to Italy. We certainly could not afford to accompany it. I suspected that if Ofelia could not go with him, the duke's remains would not go. The separation, even in death, would be too much. It took another two weeks in Vancouver for me to make all the arrangements for the duke to be brought back to Vernon in a solid bronze casket.

The day in late January that we buried the duke was unseasonably mild. Instead of fresh white skiffs and the cold burn of blue skies, there was melting snow, wet earth and the damp press of low clouds. In the days that followed, papers and magazines delivered to us carried not only the weight of dank paper but the duke's obituaries from around the world. News of his death came to us from Rome, London, Paris, Cairo, New York, San Francisco, Toronto and Montreal. The *Guardian*, *Match*, *Times*, *Chronicle*, *Globe*, *Gazette* and more gave him one paragraph, half a page, an entire article, his face speckled in shades of newsprint. I read each of the obituaries then filed them away, organized neatly in a box in the basement, while Ofelia slept.

Twenty-Five

After we buried Leone, Ofelia could not get out of bed. The mild weather at the end of January changed to a cruel cold in February. We closed the drapes to insulate against the chill, burned coal in the furnace, kept the fires lit, ate hot oatmeal in the morning, soup later in the day, and drank pot after pot of tea. Cold crept along the floorboards, licked the corners, hit us in banks as we came downstairs or passed by windows and doors. We dressed in dark colours, though it hardly mattered. With the drapes drawn, everything was cloaked with grey, dimly lit. I collected the mail and opened each letter of condolence sent to us from around the world, then took them upstairs to Ofelia. She kept her eyes closed as I read them to her, her chest rising and falling slowly, her breathing laboured.

Sveva and I waited. We waited for the day when we would leave the house and go out into the world again. The weather broke in the middle of March. We'd been in mourning for nearly three months and I thought we could open the curtains. It took Ofelia a few more days to get out of bed. Once she did, she dressed in black and walked from room to room as though the house and furniture were new to her, or so old that she had only scant memories of them. Once she had gone through every part of the house, she called me to her. "Miss Jüül, I'm so tired. Can you help me get undressed?"

She wanted Sveva to tuck her in. Ofelia ran her hand down her daughter's jaw, dropped it to her arm and rubbed the skin there. "You're such a good girl, Sveva," she said.

Sveva laughed at this, "Oh, I am now, am I? I haven't always been, though, right, Mau?"

"Oh no, you've always been our darling girl, Beo, our best girl." Ofelia let go of her and turned her head into the pillow. "Sveva, the rooms will have to be cleared."

"What do you mean?" Sveva looked to me as though I might have an answer.

"There's too much. Too much in the rooms. All these things, these things. It's all too much for me. They collect dust, germs. We don't need so much."

I nearly laughed – I had never heard Ofelia say that we didn't need much.

"You'll clear the rooms, darling?" Ofelia looked at her daughter, then to me. "Clear them of everything but the essentials. I just can't live with all these things, this clutter around me. Nor should either of you. It's not good for us."

"But the art, the china, the rugs – surely those aren't clutter?" Sveva asked.

I thought of their collections from around the world – the duke's artifacts from the Middle East and North Africa, Persian rugs, Ofelia's china, the oil paintings that had been so carefully wrapped and packed in Italy to accompany us to Canada so we could hang them on our walls here.

"We'll keep the china out. I think most everything else – except some of the furniture, of course – should be packed away." Ofelia looked at us, her head on the pillow, lids low but gaze steady. She even had the slight bow of a smile on her lips. She seemed so calm, so certain in that moment.

When spring arrived that year with flocks of early migrators alighting on exposed branches and flushing out again, the house was clean, so very clean, and nearly bare. Leaves budded, the ground softened. Between the first day of spring and the summer solstice was an increasing arc of light, leaves opening the valley. Ofelia asked us to push the windows up so we could get cross-drafts through the house, had me hire boys to replace the screens on the kitchen and porch doors so they wouldn't creak and bang the frames. The new doors would close so softly and lightly we wouldn't even hear them. Most of our belongings were stored in the basement, as Ofelia had asked of us, and the rooms were so lightly furnished that dust was visible as soon as it began to build. There were no rugs on the floors, no art on the walls. Books still lined the shelves of the library, but we pulled them out each week to dust. Sveva and I spent our days cycling through the house, washing one room after another from the first to the third floors before we began again.

After Leone's death, how simple it could have been to leave. Really. It could have been easy for me to go alone or for all three of us to set out on the train one day. Easy, simple – had we been other people. We were not. We were ourselves and where would we have gone? Ofelia's parents had died years before; her sister, Emerika, had immigrated to Argentina, then gotten ill and passed away. She had no family left in Italy. Sveva's father's family, the once-mighty Caetanis, implored her to return – the favourite son's daughter – but what would Ofelia and I do? Leone's family was so much sparser by then, the younger generation dispersed by marriage, war and misfortune. Would those left in the family have taken us in? If not, where would we go? Never mind the answers. We swung closed the gate at the end of the drive, our dogs circling us, latched closed the doors of the house.

I can still see the duke's hands, his long, slim fingers. I see them against Ofelia's back, along buttons and hems, and I shake the image from my mind. Again, his hands are there, this time bent around cards, then the flick and shuffle of them. The duke adored playing cards – for money or otherwise. Ofelia was not as keen though she humoured him. She preferred to make structures with playing decks – houses constructed of cards placed carefully and balanced in ways that could sustain their swaying weight, add enough support to hold them up. They were amazing, her creations. When she was finished, Ofelia would present them to us, then smile as though she held the sweetest cream in her mouth before pulling one, just one, card. For a moment, the structures would remain upright; then, a moment later, they would flatten around us.

It was fine if Ofelia dissembled her own structures. She seemed to delight in making a show of that as much as she did in building them. One afternoon, Sveva was playing in the study, where she should not have been, and knocked one over. She wrote her mother one of her letters of apology and asked me to give it to Ofelia like so many that I'd been asked to pass from daughter to mother. In it, she asked her darling mother, her beloved, her Mau Tau Fracapau, to forgive her for her stupidity, her selfishness, her ignorance. As with other letters, she asked that her mother please, please, please forgive her or she wouldn't be able to eat or sleep or go on. Sveva would promise her mother kittens and puppies in exchange for forgiveness. She wrote about her mother's kiss as balm on an open wound, that her embrace held more in it than the universe itself, then signed her letters *Your cruel and adoring daughter.*

In another letter, Sveva imagined her mother thinking life was not worth living, her heart beating with "only poor old Miss Jüül beside you." *Poor old me.* I have saved these letters in the basement with all our correspondence. What I wouldn't give for a house of cards, a careless child, a sudden gust.

Twenty-Six

Egypt, 1913

I was to meet Mrs. Ingeborg Brandt at port nineteen, the Iceland Quay, on the waterfront in Copenhagen to board the ship for Cairo. I'd arrived at the port early and hired a boy to transport my trunk down to the dock, then I stood beside it. I didn't want to be seated when my new employer arrived. The city was behind me but I could see it in my mind, lined up in blocks of colour, while I looked ahead at the flat, grey sea, terns and kestrels spinning in the sky. Gulls dove and shrieked above.

I had been standing for half an hour or more, an ache beginning to twist around my legs, stiffness setting in my knees, when I saw Mrs. Brandt. She was as tall, blond and distinctive as I remembered, her appearance a bit muted by the size of her hat and the grey of her coat. I stood at attention beside my trunk and waited for her to see me. She scanned over several people before she smiled, briefly and tightly, and walked toward me. Beside her, a woman who looked so like her it was unnerving held the hand of a small boy. A young woman followed behind them with a leather satchel and a small stuffed bear.

"Miss Jüül." Mrs. Brandt took my hand with both of hers. "Oh, I'm so glad that my correspondence made it to you. I wasn't sure if we'd see you here or not."

"Oh? I sent a response to you. You didn't receive it?"

"No, no, I don't think so." She turned to the woman beside her, the one holding the boy's hand. "Elspeth, did we receive anything?"

"Oh, you know I can't keep track of your things too, Ingeborg." The woman's tone was somewhere between playfulness and genuine exasperation.

"Well, never mind. You're here now." She looked over my head, as though searching for someone else, and motioned with her hand. "This is my sister, Mrs. Elspeth Anker Huugard, and Sven's governess, Miss Freja Anderson." Both ladies smiled. I had not yet been introduced to the boy. "This is Miss Inger-Marie Jüül."

"Hello." I nodded my head slightly to each of them, a bit more to the sister than the governess, who seemed barely more than a girl.

"Miss Anderson's been helping me care for Sven since we've been in Copenhagen. She won't be making the journey to Cairo. She's here to see us off."

At the mention of his governess's name, the boy tore out of his aunt's hand and toward the young woman. He clung to her leg, then raised his arms, "Up, up," though Miss Anderson's arms were full. He kept his eyes on me the whole time, wary.

"And this!" Mrs. Brandt leaned over to pick up the boy. "Is our little Sven." She held him stiffly as he struggled in her arms, reaching back toward his governess. He looked three or four years old and appeared sickly, his skin pale and body slight, a cloudiness in his eyes.

"Hello, Sven," I said. His mother placed him down and he reached his arms up to his governess again.

"Oh, Sven." His aunt took the things from Miss Anderson's arms so that she could pick up the boy.

Mrs. Brandt looked at my trunk. "Well, we'll want to find someone to get that on board as soon as possible. All of our things are already loaded and we need to ensure that everything is together." She looked around as though someone might be there waiting to help us. "Miss Anderson, can you see if you can find us a steward?"

The governess gave the boy a squeeze and then put him down beside his mother. He started to cry and reached out for her as she walked away. Mrs. Brandt looked at me. "Transitions," she sighed. "They are always hard."

"Yes." I knew something about that.

"Have you ever undertaken a journey like this?"

"Oh no. Nothing like this."

"You will be fine. I could see that when we met. That's why I've hired you. And you." She kneeled toward her son. "You will be fine as well. You're mother's big boy, aren't you?" The boy hacked out a sob and then sniffed it in. He nodded, his fists balled by his sides. I wanted to pick him up and hold him, but I knew it wasn't my place. Soon enough, his governess was back, giving him books and games and the stuffed bear for the trip, and Mrs. Brandt and her sister were instructing the stewards who had gathered around us. I could tell by the attention they were receiving that this family was important. I waited for someone to tell me what to do next.

On our sailing to Cairo, I felt more off-balance than sick, yet I wasn't able to keep food down, my body seeming to bear the roiling weight of the water. My head felt light and heavy at once. Sven Brandt missed his young governess and seemed as seasick as I was. His skin was pale and sallow, nearly yellow under his eyes. At four years old, he was so light when I picked him up that he felt like he weighed no more than a toddler half his age. Sven ate little, became weak and tired and needed to be carried often. Mrs. Brandt, her sister and I took turns carrying the boy. When I did, the deck seemed erratic under my feet, my strength tattered by lack of food and sleep. I wouldn't complain about any task I was given, so I clutched Sven's body as though he were a life preserver and moved slowly. The boy didn't seem to mind. He held onto me just as tightly as I to him. We were in the same situation, both malnourished and nervous, and became allies, too exhausted to say much to each other.

Mrs. Brandt had made this crossing before. She commented on the linens, the food, the music played by the band in the dining room. Sometimes she commented favourably, others more critically, but she always gave the impression that she had a lot of experience to confirm the validity of her opinions. I listened and tried to commit some of the details to memory. It might be valuable information in the future to know how high a thread count a napkin should have – and if it should be cotton or linen – if pickles should be soaked in vinegar or brine, if the songs played before dinner should be lively or calm – and how these should differ from those played during dessert.

I continued to call my employer Mrs. Brandt. She hadn't invited me to call her otherwise. Her sister asked that I call her Elspeth. "You'll find an interesting thing will happen." Mrs. Brandt patted her lips with a napkin at breakfast one morning. "Not many have mentioned that we are travelling without men yet. The closer we get to Egypt, the more we'll be reminded. Even though the boat's staff and travellers won't have changed, it's as though people begin to pick up on the mores of the Near East." She was right. By the third day, our dining companions at breakfast asked after our husbands, and we heard the question repeatedly from then on. Usually, I had an earlier dinner with Sven, neither of us eating much, so that I could put him to bed early and stay with him while his mother and aunt dined. That night, we were all invited to sit with the captain, and Sven was dressed in his sailor suit, the ladies in their best gowns.

"I suppose you'll stay in Cairo for longer this time?" the captain asked Mrs. Brandt. He nodded at the waiter who stood with a wine bottle wrapped in a cloth, then inclined his head toward Mrs. Brandt, so the man filled both their glasses.

Mrs. Brandt raised her glass and nodded toward the captain, touched her lips to the glass, then put it down without a real drink. "Yes. The household needs to be set up – Mr. Brandt is too busy with the business, of course, to do so properly."

"Of course. We each have our strengths – a man's is business while a lady's is running a household. It must be a challenge, though, with all the blacks and Arabs?"

"It is. I consider myself adept, but it is. I've some reliable staff in place already, most from the continent, and I've brought Miss Jüül from Copenhagen to manage the household staff. I still need to secure a governess for Sven."

So, I was now Miss Jüül from Copenhagen, Manager of Household Staff. I had a title to hang onto, a way to define myself, a role to work toward perfecting. Our plates were cleared as the orchestra began again, the violins keening out the first notes. We sat, Mrs. Brandt's and Elspeth's wineglasses full, as though it would be improper to have them as anything other than decorative, and watched as couples got up to dance. "I'll take Sven to bed now." He kissed his mother and aunt on their cheeks and then I took his hand, held it until we were out of the ballroom when I could pick him up again.

As I carried the boy to our berth, his head against my shoulder, the scent of his hair sweet enough that I could have chewed on it, I realized that the girl I'd given birth to would be around the same age. "Sven," I whispered to him. "Sven, when is your birthday?"

He was nearly asleep and didn't answer. It didn't matter.

Twenty-Seven

We disembarked with a shuffling of papers between Mrs. Brandt and someone on the dock, nothing that took more than a couple of minutes. The war was less than a year away from beginning, and one could still board and disembark ships as simply as getting on and off a train. Borders and papers seemed more theoretical than they did during or after the war. More like suggestions than divisions. We were viewed askance, but this was because we were three women with a small boy. Being without a man made us suspect. "Mr. Brandt will be here soon," Mrs. Brandt assured me. We were standing on a dock, being stared at by what seemed like hundreds but was likely only dozens of men. I'm not sure what was more uncomfortable on my skin, their eyes or the heat.

"Well, at least it's a dry heat," laughed Elspeth. "That's what the British keep telling us – *At least it's a dry heat!*" she repeated in English.

Mrs. Brandt didn't respond, looked over our heads. I held Sven. Between him and me, we had probably lost ten pounds on the sailing, and I swayed slightly with his light body in my arms. The dock seemed to move more than the ship had. When I shifted to try to alleviate the feeling, the pier kept coming up hard under my feet.

"There he is!" Elspeth pointed. Mrs. Brandt looked and I heard her make a small, almost squeaking sound in her throat before she cupped her hand over her mouth. It was the first time I'd seen such a girlish gesture from her.

It pleased me that a husband could still cause this kind of excitement. The boy was squirming in my arms, perhaps wanting to get down and run to his father, but that didn't seem safe, so I kept holding him.

"Sven, my boy!"

His son corkscrewed in my arms, and as he lurched out of them, he was caught, swung up into his father's hold. I tried to regain my balance and Mr. Brandt put a hand beneath my elbow to steady me, his son balanced on one arm. In this way, I felt Mr. Brandt before I met him. His hand left my arm when he reached out for his wife, "Mrs. Brandt," a lilt in his voice as he leaned to kiss her.

"Mr. Brandt." She held out her face and giggled. This is the only way I can describe it.

"And dear Mrs. Huugard." He leaned to kiss his sister-in-law.

Elspeth nodded and smiled. "Brother."

Following the reactions of the other two women in our small party, when he turned to me, I felt as though I should greet Mr. Brandt with some excitement, giddiness. I didn't, however. I smiled at Mr. Brandt in what I hoped was a pleasant, deferential way. I had nothing to get excited about. He was a stranger, certainly not my family, and I had little idea of what kind of employer he would be. He looked directly at me, which wasn't a given for a man of his stature, a woman of mine, and I thought he frowned slightly, just for a moment, though I may have been mistaken.

"This is Miss Jüül," Mrs. Brandt told her husband. He nodded, as both an assent and a greeting, a slight bow to his head. "We've hired her as head of household staff."

When he looked at my face again, I could see the colour of his eyes, warm hazel stippled with streaks of green. "Do you think you're up for the task?" He spoke through a slight smile, one eyebrow raised.

"Oh, don't tease her already." Mrs. Brandt swatted at her husband's arm with her gloves, held limp in one hand. To me she said, "Some find the locals hard to handle."

Without taking his eyes away from his family, Mr. Brandt made a small gesture, a slight twist in his wrist, and men came forward. Dark-skinned, white-clothed and plentiful, the men picked up everything around us, held out their arms to take what we had in our hands. They all appeared to be frowning, either slightly or quite deeply, as though we were disappointing them in some way. "It's okay." Mrs. Brandt must have read something on my face. "Give them what you can – you're not used to the heat yet, it will drain you – but make sure you keep a scarf for your hair."

Mr. Brandt led our small brigade, Mrs. Brandt and her sister following. No one thought to pick up Sven or take his hand, so I did. Several men, perhaps two dozen, followed us with our belongings. When we got to the cars, Mr. Brandt directed what luggage should go where and the ladies decided who should ride with whom and the men worked to fit the luggage into the cars. Everything the men called out to each other sounded to me like it was said in anger.

As we waited, Mrs. Brandt and Elspeth tied scarves over their hair, secured them well. I followed. "Is this in deference to local custom?"

Elspeth laughed a curt, sharp laugh and said, "I suppose it could be, yes!" She looked charmed by this idea, eyes bent into an amused smile.

"Not really," said Mrs. Brandt. "We just like to protect our hair for the drive. The dust here is different than in Europe, somehow. Thicker and, though it's so dry it can nearly choke a person, it's, well, almost oily, wouldn't you say, Elspeth?"

"Yes, something like that. Not pleasant, in any case."

"It will stick to your hair."

"Oh, of course." I secured my own scarf.

The cars sputtered through the cramped streets of Cairo. People stopped to gape and crushed toward us. There was a man in each car with a stick, swinging it to keep people back. I wondered if they supposed we were important and wanted to get a closer look, or if it was simply the cars themselves that drew a crowd. Often, it took only some stern words to let us through, but sometimes the men would poke or whack people away with the sticks. Men. They were all men. For most of the drive, there were no women on the streets. When we got through the most congested part of the city – though this was relative, every part seemed crowded – and I could see more than a couple of feet from the car, I glimpsed women down side streets, moving between doorways. A woman with a child on her hip saw us and pushed another child into a doorway as though she were afraid.

As the car lurched through the city, I wrapped both arms around my waist and held my stomach. During the crossing, the heavy weight of water pushed up against me from below, but after more than a week at sea, dry, hard land felt strange, my legs stiff. As the car jerked and slowed, my stomach felt equally, if not more, upset. How must the boy be doing? He was so quiet.

"Sven?"

He turned to me, his eyes wide and tearing at the edges. It could have been the dust. It could have been any of several things, really.

"Are you all right, darling?"

He nodded. What else had I expected? After my time on the boat with him, I knew the boy was stoic. I'd wondered from whom he'd learned this quality – his mother, I supposed. Mrs. Brandt seemed focused in a way that was steely, a little cold. I understood that she would have to be this way – living away from her husband for part of the year, maintaining two households, tacking together a family across continents, as she was.

"Won't this be an adventure?" I wanted to convince myself. Sven looked at me as though he were surprised that I was starting a conversation with him. It took a moment until he nodded. "This fascinating new country, and you'll be here with both your mother and father. Won't that be lovely?"

"I've been here before."

"Of course you have." It was me who hadn't.

"Father is busy."

"They usually are, aren't they?"

"Yes. He likes to play with me."

"Of course he does! I would like to play with you as well. You can show me the toys you have at your Egyptian home."

"I think you will be busy too, miss."

I laughed. "Yes, I suppose I will be, but I'll always make time for you, Sven. We've crossed an ocean together after all!"

The boy grinned at me.

The streets were becoming less crowded, more treed, though the shade didn't seem to provide respite from the heat. Armed men stood at gates. I could see little beyond the walls of what I assumed were estates. Everything seemed cast in shades of yellow, ochre, gold, and though it was midday, the air glowed as though sunrise or sunset. There was no blue to the sky, only washes of white and brown. The air was something separate from the sky, something made of dust and fine particles.

The lead car pulled up in front of one of the gates and two armed men pulled it open, the wrought iron squealing as they did. The cars turned into a circular drive bordered with palms and flowering plants – I could smell green, the scent of moisture that must have been required to keep this small garden thriving in front of the estate. When one after the other the men got out and began unloading our things, Sven and I remained seated. I wasn't sure what to do – would someone help us out of the car? Would someone give us directions? I watched Mrs. Brandt and Elspeth for cues. As Mr. Brandt held his hand out first to his wife, then his sister-in-law, I felt awkward waiting. Did I think I was their family? I was staff, like the men who were unloading the cars. I too should be doing something.

I stood, straightened my clothes and told Sven, "Wait, I'll help you out." Luggage was already piled around the cars. The men were moving from one to the other, picking things up, putting them down in different piles. They stepped well aside and paused when I got out of the car. I held out my arms to Sven but Mr. Brandt was there. "Let me."

"Of course."

He tipped his hat to me and then opened his arms to his son. In that moment, there was a shriek. Mr. Brandt, Sven and I all looked toward the house. Elspeth had been the one to yell and she was pointing to something. Leaving from the archway that lead into the villa was a mongrel of a dog with a large, colourful bird in his teeth. Bloody paw prints tracked across the marble floor leading from the house. Mrs. Brandt looked away and shook her head. "Good Lord," then, directed at me, "Welcome to Cairo!" She looked around until, it seemed, she had found the right person to address. "Mr. Sawalha, take care of that, please."

"Of course, ma'am." He bowed slightly, then turned and said something to the other men. It all seemed so loud, so fast to me. There was movement all around us, heat pressing up against me. We weren't inside yet when I heard two short, sharp gunshots. It sounded as though they'd shot the dog quite close to the house. I wondered what would happen to that beautiful bird, dead though it was.

Twenty-Eight

Those mornings in Cairo, I woke to a world teeming, either the heat or the noise getting to me first. I got up to respond to it all. The Brandts' estate was as sheltered from the sun as it could be, surrounded by palms and built around an inner courtyard – water slipping off the yellowed edges of plants each morning after they'd been tended – yet heat soaked into the ceiling tiles, reflected off the marble and radiated into the rooms. And the racket! The birds began shrieking at dawn, and the people were not much different. There was more yelling than I was accustomed to. More disturbing, there were insects so large that their wings and legs made noise around us as they whirred and caught.

I would dress and be in the kitchen by five each morning when the first kitchen staff arrived. I took my tea and toast with the head cook and went over the meal plan for the day. The cook was French but had been instructed to serve not only Danish food but the most British of English food as well. I'm not sure who had made this decision or why, but it was in Egypt that I developed a taste for pudding. I would next meet with the butler and we would review who was expected to call that day, when and where Mr. and Mrs. Brandt's commitments were, if there were cars assigned. Every couple of days, I would update Mrs. Brandt's social calendar and ensure that it didn't conflict with anything she was required to attend with Mr. Brandt.

There was always shopping to be done – for the pantry, the household, Mrs. Brandt's wardrobe – and staff to be sent to the best markets and vendors for each item. Most of the staff were men, the exception being the girls who cleaned the house. They needed quite a bit of supervision as it wasn't unusual to find them gathered in the inner courtyard, chattering and giggling. Sven's caregiver was an older woman named Sitto, and it was she who would reprimand the cleaning girls to get back to work. A sharp glance from her could get the lounging gardeners moving as well. As a petite Danish spinster, I hardly seemed like the right person to do so, and I often wondered why I'd been chosen as head of staff. Perhaps Mrs. Brandt saw me as someone who could keep the staff in tow while not threatening anyone or anything she held dear. A kind of nonentity in the household. That's how she treated me. Perhaps she knew that I was already ruined, as they called unwed mothers then. Whatever her reasons, aside from disciplining wayward staff, I did my job well.

I found ways to see Sven throughout the days, made a pretense of checking in on Sitto and asking after her when it was the boy I wanted to see. When I glimpsed her giving him sweets one afternoon, I teased her, wagged my finger as I took the bag from her hands. "Not from Sitto! Sven needs to listen to Sitto." She smiled in response, and I believed she understood me. Instead, it was I who carried a small paper bag with me so that when I was able to spend a little bit of time with Sven, I could slip him sweets. Sitto humoured me, seemed to know that I was trying to fill a need that was beyond confectionery.

One afternoon, I was in the small room adjacent to Mr. Brandt's office where I updated the calendars and made lists of tasks and supplies. Sitto knocked on the door and ushered in Sven, pale and listless. "Not good, miss," she said and nodded toward the boy. "Not good."

I came around the table and knelt in front of him. "How are you feeling, Sven?"

As soon as I asked, tears were in his eyes, but he neither cried nor spoke, just shook his head and looked down.

"Not good?"

He shook his head again. I took his hand in one of mine and put the back of my other on his forehead. He was so cold. It was hot, even indoors, and the boy was cool to the touch. "I'll call for the doctor." Sitto nodded. I knew she understood English, which was the language we used with the staff, even though she couldn't speak much. "I'll call for Mrs. Brandt as well. She'll be home soon." Where was she that day – her bridge game, playing tennis at the club? I should have known but would have to check. "Your mother will be home soon." In that moment, he lurched forward and I fell back slightly, hanging onto the boy as he clung to me.

Plans were made quickly and I wasn't the one to make the calls and arrangements. I could hear Mr. and Mrs. Brandt, voices raised against each other. The house was strange that way – some parts of it swallowed sound and hid it away; in other parts, voices slipped along chambers, turned corners, emerged in other rooms completely.

"A sailing, at this time? You know the conflict – things are about to erupt –"

"Not at sea, not so soon – if we stay, he may not –"

"– no one should be travelling now."

"We can send for someone –"

"Overland, perhaps."

"– not last that long – our son!"

The words travelled down the halls, sometimes in complete sentences, other times singularly – *no, her, how, home* – though nothing was said to me until the next morning. I jumped when Mr. Brandt's office door opened into the area where I sat as I sorted through the appointments and household arrangements for the day. I hadn't expected to see him so early and said nothing, no morning greeting. Mr. Brandt looked pale, his eyes heavy as though he hadn't slept. I didn't look at his face for long. "My wife and son need to be back in Copenhagen. He's –" He stopped.

"I'll make arrangements immediately."

"No, no. That's already been done. I just wanted to let you know."

"Of course. I'll cancel all of Mrs. Brandt's appointments."

"Yes." Mr. Brandt didn't move, stood facing me, though I knew from a glance at his eyes that he couldn't really see me.

"Your son –" I started.

"Yes."

I felt like I shouldn't continue, as though it was too personal to talk about his family. I'd started, though, so I continued. "He'll get the care he needs in Copenhagen. He's a strong boy, Sven." He was frail physically, but I'd seen him withstand so much already – rough ocean travel, transition into an entirely different culture and climate, long days in the company of people who didn't speak his language. He did all this without complaint and with little comfort from either of his parents. I didn't say this, but I thought it might be good for the boy to have an extended period of his mother's attention, even if it was in such unfortunate circumstances.

Something occurred to me then. "Should I plan to go with them?" I knew that I'd not been hired to care for the boy and I had seen him less than I would have liked to once we were in Cairo.

"Oh no. No, Mrs. Brandt will be able to travel with the boy and our staff will be waiting in Copenhagen. My wife is going to expect you to keep this household running, to keep everyone in line. She doesn't think I'm capable of doing so." He pinched the bridge of his nose, breathed in and released a long, slow sigh.

I reached for my papers on the table as though they might have instructions for what I was to do or say in this situation. I found none. "Of course. She'll be able to depend on me."

"Presumably." He glanced at me, that quick frown caught between his brows I'd seen the first day we met. "You can go now."

Twenty-Nine

When Mrs. Brandt left to sail back to Denmark with their son, she wished me luck in holding up to the blacks. It was the Arabs she was speaking of. "If you're not able to handle them, it will be no weakness on your part. They are an ugly, brutish people. Just let Mr. Brandt know that you need help." I wondered what her husband would do, what kind of help he could offer me. Most staff were not Arab. The chef was French and the house girls who worked in the kitchen and as cleaning staff were Spanish and Portuguese. The gardener in the inner courtyard was from Italy. It was the groundskeepers around the compound who were black, as we called the Arabs then.

One morning, Sitto came back. I hadn't seen her since Mrs. Brandt and Sven had left. "Madam, something wrong." I was a miss, not a madam, but I didn't correct her.

"What is it? You received your pay?" I felt badly as soon as I asked. I hadn't assumed that she was coming to me for money and yet it was the first thing I said.

"No, no. It is the girl, Marta. She not good."

As with Sven, Sitto came to me when things were not good. Marta was one of the girls from Portugal, a housekeeper. "I don't understand. Has she done something wrong?"

"No, no! Not Marta. She no wrong. The men, so bad. Animals, they animals."

I understood. "Where is she now?"

"She come to Sitto. She sleeping at Sitto's daughter's house."

"Does she need a doctor?"

"No, Sitto take care of her."

"Can you take me to her?"

Sitto looked frightened, wary.

"I need to see that she is okay."

"She not good."

"Sitto, listen to me. I will make sure that none of those men work here anymore." I wasn't sure of this, at all – that Marta would identify the men, or that I would be able to dismiss them – but I looked directly at Sitto as though to assure her of my ability to do so.

She wouldn't meet my eyes. "It not them, miss. Not them."

"Not who, Sitto?" She didn't respond. "I need to see her, Sitto. Will you take me?"

I wanted to call on one of the Brandts' drivers, but Sitto convinced me to walk. We left the broad, palm-lined streets and went through narrow and narrower lanes until we were on dirt tracks between walls. I followed Sitto down a deep flight of stairs cut into the wall. At the bottom, though we were still surrounded by city, the dirt gave way to sand. I could hear the river somewhere near us, feel it on my skin, but I no longer knew where I was, didn't know in which direction the water ran. Tents circled an area the size of the Brandts' villa and compound, and smoke from small fires rose in thin columns. The smell of meat, spices and incense blended with that of urine and animal dung.

Sitto led me into a dark tent, heat and smoke choking the space. When my eyes adjusted, I could see Marta lying on what was likely a straw mattress on the ground covered in layers of rugs. I knelt beside her, saw in the low light how her eyes were swollen, her lip cut, face bruised. The air was hot, closed, and yet she was covered in layers of thick blankets. By the foot of the mattress, I saw a bundle of fabric, the dark stain. I could smell the rust of blood.

"Sitto, she needs to see a doctor."

"No, no, madam. Not here, no doctor here."

"Well, then I'll have to bring her to a doctor."

"She cannot move. Must rest."

Marta's hand hung over one edge of the mattress. I moved it so it was on her chest. Her skin was moist, so hot. "I'll be back, Marta," I told her, though there was no indication that she could hear or understand what I said. When I stepped into the yard, the air seemed clear, fragrant in comparison. Children appeared from somewhere – so many children, pushing up against me and staring.

"I will come back with Mr. Brandt. He will understand. I promise you that he will not be upset." Again, I made pronouncements about things I could not control. "If we cannot bring a doctor here, we will take her to one."

Sitto didn't look pleased with my plan, but she nodded.

"Please, stay here with her until I return. Make sure she is okay." I climbed the steps back toward the streets and heard Sitto yelling behind me. She wasn't speaking in English but she was pointing to a young boy who was running my way. I understood that he would show me the way back to the Brandts' compound. More than that, this twelve-year-old boy would be my safety; without him, I would be a target.

I called the doctor, summoned the car and driver and located Mr. Brandt, who came home dressed in white, directly from the club. He wanted to change but I told him that we didn't have time. He listened to me. The doctor listened as well when I told them that only Mr. Brandt was to come into the circle of tents. I gave coins to boys and told them to protect the car as the doctor waited. Mr. Brandt looked absurd, dressed in his club attire, but he carried himself as though we were meant to be there, in that part of the city, entering a tent that was only for women. Sitto stood when we did, then bowed slightly to Mr. Brandt. He looked at Marta, touched her forehead, her hands, things that would not have been permitted if he had been a Muslim man and she a Muslim woman, but we were each something other, moving through their world. Mr. Brandt picked up Marta, still wrapped in the heavy blankets, and carried her out of the tents and up the stairs to the car. Behind us, children trailed, their voices lilting, almost cheerful sounding. This was exciting for them.

Marta was put in a bedroom in the family quarter of the villa, away from the other employees. "She has an infection," the doctor told us. "She will likely recover but she will need rest and clean conditions." I gave the girl her medicine, cleaned her wounds and kept the shutters closed against the sun. One afternoon while she slept, I went to Mr. Brandt in his office. I knocked quickly, then entered already speaking before I lost my resolve. "The groundsmen – all of them – will have to be let go."

Mr. Brandt was standing behind his desk, facing the papers spread over the surface. He looked up slowly, as though coming out of thought, then focused on me, eyes across my face, his brow lowering. "Of course."

I wasn't expecting he would consent so quickly. I kept speaking. "Sitto will help me rehire. She will know who we can trust."

He came around the desk. "Will the girl be all right?"

"I think she'll heal physically if that's what you mean," I answered. "I'm not sure that she should stay, though."

Mr. Brandt leaned against the front of his desk. "I'm not going to fire her for this. That wouldn't be right."

"No, no, of course not, but I think you should pay her way back home to Portugal. You should give her a month's wage as well."

Mr. Brandt crossed his arms over his chest. "Really? You wouldn't make a good businesswoman, Miss Jüül."

I ran my hand along the top of one of the chairs, looked toward a wall in the opposite direction. "I never claimed that I would. It's the right thing to do."

"It goes against my instinct, but if you think I should, I'll do it."

I looked back toward him. "It goes against your instinct to be kind? To do what is right?"

"You've misunderstood." He stood up straight.

"That's what you just said."

"I meant that the girl is a good employee. I don't want to lose someone like her." He rounded the desk, straightened papers as he did. "How will it be right to send her home as though she's done something wrong? What will her family think?"

He was right. I'd been thinking of myself, how I wouldn't want to stay in a place after what had happened. Yet, would I be able to go back home if I were in the same position? I'd never returned to my family. "You're right. You should ask her, give her the choice."

"You can ask her, when she's ready." He stared at his hands. "And then you will tell me what to do." He looked up, eyes on mine.

I hired groundskeepers based on Sitto's suggestions. They were younger, more boys than men. Their clothes were clean each morning and they spoke quietly, bowed their heads to Mr. Brandt and to me. I told him that he should increase their pay, just slightly. Before leaving for Copenhagen, Mrs. Brandt had briefly considered taking Sven to the family's other residence in Alexandria, where the sea air might have bolstered his health. I told Mr. Brandt that Marta should be sent there to escape the heat and crowds of Cairo. I don't know why I spoke to him so much, gave him my opinions. In all matters, he listened to me. I suppose that was all it took.

THIRTY

The heat was constant in Cairo. I had been told that I would get used to it but it had been months and I had not adjusted. It had been two weeks since the incident and Marta had recovered physically, but when she stood and moved, it was as though she were somewhere else, her body a kind of stiff costume.

One morning, I was filling out the calendar on the small table outside Mr. Brandt's office. "I've taken your advice." He startled me and I jumped, banged my knee on one of the table legs. "I'm sorry," he said without looking at me.

"No, no." I stood. "What advice, sir?"

He looked out the window into the courtyard. "To have Marta relocated to our residence in Alexandria."

"Good. I'll ensure that she's ready to travel."

Mr. Brandt turned from the window and looked at me briefly before his eyes flicked away. "By tomorrow. We'll leave then." He touched the back of a chair. "I know this means you'll need to rearrange my appointments once again. I'm sorry." He didn't look sorry; he looked harried, tense.

"No, sir. Let me know what arrangements you'll need."

"Book a first-class ticket for each of us – you as well. I'll need you to acquaint Marta with her new duties there." He drummed his fingers along the top of the chair. "I know it is late notice, but I'll need you to find some more staff. It wouldn't be right to have her there on her own." Mr. Brandt looked toward his hands, now still.

"Of course."

"And you can meet my brother. You'll like him. Most women do." My surprise at this comment made me blush. "Oh, I'm sorry. I didn't mean to imply anything." Mr. Brandt may have been embarrassed as well. "My brother, he's – I'm sure you'll like him. And he you."

Mr. Brandt knew little about my preferences, for people or otherwise.

"Cancel my appointments for the week. My brother will convince me to stay longer than I intend – he always does. I could use some time away." Mr. Brandt stepped toward his office, then turned. "Do you ride, Miss Jüül?"

"I beg your pardon?"

"Horses – do you ride horses?"

Was there a right way to answer this? "I used to."

"I thought that you might have." He smiled and turned to look out the window, then back at me, his eyes clouded with distance.

Mr. Brandt's brother met us at the station in Alexandria. He was taller and fairer than his brother. I recognized something in him. "Call me Onkel," he said, as though I were a family friend, not his brother's staff. He winked at me and gave his moustache a quick twist and I knew whom he reminded me of – Knud, in Zealand.

"Your carriage awaits." He threw his arm in the direction of a car and driver. "I'm afraid that I'm not as minted as my brother here. It will be one car for the four of us. I hope it will suit you ladies."

Marta stared at Onkel, without expression, then turned to me with a slight smile.

"We will be fine." I took Marta's elbow to lead her to the car. As far as I knew, a man had not touched Marta since the incident. We got into the car, Marta and I in the seats facing forward, Mr. Brandt and his brother on seats across from us. It seemed improper to look directly at either man, so we watched the passing city.

"You could've called for one of my cars, Onk." I turned to see if Mr. Brandt's expression was serious or jesting. When I did, he was looking at me, so I quickly turned away again, tightened the scarf under my chin.

"I know – just as I know that this car and driver are yours as well, really. Don't reveal my ploy, Bror." He spoke with a lilt, obviously the younger of the two. "I always prefer travelling with ladies."

I hadn't glimpsed the Mediterranean yet but the air was laced with the sea, so different from the dense heat in Cairo. I was used to being by the ocean, the smell of it, and for the first time in Egypt I felt a familiarity. Something that was not like home but was not as foreign to me.

Mr. Brandt's Alexandria residence was near the shore, a French-style apartment with tall arched windows and stone balconies. "Onkel's apartment is connected to ours, but I won't be comfortable with you here alone. Miss Jüül will help find another staff member for the residence, a girl to help you." It seemed extravagant and unnecessary. As though thinking the same, Mr. Brandt added, "We'll want more staff. Mrs. Brandt and our son will want to spend more time here when they return. The sea is so healthful." Marta and I both nodded. "I'm here quite often as well. Onkel takes care of the shipping end of the business, but every little brother needs supervision once in a while, yes?"

Again, Marta and I simply nodded. I wasn't sure what was appropriate in this circumstance and neither was she. Mr. Brandt looked from one of us to the other. "Marta, I will show you the staff quarters. You can get settled in," though she had very little to settle. They started down the hall and I stood in the entry and waited, wondering what to do. Mr. Brandt was back in a few minutes. "Miss Jüül, you'll join me at my brother's?"

"Of course. Should I make arrangements with Marta?"

"She'll be fine. I'll have the hotel staff bring her some dinner."

I left my own bags where they were in the foyer and followed Mr. Brandt to his brother's apartment. Onkel was now wearing a long white tunic like Egyptian men wore, and he had taken off his shoes and socks. I was not used to seeing the bare feet of men, and I tried to not keep looking at them, ill-formed and bony as they were. Onkel brought us each a drink. The glass was cut crystal and I could smell alcohol. "Egyptian whisky." Onkel paused. "I know, it seems like an oxymoron, but it's actually quite good."

"An acquired taste, really." Mr. Brandt raised his glass. Light refracted off it, glinted as he took a drink. I stood looking dully at mine. "Go ahead." Mr. Brandt tilted his glass toward me. "See what you think."

Onkel was grinning like an eager child. I wasn't sure why I was with these brothers instead of with Marta or what was expected of me. I tipped the glass and touched the drink to my tongue, not enough to swallow. I licked my lips. It tasted like the whisky Carl had once shared with me at the lighthouse. "Well?" Onkel raised his eyebrows at me.

"It's warm." I suppressed the tickle in my throat, the desire to cough.

"Warm!" He clapped his hands once and clasped them in front of his chest, beamed at me. "Well, aren't you lovely? Isn't she lovely?"

Mr. Brandt smiled in response, didn't look at me directly. It was, of course, inappropriate to answer.

As though sensing this, Onkel asked, "Aaannnd," he elongated the word, "your lovely wife, Bror? How is our Ingeborg?" Onkel waved his arms to guide us into the apartment.

"She's as well as she can be. Sven seems to be receiving good care in Copenhagen. It's difficult, though. With so much talk of war –"

Onkel pointed to chairs turned toward open doors to the balcony, heavy drapes pulled open so that the white curtains underneath billowed with breeze off the water. The ocean was so close that I could smell the thickness of it. I wondered what Marta was doing. Had she opened the doors to let in the air?

Onkel stepped onto the balcony and turned around, leaning against the stone railing and facing Mr. Brandt and me, still standing inside the apartment. "We'll have to do something while you're here." It sounded as though we were together on a special visit. "All my brother does is work and, admittedly, he's good at it, but that is so boring, yes?" His question was directed toward me but I wasn't sure if I should respond. All I'd done in Egypt so far was work, after all. "What do you like to do, Miss Jüül?"

"Read." I hadn't thought before I answered, felt embarrassed – it wasn't an answer that involved anyone beyond my own mind, and in this way, it was rude. I looked at my hands.

"Read! Well, I'm afraid the library here burned down." He chuckled at his own joke.

"Onk, really." Mr. Brandt's tone was admonishing.

"I'm sorry. You know I've nothing but respect for you, Miss Jüül." How could he? We had just met. "My brother always hires the most intelligent staff. I don't know how he does it, really."

I hadn't had more than a taste of the whisky, but I was bold to say, "It was Mrs. Brandt who hired me."

"Of course! Well, that's it, isn't it? He knows enough to leave some things to the lady of the house."

I could sense Mr. Brandt shifting uncomfortably beside me. I took a drink and then had to clench my throat so I wouldn't sputter it back up. From below, a herd of goats griped as a boy yelled. I could hear the switch of his stick, to keep the animals moving, presumably.

Mr. Brandt cleared his throat. "Miss Jüül likes to ride." I turned toward him, stifling a cough in my mouth. He slipped a glance at me, a quick smile that wavered at the corners of his mouth.

"Oh good! We'll go riding then! Have you ridden in the desert yet?" Onkel asked me.

"No, I've not." When did he imagine I would have had the chance?

"Oh, my. You are going to love it. Won't she? Riding in the desert is like nothing else."

"Well, the sand in one's eyes is like nothing else." Mr. Brandt had put down his drink and was rubbing his hands along each thigh as though he were about to stand, but he settled back into the chair again.

"Listen to him! Spoilsport. Don't mind my brother. If one has the correct form, one won't get too much sand in the eyes. And the light! It's so, I don't know, diffuse – diffusssse. The smells! Did you know that the sand has a scent?"

"No, I suppose I didn't."

"Not in the cities of course – well, there are smells, of course – ugh, the smells! – but not the ones I'm thinking of. In the true desert, it's got the most delicious, fragrant scent, doesn't it, Bror?"

Mr. Brandt had picked up his drink again. He looked at his brother, surprised, as though he hadn't heard the question.

"Oh, I don't know why I bother asking you. If there is anyone who needs his senses awakened, it is you!"

"And if there's anyone whose senses are perhaps too awake, it is you, dear Onk." I could tell that the two of them had played this game for years – responsible older brother, mischievous younger one – their roles well defined. Mr. Brandt's annoyance seemed light-hearted, as did his brother's teasing. "I suppose we should think about dinner."

"Why think about dinner when we can have more to drink! Miss Jüül?"

I looked at my glass. I didn't need any more. I shook my head.

"Are you trying to corrupt my staff?"

There it was, then. For a moment, I'd felt like I was, if not quite an equal, a social guest of these two men. Of course, I wasn't.

"Someone needs to." Onkel winked at me. "There is a new chef at the Monte Carlo."

I leaned toward Mr. Brandt, whispered, "Marta."

"I'm sure Miss Jüül and the girl would like some rest after a day of travel. Do you not have a cook anymore?"

"Why have a cook when I never eat in?"

"Then we'll order from the hotel kitchen."

"What? And keep these lovely ladies in their rooms like a couple of caged birds? You want to stretch your wings, don't you, Miss Jüül? I can see it in the way you move!"

"If you'll excuse me, can you point the way to the powder room?" I knew that it would be inappropriate for us to dine out with Mr. Brandt and his brother. There were no ladies or children to care for, and Marta and I were not here to provide men with the kind of company that was only appropriate for family. Mr. Brandt knew this, as did his brother, likely, though Onkel didn't seem one much for social conventions.

When I returned, Mr. Brandt said, "I'm sure you'll want to rest back at the apartment, Miss Jüül. I'll order some food and have it brought up."

"And then I'll come by later," interjected his brother, "to whisk you off for a night on the town."

Mr. Brandt got up, cleared his throat. "He won't."

"That's where you are wrong, Bror. I will! Won't I, lovely Miss Jüül?"

Mr. Brandt stood, hands clasped in front of him like a guard or butler, and I realized that he was waiting to walk me back. We said nothing until we got to the door of the other apartment, then he apologized for his brother. "And I assured you that you'd like him. I'm sorry. He's too brash, too presumptuous. He always has been."

"No, not at all. I like him. You were right."

Mr. Brandt nodded slightly, his jaw tight. "Your dinner should be up soon. I hope you enjoy it."

"I'm sure I will."

He backed away from me, nodded again. "Goodnight, Miss Jüül."

"Thank you." I wondered why I was so eager to be easy to please.

Before I fell asleep that night, Marta turned in the bed across from mine, whispered, "It wasn't them, Miss Jüül."

I rolled toward her. "It wasn't who?"

"It wasn't the groundskeepers who hurt me."

Cold cut through me, even though the night air was stifling. "What do you mean?"

"I let you assume it was the groundskeepers, but you should know, it wasn't them. It wasn't any of the staff."

"Who then, Marta? Who was it?"

"Some stupid, stupid boys at a club."

"What club? The Brandts' club? Does Mr. Brandt know?"

"No – and don't tell him. Not that club. The Foreign Service Club. I let Leonore convince me we should go there for a coed party after hours. They seemed so young and harmless."

"But what happened, Marta?"

"It doesn't matter what happened, does it? It happened. It's over. And now I've been sent here, as though that could protect me, as though anyone could actually protect us, Miss Jüül."

"No, this isn't right, Marta! I'll talk to Mr. Brandt, I'll –"

Marta sighed loudly and I could hear her turn. When she spoke again, her voice was against the wall. "No, please don't, Miss Jüül. There's nothing you or I can do. It's best if we forget about it."

The feeling of cold left me, and air pushed down, weighted me to the sheets, damp beneath my body. I couldn't sleep. Occasionally, a breeze would shift the drapes, but barely, as though even the air was too lethargic to move. I was thirsty but too tired to get up, too awake to chance not being able to fall asleep. I'd fancied myself smart and savvy, the head of household staff. But I'd been play-acting, even if I hadn't known it myself until then.

THIRTY-ONE

Onkel did not come back to the apartment for me that night as he'd joked he would, which was probably best. The next morning, sound entered my dream, the whirring screech of an enormous insect. I opened my eyes, unfamiliar with where I was. The light was clearer, more defined somehow than in Cairo, but it had the washed-out quality of very early morning. I felt like I hadn't slept long. The ringing continued, a bell. I put on a robe and went to the door.

"Good morning, lovely!" Onkel spread his arms as though he wanted me to hug him. "I'm sorry that there is not someone more appropriate here to call on you at this early hour but, as my brother keeps reminding me, I am short-staffed." I stood holding my robe and looking at him. Was I supposed to invite him in? What time was it? "So, I am your wake-up call. Breakfast will be sent up soon. And then – we're going riding this morning!"

"Riding?"

"Yes, riding, love! We'll try to beat the heat of the day."

"When should Marta and I be ready?"

"I'm sorry, just you, Miss Jüül. Marta will be working today. As for you – your breakfast will be up shortly. Eat well, dress for riding, then come to my apartment. We will be ready when you are."

I had no riding clothes, but I knew that wasn't expected of me. At the farm, I'd worn woollen trousers. A woman couldn't wear pants while riding in Egypt – she hardly could in the higher circles in Copenhagen – so I dressed in the heaviest skirt that I had. Onkel drove us out to the stables himself. He yanked on the wheel sharply to get us through the crowds in the city. As we lurched from side to side, I kept my eyes forward. Goats ran alongside the car, donkeys ambled by and when we came across camels, we stopped to let them pass. Once we were out of the city, it was better, though eventually there was no road, only hard-packed sand. "Soon we won't be able to drive," Mr. Brandt said. "The sand gets finer the further from the city we get." I turned my head, the city retreating behind us, the desert burning gold along a wavering horizon.

British expats ran the stables. Onkel had obviously been there before and staff greeted Mr. Brandt with a kind of respectful familiarity. A man turned to me and said, "You're looking well, Mrs. Brandt." I opened my mouth to correct them but swallowed a laugh instead. It was inappropriate, but I had so few similarities in appearance to Mrs. Brandt that it struck me as funny. The moment passed when I could have corrected the mistake. A stable hand led to me an Arabian, muscled and lean, its coat a light ginger tone. He lifted me to ride her sidesaddle. I hadn't ridden in years by then and had rarely ridden sidesaddle. I gripped the reins, feeling unstable, and resisted lifting my leg to the other side of the horse so that I could ride properly. The stable hands trotted the horses with us on their backs once around the arena and then led us out into the desert. Older men in white robes met us, leading horses draped in patterned, deeply coloured fabric and saddled with bags. "These will be your guides," said one of the stableboys.

Mr. Brandt said something in a low voice to one of the guides and they bowed to us and left.

"Probably a good decision," said Onkel.

Mr. Brandt turned to me. "We've found that the guides here have very specific ideas about what we should see and how we should go about doing so. It usually involves stopping for tea and hookah ceremonies every ten or fifteen minutes or so, wouldn't you say, Onk?"

"Yes, and the distinct feeling that they amuse themselves by riding us around in circles – it's hard for us cold-blooded people to get our bearings in the desert, after all. I suppose not everyone believes in riding headlong into unknown territory." Onkel trotted ahead a bit, then turned to face me. "How about you, Miss Jüül? A slow, circular jaunt or headlong?"

His question felt like a kind of dare. I was riding tentatively, holding the horse at a trot slow enough that I could feel its hooves sink slightly with each step, hear the swish and hiss of sand. Mr. Brandt and Onkel rode on either side, slightly ahead, throwing their words back at me. The desert had its own kind of quiet, as though there were an edge to it off which sound slipped, disappeared. My hat was enormous, chosen for sun protection, but it surrounded me, blocked parts of my vision. The way I was riding, the encompassing hat, the heavy skirt and the building heat made me feel small and contained, the desert huge and shining around me. I remembered home, my legs clenching either side of the horse, the cool balm of air, tall grass and rolling hills instead of sand and dunes heaving in the distance.

For a while, none of us said anything. We continued at a trot that I could maintain riding sidesaddle. I felt as though the men were holding back for me, so I quickened the pace to a canter. If I angled my chest toward the horse, arched my lower back and steadied my hips, I could achieve some sense of stability. The sky was turning from a bleached-out white to a high, aching blue. The desert lifted and fell like eerily solid waves around us. What scrubby plants and trees there had been when we had begun our ride were gone. Riding in the stance I was, I felt like I was expending a lot of effort to not go very far. When we slowed and eventually stopped, Onkel said, "You don't look very comfortable, Miss Jüül." Was it that obvious?

"She seems like an accomplished rider to me." Mr. Brandt wiped his forehead and glanced toward me, something of an apology in his expression – or was I imagining that? It was strange to be spoken about between brothers while sitting on a horse between them.

"I'm fine." I shifted on the horse again. "It has been some time since I've ridden, though."

"I sense you'd be much more comfortable riding the horse as it's meant to be ridden," said Onkel.

I laughed. "Is that what this is about? You'd like to see me ride like a man?" Something about Onkel made me feel bold. I spoke to him in a way I wouldn't his brother.

"A man, perhaps, or perhaps just a person in the best position to ride a large animal." Onkel was teasing me, goading, and while part of me appreciated his banter, part of me was annoyed. I knew this wasn't just for me; it was for his older brother, as well. I should have ignored his prod but it frustrated me. I let go of the reins and slid off the horse. Mr. Brandt dismounted as well and reached out to help me, his hands briefly on my waist as if to lift me onto the horse again. I moved away from his hold. "If your brother wants me to ride like a man, I'll mount the horse like one as well."

I am a small woman. The Arabian was a good size, as were my skirts. It took some time for me to gather them in one arm as I got my foot in the stirrup. I paused. It would take momentum and strength to get me up on the horse in one motion. I was in an awkward position, in the desert with two men, near strangers, with whom I shouldn't have been riding, really – and there I was, trying to prove something. I gripped my skirts under my arm, the rein with my hand, and propelled myself up. I hit the horse off-centre, sloping toward the side from which I'd mounted, but righted myself, settled my skirts around me and took the reins.

Both men were quiet – I could feel them watching me – then Onkel said, "There we go! That's much better, yes?"

"Yes." I lifted the reins, clucked my tongue at the horse and dug my heels into its side. I wanted to ride in a way that I could forget that I was anything other than a person on a horse. To forget that I was an employee and was perhaps acting improperly. To ride away from Marta at the apartment and what had happened to her. These two men, so different, one of whom – Onkel – seemed to want me to prove something to him, though I wasn't sure what. The other, the one who paid my way, I knew so little about, and yet I knew it was Mr. Brandt whom I wanted to impress more than I did his brother. To be simply a woman on a horse. To ride as though I knew how. And so, I did.

I brought the horse to a gallop and the desert stretched out in every direction, the men somewhere behind me, where I was determined to keep them. I rode toward the hills beyond the dunes. We crested a dune and distance did strange things. First, there was a caravan of camels far enough away that I saw them as if in silhouette, and then I was pulling the reins to stop the horse from plowing into them. I saw the brightly patterned cloths against the camels, the rough sacks they carried, men in white robes.

I pulled the horse back in time, with Mr. Brandt and Onkel not far behind me. The horse snorted in exertion, puffs of condensation hitting the dry air. The camels kept moving by us but some of the men had stopped, were pointing at me and yelling. Onkel pulled his horse between the men and mine and yelled back in their language. The men glared toward me, but they were silent as they moved their camels past us.

"What did they say?"

"Oh, it hardly matters," said Onkel. "I know enough Arabic to tell them to mind their own concerns. That in some matters, Europeans are always right."

"And they accept that?"

"Perhaps more accurately, businessmen are always right. Everyone understands that, don't they, Bror? Even silly little me."

"I'm not sure about that." Mr. Brandt had brought his horse up beside me. "I think people attribute more power to businessmen than we have." He said this as though he were speaking to me directly. I didn't know what to read into his statement.

"Wishful thinking, Bror. If the war they're predicting arrives, we'll discover just how much power we do or don't have." Onkel now rode on the other side of me.

"We are not bringing that up, though you just did." Mr. Brandt spoke over me to his brother.

When we'd been riding, I'd been outside of this, beyond the banter between brothers, the business of being a man in a foreign country, the reality of being a woman. I could feel the heat bearing down as well as the warmth of the animal pushing up through me. My clothes felt heavy, restrictive, my hat so enormous that it seemed to block my breathing. I lifted it off my head and let it fall to my back. I put my hand on my chest and took a deep breath, closed my eyes. The men were still talking; I could hear their voices though no words until Mr. Brandt said, "Miss Jüül?"

My eyes were still closed. I swallowed and reached out my arm to indicate that I needed a moment before I could speak. Mr. Brandt misunderstood. I heard him dismount, felt his hands on me, pulling me down from the horse. I opened my eyes and pushed away from him. The ground was both so hard and so unsteady beneath me. The sun seemed to reflect off the sand and hit me full in the face. I moved away from the men, wanting nothing more than for them to remain quiet, not question me. "Miss Jüül?" Onkel asked.

"Leave her," I heard Mr. Brandt say, and for this I was thankful. I looked for shade, a place to sit, and saw nothing. I stood, one hand on my chest again, one on my stomach, and breathed. I concentrated on the sound of my breath, the movement of my stomach in and out. I told myself it would pass. I turned back toward the men. I may have even attempted a weak smile.

Mr. Brandt came toward me, his arm held out. I didn't take it, but he stood beside me. "It's likely heat exhaustion."

Onkel looked pale himself. He held back, behind his brother. I could tell then that he wasn't someone who dealt with illness well. I nodded toward Mr. Brandt. "I'll be fine."

"You will."

"We pushed you too hard," Onkel said.

"No, you didn't. It was my own fault."

I wanted to say more but Mr. Brandt interjected. "We should have warned you about the heat."

"I'm not that new to Egypt." Though Mr. Brandt knew exactly how long I'd been there, I didn't want to seem inexperienced.

"No, but it can sneak up on any of us."

"We should get back." Onkel's joviality was gone. Had I disappointed him?

"Are you all right to get on your horse?" Mr. Brandt asked.

I took a breath, placed my hat back on my head. "Yes."

I mounted my horse to ride back to the stables, which now seemed a great distance away. I felt unsteady, my stomach heavy with unease, the rest of my body so light I felt like I could slip off the horse. I held tight the reins, clenched my thighs, swallowed and swallowed against the nausea, willed my eyes to focus.

"Miss Jüül, you don't look well. Are you still able to ride? Come with me. I can rein your horse to mine."

"No, no, I am fine. I can make it back."

When we got back to the riding club, I vomited in the ladies' room. I rinsed my mouth and splashed water on my face, tried to pretend I was fine when I rejoined Mr. Brandt and his brother. "Miss Jüül, you look awful," Onkel said as soon as he saw me. "Doesn't she?"

"You don't look well," said Mr. Brandt. "We'll get you back."

This was not the way it was supposed to be. I was staff; I was not to be taken care of by my employers. That night, before I fell asleep, I thought of Mrs. Brandt telling me before she left for Denmark, "Mr. Brandt is a wonderful father, but he doesn't deal well with illness. Not only will it be better for Sven, no doubt, to get proper medical care, it will be easier on Mr. Brandt."

When we were back in Cairo, my fever mounted. I spent days in bed, the high ceilings and tiled borders going in and out of focus. It felt like we were alone in the villa. The other staff were there, of course, but no one came to me to ask for instruction. Later I would find out that Mr. Brandt was keeping the staff and their questions from me, letting me rest.

He came to me, often it seemed. How much time passed? At first, he stood at the door and spoke to me from the arched frame, then, I'm not sure how much later, I woke to him sitting on the side of the bed. Toward the end of that time – had it been two or three days or more? – Mr. Brandt had reached out and placed his hand on my forehead. I remembered how he had tried to help me on my horse, his hands on my waist so briefly. In my illness, I regretted having moved away. I rolled my head and his hand left my forehead, moved along my cheekbone, my jaw. My fever broke, but I could still feel his hand there.

Thirty-Two

One afternoon when I was well again, Mr. Brandt asked, "Miss Jüül, where do you usually eat?"

"In the kitchen with the girls." He must have known that.

"Dine with me tonight. I'm getting bored of my own company. It's time to bore someone else with it, I suppose." His smile was tight, uncomfortable.

"If you like, I can invite someone for dinner – a business associate, perhaps?" This was something I'd done often when Mrs. Brandt was in Cairo, arranged dinner company for them, whether at their villa or out with others.

"No, that's fine. I'd just like someone to talk with about home."

"Home?"

"Denmark. Do you miss it?"

I missed the climate. Here, I felt like heat was a parasite inhabiting my body.

"Wait." He held out his hand. "Don't answer, we'll talk at dinner."

That night, the conversation began forced, flat. Mr. Brandt talked about Copenhagen. I wasn't sure how much I could add. I'd spent most of my time in the city between a dress shop and the library, later in the homes of the ambassador and other government officials. The conversation faltered as one of the kitchen girls cleared away the soup bowls, set down plates of beef and potatoes. I smiled at her but she didn't look at me directly.

Mr. Brandt began cutting into his meat. "Where did you learn to ride?"

I kept my hands on either side of my plate, not picking up my utensils. "I grew up on a farm in Jutland. We rode a lot there."

Mr. Brandt nodded and looked up. "Gudum, yes?"

Of course, my employers would have my papers, my birthplace wouldn't be a secret from them, but it seemed strange. What else of my past might he know? "You've heard of it?"

"My family's from Klitmøller – now, have you heard of that?"

"I have. I've an uncle, a fisherman, who told me how fierce the waves were there." I felt more at ease, began cutting my beef. "Is your family still there?"

"Far as I know."

"You don't keep in contact with them?"

"They weren't happy that I didn't want to take over our fishing fleet, tiny and feeble as it was. It's what our family had always done. Once I left, they made it clear if I wasn't part of that, I wasn't part of the family."

"Oh, that's too bad."

"Not necessarily." Mr. Brandt raised his water glass toward me then took a drink. "We should have something more than this. I'll have them bring in some wine."

"Oh no. I can't – wine doesn't agree with me." It was no more appropriate to drink wine with Mr. Brandt while his wife was out of the country than it had been to have whisky with him and his brother. I'd convinced myself that a meal and conversation with him were fine.

"Your own family?" he asked. "Are you still close?"

"Close, no, not close. There's no estrangement, though, I suppose."

"No, I would guess not. You still receive letters from them, don't you?"

I looked at Mr. Brandt instead of answering, but his attention was on his plate. I'd little idea that my presence in the household was so noted. Was I being monitored in some way?

He looked up, a piece of meat on his fork. "They must miss you."

"They write that they do, but I don't think I'm missed in any real way."

"I have a hard time believing that could be true."

I didn't know if he was speaking about me, personally, or in a general way about family members, distance and time. Before I could respond, the kitchen girl came in again, and as she was refilling my water, I faltered, tipped my glass, soaking both the tablecloth and my skirt. I jumped up and knocked my cutlery clattering off my plate.

Because of Mr. Brandt's schedule, we didn't have dinner again for another week. I thought about things we could talk about, topics that might make me seem more interesting. I had decided to tell him about my time at the lighthouse on the island. Not about how I'd been rejected by a man I didn't love and taken in by another who wanted more than I could give him, but about the wind, the dark stain of night, how I'd had some control over the light flashing through it. I was going to make it sound intriguing, adventurous, but as I was about to speak, the bell rang at the front door. A few minutes later, the butler came to the dining room. "Excuse me, sir. It is important." Mr. Brandt left the room and I waited without eating.

When he came back, Mr. Brandt sat for a moment, leaned his forehead into the heel of his palm before he straightened, reached for his spoon. He took a mouthful of soup and I did the same. When he put down his spoon, I did mine. He looked across the table at me. "Russia's mobilizing along Serbia's border." I blinked back at him. "Word is the British will be the ones who declare war, but the others won't be far behind."

We'd known it was coming, I suppose. My brothers kept telling me so in letters.

"They'll have to stay."

I wasn't sure about whom he was speaking.

"Mrs. Brandt and the boy. They'll have to stay in Copenhagen. It won't be safe enough to travel, especially with Sven still not well."

I remembered the conversation I'd overheard between Mr. and Mrs. Brandt as she'd prepared to leave. "Will you go to them?"

"No. The time's passed when I could have left. Business will change – the ports will be restricted – and I'll have to stay, do what I can. It may arrive sooner than we expect – there are so many stakes here: the British, of course, but also the Russians, the Germans. They'll be here eventually."

It didn't seem to me like war would reach North Africa. It was as though we occupied a different world, one encased in heat and the strange sounds it held, and I could hardly imagine Europe's war affecting us.

Neither of us ate. Mr. Brandt turned silverware over in his fingers. "There may be a way to get you out, if we do so soon." He stopped fiddling. "All travel will become limited, but there will be a window now of expats returning home."

To what would I be returning? Likely a train out of Copenhagen, back to the farm to do my brothers' work once they left for the front. Rations, perhaps. But if I stayed? I'd be a single woman far from the protection of my own country. My world was already circumscribed in Cairo; how much more so would it become? I felt, in that moment, as though it could get as small as that villa, that room, that table. I was not going to scare that easily, especially since I'd little idea of what I would be avoiding, to what I'd be running. "I'll consider what to do."

"Would you like to wire your family?"

"I would, but I don't need to immediately. I can wait until tomorrow." I had so little sense of urgency then – or perhaps so much. I knew as soon as I wired my family, they would implore me to come home – why wouldn't they? It was reckless to stay, and perhaps unnecessary as well. Mrs. Brandt and Sven were gone, and if the war did come to Egypt, staff would be lessened by necessity. I didn't want to think of any of that. I knew things would change in ways I could not control – of course they would. They always did, war or not. I wanted to sit at that table, eat slowly, draw out conversation, awkward as it was, as though my own words and actions could slow time or forge new paths into it, my desire casting a fluid line of my own future out in front of me.

Thirty-Three

War came to Egypt sooner than I had expected. I'd wired my family in the first days of the war to let them know that I was safe and I was needed by the household in Egypt. This was untrue, but I'd made up my mind to stay in Egypt nonetheless. Mr. Brandt had me cut back on staff and their hours. With Mrs. Brandt and Sven not returning, less household help was needed, but decreasing his staff was more a matter of safety. "War brings out the worst in some, that goes without saying, but you never know who it will turn, and how."

Sitto rang the bell of the villa one morning. I hadn't seen her since Marta had been relocated. "Sitto!" I greeted her as though she were a beloved old friend.

"Miss." She bowed slightly, seeming stiff, almost formal. I offered her tea and she declined. "There is something I must tell you, miss."

"Yes?"

"Some people, they listening to bad things about war."

"What do you mean?"

"They thinking British bad, Allies bad. You are in some danger."

"But they know that we – that Mr. Brandt has little to do with the actual conflict?"

"They know Mr. Brandt do business with British. I come here to tell you be careful."

"Careful of what? What should I tell Mr. Brandt?"

"Tell him, yes. A warning."

That was all I could get from Sitto. She backed away from me, looking both ways as she did, turned quickly and left the courtyard. I was alone again with the house girls in the villa. One or two of the groundskeepers would be outside. I'd felt safe with those young men around, as though they could protect us. Now, I felt nervous.

"There's something bothering you," Mr. Brandt said at dinner before I could tell him about Sitto's visit. We were eating dinner together most nights. We'd lost some awkwardness and formality with each other, though I told myself, often, to not become too comfortable.

"Sitto came by today."

Mr. Brandt waited for me to continue.

"She had a kind of warning for me – for us, rather."

He tightened his jaw and looked at me, his eyes narrowing slightly. "Yes, I've heard some rumblings." He looked wary, tired.

"You don't think we're in any danger, do you?"

Mr. Brandt moved his hands off the table. He glanced toward his lap, his face a mask of exhaustion, and then toward me. "Miss Jüül, do you know what our company does?"

"Imports and exports." I'd heard this from Mrs. Brandt. I hadn't asked for any details beyond that.

"We purchase sulphur and saltpetre in North Africa and the Middle East and import it into Denmark." He said this in a rote way, as though he'd done so several times, pinched the bridge of his nose and closed his eyes as he did. "In Denmark, we manufacture bullets and casings, then export ammunition into the rest of Europe – and back into Africa and Asia."

I blinked against the sudden pain behind my eyes, the high-pitched knell in my ears.

Mr. Brandt looked directly at me when he continued in a voice that was a beat slower, more hushed. "I am not going to assure you that this business is completely neutral. It's far too complicated for that."

"I don't feel safe, knowing this."

"And you may have reason not to." Tension stitched between his brows. "I'm sorry, Miss Jüül. I should have told you earlier. I assumed you knew, but I should have told you."

I didn't say anything in response.

"I can still arrange passage home for you."

"You weren't concerned enough about my safety to do so a few days ago, but you are now?"

"It was selfish of me. I was only thinking of myself – I didn't want you to go."

"Your wife and child are in Europe, and you wanted me to stay? Why? For a dinner companion, light conversation around the table?"

"Miss Jüül, I'm a foolish and selfish man. My wife can tell you that."

"She can't. She's not here."

"I know that. I know, Miss Jüül."

"I'm not going." I must have known it was imprudent, what we were doing – foolish, yes, but also reckless, this playing at innocent chatter over dinner as war encroached. Mr. Brandt wasn't the only selfish one. I'd already shared meals, played house with a man, and I knew where that could lead. Carl had been a widower. Though Mr. Brandt's wife was gone, she was certainly not dead. It wasn't up to me, alone, in any case, and if Mr. Brandt grappled with any kind of inappropriate desire, it wasn't apparent. There were much larger tensions to contend with than our petty domesticities. I told myself that, in everything, I would be careful.

Mr. Brandt sighed heavily, leaned his brow against his fingers. "If you're going to stay, we should reduce staff to only those necessary. The groundskeepers are all young men, the ones most likely to be swayed by those who believe I'm arming the enemy."

"Are you?"

Mr. Brandt rubbed his mouth once, briefly, and looked to the far corner of the room. He cleared his throat. "That, Miss Jüül, is a difficult question to answer." His eyes moved back to mine, his expression seeming like both a challenge and an apology.

"Is it?"

"I suppose our company is part of the vast machine which arms, well, everyone – enemies and allies and those who go from side to side and back again, depending." He drummed his fingers along the edge of the table, watched their movement, then stopped. "It's just going to get more difficult to figure out where anyone stands in this. It's likely going to be best if we let all the groundskeepers go and don't rehire for a time."

"Who will care for the grounds?"

"Well, I was once good with a rake and shovel."

For a moment, I thought he was serious, but I saw the slight pull of his grin. I looked back at him, stiff-faced. I didn't feel much like joking and didn't think he should either.

"Perhaps no one will. Perhaps we'll sequester ourselves in this villa surrounded by withering and overgrown plants." I could still hear the twist of his humour.

"That doesn't sound very pleasant."

"War never is. This is going to end someday, Miss Jüül. I don't believe we're in real danger, or I wouldn't let you stay here, but I want you to believe that. I want you to feel safe."

"Should I dismiss them tomorrow?"

"No, I will." I was relieved. I'd already wrongly accused an entire group of groundskeepers of hurting Marta. I didn't want to be responsible for letting go another crew.

A few days later, one of the staff approached me inside the villa. He was a bit older than the others and was the one who spoke for them. He didn't ring or knock. I wasn't aware he was there until I felt him behind me. I turned and he was so close that he had to bend his neck to look at my face. "I know what you say about us," he said in English.

"I'm sorry?"

"As you should be. We Africans are not good enough for you?" He spoke through closed teeth.

"No, I –"

"You think we are too black? Savage, dangerous?" The man elongated the last word, said it with a French pronunciation.

"I, Mr. Brandt –" I began again, though I could think of nothing to say. The man took one of my hands, twisted my arm behind my back and yanked me into him.

"Mr. Brandt, Mr. Brandt. I hope he is enjoying you while his wife is away." He said this into my ear, the smell dense with chewing tobacco. I closed my eyes and swallowed. Then he let me go and laughed. "You'll be gone soon enough. You all will be. Egypt isn't yours. Africa isn't yours; it's ours."

That night at dinner, I told Mr. Brandt what had happened. He looked first at the table and then lifted his head, looked directly at me. Our eyes held. "That shouldn't have happened to you." We kept our eyes on each other. I could sense a waver, but he held it steady and so did I. Then he banged the tabletop with the flat of his hand, the silverware ringing out. "I should have made you go."

I pushed away from my seat. "That's your solution? Send the ladies away so that the men can play war with themselves?"

"How is that any better than letting you stay so you can prove some sort of point? You shouldn't be in this kind of danger."

"I wasn't in real danger."

"You don't know this."

I started picking up plates.

"Don't do that. You know you don't need to do that."

"I am an employee. I can help the others."

"Come with me," Mr. Brandt said roughly as he stood. "I mean, please." He adjusted his tone. "Come join me in the study." He held an arm out to me as though to take my hand.

I didn't move toward him. "Why?"

He dropped his arm. "We need to figure out how we're going to ensure your safety. Leave those."

I put the dishes down and followed him to a separate wing of the villa, into the office, where he closed the door. Mr. Brandt went to the sideboard first, took out two glasses and turned to me. "Do you think you've developed a taste for Egyptian whisky yet?"

"When? During one evening with your brother? No, I don't think so."

"Brandy, then?"

Mr. Brandt was already pouring. He walked toward me, the glass held out, but when I reached for it, his arm moved past, put the glass on the desk behind us. He was up against me, his body giving off warmth as I took a breath. I could feel how my rib cage moved his arm. He ran his hand lightly against my jaw, then cupped the side of my face. He leaned toward me or I reached toward him, it didn't matter which. It was skin and lips and breath, the scratch of stubble on his chin, plump warmth of his mouth, smooth insistency of his tongue. He backed away from me. "My God, I'm sorry." He picked up his glass, considered it. "I don't want anything to happen to you."

I took a step and stood in front of him. "Something is always going to happen."

He put his glass down, brought his thumb along my lips, against my teeth. Hand over my hip, the top of my buttock, pressing into my lower back, pushing it against his thigh. "Not here." Where would we go? Not the room he shared with Mrs. Brandt, I hoped. Please, not my own staff quarters. Mr. Brandt circled his thumb against my palm as we walked. Desire carved a line directly through me. When we got to a bedroom in the guest wing, he closed the door and we stumbled up against each other, fell onto the bed. Balanced over me, hand from my sternum, around each breast, palm flat on my stomach, pressure steady, he circled my waist, lifted my pelvis to his, heat pushing through our clothes. I could smell the salt and musk of his skin, pulled his shirt open, brought my mouth to his chest, licked and bit. I wrapped my legs around him, each of us pushing away our clothes. For a moment, we stopped, looked at tiny versions of ourselves reflected in each other's eyes. Mr. Brandt lowered his mouth, waited. I ran my hands through his hair and tugged slightly. He nibbled at my lips, then licked as though to soothe them before he slipped his tongue into my mouth. I pulled at his hips, desperate, but he backed away from my face, began kissing his way down my torso. "Where are you going? I want you here."

"Shhh." He kept one hand on my breast, the other under my hips. The room spun, bed rocked like a boat. I gripped his head between my legs with two hands, bucked and gasped, and then he moved along the length of me, face to face, his body mine, mounting wave rising and rising until it broke, flooded crown to soles, the retreat as intense a sensation, a mass of water sucking away from shore, then calm, sweet collapse.

I rolled away from Mr. Brandt, kicked off the sheets tangled around me, lay open to the ceiling. He propped himself on one elbow. "I've wanted to do that for so long." Traced my body with his fingers.

"You have?" I rubbed at the places he'd touched, a tickle rising, stifled a giggle.

Mr. Brandt raised one eyebrow. "You haven't?"

I shivered, gathered the sheets around me. "Are you going to tell me now that we can never do that again?"

"Good Lord, why would I do that?" He pulled the blankets over us, rubbed my skin.

"Because you're married." As soon as I said it, I wished I hadn't.

"I am." He stopped rubbing, lay his hand flat on my stomach. "I'm not going to try to convince you of anything, Miss Jüül – of what will happen now, or later – all I know is I want to be with you."

"What if you can't?"

He looked surprised and, in that expression, I saw the slight frown that had been on his face when we first met.

"You want to, but we shouldn't be together, we both know, and there will be a day when we can't – what then?"

He took me by the hips, moved me so I straddled him and ran his hands from waist, along breast, collarbone, until he held my face. "What then, indeed?"

Night came on quickly, brought darkness but didn't ease the heat. The sound of squalling birds filled the courtyard with morning. The sticky salt of sweat was dried on my skin, then heat broke along my body. I slipped into the cool water of a full bath, my head tilted back along the edge, throat exposed, Mr. Brandt's – Hermann's – lips there for a moment and then gone.

Thirty-Four

War made Cairo something other than it had been. So many Europeans left the country, and those of us who remained had a new kind of freedom. Oddly, the streets seemed safer to me. I walked on my own, as I hadn't before in Cairo, for hours, out of the wide, palm-lined streets of Garden City into the tighter-wound, dusty roads that circled Ismailia Square. I would pass Shepheard's Hotel, where Europeans stood on the balcony, umbrellas and parasols shielding their heads from the sun. I didn't join them but walked among the Egyptians, all men and mostly touts who called up to the Europeans, offering them transport, assistance, even instant entertainment, prodding at small monkeys in red caps and little jackets until they jigged on demand.

Sometimes, I saw Egyptian women when I went into dress shops. Those in the same shops as I entered wore European clothing, yet their faces were most often covered with gauzy white fabric. Some smiled at me, eyes shining above their veils. Others kept their expressions wiped blank. In dressing rooms, shopgirls rolled silk stockings over my legs, slipped dresses over my head – all as I had once done for others. I had become used to the feeling of Hermann's hands on my body, our skin together, and though my time in the dressing rooms with the girls was completely innocent, it was drawn of this need for more touch, a hunger. I had them pull dress after dress over me, to tie, hook and button them until I found those that made my body sing with how the fabric held tight or dropped loose from my body in the exact way I wanted. The way I wanted Hermann to see me.

One afternoon, I was fitted for a new kind of corset, one without boning, the soft fabric stitched instead with flexible seams. The shopgirl had to bring in several before we found one that fit as it should. "Still a bit complicated, but it feels wonderful," I said.

"Doesn't it? I've got one on as well. Just think, someday soon, you and I won't have to wear them at all."

"Imagine." I knew from talking to girls like her in the shops that women's fashion was increasingly considered a frivolity. Food and supplies were being rationed and eventually someone would object to the materials used in even corsets. I told myself it was for the war effort that I wore nothing under my dresses when I was at the villa, though one woman scoffing at corsets and slips did nothing, of course. Nothing and everything. For so long I'd held my body as a little fortress, seams and stitches and the fine bones of corsets holding me in place. Now, I wanted as little between me and the world as possible.

I didn't confine my outings to the European districts. I walked block after block of markets, spices and textiles hanging along the roads, cats and kittens weaving in and out of my legs, mewing. Some days, I would keep going until the streets became narrow lanes, the haze thick with dust. Donkeys and goats pushed past me with their rank smells, children toddled barefoot alongside feral dogs, and I could feel the gaze of women from behind veils heavier and darker than those of the women in the European quarters. Alleys twisted into cramped squares where men gathered, pointed and yelled, though not at me particularly. To escape the noise, there were times I would find my way to the river and hire a boat to take me out as far as they could to where it widened toward the gulf. From there, Cairo was a wash of grey and green, a diffuse glow to the city as though perpetually in sunrise or sunset. On the river, I could finally feel a breeze, the air seemed clear. The city retreated and the hills were bright and golden, a belt between water and sky.

I went to the pyramids alone one afternoon. I'd been looking up at them for months from inside the city. At the base, I hired two Bedouin guides. "Take me to the top."

"You, madam? You will make it?"

"I will try." It was difficult to keep my skirts from catching on my boots as I climbed. The stones were both rough and as soft as powder. With each step, I felt like I nicked the stone a bit, looked back to see if I'd left a mark, scarred the surface. Toward the top, the heat pushed into me and my palms felt raw, calves burned with exertion. The Bedouins circled me, one taking my hand, the other behind me, steadying my wobbling steps or pushing lightly on my back. They managed to coax me to the top. Once there, they held out their palms, put their fingers to their lips as though to silence me and looked carefully down the four sides. "No soldiers," one said. Below us, reservist troops were setting up camp, white canvas tents like rows of miniature pyramids in the desert.

"Australians, like they are on adventure holiday," the other said. They spoke over each other about each country's troops as they asked me who I thought were the strongest fighters.

I was being asked questions like a man, like someone who might have opinions that I could offer. "Well," I began, "I don't know much about the Australians, but I think the Germans might be the best soldiers, physically."

They nodded, serious.

I repeated something I'd heard Hermann say. "But perhaps the English are fiercer. The Germans shoot soldiers in the back, but the English hit entire countries in the bank."

The men grinned, delighted. "Yes, yes, madam! This is exactly as we think!"

So, I'd gained some allies in this war. Two impoverished Bedouins with a Danish mistress masquerading as a wife, pretending to have opinions about war and force. I was simply someone carrying on an affair in a country of dusty ruins that I'd once considered one of the wonders of the world. From where I was, the pyramids seemed made of stone so soft that I could have cut into them with a penknife. Below, more tents were erected. When we came down, soldiers stood and lifted their hats to me, said, "Ma'am," in Australian accents, and I wished I'd said something more generous about them.

On my walks alone, I did not get used to the times I would take a wrong turn into a lane with painted ladies pushed out of doorways onto street corners. Men saw me and propped these girls and women out in the open and pointed, as though I might be interested in them simply because I was white and I was alone. By that time I was wearing the most recent European styles, looser fitting dresses that stopped mid-calf, some with dropped waists and sailor collars. Perhaps the way I looked confused them. The girls they pushed toward me looked as young as eleven or twelve, and those older than teens seemed to be all one age to me, though I wasn't sure how old. My own age? Under the paint and robes, the women and girls alike were dead-eyed, some dotted with scabs. I wondered if I could do anything for them, find someone, an organization perhaps, that would take them away from these men, give them shelter. The world was at war. Who was I to walk free along the streets of Cairo, tucked into my new soft corset, my light fabric skirts swinging around me? I was no one, I knew, and I could do nothing. This is what I told myself.

Staff continued to return to Europe until only three remained. Hermann went to work each morning, and I was left in a nearly empty villa. Mail arrived sporadically and what news I got from home told me about the financial troubles of our farm holdings with rations lean and both Anton and Soren gone to the front.

One evening, when I returned from my walk, Hermann came into the foyer, stood and watched me before he said, "You were out on your own again."

I had taken off my hat and was pressing the pins back into my hair, damp with humidity, as I turned to him.

"You know that I don't like that. It worries me."

"And you know it's no more dangerous out there than it could be in here."

Hermann stepped toward me, ran his hands down my arms. "I've taken precautions against that. Out there, in the city, if you get into danger, there's nothing I can do about it."

"That's right." I felt like this much of the time – like there was so little I could do to control my environment, the people around me, what they might do, for good or for bad. I hadn't expected that Marta would be attacked, that I would be threatened. Hadn't expected that I would be with Hermann now, spending nights with heat rising off our skin, fans cooling us enough to fall asleep beside each other.

Hermann pulled me to him, took more pins from my hair, unwound it. "I want to keep you safe. I don't want to lose you."

"You want to keep me." *A kept woman.* "But what happens when she returns?"

"We won't talk about that now."

Later that night, I woke to sticky heat on the sheets, felt wetness between my legs, under me. I didn't move, tried to think of what to do. It was only blood, a regular part of each month and a fortunate one for me, really, yet I wouldn't leave rust of my body staining the sheets. I got out of bed gingerly, looked at the mark I'd left. It was the first night, the heaviest. I folded the top sheet away. In the bathroom, I took off my nightgown and rinsed it in cold water, rolled and twisted it until the sink ran clean. In the darkened bedroom I scrubbed lightly, rhythmically, in hopes that the constancy of the movement wouldn't disturb Hermann's sleep. I worked steadily and quietly until the sheets were no longer deep red but light pink.

I was crouched, naked, beside the bed when he turned from his back to his side, arm falling over the damp spot. I stopped for a moment, breath blocked in my throat. When I thought he was still asleep, I began to stand and he said, "What on earth are you doing?"

I didn't move, looked at him, his eyes closed, watched a small smile play on his lips.

"Hmm, my Jüül, my love?" He said my name with the English pronunciation: *jewel.*

I stood motionless, didn't respond. For a moment, neither of us moved or said anything more, and then Hermann stretched and reached for me, his eyes closed. He opened them when he pulled me on top of him. "Had a bit of an accident, then? Made a bit of a mess?" He looked at me, every part of his face smiling. "Marie, you don't have to clean this up. We don't have to keep any secrets between us, do we?" Between us, perhaps not, but my blood on his sheets would mean that the meagre staff would know where I'd slept. Hermann didn't seem to care. Should I?

His hand on my back, the other hooked under my legs, he flipped me over with one smooth movement onto the damp, cool sheets. "Besides, we'll just make a mess of them again."

I twisted out from under him, spun and jostled Hermann until I was on top, his back against the soiled bed. "We will." My thighs clamped around his hips. I squeezed each of his earlobes between thumb and forefinger, and then moved my hands along his collarbone, his chest, pinched his nipples, kept moving downward. Hermann pushed up, toward me, but I hooked my feet around his shins, braced my legs against him and rose farther. I placed my hands between his torso and my legs and found his hips, held them, then found him, slipped him inside and moved against him until he was bloody with me.

When we were lying, spent, slicked in my blood and both of our sweat, he turned to me. "It was never anything like this."

"What wasn't?"

"I left Klitmøller because I knew that I'd get trapped there in charge of ailing, old fishing vessels if I didn't. I wanted something more, somewhere else, somewhere bigger – you can understand."

I could.

"I went to Frederikshavn, figuring, if nothing else, I could still find work as a fisherman for a bigger fleet. Instead, I got work at the munitions factory. Ingeborg worked for her father in the office. I won't say I wasn't drawn to her, but it was how stiffly she held herself, how cool. A woman who worked, who was my superior. I wanted to breach that haughtiness."

"And so, you did – Hermann, I don't want to hear about that."

"It was never like this, though."

"She was a conquest, was that it?"

"I suppose. And I got her pregnant. If I married her, she'd maintain her virtue. I could work under her father, learn how to run the company abroad."

"You both got what you wanted."

"I thought so, at one time. There's Sven – I cannot imagine my life without my son."

And yet there we were, living without him, month after month.

"But it was never like this – never."

It hadn't been for me either, but I wouldn't say it. Instead, I told him, "I've had a child before."

Hermann shifted so he was propped on one arm, his eyes from one of mine to the other.

"You said we didn't have to keep secrets from each other. That's my secret." If he was going to think of me as something other, a safe place, I wanted him to know I wasn't unsullied.

He didn't say anything for a moment, brushed the hair from my face, traced my eyebrows, lips, jaw, then laid his hand on my chest, between my breasts. "I wish it could have been mine."

I looked up at him. Breath wound around my ribs. I pushed it up, and air sputtered out of my throat as a sob while Hermann held me, bloodied and damp.

Thirty-Five

During the war, Onkel came to Cairo more often and stayed with us at the villa. We would go out together evenings, the attention deflected from me being alone with Hermann. Without much household or kitchen staff, we most often ate out, either at Italian or French restaurants or, as the war droned on, at the consulates or official residences of the diplomats who remained. Hermann brought me delicate glasses gleaming with wine. He caught my eye across rooms as he talked with politicians and diplomats. He didn't need to wink. I knew that flicker, that warmth. Other women spun me around. We tipped back glasses and held each other's waists, even danced. The world was at war and we were in fortified villas in Cairo, pretending to be different, pretending none of it mattered, at the same time we were terrified our lives would never be the same. They wouldn't be, of course, and I believe we knew that then. The ways in which I thought mine would change were so very different from what would happen, though.

There were times when we could leave Cairo. Hermann had business in Alexandria, and it was there where I felt most comfortable. The heat didn't inhabit me so heavily on the coast. I was responsible for organizing nothing beyond our train bookings. Once there, I was alone with two men, but it didn't feel like I was in anyone else's home. After a couple of days of work, the men would be free. Mornings, we rode horses; afternoons, we read; evenings, we dined. Nothing could be simpler, nothing more luxurious. The world was at war, the fighting not far from where we were, and yet these were our days, ones of privilege.

I see us at the apartment in Alexandria, the nights when I licked the heat of whisky off my lips. Onkel tried, he did, to have me develop a taste for it. I did it for them, Hermann and his brother – for their goading and their laughter – I tried the whisky and every time made faces and grabbed my throat. Later, it would be sweet H with his hands along my neck, fingers lacing my sternum. He and I knotted in white sheets, the curtains full of salt air. Mornings, we took out the horses. I could still ride bareback if I wanted, and sometimes I did. "Jüüly, slow down," Hermann would call behind me. "You're scaring me!"

The middle of the war, a foreign country, a married man. I felt so safe.

Hermann had to return to Cairo early. "You stay with Onkel. He likes your company. Stay here while the heat is so bad in Cairo. I'll be back in a couple of weeks."

"A couple of weeks – you'll be all right without me for that long?"

We were lying in bed. I was on my side and he slid his hand along my back, down my buttock, then gave me a little slap. "Barely. You know that." He burrowed his face into my neck.

After he left early that morning, I rolled over and slept more. When I woke, I put on my riding clothes, but Onkel didn't want to take out the horses without his brother. "Why not?"

"It doesn't feel entirely safe, out there with fighting so close."

"You know that there's no fighting right around Alexandria."

"I don't want to risk anything. Not with you. My brother's the brave one."

"Yes, but you're the brash one. And I'll be fine. I go out walking on my own in Cairo. Hermann knows that."

"For as much as my brother wants to protect you, he also believes you're stronger than you are."

"What's that supposed to mean?"

"I can see how fragile you are, Marie."

"Petite is not the same thing as fragile."

"Of course not."

He'd brought me a coffee in a small silver cup. I perched on the edge of one of the chairs so low and deep that if I sat back, my feet wouldn't touch the ground.

"She's coming back, you know." He walked toward the window, his back to me.

I watched him. "Who?"

He turned, took a drink of his own coffee. "Mrs. Brandt. She and the boy."

I blinked at him. "Yes, of course they are."

"Soon."

I nodded, took another sip of coffee as though for a reason to swallow.

"He's told you, then?" Onkel must have known that his brother had told me nothing.

"Hermann? Of course he's told me," I lied. "He's excited to see Sven."

"What else has he told you?"

I lowered the tiny cup to my lap, watched my hand wrap around it.

When I didn't say anything, Onkel continued. "There's a chance she'll find out – if she hasn't already. Our friends at the consulates aren't the souls of discretion. I know this." He laced the word *friends* with derision. I thought of the women in their gowns, me in my own, how we put our arms around each other's waists and laughed.

I took a long gulp of coffee, felt its heat down my throat, then put the cup down. "Why are you telling me this now?"

"I thought you should know."

I stood and walked toward the doors to the balcony. "And what is it that I am supposed to know?"

"When she finds out about you, Marie, you'll have to go."

"Go where?" I struggled with the door handle, my palms itchy with sweat, heat prickling over every part of me. Onkel put one hand on my arm and I stopped.

"I don't know. Somewhere that isn't their household – isn't her home."

I was still holding the handle. My voice was low, nearly a whisper. "It's hardly her home, you know that."

"No, but it's certainly not yours and she can lay claim to it." He took my hand off and opened the door, salt air pushing into the room.

She could lay claim to so much. What was mine? Even less than I had once thought.

Onkel and I were on our own in Alexandria. Marta had returned to Portugal when the war started, and the Egyptian staff came only once a week. We went out to eat or ordered meals from the hotel next door, left the dishes in the hall of the apartment until the next delivery. I tidied the apartment but told myself I would not do much. I was not in this apartment to be a housekeeper. Who was I to be?

Evenings, I read. Sometimes, Onkel would stay in with me, but he couldn't sit still for long. "Is this really what you do together, you and my brother, lie around and read?" I looked up from my book, raised an eyebrow, and he laughed. "Of course," he said. "Well, I'm going out." The first night he announced this, I thought he might invite me along. After a couple of evenings of him returning to the apartment late, his skin rosy, a warmth still rising off him, I realized that he was going to the baths.

One night, Onkel didn't return. It wasn't unusual for me to go to bed before he came back, but that night when I woke hours after falling asleep, it seemed darker than usual, the quiet thicker. When I got out of bed, a shiver kicked through me though it wasn't cold at all. I walked through the apartment, the furniture looming larger in the dark than it did during the day. I had closed all the windows and patio doors before going to bed, and the drapes stood tall and motionless. It was too quiet, too still in the apartment. I walked in and out of each room before I stood in front of the door to Onkel's bedroom. I felt movement, heard a noise from within, a faint knocking. I opened the door and the noise built. It took me a moment to realize it was the panicked whirring of large insects hurtling themselves around the room, hitting furniture, the walls. I closed the door quickly.

Onkel must have left the window open, the insects drawn in by a source of light. I stood in the hall for a couple of minutes, then sucked in a deep breath and opened the door, arm held up in front of my face. A large mirror leaned against the wall opposite the open window and reflected the lights of the harbour. Scarab beetles were flying headlong into the reflection of light, then ricocheting around the room. I reached the bundle of bedclothes piled at the end of the bed and threw a dark blanket over the mirror, batting scarabs away as I did, then opened wide the door to the patio. I lit a gas lantern outside and waited until I thought I'd drawn most of the insects out of the room before going in, closing the patio door. I could still hear a few beetles crashing about.

In my own bed, I couldn't sleep, waited for morning to colour the curtains, thought of what to do next. I had no hold over Onkel, he none over me. We were friends living like family, though we weren't that. Where he went and what he did were his own. Nothing was quite my own, but he didn't ask many questions of me. I spent the day in the apartment, wondering what to do next. When he didn't return by early evening, I went out, crossed a thin lane to the hotel. I would ask after Onkel and perhaps order a meal for myself. I hadn't eaten much that day, just pieces of fruit and bread. A slight nausea hollowed my stomach, growing like hunger, but without the desire for food.

"Ma'am?" The concierge came up to me as soon as I entered the lobby.

"I'm sorry," I began, though for what was I sorry? "I'm from next door, staff of Mr. Brandt?"

"Yes."

"Have you," I began. "Have you seen Mr. Brandt at all in the last day? Has he been into the restaurant, perhaps?"

"One moment please, miss." The concierge went to the front desk, and he and the man there spoke in low tones, their foreheads close together, neither looking directly at the other. It was the man from the front desk who came back. He nodded and reached toward me as though to take me by the arm, but he didn't. "Will you come this way, miss?" He inclined his chin toward the side of the lobby.

"Yes." I followed him.

The man looked around before he spoke. "Miss?" Was he looking for my name? I wouldn't say, nodded for him to continue instead. "There were raids at the baths last night."

"Raids?"

"A number of men were apprehended."

"Apprehended? For what?"

"I'm afraid I cannot say."

"Does this have something to do with, with the war? The Allied forces? I'm not sure what –"

He held his hand between us. "Not the war specifically, miss." I waited for more. "The clerics believe the country's morals are being corrupted by foreigners, some here because of the war, some not." I nodded as though I understood. "Decency laws." And then I did.

"What did they – Where did they take those, those apprehended?"

"I can't tell you because I do not know, miss."

Onkel didn't return to the apartment the next night, either, and I began to feel ill. It started as heaviness in my stomach, lightness in my head. I thought it was worry. I couldn't stay there alone with no one to speak to, no clear idea of what my role was or what I was supposed to do. I packed my small bag, closed all the windows and drapes in the apartment and walked to the train station. There, crowds of Egyptians were going in as regiments of Allied soldiers came out, one after another – British, Canadian, Australian. A soldier stopped me, his hat removed. "Ma'am?" he began, but I didn't want to hear more, didn't want him questioning me, who I was, where I'd come from and why I was alone. I turned and jostled through the crowds, continued to push until I'd purchased my ticket and boarded the train.

The feeling of unease in my stomach grew as the heat barrelled in, rolled through the train. I could feel sweat break out on my forehead and cheeks, under my clothing. I clasped my hands in my lap, gripped and released, tried to bring my mind back to them tightening and loosening, then pulled out a handkerchief, ran it along my forehead and held it over my mouth. I thought I might be sick; I couldn't be sick, not now. I remembered the last time I had felt that kind of nausea, in the bakery in Zealand, a lifetime ago. No, it wasn't that, couldn't be that, not then. But of course, it could.

Thirty-Six

We'd always had cars waiting to take us from the station to the Brandt villa. This time, I hired my own and directed it. When I arrived, the gates at the end of the drive were closed and I didn't know the man who approached the car.

"I am Miss Jüül," I told him. "I work here."

He had his chin raised, and though he seemed to be looking directly at my face, it seemed as if he couldn't see me. I sat in silence until he said, "Wait here." I paid the driver, took my bag and got out of the car.

The guard hadn't returned and I gave the gate a nudge, discovered he'd left it unlatched. No harm going in. I walked the length of the drive around the fountain, dry of water, and wondered if I should go to the front door or around the side, through the courtyard. I went in through the front. It was quiet and cool in the marble foyer, the smell so familiar but one I couldn't name – faintly of irises and cigar smoke, something honeyed, something else like dust or incense. I stood, bag in one hand, the other on my throat, trying to identify the scent, when Hermann came into the foyer. I recognized his step, though it was quicker than usual, and turned to smile at him. His brow was lowered and behind him was an older woman I didn't recognize.

"Hermann!"

He came toward me and I was about to reach for him, but he took me by the forearms and pulled me into an antechamber off the foyer.

"Hermann? Who's that?" He let me go and I dropped my bag. He looked confused for a moment, so I looked around him at the woman. "I'm Miss Jüül." The woman smiled slightly and nodded. "Hermann?"

He turned to the woman and she backed away from us and into the foyer. "That's Mrs. Nielson." Hermann still hadn't looked at me directly. He ran his hand through his hair, exhaled. "Miss Jüül, you can't be here right now."

"Who is Mrs. Nielson?"

"New staff." He'd lowered his voice to a whisper. "She's back, Marie. Mrs. Brandt has returned. You can't be here."

"Where am I supposed to go?"

"You are supposed to be in Alexandria with Onkel."

"That's why I'm here. Onkel, he's – he hasn't returned to the apartment. I went to the hotel. They told me there's been a raid on one of the baths, that he's likely been apprehended –"

Hermann took both of my hands and looked at me for the first time. "Miss Jüül." I felt the burn of tears in my eyes. He reached for my shoulder. "Marie, this has happened before. Don't worry. Onkel knows the right people to call. He may have to spend a couple of nights in prison, but he'll be out –"

"Don't worry? Your brother's in an Egyptian prison, I'm sick with worry and God knows what else, there is a strange man guarding the front gate, and look –" I lifted my chin in Mrs. Nielson's direction. "Your new staff member is staring as though she's scared of me. Don't worry, Hermann?"

He backed away from me and turned, held out an arm, palm open toward me, as though trying to hold still a pet or a child. "Mrs. Nielson, will you please take Miss Jüül to the –"

"Take dear little Miss Jüül where?" Mrs. Brandt's voice was in the foyer. Hermann's arm dropped, his hand by his side.

"I haven't even had a chance to say hello, have I?" Mrs. Brandt walked slowly across the foyer and I watched her – we all did. Her height sheethed in a simple light-green gown, fair hair rolled and gathered, her steps heavy and slow. "Miss Jüül, let me see you." She motioned when she reached the middle of the foyer. I stepped toward her.

"Ingeborg," Hermann started.

"Hush." She held out one finger to her husband but her eyes were on me. "You said that Miss Jüül was on her way back to Denmark and yet, look, here she is."

I stood, so small, in front of her, felt myself red with heat, with something more – anger, perhaps, shame.

"Where have you been hiding her, darling?"

"Mrs. Nielson, could you –" Mr. Brandt started.

Mrs. Brandt interrupted him. "Come a step closer, Miss Jüül." I moved slightly toward her, willed myself to look directly in her eyes. "You don't look very well, Miss Jüül. Is there something wrong?"

I didn't answer.

"Are you unwell?" She took a step closer. "Did you come here for my husband's help?"

Still I said nothing.

"I'm afraid you may be confused. It is you who we hired as help, and I've been told that you were not good help. Not good help, at all. In fact, I've been told that you were neither reliable nor trustworthy." She leaned toward me, her mouth close to my ear. "You thought you could keep things from me, did you?"

"Ingeborg, that's enough." Hermann pulled her away.

"It certainly is enough. Get her out of here." She came toward me again, her neck splotched with pink.

Mrs. Nielson stepped between us, her hand on my elbow.

We'd gone a couple of steps when Mrs. Brandt said, "Miss Jüül?"

I turned to her.

"I trusted you. Remember that."

I shook out of Mrs. Nielson's hold. "It wasn't trust. You didn't see me as a threat, as someone your husband could –"

There was a sharp pain across my cheek, the sound of a slap. I hadn't realized what happened. Hermann had his wife's arms behind her as she yelled, "Get her out of here!"

I brought my hand up to my face, felt the heat there, and Mrs. Nielson pulled me away.

A car was waiting, the guard from the front gate opening the door. Once he shut it, I saw him say something to Mrs. Nielson before she got in, but I couldn't hear their words. The car circled the dry fountain, left the grounds. "Where are we going?"

Mrs. Nielson looked as though she were tired the way those who care for children are tired. "I am escorting you to the station, Miss Jüül, where I will purchase a ticket to Alexandria on your behalf and see you onto the train." Her tone suggested that I shouldn't ask more questions.

I tried to close my eyes against the heat. Nausea rose again and I clasped my stomach with both hands. I didn't want to say anything more to Mrs. Nielson, so I leaned forward to the driver. "Stop the car, please."

Mrs. Nielson put a palm on my chest and pushed me back. "Please, sir, keep driving."

"I'm going to be sick!" My body began to shake as a retch spasmed up my throat. I held it back but as soon as the driver pulled over and stopped the car, I stumbled out and vomited. When I turned back, Mrs. Nielson passed me a handkerchief, holding it out of the door with two fingers. I took it and daubed my mouth, got back into the seat. "Thank you."

"You shouldn't have done that." She must have known that if I could've prevented it, I would not have been sick. "You should not have come back to the family home." What did this woman know about the family home? So little. What did I know about what I should and should not do? Nothing.

I was sick most of the way back to Alexandria on the train and hadn't slept in more than twenty-four hours. Onkel was there when I returned, his lip cut, a bruise around his swollen eye. I dropped my bag and went to him. "Onkel! What happened?" I put my hand out toward his face, then stopped. I didn't want to hurt him.

"I could ask you the same, Miss Jüül – you don't look so good either, love – but I know what happened. My brother wired. Quite a pair we are."

"I went there to tell him that you were gone, what I'd heard –"

"I know, and for that I'm thankful. I suppose my brother told you that I could sort it out myself?"

"He did."

"Well, seems money is speaking less during the war rather than more, which is surprising. Or perhaps my powers of persuasion aren't what they used to be. In any case, after a three-day stay in Alexandria's least-illustrious cells, I'm now out." I nodded, wondering if I should feel relief. None of this seemed comforting. "Don't worry, your Hermann has sent word. He's going to try to get here as soon as possible. It may take some time to get out from under Mrs. Brandt. In the meantime, you, my dear, need a nice long sleep."

I left my windows open that night. With the sheers closed, I listened to the sounds of insects struggling against the fabric, the long, low horns of boats in the harbour.

I'd been careful. I'd counted months in cycles, made notes in my calendar, blocked off days. And yet, there was the tenderness in my breasts, cravings for salted fat, jellied sweets, chips of ice. If I did eat, my stomach lurched, saliva pooled beneath my tongue. Onkel found me one day, my hands gripping the back of a chair, bent at the waist, hanging my head. "Good Lord, Miss Jüül, are you not well?"

I stood upright and turned, kept a hold on the chair with one hand as the room spun. "I'm fine." I pressed my forehead with my fingertips. "Just tired. I'll go lie down for a bit."

"It's all taking a toll on you, isn't it – the separation, the secrecy?"

What secrecy remained? Perhaps Onkel was thinking more of his own situation. "I suppose it is – and I suppose it should."

He didn't say anything more as I left the room.

I lay down, palm against my stomach, and Onkel knocked lightly, came into the room with a damp cloth. "Put this over your forehead. It may make you feel better."

I thanked him. Where there had been Knud before, there was Onkel now. How was I in this situation again, alone but for a single man unconnected to the trouble I was in? My mother had told me, as a child and young woman, *what challenges we do not meet, God will keep sending us opportunities to improve.* Perhaps he also sent me the same kind of helpmates, as though to set into relief my pattern of lack.

THIRTY-SEVEN

A month later, word came that Hermann was arriving. Everything was arranged. Someone other than him, a secretary, wrote the letter. Could it have been Mrs. Nielson? Sunday, June thirteenth. Through Onkel, I told him I'd meet him at the station, wanting every moment with him in Alexandria. I watched Hermann looking for me, hand hooked at his hip, the other tapping an unknown beat into his thigh as he scanned the platform. When he saw me, he smiled like a boy, but as he came toward me, I saw his eyes were dull, his cheeks hollowed out. I felt pain twist in my gut. He pulled me to him. "Thank God, Marie." His breath traced along my jaw to my ear. "Have you been all right? Has my brother been taking care of you?" He backed away from me just enough to cup my face, then ran his hands along my neck, shoulders, arms. "I'm so sorry that all this has happened."

I wanted nothing more than this.

When we got back to the apartment, Onkel was out. Hermann dropped his bags inside the door and came to me. "My God, I've missed you." I backed away from him and led him to the bedroom where, without saying anything, I started to undress. A sound came from his throat – a soft growl, a moan – desire across each of his features so fierce I thought he might cry. My hands mapped each part of his body. He'd lost weight and his ribs were visible, clavicle close to the surface. But he grew with my touch, reddened, and I believed that I was a balm for him, a cure. The sounds he made moved from his mouth to his throat into his chest and then through him into me. We were resonant with each other. I believed this.

The next morning, Hermann seemed distracted, his thumb and fore-finger along his brow again and again. I sat across the breakfast table from him. "What is it? Is it –" I was going to say her name.

"Marie." Hermann made a triangle with his hands on the table, seemed to examine them. "I know about –" He looked up. "I know about your condition."

I didn't say anything for a moment and he kept his eyes on me. There was a kindness there, but he looked so very tired. "How? I – Was it Onkel? – I haven't said anything –"

"Jüüly, I know you too well. Onkel told me that you haven't been well, have been getting sick a lot, but I knew as soon as I saw you."

I looked at the table, the grain patterned across wood like water against sand. "I'm sorry."

For a moment, neither of us spoke nor moved, then Hermann pushed his chair from the table and stood enough that he could pull me onto his lap. "We'll find a way to make this all right."

I sobbed with something like relief. When he said we'd find a way, I thought it would be all right for both of us.

In the afternoon, Onkel was there, a forced cheerfulness to his voice. "Well, lovely Marie, are you ready for your appointment?" He held out his crooked arm as though to lead me to a dance floor.

I turned to Hermann. "What appointment?"

"I've made an appointment with a doctor, for peace of mind. I want to know that everything is – that you're all right."

"Are you not coming?"

He smiled at me, encouraging, then looked away. "I need to inquire about some tickets."

He was being so vague, withholding; yet he'd said *tickets*, plural.

At the office, the doctor shone light in my eyes and ears, pinched my skin to see how much colour it retained, laid a stethoscope, like a disc of ice, on my chest, my belly. He took my measurements, tape to skin, and scratched his pencil against a pad. I wondered to where Hermann was booking tickets and what would happen to the Cairo household. There was so little there that either of us needed; nothing that couldn't be replaced, apart from ourselves. We had our skin, we had our hair. We had the parts of each other that fit together, the parts that we could each hold. Other than that, what was there? Measurements and records. Paperwork and legalities. Documents would be sent from his Cairo office, and certainly Onkel could handle the business for a time. Once we'd relocated, Hermann could continue in his capacity. I thought of Sven. Would he send for the boy? I adored him, but I was sure Mrs. Brandt wouldn't be separated from her son.

The doctor tore paper from his pad. "You can get dressed now." He looked at my face for the first time, his lips pursed and then moved into a quick, tense smile before he turned and left the room.

When we met back at the apartment that afternoon, Hermann said, "I have a surprise." Tickets, I imagined, though I didn't know to where. "But first, shopping."

"Shopping?"

He put his hands around my waist. My shape hadn't changed much yet. "I thought you'd like something new." He took me to the part of Alexandria where the society ladies shopped. I was measured, again, and fitted, as I'd once fitted the ladies who came into the shop in Copenhagen. How long ago that seemed. *I'll never be that girl again*, I thought. I'd never be a shopgirl again.

In the last shop, H slipped into the dressing room after the girl had left. "Do you need any help, miss?"

"Oh, these stays – they feel a bit snug. So tight. You wouldn't be able to loosen them, would you?"

"I'm at your service." From behind, he unhooked each eye with one hand, the other pressed between my legs. He turned me around, peeled away the undergarments like a husk and kissed his way down my torso. He stayed there, his heat and his mouth between my legs, warmth mounting there, until he spun me around again, and I gripped the back of the chair. We watched each other moving in the mirror until I closed my eyes and clamped my mouth to stop from calling out. The shop ladies averted their eyes or looked at us with disapproval as we left the store, both of our arms weighted with bags. I wanted to laugh, to say to them, "It doesn't matter! You don't matter! None of this matters!" Because none of it did then.

Hermann had hired a car and he loaded the dress, hat and boot boxes into the back. "One more stop." He took me to a photo parlour. "I want a photo of you, something professional. And one of you and me together." The photographer sat me on a chair, then took my hat off and tucked a flower behind my ear. He adjusted my shoulders, tilted my chin, a hand down my spine as he said, "Like this," and marked the angle I should sit. Hermann watched. Once the photographer had taken some of me on my own, Hermann joined me. This time, the photographer did nothing. We knew how to be together, though for the photograph we sat formally. The photographer disappeared underneath his black hood, and we were washed in white light before the flash crackled and burst.

Thirty-Eight

When we returned to the apartment, I saw new luggage lined up in the hall. I was giddy with it – the smell of soft leather, the starred patches of light still in my vision from the photographer's flashbulb. "Leave everything here except what you want to wear to dinner," Hermann told me. We left the apartment and Hermann pointed to a motorcycle parked in front of the building. He placed a helmet on my head, ran his fingers along my jaw and strapped it under my chin, then reached for his own. I pulled up my dress to ride to the restaurant, felt the heat of the machine between my legs and the warmth of his back as I pressed against him. Everything was vibration and warmth, not only our bodies but also the place we met the world, air and skin humming on contact.

At dinner, Hermann leaned to me. "Oh, Marie. Do you have any idea how beautiful you are?" He paused. "I want to – This isn't –"

"What?" I laughed, light-headed with what he might say next. A proposal of some kind. Not of marriage, of course – he was still legally bound to Mrs. Brandt and I knew that dissolving their marriage would take time.

"I can't believe –" He turned his face toward the room, tightened his jaw, then looked back at me. "I can't believe that this will be the last."

"What are you saying? The last what?"

"No, you're right, this won't be the last. I won't believe that. It will just – it will take some time."

"What will?"

"You know that it's not safe for you here now, in Egypt. Cairo is out of the question and I had thought – I thought that I could keep you in Alexandria for some time, but things are precarious here."

"It's not as though we're anywhere near the front."

"Mrs. Brandt, Marie. She already suspected, but then you came to the house –" He looked at me as though he were both guilty and complicit, helpless on both accounts. "I've managed these couple of days away, but she'll find out somehow. I just can't – I can't keep you hidden away here. And there's the –"

He couldn't finish the thought so I did it for him. "The baby."

"Yes." He reached across the table for my hands. I pulled them away. He sighed, looked around the room before back at me. "I know of a place, in Italy."

I waited.

"A cloister, but not strictly religious, more of a sanctuary."

"You're sending me away to a cloister?"

Hermann didn't answer, nor did he look at me. He spoke evenly and quietly to a place on the table in front of him. "You can rest there. There's a doctor. He'll know what to do." He looked at me then, his eyes steady. "About the child – a safe delivery and a way to find a home for it. You'll be well taken care of."

I stared at him, heat building behind my eyes. "Our child!" I said so loudly that several other patrons turned, stared at us before averting their eyes. I lowered my voice. "You're suggesting I give our child away? That I'll be 'taken care of'? What about you?"

"We can't – I can't – don't you see? The situation is impossible."

"You've decided the situation is impossible."

Hermann looked around the restaurant, tugged on his earlobe, rubbed his jaw with his palm before turning back to me. "For now. My son is here. We're in the middle of a war. I'll make sure you're cared for until I can come."

"Oh yes, the war."

"The war, my business – Marie, what else do you expect me to do?"

"And so, you'll remain in Cairo, with her. You'll just carry on."

"I'm not letting you go, Marie. I'll come for you. It just can't be now. You can wait, though, for me? I know how strong you are."

"And you?"

He dropped his head, ran his fingers along his hairline and then gripped his forehead, his hand a small vice. "I'm not as strong."

"You certainly aren't." When I stood up, the chair scraped across the floor, caught on the bottom of my skirt, then toppled. I walked at a quick but measured pace out to the street, turned in the direction of the apartment. After a few minutes, I heard the drone of his motorcycle slowing behind me. I turned and yelled, "Don't follow me!"

Hermann got off his motorcycle. I moved away, but he caught my arm, pulled me toward him. "I will follow you." His voice round with heat, filling my ear. "I will keep following you." He pressed me into him. I told myself not to believe him. I believed him.

At the harbour the next morning, soldiers lined the docks. When we came to the port where I was to board, one thrust his hand at us. "Tickets."

"Just for the young lady." Hermann's tone was hurried, dismissive. "I'm seeing her off."

"Only ticket holders beyond this point, sir."

Hermann tried to ignore the soldier, push past him, his hand on my elbow, but more men stepped in and barred the way. "Admittance only to ticket holders."

"That's ridiculous. I've always been able to see my wife board safely." When he said *wife*, they would assume he referred to me.

"War measures, sir. No exceptions."

"It's fine, Hermann. I'll be all right."

We held each other as the crush of people knocked into us. "I'll come for you in Italy. Wait for me, Marie. I know you can." His face was so close to mine. I tried to look away but Hermann took my chin gently, turned me back to him.

I nodded, pressed my lips against my teeth so I wouldn't sob.

He leaned forward, put his lips on my forehead like a seal of heat, then backed away and passed me my bags. "You shouldn't have to carry these on your own." But of course, I'd be carrying it all on my own now. He pulled me toward him, put his mouth on mine and for a moment, we each just breathed. When we kissed, it felt hurried, forced. I turned from him and shouldered my way through the crowd. I stopped to look back at him and I saw only groups of strangers, soldiers, rising steam and smoke from the boats.

I queued with passengers to board the boat to Sicily. Alongside us were carts loaded with supplies for the naval ships, makeshift corrals of horses, donkeys tied to each other, their brays like guffaws at the indignity of their positions. When the air shifted, I could smell the animals and it reminded me, briefly, of home. The passenger ferry pulled away from the dock, the sound of its horn reverberating along the water, and I stood on deck, strained to see Hermann amongst the crowd, but it was impossible. All was uniforms, loaded carts and battle animals. I watched men strap a mule into a large harness and then fasten it to levers that lifted it toward the deck of a naval ship as our own boat lumbered into the harbour. When the animal left the ground, it cocked its ears forward and held its limbs stiff, as though immobilized. A horse was lifted next. Unlike the mule, it struggled as it was raised, muscled legs kicking air, flailing its head from side to side. I imagined its nostrils wide, huffing indignantly, but by then I was too far away to see that closely. I looked from its writhing silhouette to my hands, pink and raw on the rusted handrails of the ferry, then back to the coast, retreating. The last image I have of the port of Alexandria is the horse suspended between sea and boat, thrashing against the sky, my bare hands wrapped around a rail.

Thirty-Nine

Canada, 1946

I understood that my job, in part, was to turn people away. I was reasonably good at it – adequate, in any case, as we remained alone with few intrusions. The ladies stayed in and I kept other people out. We each had our habits, our rhythms, and these became our lives. It was surprisingly easy to stay in once it became a daily routine. Newspapers, magazines and books were delivered each week, so we were not without contact with the outside world. I placed them on the table in the hall and Sveva carried them away, the papers returning to the breakfast table the next day. Ofelia read no papers. I read some, then stacked them by the fire as starter. Sveva ordered her novels and books about scientific discovery every month and read through them so quickly, she was often finished before the next arrived. She recommended some to me. Once, I'd considered myself a great reader, but I rarely had the concentration required for that kind of reading anymore.

Ofelia's doctors made house calls and the pharmacy sent a boy to drop off medications. Early in our seclusion, we could take delivery of milk and dairy, groceries. Ofelia became increasingly particular. Meat, for example. No longer was she fine with having it delivered from the local butcher. Instead, a farmhand collected me in his rattling truck twice monthly and took me to a narrow valley east of town where I watched as freshly slaughtered meat was cut and packaged by men in heavy aprons splattered with blood. I was not entirely sure why I should be there to bear witness to the butchery. I told Ofelia that I was no safety inspector, but she only laughed. Of course I wasn't. The things I wasn't had become funny, a source of humour. The drive to and from the farm was lovely, in any case – out of this small Western Canadian town to which we still weren't completely accustomed and into a valley where the sun stained everything golden, cows lay down with horses in fields, light sparked off creek water flowing through the tall grass. Some might have called it charmed, magical. To me, none of this – our lives – was magical, but all was surreal. When I returned home, I packed the meat into an icebox in the pantry off the kitchen because Ofelia was still resistant to electrical refrigeration. I thought it would be fine – perhaps even safer, more reliable – but I followed her wishes.

Though she'd travelled the world as a girl, the map of Sveva's own life had become smaller and smaller until it was a blueprint of the house. I'd worked on Ofelia for years. It had been up to me to do so, after all. Sveva seemed so strong-willed, so tall and certain of herself, but when up against her mother's wishes, she knew how to bend, submit. When I returned from the druggist downtown with prescriptions for each of them, I listed to Ofelia her daughter's medication every time, as though to remind her of Sveva's condition, passed through the long limbs of her father's side of the family – the result, perhaps, of generations of noble lines marrying amongst each other. The syndrome makes joints stiff, eyes ache. I read to Ofelia articles on the benefits of fresh air and exercise and suggested on Sveva's behalf that she be allowed outdoors to stretch her legs, give her eyes more range in the natural world. I'd even commented on how difficult it would be to have another family member fall ill. That might have been what convinced Ofelia. In any case, after a decade, Sveva was allowed outside again, though only as far as the veranda, never the property. Still, I had done my small part.

One afternoon, I took a photograph of her on the veranda, leaning against the door, her frame statuesque in a smart, tailored suit, hat tilted at a jaunty angle, one side of her mouth pulled in a slight grin, as if she held a secret joke. She looked both confident and delighted, about to embark on a small adventure, but it was only a photograph, a way to pass the time. Sveva hadn't gone anywhere but back inside that day, as she did every day.

When I was at the Mayo Clinic at the duke's bedside as he wavered in and out of consciousness, I began to trace my stories back to other times, other places. It had been his request, scribbled on a note when he was in too much pain to speak, that I tell him of my time in Egypt. My voice seemed to soothe him, and my words filled the time that stretched around us both in those long, bleak days. One afternoon, he turned his head slowly along the pillow and faced me. His voice came and went, and on this afternoon he could speak. He said, "I didn't know it was him."

I felt my heart ricochet in my ribs. "I'm not sure what you mean."

"Mr. Brandt. I had some contact with him before the war, when Italy was set on attacking Libya." A cough rasped out of his throat. "His wife's family's company was to supply arms and he was the chief officer. I went to speak to him about preventing sales."

"And what did he do?"

"He told me that if they didn't supply arms, the black market would, and dirty weapons would end up in the wrong hands." The duke's voice lowered to a strained whisper. "His company supplied Italy, but I believe Mr. Brandt was sympathetic to our cause."

"What does any of this have to do with me?" I knew he wouldn't be able to speak much longer.

The duke closed his eyes, asked for water. "His wife wrote me a few years later, wondering if I might need household staff with experience in Egypt. She knew I was an Islamic scholar. I had no plans to return to the Middle East then, but I always felt that I might – that we might – with Ofelia and the baby. I knew we'd have to leave Italy.

"The wife told me that there'd been an incident between a member of their staff and her brother-in-law – I took this to be more predatory than romantic."

I blinked at the duke, bent my head to the side as though listening for something from below, something to help me understand what he had just said. "I was that staff person?"

"I believed that there was some danger to you, some threat from the man. She said it would be best if you were taken into a respectable family and protected, and that contact with her family should be cut off. I expected you to be younger, to be honest."

I laughed at this, though with no joy or levity.

"One of the Brandt men came for you once, in Rome. I didn't see him but I'd already given the staff instructions to turn him away. I thought I was protecting you."

"Oh." It was a great strain for him to speak for so long, and part of me wanted him to stop.

"And, I thought that you would likely have some sympathy for the state that Ofelia was in. You both needed a friend then, and you've been that to each other these years, haven't you?" His voice was fading.

"We have."

The second war had ended and life carried on – for other people. In October, I went to the pharmacy to pick up some of the ladies' prescriptions, and there were bins of candy lined up along the glass apothecary cases. The woman behind the counter apologized for my having to reach over them. "Mr. Nolan wants to supply a good variety of Hallowe'en candy for the kids," she said in explanation. "I'm not sure we should be stocking so much, but Chester is determined. Perhaps it's a way for us to shake off the last demons of the war."

"Do you think so?"

"Well, that's one way to look at it. Mostly harmless fun, in any case, and we could all use a bit of that."

At dinner that night, I explained the custom to the ladies. "Children go from door to door in masks and costumes, asking for candy."

"They do?" Ofelia asked. "That sounds so strange. What if they get no candy?"

"That's the trick part – if they're not given candy, they play a trick, but Mrs. Nolan assured me that was mostly talk, bluster. Those who don't want to take part just keep their gates closed and lights low."

Sveva huffed. "Mau-Mau, I explained to you all about Hallowe'en when I was at Crofton House – you must remember."

"You'll forgive me, Sveva. There are many things from that time in our life that, no, I do not remember."

"Well, now is our chance. I think we should take part." Sveva looked from one of us to the other and wiggled her eyebrows, challenging us.

"Sveva, no!" Ofelia responded. "Why would we want to do that?"

"Oh, come on, Mau – wouldn't it be grand? We could see some of the neighbourhood children, all dressed up, and there would be absolutely no expectation that they come in. We'll just say hello and give them candy and off they'll go. It will be fun!"

"Sveva, really."

Ofelia stared at her daughter, mouth open slightly as though she were trying to think of a way she could refuse. Instead, she said, "What kind of candy do you imagine we should give the children?"

Sveva looked at me, lips suppressing a smile. "Miss Jüül? What do you think?"

"Oh, I think it can be anything really. They've certainly got enough at the pharmacy – hard candy, toffee, gumballs. I can pick up any of those."

It was Ofelia who said, "Well, we'd want to give them something quite nice, I think, some Swiss chocolates or Italian sweets."

"Mother, I'm sure they're used to getting cheap Canadian confections."

"Yes, but we are neither cheap nor Canadian, are we?" Ofelia asked. "And wouldn't it be nice to give them a taste of something truly special?"

Sensing her opening, Sveva said, "It would. Of course! We'll give them a taste of the Caetani experience!"

"Not too much, Sveva. We don't want vagrant children hanging around the property."

"Mau, I'm not sure Vernon has many vagrant children roaming the streets. We're not in Rome."

"We certainly are not."

It was Ofelia who ordered the treats from European confectioneries in Vancouver and Calgary – chocolate from Belgium, caramel from Rome. Sveva sewed little satchels to hold them, using fabric from our basement – not her mother's fineries, of course, but things stacked up down there that were already going to ruin – heavy velvet drapes that Ofelia had us take down because they harboured too much dust. I picked up some scraps from the fabric store on my trips to town for her to use to create little black cats, intricate stars and slivered moons.

On Hallowe'en, we put the dogs in the kennel – not only were they bound to try to run off, they would scare the children – and opened the gates at the bottom of the drive. When the children came, Ofelia retired to her room and Sveva and I passed out the candy. We must have made such a curious pair, a looming Amazon and her diminutive companion, both of us so eager to see the children in their costumes, clapping as they roared or twirled or acted their parts. I felt just as much or more for the children who came to the door looking petrified, their eyes wide, hands trembling as they held out their bags. These children were too scared or shy to say much, if anything, beyond a squeak of "trick or treat." There were others who chatted and carried on, and some who even asked us questions: "Are you a countess?"; "Are you really trapped in this house? My mother says you are."; "My father can do handiwork if you ever need anything done," and so on.

I was patient as I answered each one: "Yes, the ladies are descended from royalty," "Yes, we do live here alone," and "No, no, we don't need much help. We'll be fine."

The gravel drive crunched all evening with the feet of children. When we ran out of our little satchels of sweets, we closed the gate and turned off the lights.

FORTY

On Good Friday, I let the dogs out to run around the perimeter of the property before I called them back into their kennel. I thought I might bring them indoors later to cheer the ladies, though Ofelia might not approve on a holy day. She hadn't yet emerged from her room, though that wasn't unusual. I was in the kitchen, setting out the hot cross buns I'd baked the day before. Aside from a light midday meal, these were what we would eat that day. We'd had nothing but tea so far. Sveva was on the veranda, drawing. I didn't think her mother would approve. We were supposed to be engaged in dreary activities on Good Friday, though the sweetness of the buns seemed a bit too cheerful, the warmth in the kitchen not dire enough. I heard the front door open, Sveva's steps in the hall. She came into the kitchen, shaking her limbs and rubbing her face as if she was coming in from doing calisthenics. "I was up too early. I'm going up for a rest." She started up the back stairs. "Call me for lunch, will you, please?"

"Yes, of course."

A few minutes later, Ofelia entered the kitchen without me hearing. When I turned from the sink, I jumped at the sight of her standing beside the table in a grey jacquard dress. Despite the colour, the dress didn't seem dull enough for the day, though who was I to say? She had a way of making even the plainest garments seem regal, so it was hard to know if it was the dress or her way of carrying herself.

"The buns are ready," I told her. "Would you like one with tea?"

Instead of answering, Ofelia asked, "Where is Sveva?"

"She's gone for a rest."

"She shouldn't be napping. Christ was not able to lie down on this day."

"No, of course not."

She hadn't answered me about the tea and buns, so I put them on a tray and took them into the front room. Ofelia followed me, then stood looking out the window to the veranda. She didn't move her arms from her side, just stared and asked, "What are those?"

I turned my head to look out briefly, then back at my tea. "Sveva's sketches, I suppose," I answered. I wanted her to believe that the drawings were nothing to look at. I knew that this hope would be wasted. When Ofelia left the room, I trailed her to the veranda. I was nervous about her being outdoors and, I'll admit, I was curious to see Sveva's work. It was always striking.

Her mother stood in front of the sketches, three hung from a line with clothespins. I suppose this was to prevent them from smudging or blowing away, though it seemed like they were on display for us. Sveva had never been practical, but this gesture seemed like a taunt. Ofelia cupped her mouth with her hand as we both looked at a drawing of a chain of elephants, trunks wrapped around tails, lines of charcoal making their large, rounded hind ends appear to sway in the foreground. The curve and form of each elephant appeared to get more detailed the farther in the background it was. The drawing gave the impression of elephants marching endlessly.

In the middle of the next drawing was a circle of black men, their skin shaded so finely with graphite that I could see the angle of the sun on their skin. Around them, all was colour – red and white tents, green trees mottled with amber, sky vivid blue. The third drawing was the most unfinished, and I suspected Sveva stopped working on it just before she went for a nap. She should have taken it with her.

The sketch was crude, barely more than lines, but even so, the figures were clear in the set of their limbs, the tilt of their heads. It was Sveva and her father, walking somewhere, although there was no context but the blank page around them. Perched on each of their shoulders, with one leg on each of them and long arms wrapped around their foreheads, was a large monkey.

The animal was in colour. It had a red fez cap, but instead of a vest or suit, it was wearing a red-and-gold gown. Gems hung from its round ears. It was a rudimentary sketch and yet, I could see something of Ofelia's expression in the monkey. I might have been imagining that. Behind the figures was a rough sketch of a wolf, done so well that I could tell what it was even though it was only a few lines, a smudge of shadow.

"What are these?" Ofelia demanded. I didn't think she expected a response from me. "They are ugly, lurid. What is she doing, making these and then leaving them out for me to see?"

"I don't think that was intentional, Ofelia."

"Everything," she began, still looking at the drawings. "Everything, every act and gesture has an intention, Marie." She rarely called me by my first name. Her voice was small and controlled, both angry and intimate at once, a tone I'd heard her use often with the duke. I watched her clench her hands, push her fingers into her palms and then open them. When she looked at me, her eyes were moist. "I can't take this kind of stimulation. You know that, Miss Jüül." Ofelia sniffed, cleared her throat. "Get rid of them, please."

I knew what she wanted me to do, of course, but I asked, "How?"

She turned, held the railing. "In the fire would probably be best. The church encourages cleansing the home on Good Friday. Leone always thought heat was purifying."

"Should I wait for evening?"

"It will be better now. Our Sveva is so hard to convince when she's got her mind set, but it doesn't take her long to accept things once they've happened. I sometimes wish I could move into acceptance as easily."

I lit the first fire of the day. As well as wood kindling, I had a small chest near the fireplace full of my own personal papers. For everything of Sveva's that I fed to the flames, I offered something of my own. I was moving backwards in time and most of my more recent correspondence was gone. I hadn't gone back past 1930 and I didn't yet know if I would. That would mean erasing all traces of him, of H. I didn't think I could do it. Nevertheless, Sveva wasn't the only one whose chronicles were being purged. I thought it could do us both some good to prune back a little. Our minds were too dull to confront the task, so I had the fire to spark the process instead. Once the fire was licking the kindling, flames wrapped around it, I lay the sketches on top, watched them curl and grow smaller.

I didn't hear Sveva enter the room. My hearing was usually so acute – all my senses sharp, really. Perhaps it was the heat and crackle of the fire but, no, I didn't hear her until she cleared her throat. I turned and there she was, looking at me from the doorway. Her stature and expression seemed to fill the entire space. Her height and the way she held her chin were her father's. Sveva's mother had given her the tone of her skin and the cast of her eyes. These women and their eyes.

We watched each other as we had so many times – Sveva unblinking, mouth and jaw set in that haughty, accusatory way, me looking back, trying to soften the same things that she held so tightly. If I let my eyes, my mouth, my posture loosen and yield, I would signal that I had accepted this. I had, hadn't I?

Sveva turned and left the room. I heard her pause in the hall and imagined that she was deciding where to go, though her options were few. I heard her move back down the hall, her steps heavy on the stairs. I moved closer to the fire. The paper was all ash now, the kindling glowing coals as the larger pieces of wood cracked and hissed. How good the heat felt.

FORTY-ONE

The few people who passed our threshold administered to either the body or the soul. Doctors made house visits and did what they could for Ofelia. The church sent its redeemers. Often, Monsignor Miles himself would come to take Ofelia's confession without any cloak of anonymity for her, administer rosaries and prayers, the rolling timbre of his voice with the plaintive murmur of hers. When the monsignor was not able to attend to her himself, he sent others, deacons from the church or young acolytes who hadn't yet received their own parish clutch.

I was not often near her room when she received her religious guidance. I would find reasons to busy myself below – there was always cleaning, always the kitchen, always the fires to tend. On a day when one of the young priests made a house call, I'd gone up to get the iron so I could smooth the table linens. I was in the hall, weight of the iron in my hand, when I heard the noise: a shuffling crackled with strips of sound, like static broken with sudden high notes in a minor key. A cry, the sound of broken air.

My rib cage tightened, heart ricocheted, jittered with fear. I wouldn't stand here, iron in hand, couldn't stand silent. I put the iron down and knocked. The sound stopped. For a moment, nothing. I knocked again – "Ofelia?" – and the young priest opened the door, lock of hair fallen across his forehead, cheeks bright. I looked around him to Ofelia, standing near the window, curtains pulled closed, light beside her bed casting half of her into shadow as I stepped into the room. "Ofelia, are you all right?"

She turned to me. "Of course, Miss Jüül, of course! The only pain inflicted is my own. God has granted me salve. He is my balm." Her voice wavered, broke. Her face was wet with tears. She held her blouse against herself and I saw, reflected in the mirror behind her, that the buttons down the back were undone.

I heard the young priest murmur something to her. I saw then that she held a kind of whip, a handle rooted with cords of twined fabric. The priest had his hand on her forehead as he crossed himself and went into the hall without looking at me, his steps a web of creaks and small sounds. I backed out of the room and watched him pause at the top of the stairs, cross himself, lean toward the icon of the Virgin and kiss it, then descend. When I went back into the room, Ofelia held out the whip as though encouraging me to take it, so I did, felt its weight in my hand.

"The priest told you to do this?"

"It was monsignor who suggested it might help me express my faith, my subservience to God, my remorse."

"Remorse for what?"

Ofelia ran a palm over each of her cheeks, seemingly still wet even though her eyes were now dry. "For everything, Miss Jüül."

Pins and needles tore across my skin, my cheeks burned and a flush crept up my neck. Fear or anger or both. "No one can tell you to do that to yourself, Ofelia."

"He didn't tell me. I asked if I could."

"And he sent a priest right out of seminary, someone untested, to bring you a whip? A whip. Ofelia, this isn't right."

"You don't understand, Miss Jüül. You're not Catholic. It doesn't feel bad – it hurts, yes, but it's a purifying pain. It's sanctioned – His Holiness Pope John approves, does it himself."

It wasn't the practice itself that I disagreed with (though this was part of it, true) so much as the young man. The priest. I'd seen how his skin was ruddy when I opened the door, saw the bright moisture in his eyes before he looked away, furtive. He was barely more than a boy and I knew that look.

He'd been aroused. Spiritual arousal or otherwise, I wouldn't let her open her blouse, bare her skin – for pleasure, pain or redemption. Whatever the reason, I wouldn't allow it. But what could I do? What I allowed or didn't allow made little difference.

The nights when Ofelia would wail became better than the ones when she didn't. I would wake to silence and it leached into everything, hollowed it out. I would creep down the stairs from my third-floor perch to the second floor to listen, make myself light enough that I could move without sound, then wait outside Ofelia's door. Sometimes it would come, the swish of air with the switches of what I could only call a whip. Switches through air – *swish, slap* – her skin bared to herself, her guilt, her own penance, but it was too much for me. I would open the door, say her name again and again until she heard me and stopped. Part of Ofelia seemed to be asleep those late nights or early mornings. When I could get her to stop, she'd turn to me, her eyes glazed and colour heightened much like that young priest's had been. She would stare at me through a haze of dream, remorse, incomprehension. I'd try to wrest the whip from her, bring her back.

One night, Sveva found us: the light from a small lamp weak in the room; Ofelia on the bed, her cotton nightgown unbuttoned, rolled down to her waist, nothing covering her breasts, flat and fallen by then, her back exposed, baring strips of red welts; me, having wrested the whip from her.

Sveva yelled, "Miss Jüül! What is going on?" She lunged at me, pulled the whip from my hand with such force that I felt my own skin tear along the handle.

Ofelia came to then, the glazed mask over her face falling away, her eyes sharp, mouth tight. "Sveva, put that down."

"Me put this down? What has Miss Jüül been doing? This is absolute insanity, Mother! Why – what have you let go on?"

Ofelia looked from Sveva to me, back again, her eyes quick, her mouth loosening, hands reaching out for the post of her bed, for something, anything. I could see confusion in her movements, her expression, as she tried to gain bearings, shore herself up. I reached out for her other hand, wanted to communicate that it was okay. It would be okay. Once I made contact with her, felt the smooth skin of her hand in mine, Ofelia sighed and sat on the bed, pulled her nightgown up so that it was partially covering her torso. Head toward her own hands on her lap, she said, "Miss Jüül has nothing to do with this, Beo. She was just trying to stop me, as you'll try to stop me. It's a spiritual practice – a penance, purifying."

"Try to stop you from self-flagellating? Of course we will!"

"Call it whatever you like, I won't stop. It makes me feel better." Ofelia then lowered herself slowly back onto her bed, lay on her side. I wanted to pull up her nightgown completely and cover her with bedding, but Sveva moved so that she was between the bed and me. I backed away and let her settle her mother. She brushed Ofelia's hair off her forehead with her palm, murmured in Italian, and I went out of the room as quietly as I'd come in.

Later, Ofelia's voice sliced down the hall: "Sveva, my Beo! Sveva, darling!" I started down the stairs from the third floor, heard the shift in floorboards as Sveva went to her, moan of the bed's wood as Sveva got in.

I went back up to my room. Minutes later, I heard Sveva getting out of her mother's bed and coming up the stairs. I was at my door before she knocked. "Mother," she said as an explanation.

"She's not able to sleep?" *Obviously.*

"She's got all the windows and drapes open. The sheers are billowing around the room like so many ghosts."

"Is she speaking?"

"Speaking, intoning, she won't stop – keeps asking me what I remember most."

"About?" I rubbed my hands up my arms.

"Father. Our life, before."

"What do you tell her?" Not that this mattered. I was curious.

"I've told her that what I remember most about Daddy is his face, his hands, his voice – I suppose I feel like I remember everything, really. It doesn't matter what I tell her. It will never be exactly what she wants to hear."

True.

"I need to get some sleep, Jüül. So does Mother."

"Of course. We all do."

"Can you close the windows, try to calm her, even just a bit?"

When I went into Ofelia's room, a cloud of cold air hit me. She sat up in the bed, a silhouette against the weak light coming through the windows. She clutched at her neck as though she were choking, a sob caught in her throat and then torn out like a wail. I'd find a way to calm Ofelia, get her – all of us – to sleep. I took her hands from around her neck, prying them while trying to be gentle, gentle. She was so thin then, our Ofelia, and her hands didn't feel quite real – too soft, too papery. Even so, I felt the steel of Ofelia's resistance as she pushed back against me – the strength she still held, coiled tight, somewhere inside her. I pulled her hands, then arms, slowly, first away from herself and then toward me. When I placed each of her hands along my side and tightened my own arms over them to hold her steady, I felt her tension ease. Ofelia moved her hands until they were on my back and I felt her breath, held so tight in her lungs, her throat, leave her mouth in a long, smooth sigh.

Ofelia shook and I thought she would put her head on my shoulder, as she'd done so many times. I would stroke her hair, tell her to sleep. We had practice in these roles, her nocturnal disturbances, grief raging through her, my ability to calm her, to tuck the sloppiness of her melancholy in for the night, guide her back to something approaching sleep. That night, though, Ofelia's hands moved swiftly from around my back until she was pressing down on each of my shoulders and she reared back, pushed against me. I thought that she might use me to launch herself to standing. I wasn't prepared when, instead of standing, she brought her face directly in front of mine, looked at me, one eye to the other because we were too close to hold both in focus. Then Ofelia gripped my head in one of her hands, her fingers a vise around the back of my skull, and slammed her mouth into mine, splitting it open with her tongue, the heat and smoothness of it a shock. She pulled away as abruptly, looked toward the ceiling and released a short, sharp laugh before she closed her eyes, opened her mouth wide and let out a cry like a long howl. I backed out of the room, closing the door.

Sveva was in the hall, hands in the mess of her hair, and I could see the tension along her neck even in the low light. "It's okay." I reached for her.

Sveva backed away, flung out her arm as she turned from me, then back. "It's not okay, Jüül!"

"You go back to bed. I'll calm your mother."

Sveva dragged her hands over her face, along her collarbones, around her own waist until she was hugging herself.

"Really, go back to bed. Listen." There was no noise now from Ofelia's room. "She's already quieted."

Sveva looked at me, her eyes black in the dark, then turned back to her room.

That night, I gave Ofelia a mild sedative, something the doctor had assured me was fine, harmless. She needed rest, not a night of ragged rumination as she questioned what kind of God would pillage a family such as hers over and over again. Ofelia, for all she'd been through, didn't question him. She was utterly devoted. As was I, in different ways. I took a sedative myself. When sleep came, it was swift and heavy.

The next morning when I checked on her, Ofelia was still asleep. She usually laid with her limbs held close, folded around her, her face pinched as though sleep pained her. That morning, her arms were flung over her head and I could see her legs spread under the duvet. Her hair was loose, mouth open, face soft and slack.

I placed the tea service on a small table and turned away to crack open the window. Sveva came into the room. "What is wrong with her?"

"Wrong? She's sleeping. I gave her something to help last night."

"Something? A sleeping pill? I've asked you, expressly, to not give her any Veronal. I cannot believe I need to ask you again."

Yet this hadn't come up the night before when I'd intimated I'd be giving her something. "And you know how she was last night. It won't do her any harm, not so infrequently, and far less harm than she can work herself into."

"So, you ignored my wishes?"

"I chose to do what I believed was best for your mother."

"However you term it."

"It is your mother who employs me and I believe she will have appreciated the sleep. Once she wakes up, I believe she will respect my choice."

"There's no need to talk about employment, Jüül. You're family, you know that."

I wiped my hands on my apron. It was a habitual movement, the apron an adornment of habit as well. I wore one each morning as I rewashed the cups and spoons and prepared the tea service. It made me look like a maid, of course, but it was practical. Sveva wore one at times, as well, hid slips of sketched-on paper in the pockets. I'd laundered her aprons to remove the smudges of graphite that might have alerted her mother. I always replaced what I found hidden. After all these years together, part of her remained a mystery. I was glad. I hoped that part of me remained a mystery, always, even to those closest to me.

Forty-Two

With each year, fewer things were delivered to our door. Large book orders, which Sveva made every month, now had to be picked up at the train station. When I went to collect them, instead of going directly inside, I would go around the building, stand on the platform and watch trains arrive and depart, as though to reassure myself that people could still do this – come and go at will. Teenaged boys queued in a row along one side of the brick building, pants rolled to their ankles, smoking cigarettes. They didn't see me as I passed. Why would they? I was invisible to them, an old woman – there was nothing for them to see. They felt dangerous to me. Dangerous and so fragile, as boys and men are.

I could hear a train coming, the daily from the coast. Even though I knew no one who would be on it, my anticipation built as it pulled in, as though I could feel the quickened blood and heartbeats of those who were waiting for loved ones resonating in my own body. I didn't look directly at the train but let my vision blur into the middle distance as people moved around me, a stone in a current, until there was nearly no one on the platform. I was about to turn and leave when I saw him.

I saw his face. Hermann. My H, but older, much older. I watched his face shift with recognition but he was already moving away from me, the train pulling out of the station. He leaned against the window, straining to keep his eyes on me. I raised my hand as though to say – what? *Yes, it's me*. Or, *come back*. Or, *goodbye again*. The train was heavy on the tracks, then the rhythm increased in speed. I began to run. At first, it was as though I was lumbering through a dream, my limbs oddly heavy, waterlogged, but I picked up speed. I heard my footsteps, as rhythmic as the train on the tracks, my heartbeat like roaring water in my ears. The platform ended but I could keep running on air down the tracks. I reached out, as though to pull the train back, but there was a hand tight around my arm. I didn't turn; I wanted to see him again, my H. I tried to mark the moment when I could no longer see his face, when we were no longer looking at each other but only the moving distance between us.

The other person pulled more insistently. I turned around – a man, a stranger – "Are you okay, ma'am?" He put his hand on my other arm to steady me. I pushed him away, but the train was already gone.

I was sure it was him I saw. Hermann. It was his face, older. He had leaned against the window, tried to keep his eyes on me. I had raised my hand as though I could reach far enough back in time that I'd be able to touch him. I'd been pulled away, and now the train had left the station. It was gone and I was simply an old woman again, clutching my chest, a knot of pain. I looked at the tips of my shoes on the platform, ran my hands along the fabric of my dress at the hips and cleared my throat before I turned back to the station. The other man had stepped away, and no one else showed me any interest.

Was it really Hermann I'd seen? It couldn't have been. It could not have been him. I was so tired. I hadn't been sleeping well, waking often to listen for noises from Ofelia's room. Many nights, I was up two or three times, either unable to sleep for the listening or helping Ofelia back to bed. I was tired, perhaps delirious. It couldn't have been him.

I went into the station to pick up the parcels, unfolded my wheeled metal basket to trail them home. As I walked, a magpie laughed and others joined in. There was a sound from behind me, a kick of gravel, a warm whooshing noise. The blare and then sputter of a horn. I stepped away from the edge of the road and a car passed, a woman's face in the passenger seat turned to look at me, her lips painted dark red, mouth open as though she was saying something. The car passed and with it, sound – the crunch of gravel, whir of motors, noise of the horn trailing in the air, magpies jibing – and then there was nothing. I stood on the side of the road and lifted my chin to feel the sun like a warm mask on my face. One car passed, two, before I started to walk again.

When I got home, I closed the gate behind me and walked up the drive. As if on cue, a flock of waxwings smudged the sky. They swirled and contracted, then formed a dark crease and descended into a tree at the base of the driveway. The click and whir of the birds' calls caught on each other, hooked into the trees, the air, all of it too loud. Inside, the house was quiet. I locked the door and decided to lie down for a bit, just for a bit. I thought of him, my H. He was no longer mine. He hadn't been for years, had never been. I thought of his face, his lips, his hands on me. I pressed up against myself, rose and rose and fell, felt sleep wash over me then retreat, over and over. I turned my head toward the window and watched light leach out of the sky. Darkness built until it was too much and had to be pricked through with the pinpoints of stars.

THREE
Elegy to a Neverland

But must words be words?
Wings are a wanting:
All reasonableness defying,
They leap not just to land, rather
To bear and beat away.

– Sveva Caetani, "A Psalm of Birds"

Forty-Three

Canada, 1960

There were days and nights when the fist of loneliness that clenched in my chest would open up and the pain would cramp through my body. Did it seem normal, our life? Well, no, but then it never had. There was some comfort in knowing that I had once lived such a full life. The choices I made became the life I'd led – more than that, I'd become the choices I made. Only I knew the curves and relief of my own topography.

I had once sent letters to my own family in hopes that I could trade the stories of my life abroad for a place in theirs. I asked them to write to me of their spouses, their children. I still have photos of my nieces and nephews in christening gowns, later perched on top of horses or standing stiffly in front of gates in their Sunday best. We kept writing, my siblings and I, through the first war, though our letters arrived months late and some didn't make it at all. I learned what a struggle it had been to keep the farm during the war and of my brother Soren's money woes afterward. *I've had to sell all but one horse, Marie,* he wrote, and I knew how much this would have pained him.

When I was in Egypt, my cousin Kristine had married. *No longer in anyone else's service,* she wrote. Her husband was an admiral in the army, and she lived in the best homes on the bases, had her own staff. It was staff who kept her company on her husband's tours of duty, staff who comforted her when he didn't return from his last post, only days before the end of the war. They hadn't had any children and now she was a widow. *Do you ever have regrets, Marie?* she asked in one letter.

They had each implored me to return home. I'd used the First World War as an excuse for not returning earlier. When the fighting ended, however, my excuses were just that. My sister, Johanna, and her husband now ran a shop in which they built coffins and caskets. *You could join our business, Marie,* she wrote. *We're busier than we can keep up with and now I have the children to care for.* I could not go back to that small place to help bury the dead. In Denmark, I had nothing but memories of my childhood on a farm, the mistakes of my youth. By the time I arrived in Italy, I carried the mistakes of a woman. I packed these with me to Canada instead. I expected that the letters would become a record, would become memories themselves when I was finally reunited with my family. Our correspondence continued, and then it ended sometime after the duke died, when it became likely we wouldn't be travelling back to Europe again. When exactly it stopped is hard to say. If I went back and looked, I might be able to find the final letter that I received from Kristine, and from each of my siblings, none of us knowing it would be the last.

One afternoon, Sveva came up from the basement and asked, "Why do you think there were so few letters between Mother and Father?"

"I imagine because they were together most of the time."

"I suppose. I can't even find their marriage certificate."

I said nothing beyond, "Hm."

That afternoon, Sveva offered to help me clean and bandage the ulcers that had developed on Ofelia's legs. She was rarely out of bed now, and the dressing needed to be changed every couple of days. Sveva did as I asked, held damp cloths, gauze and pins, though they kept falling out of her hold. She was distracted.

"I'm getting some papers together, Mau."

"What for?" Ofelia was propped somewhat upright on pillows, rolling her wrists, watching her hands.

"Perhaps I like a sense of order as much as you do, Mother."

Ofelia dropped her hands to her lap.

"I haven't been able to find your and Daddy's certificate of marriage."

"Oh?" Ofelia tacked a small smile on her lips, turned her face away from us to the window.

"Do you know where it is?"

"Of course I don't." Her chest rose and a sigh came out ragged from her mouth.

"Could it be back in Rome? Should I ask Auntie Nella?"

Ofelia turned back to her daughter, brow tight. "Your poor old aunt. I'm afraid she doesn't need to go on a mad search for a piece of paper she's unlikely to find. She's too old, Sveva. We're too old. Be easy on us."

"You are not that old, Mau."

Ofelia looked toward the window, lowered her voice to nearly a whisper. "When I am gone, Sveva, you will have so many friends."

"Mau, I don't want to speak about when you're gone. You won't be gone for a long time."

Ofelia continued as though she hadn't heard this. "They will gather around you and take care of you as you've taken care of me. They will be your reward."

"I need no reward for this, Mau."

Ofelia turned toward her. "I know you don't, but I can see how they'll help you. They will protect you." She had always claimed to know what would happen to Sveva, warned her that misfortune was lurking, waiting for her. "Your father thought democracy and freedom were the ideal, but they were a bane to his family."

"What are you talking about, Mother?"

"I suppose no one has told you about the curse?"

Ofelia was taking several different prescription drugs each night, and the priest was making house visits at least once a week, sometimes two or three times. Her mind addled by prescription drugs and religiosity, it didn't surprise me that she would be muttering about being blighted.

"Yes, Mau, you have told me about the curse." Sveva sounded bored, like a teenager again. How we each kept to our roles, even though she was in her forties now, middle-aged, as the young women Ofelia and I had once been became trapped in old women's bodies.

"So, you'll remember that Pope Pius cursed the Caetani family line to die out within two generations."

"That's absurd. Why would he do that? Besides, there are still my cousins Leila and Topazia."

"Absurd, yes, but there are fewer Caetanis with each passing year, and no male heirs, but you are a Caetani. It has been up to me to protect you."

"Don't be ridiculous, Mother."

"Ridiculous or not, it's been my lot."

When Ofelia closed her eyes, there was a tremor in her lids, as though it took some will to keep them shut. Sveva and I looked at each other across the bed. Her lot had become both of ours. In what ways did we enable her fears to become what kept us together? We were each grown women, after all. You might assume we'd have the agency to make our own decisions. It felt as though the things that bound us were both too subtle and too numerous to see clearly. Like a spider's web, invisible until we stepped into it.

I took the back stairs to the kitchen and met Sveva as she was coming up from the basement again. "I'm afraid I've left a bit of a mess down there," she told me, her curls standing on end around her face, dark smudges beneath her eyes.

"What are you looking for, exactly – a wedding certificate or something more?"

"I'm not really sure, to be honest. Something, some kind of document that will make sense of all of this – where we are, what brought us here, our lives."

"Sveva, sometimes few things make sense, regardless of what is written and what we read."

"I suppose, though you can't blame me for searching, can you?"

"No, though I can blame you for the mess I'm sure you left down there."

Sveva flung a hand at me and snorted a short laugh, touched my shoulder briefly, then walked out of the kitchen.

I didn't need to go to the basement. I could have left the boxes tipped, papers strewn across the floor, and waited indefinitely for Sveva to clean up after herself. Instead, I gathered the documents and tried to find each one its proper box. Family correspondence, bank and investment statements, drafts of the duke's publications and his unpublished drafts, Sveva's. There were file boxes of her essays – written for what readership, I didn't know – copies of the letters she had sent to editors of papers around the world – this had been an occupation of hers for a time, to write letters in response to articles in papers and magazines, praising or scorning them or, often, both.

There was at least a box worth of articles cut out of papers, a folder devoted solely to obituaries for the duke. These mentioned his lineage and professional accomplishments – his time in parliament, publications, the *Annals of Islam* that still distinguished him as a scholar of the Middle East, even though his life as an academic ended when we left Italy. There was little of his personal life, no mention of Ofelia or Sveva in any of them. As I collected the newsprint, some of it crumbled in my hands. I lifted everything gingerly, placed the documents in piles. When I found envelopes, I tried to tuck the corresponding letters into them to protect the paper.

I had little idea of how much time passed. There was no natural light and the bulbs dangled bare from wires slung from the ceiling. It was warm down there. We had a gas furnace by then, and it clunked, chugged and rattled, the sound blocking out most others. Both the wood and the coal furnaces were gone, but there were still dark stains on the concrete walls and floors. In places, I could see where the concrete was cracked along both walls and the floor, the crumbling along these unintended seams. We'd been told that the foundation of the house was built into ground packed with clay, that the pressure on it would build with time.

I found an envelope tucked between a furnace duct and the concrete floor. I pulled it out and looked at the names printed on the surface, then I turned it over again, held it with both hands, shaking. It was addressed to me, Inger-Marie Jüül, at our address on Pleasant Valley Road. His name. The handwriting was firm and clear, though not overly neat, and I recognized the peaks and curves of it. Heat jolted through me, blazed the surface of my skin with pins and needles. The return address was in Vancouver, the envelope postmarked September 1935. I turned it over again, ran my fingers into it, but there was nothing there. No letter.

In one of the last letters I'd received from Onkel, he'd written, *Please, please, I implore you, Miss Jüül, do not write again until neither the censors nor the war itself exists.* The war ended when I had been in Italy for three years, with the Caetanis for two. When peace was declared, I wrote again, the tone different from the desperate appeals I'd sent from the cloister. I told Hermann I was well, I'd found good employment in Rome, that I lived amongst nobility now. I told him that I would wait until I heard word from him and then – I had paused there in my letter. *I would welcome a visit from you, or an invitation for us to meet. I travel widely with the family and could likely arrange to meet you in any of the prominent cities in Europe.*

I'd waited for word from Cairo or Alexandria – a letter, a telegram – but none came. How had Hermann known to write to me here, in Canada? In September 1935, I'd have been nearly fifty years old. By the following winter, I would have retreated into seclusion with these two women. What had become of the letter, and why hadn't he written again? My hands were moist and they itched with a sudden sweat. I sat on one of the file boxes, felt it give slightly under me, and scratched each palm until both were raw, streaked with pink and red marks.

All I had was an empty envelope, his handwriting. His name, mine. I carried it upstairs and circled the main floor, turning off lights and closing doors as I did. I stopped in the parlour, where the wood floors were cold; a draft came from the windows on either side of the room and a chill dropped down from the ceiling. I stood, envelope in my hand. Perhaps I would drink to things falling away, or to things returning. So rarely did I have a drink, certainly not socially in decades by then. I lit the fire, a roar of kindling followed by a desperate fanning of the flames until it was going. Once that was done, I took the decanter from the sideboard, poured myself a finger, two, of brandy.

The fire hot on my skin, the drink a small flame in my throat, bloom in my chest, I thought of seeing the man who looked like Hermann on the train. It had been H I'd seen; I was sure of it then. I would write to him at this address, but where would I begin – seeing his face blurred through the glass of a train window? Perhaps I'd begin with that day in June, the last we were together, the ferry pulling away from the wharf. I thought I prepared myself to be apart from him for weeks, a few months at the most, and this – the time not yet lived – already seemed too long to get through. Instead it had been a lifetime since I'd clutched the rail of the boat and watched the water widen between where I stood and what I'd left behind, a horse kicking against the sky, the retreating shore.

I sat with the pen balanced over paper and decided I'd write none of this, but simply:

Dear Hermann,

I am not sure if you can be reached at this address or if you will receive this letter. I believe that you wrote to me in Vernon in 1935 but, I regret to say, I never received the letter. I have just recently found the envelope that may have contained it, and I am writing you in hopes that you can still be reached here. I think of you, and our time in Egypt, often and with great fondness. If you receive this letter, please do respond.

Here I paused. With what sentiment would I sign my name? If I were to write *With respect* or *With admiration*, I would be dishonest. I wasn't sure I had respect or admiration for Hermann, who must not have persisted for long in trying to contact me, despite the envelope I held in my hand. I was not so hard to find; I had rarely left the same house for three decades. I wrote:

Yours truly,
Miss Inger-Marie Jüül

I had never been his, truly or otherwise, and he had never been mine, but I could offer myself to him again, at least symbolically. After all, I had so little to lose.

FORTY-FOUR

I sat beside Ofelia as she lay in her bed, turned her head to the window. "It's already getting dark so soon."

"Just a month and it will be getting a little lighter each day."

"Well, hardly. Seems a long way off, in any case." She turned her face. When she looked back at me, her eyes were red. If I'd followed the doctor's schedule, I would have given her the prescriptions a half an hour before. I could tell that pain was building, her body stiffening against the bed. Part of me wanted to reach out and touch her hair, smooth it from her face. Part of me wanted to take a fistful of it and yank her head back, expose her throat. As if sensing this, Ofelia turned toward me and pushed her hair off her forehead so that it rose up on the pillow behind her.

I smiled in a way I hoped seemed genuine. Ofelia reached for my hand as though to squeeze it, though her hold was weak. I didn't respond, my own hand limp, and she coughed, held her chest. Pain cinched along her neck, her face. She took a ragged breath, then reached out to me again.

I pulled away from her touch, felt sparks of pain travel along my arms and into my fingers, across my cheeks until they burned with nerves. I took a shallow breath. "Ofelia, I found an envelope in the basement. It was addressed to me." I paused. "From a Mr. Hermann Brandt."

I thought I saw a tremor set off in the skin below her eye, a slight jump in her hand, open-palmed on the bed between us. Ofelia looked directly at me. "Yes, and?"

"I never received the letter. Do you know what became of it?"

"No, of course not. You are the one who handles the mail, Miss Jüül." Ofelia smoothed out her bedding rapidly, as though brushing off crumbs that were not there.

"This was from some time ago – 1935."

She stopped brushing and threw up her hands. "Nineteen thirty-five! How am I to remember correspondence from 1935?" Ofelia met my eyes, but her expression wasn't calm or even neutral; it was challenging – or I may have been imagining that.

I tried a different tack, spoke in a soft, even tone. "Ofelia, the duke told me that he turned a Brandt man away from the villa in Rome so many years ago. He believed that he was protecting me." I took her hand in my own, tried not to squeeze it too strongly. "Were you trying to protect me, as well?" *Just tell me, tell me something.*

She slipped her hand out of mine, brought it to her chest. "Of course, I've always wanted to protect you – to protect all of us – Sveva, myself."

"You remember the letter then? Do you remember what you did with it – did you read it?"

"No, I don't remember any of that, Marie." Ofelia faced the wall, ran her thumb and forefinger along her slight eyebrows. "Who was he?"

"My employer in Egypt."

She turned, looked at me without blinking. "And your lover?"

"Yes."

She broke my gaze, tucked her bedclothes around her hips. "Nothing good could have come of it, you must know that, Miss Jüül."

"You can't say that, Ofelia. You can't know that to be true."

She slapped the bed with her palms. "Can't I? Look at the choices I made and where I am now. My actions were never intended to be noble and – as if reminding me of every one of my weaknesses – God has granted me *this* life."

I leaned toward Ofelia, took her hands in mine. She wouldn't look at me. "The letter arrived when I was at the clinic with the duke, but it was addressed to me. It was mine to open and read."

Ofelia turned her face toward her pillows so her speech was slightly muffled. "I suppose Sveva could say the same of those letters addressed to her, but we haven't always thought it in her best interest to read them either, have we, Miss Jüül?" She looked directly at me.

"Please, just tell me, did you read the letter, Ofelia?"

She pulled her hands out of my hold, ground them in fists into the bed beside her and faced the ceiling, as though appealing to it. "Miss Jüül, Marie, I honestly cannot remember. Why does it matter now?" She turned toward me. "Now, after everything Leone and I did for you? Taking you in, inviting you into our lives, treating you as one of the family. We rescued you, Marie, and you've led a good life with us."

"Rescued me? Is that what you believe, Ofelia?"

"Yes, of course. Do you not? Tell me, where do you think you would be without us?"

"Without *us*? I've been caring for you for more than half of your life, Ofelia! A life that Sveva and I have tried to make as comfortable as possible for you. I have not left – you, this house, this way of living – because of my care for *you*, Ofelia, and you believe it's me who's been rescued?"

"You have been so good to me, Marie, there is no question of that." She ran her fingers through her hair again, left her hand around her neck and sighed heavily. "And, it's been a mutually beneficial relationship, yes? Leone and I gave you a life that there is no way you could have led otherwise."

"Yes, and after he passed I stayed with you, Ofelia, not for my own good but for yours."

Ofelia rolled to her side, tucked her knees into a fetal position. "I've forced you to do nothing, Marie."

Her voice was so quiet, but I had heard what she had said. Was this true? I supposed it could have been, but then it was so difficult to parse out what was truth, what was fallacy, where reality lay between the two, if there was such a thing.

Each day I waited for his response. I had always monitored the mail – what was brought into the front hall and placed on the sideboard, what was opened and dealt with between me and Ofelia and what was burned or disposed of before Sveva might happen upon it. I had been to the mailbox at the end of our drive nearly every day of our time in seclusion, an act of interference as much as anything else. The letter came three weeks after I'd sent mine, but it wasn't H's handwriting. It was addressed to me, and the return address was the same, but the handwriting was smaller, boxier, more contained than I knew Hermann's to have been. Not knowing where else to go, I opened the letter in the dog kennel, crouched on a bed of straw.

The envelope was so thin. Inside was one page:

Dear Inger-Marie Jüül,

I received your letter addressed to my father, and I am writing to you on behalf of his estate. I am not certain if you remember me, Hermann's son, Sven Brandt. I remember you warmly, though vaguely, I will admit. I was quite young when we last saw each other. I know you and my father were very close and kept in some contact after your departure from Egypt.

I am sorry to write you now with sad news. My father passed away last year. It has taken me some time to go through his estate. I have found some things that I believe he would have wanted you to have. Now that I know where you can be reached, I can send these things by parcel post, or perhaps drop by with them when I'm next in the Okanagan. Please advise. I can be reached at the phone number above should you wish to speak to me.

With fond memories of long ago.
Sincerely,
Mr. Sven Brandt

How easy this sounded, to simply stop by on one's travels. I thought of my passage from Alexandria to Sicily, how sick I was. I remembered my days at the cloister, the letters addressed from Onkel, when sometimes I would get just one sheet of a letter that referred to so much more, pages that weren't there, communication broken, lost. There was a sea between us. Years later and how easy it was for Sven Brandt to write, to suggest he stop by.

I read the letter over again, and then two, three, four more times. Heat surged in me, became a pain on the crown of my head, a sting in my eyes, then drained and left me so cold I shook. My mouth slackened as it filled with moisture that then poured out of me – tears, mucus, streams of spit from my mouth. I crumpled the letter in my hand and slumped over onto the dogs' bed, straw sharp and cool against my cheek, the smell of animal both comforting and rank at once. *Get up*, I told myself. *Get up. Keep going. You always have.*

Forty-Five

A faint line of smoke rose from the chimney, and I was both pleased and surprised that the ladies had thought to build a fire without me. I came up the steps, slick with new rime, and made note to throw down some salt. It was early afternoon, but the sky was already fading. I opened the door quietly in hopes that I could move through the house unnoticed. The only smudge of light I could see flickered from the parlour. As I was about to take the back stairs, I heard, "Oh, Miss Jüül?" I went toward the voice. There were no lights on, and the fire was struggling. "You'll help me with stoking this?"

I was astonished to see Ofelia out of bed, standing. At first, I thought she had cinched a robe tightly around her, but when she turned as I came closer, I saw that she was wearing one of the gowns I'd packed away in the basement years – decades – before. She had arranged her hair, pulled it into a messy topknot. Ofelia smoothed her skirts and raised her chin, as though to say, *Yes, and?* I couldn't see very well but knew that the dress hung from her. Where it had once skimmed her curves, it now fell like fabric from a hanger. I hadn't seen her on the main floor for months, had rarely seen her out of bed.

"Ofelia, are you –"

"Shh." She backed away from me, finger to her puckered lips, then placed both hands on her cheeks, raised an eyebrow and leaned toward me. I stared and her expression fell. She dropped her arms to her sides and then pointed at the fire. "Please, get that burning, Jüül. I cannot keep it burning."

I tried to meet Ofelia's eyes, but the light was too low and she had raised her chin, cast her gaze to the sides of the room. I waited a moment, then moved toward the fire. It was clear that she'd had no help in building the fire so far. There was a pile of ashes topped with small pieces of paper and a couple of logs, charred by attempts to light them, lying dormant in the fireplace. "I'll need more kindling."

"What do you mean, you'll need more kindling? What do you think that is?" Ofelia pointed toward the scraps of paper covered in full-sized logs.

"That's good," I started. "We'll just need something more, some smaller pieces of wood to keep it going, or once the paper burns, it will be out again. I can split up larger logs with the hatchet."

"The hatchet!" Ofelia put both hands over her heart, bowed her head and sucked in breaths against her ragged throat.

"Yes, the hatchet. It's what I use to make kindling."

"It sounds dangerous."

"Where's Sveva?"

Ofelia dropped her arms, then stood straight. "Where *is* Sveva? I suppose she's in her room, brooding over those ridiculous sketches." Ofelia pointed toward the fireplace, all flames now extinguished, small embers remaining, smoke entering the room. "I tried." When she first said this, it was a whisper, and then louder, "I tried, Miss Jüül!" She smoothed the fabric of the gown that hung off her as though she were a child playing dress-up, took a breath and continued speaking in a smooth, moderated tone. "I tried to tell her that she need not disappear into those pointless sketches. Sketches! There are far better things to do with her time. I suggested that she and I play cards."

Ofelia hadn't played cards in years by then. "Sveva wasn't as interested?"

"Interested? Sveva was as spoiled as you might expect she would be. She was more concerned with her precious sketches – which are not, I might add, very good at all. Nothing worthy of being treasured – than with spending time with her mother."

The room felt like it was getting cooler by the moment, the fire all but out. Ofelia began to sway. She reached for furniture to steady herself. When I motioned to take her arm, she jerked away from me and knocked into the table. A vase rocked against the surface once, twice, then rolled off, as if in slow motion, and shattered on the floor. Ofelia screamed and I moved toward her instinctually, but she backed away from me. "What have you done?" she yelled.

"Ofelia, I . . ." I wanted to be able to do something – to calm Ofelia, or light the fire, or get us both upstairs and into our beds. I wanted to know if and where Sveva was in the house and what she was doing.

"You what?" Ofelia was now on her hands and knees and appeared to be looking for something as she yelled at me. "You what, perfect little Miss Jüül? You just want to help? Is that what you're going to say?"

I didn't respond. That was, perhaps, one of the things I might have said.

"Haven't you helped enough?"

"I will just get the fire started, Ofelia. If that is help, so be it. I have years of practice in getting the fire going. After that, I will leave you to do as you choose."

"You will leave me, will you?"

"I will go to bed and we can talk more in the morning."

"What makes you think I want to talk?"

"If you don't want to, we needn't." Fear spiked through me. I'd been with Ofelia when she was unpredictable, but this seemed different. It was silent for a moment, then Ofelia howled, her cry as plaintive and sustained as I would have imagined a wolf's. Then it died in her throat and she stood shaking, a silhouette in the room. I didn't move, waited for her. Ofelia picked up the skirts of her gown, raised her chin and walked past me without a word. I stood still some time after she left, then went to the fire and pulled out the papers. They were Sveva's simple, almost comic-like sketches of herself as Beo, the nickname her mother had given her. Not great art, perhaps, but it was one of the only artistic outlets for Sveva after Ofelia had burned all her watercolours and pastels, or had me do so. I brushed the ashes from the papers and slipped them into my pocket before I went upstairs.

On the landing I stopped and listened, heard nothing. There were no lights visible on the second floor. I opened the door to the stairs that led up to my quarters. When I turned on the light as I entered my room, I saw Sveva curled against my single bed, her body too big for its frame. I took off my cardigan, not wanting to disturb her, not knowing where I would go if she remained asleep on my bed. I had my back to her when I heard her sit up. "Miss Jüül."

I turned. "Sveva?" I spoke as though it wasn't unusual that she was there, lying on my bed.

"She found my sketches."

"Yes, I know."

"They weren't much, but they were the last thing I had that was only mine, I suppose. What I wouldn't give to be able to paint, to draw – to live! – but without any of that, at least I had my measly sketches. Now, even those are gone."

I went to my cardigan, hung over the back of a chair, and pulled out what I'd salvaged from the fireplace, handed them to her. Sveva took them, looked at each one as though studying it, seeing it for the first time, then she pulled me to her. I felt a sob break out in her chest. She backed away from me, dragged one palm, the other, against her eyes and cheeks, offered me a weak smile. "Thank you, Miss Jüül." She leaned to me, pressed her hands on either side of my face so that I heard nothing but my own blood moving in my ears, and kissed the top of my head.

Forty-Six

There was another Christmas, the twenty-fifth that had passed since the duke's death. Every year, the holiday was far more melancholy than it was celebratory. We had both the birth of Christ and the death of the duke to observe, but only one of them had risen again, and so far he did not seem able to save us from our self-imposed exile. Nonetheless, I prayed for some kind of release from our situation, as I did every year, asked for signs, divine intervention. If they came, I was unqualified to recognize them. It seemed nothing changed, nothing would ever change, and we were stagnant as time moved through us. We were steeped in so many times, so many places and yet, as the rest of the world spun on, we remained in continuous retreat. Each year on Christmas morning we handed each other embossed cards, finely wrapped Christmas gifts of French-milled soaps and tiny bottles of perfume.

In the last week of 1960, Dr. McMurthie made house calls each day between Christmas and New Year's Eve. On the last day of the decade, I sent him home. "You'll want some time with your family."

"I can stay. Mrs. McMurthie will drag me out to some kind of party, but I'm really not one much for them."

"No, no, go." I didn't say that his wife needed him – that wives need husbands, and wives need celebrations.

"I'll be by tomorrow – you'll be all right until then?"

"Of course."

He showed me again the row of prescriptions and explained what to give Ofelia when. "I know that you are experienced in giving Ofelia her medications, but it is up to me to remind you to give her some time between these three – and none of those with alcohol, of course, despite the season."

"Of course." Ofelia hadn't drunk any alcohol in years by then, not a sip of wine or touch of brandy to her lips.

"Best you keep the medication with you. The Dexamyl in particular seems to cause a kind of temporary amnesia, and patients may be quite convinced to take their dose over again." How good a temporary amnesia sounded. "You can always call. Despite Mrs. McMurthie's wishes, I won't be out late."

I circled the house to make sure the drapes were pulled shut against the cold, the doors closed, then went upstairs to Ofelia. "Can I get you something to drink – water, tea?" I thought of the duke, calling for water again and again, trying to soothe his ragged throat in the months before his death.

"There's nothing." Ofelia turned her head from side to side. I saw the smear of tears on her face. She took a long, rough breath. "We were loved once, weren't we, Marie?"

"Yes, of course." My voice was forced, flat. "The duke loved you very much."

"He did. And Sveva. He loved her so very much. She knows that. He tried to leave us in a good place in this world." Ofelia laughed at this – the sound came out like a cough and she held her chest. I watched the pain bind along her neck, her face. She looked at me. "You were loved once too, Marie." Her voice was quiet, a rasp. "Do you ever say his name?"

I didn't answer her.

"Now there's no one. No one for me, no one for you. And Sveva, dear Sveva." Ofelia seemed as though she wanted to say more about her daughter but stopped. She looked away again, as though out the window, but her focus seemed dull. "What have I done?"

What had either of us done? Only what we could, what we knew to do. Somehow, that had led to us spending a quarter of a century shut away together, but even as I traced back my role in this, I wasn't sure how it had happened. There was one day and then the next, one year and then the next.

At first, it seemed like there was so little time to question our lives, and then time became a pool around us, and its depth only hid its currents.

"Ofelia." She was so still, I wondered for a moment if she was breathing. I put my face close to hers, turned my cheek to her mouth. "Ofelia," I said again. Nothing, and then she began to shake. I knew she was too weak to cry so I held her, her body so thin against mine that I made sure my hold was light, as though I could hurt her with just a bit too much pressure. Her shaking calmed and it was then that it travelled from her body to mine like a tremor.

Wind pushed thin branches of trees against the house and they scraped against the window. I twitched on waking, as though the limbs were scratching my skin. I thought I heard a bough dragged along glass. It began as a shrill rasp, a keening of air, and then it tore and I recognized Sveva, her voice coming from Ofelia's room. When I came in, she was sitting upright in her mother's bed, her mouth open. She pulled in breaths, holding her throat as though she were choking, then she coughed out barking sobs.

I went to Sveva, pulled her hands from her neck, put one of my palms on her back, one on her chest, as though to guide her breath. I saw Ofelia, her eyes open to the ceiling, looking at neither her daughter nor me. I wish that I could tell you she looked peaceful. Her face was no longer closed around the pain that she'd felt. It had been so long, I realized, since I'd seen her without pain. It wasn't peace that replaced this, though. What was it? There was nothing there. Ofelia was gone, and in her face I saw only absence. Something rose in my chest, along my neck – tightness, heat, bile. I felt as though I would be sick; then it was as if all the sensation hit the ribbed roof of my mouth and drained away, a hollowing.

I didn't cry, not yet. I made calls, first to the doctor, then to the priest. They arrived in that order, the doctor pronouncing her death, Monsignor Miles asking me to fold back the bedding so that he could sprinkle holy water on her body. I tried not to touch her skin as I moved the bedclothes. It didn't seem right, death both the ultimate vulnerability and nothing to do with Ofelia at all. She was already gone. I didn't want to touch what was left behind. It wasn't her; it wasn't anyone. While I pulled the blankets down, Sveva stood beside me. The way her body shook seemed to disturb the air. When Monsignor dipped the aspergillum into the holy water, she began to wail. He sprinkled the holy water on Ofelia's nightgown and Sveva howled like wind, a storm in the room.

Ofelia left us so late on the last day of 1960 or so early on the first morning of 1961 that it was hard to tell. Just as she had lived, her death straddled two worlds. It was hard to know where one ended, one began. I called the funeral home. Sveva sat beside Ofelia's body while it was blessed and prayed over, and when it was removed and prepared for burial, she lay in the place in the bed where her mother had been, the space she'd left behind. I could hear her sobbing. When she emerged, her face was swollen, skin wet. She spoke to me as though her tongue were fat and numb. "I feel like I've been beaten, Jüül, hit all over with something wet and dull."

I followed my lady's request and she was brought to the cemetery by horse-drawn sleigh, the first time one had been used in twenty-seven years. When we got into the coach that pulled the sleigh, I felt like a child sitting beside the towering Sveva, my feet not quite reaching the floor, each jostle riding the small bones of my legs, tilting my tiny hips and laddering my spine. I hadn't cried yet. Small cramps and shudders travelled my skin. I wished that Ofelia could have seen the attention we drew as we made our way down Pleasant Valley Road – imagine, a horse-drawn sleigh! As much as Ofelia had sequestered herself during her lifetime, I don't think she would have minded making a spectacle of herself in death.

At the cemetery, everything but the gaping grave was covered in a hard crust of snow. The hole in which the coffin was laid was cut away from the earth so neatly, the ground so hard, it seemed it was being lowered into concrete. Sveva stood over it. She had stopped crying and flailing her arms in exaggerated grief and was holding herself still, standing so tall. It wasn't quite snowing, but a few flakes were in the air, floating around us as though they didn't know which way to fall. Sveva wouldn't meet my eyes and I knew that if she did, she would begin to cry again. When we returned to the house, she went to her room. I opened the door to Ofelia's quarters to the smell of camphor and closed air. The bed hadn't been stripped since the monsignor had blessed the body.

I pulled back the bedding and released a scent – not the odour of sickness, but that of her, a smell I'd lived with for forty-three years, the length of Sveva's life. In that smell, I saw the roundness of Ofelia's young face when pregnant, her pink cheeks, her full lips smirking. I saw her four years later, on our sailing to Canada, how sallow her skin, the dark smudges under deep-set eyes. I saw her looking up at Leone, her mouth open, the red wet of it those times she would laugh, the times she would yell at him. I saw her reach for Sveva, a small hand along her daughter's long arm. How even until her last days, she would pull her daughter toward her, kiss the top of her head as forcibly as she could. I felt the shock of Ofelia's tongue in my mouth that one afternoon. In that smell, I saw us both from above on her last day as I held her. I felt the memory of Ofelia against me, her bones so close to the skin, so thin it was as if she'd been leaving her body for years by then. When I cried, it was like I could feel a shiver in her body ride my skin.

Forty-Seven

We didn't understand how little was left for us until Ofelia's will was read. She had named Monsignor Miles, the priest of St. James Catholic Church in Vernon, as the executor of her Italian property, a villa in Rome. "She advises the church to sell it," the lawyer explained, looking at the document. "And to use all proceeds for what's called the Society for the Propagation of the Faith."

Sveva and I looked at the man. I'm sure neither of us knew what to say in response.

The lawyer cleared his throat. "The proceeds of the sale of that property as well as the proceeds of any of her investments held in Italy will go to the society."

"I was under the understanding that there was not much left to her investments," I said.

"Now that Monsignor Miles is named as the executor, he's the only one privy to that information."

"I would have thought . . ." began Sveva, but she didn't complete the sentence. I supposed the monsignor would know soon enough what he'd been bequeathed – and if it was worth anything. I knew well that the ladies had yet to see any income from that property. I suspected he'd be left more debt than revenue, but I couldn't be sure.

To me, Ofelia left a modest monthly stipend. The lawyer explained,

"This stipend is only provisioned – and I'll stress *only* – if you remain living in the same household as Miss Sveva Caetani."

Had Ofelia thought I would leave Sveva? The day when I could have done that had long passed. "I wouldn't think of doing anything otherwise."

"I'm not suggesting that you would, Miss Jüül. I'm simply reading your lady's wishes."

"Of course."

He continued. "It states here that all of Miss Ofelia Fabiani's household possessions should remain in the care of Miss Sveva Caetani di Sermoneta. This includes all artwork, china, garments and jewellery."

I waited for the lawyer to go on. When he didn't, I said, "And the duchess has left something else – a stipend, perhaps – for Sveva as well?"

The lawyer cleared his throat and lifted his hand as if to loosen his necktie before he dropped it again and straightened the papers with both hands, stacking and then smoothing the pile. "There is no specific stipend. I understand that Miss Fabiani's possessions – the jewellery in particular – are of considerable value."

"Her possessions, her possessions!" Sveva said. "Of course they are of some worldly value. That hardly makes a difference when she is gone. She – my mother – was of considerable value, and now she is gone!"

"Of course, this is difficult. I believe that Miss Fabiani –"

"Why on earth do you insist on calling my mother by her maiden name?"

The lawyer's cheeks fell and he tightened his mouth, wide and thick-lipped, giving him the appearance of a sad clown. His eyes darted from me to Sveva and back. "That is her legal title. As such, it is the name that appears on all her legal documents."

"Her legal title? Her legal title is Duchess Ofelia Caetani di Sermoneta."

Some of the tension left the lawyer's face, and when it did, he looked defeated. He rubbed his hand against his forehead once, briefly. "Miss Caetani, your parents' union was one that we would term common-law. Your mother was known as Mrs. Caetani in this country, but this was not her legal title."

I didn't look toward Sveva.

"No one knew her as Mrs. Caetani! She was known as Duchess Caetani di Sermoneta. Who is this *we* that you refer to? What do they – you – know about my parents' marriage?"

"I'm not sure if you're aware –" The lawyer cleared his throat and squared his papers again. "Your parents did not legally marry."

I remained looking at the large desk. He kept all his papers close to him and the rest of the desk was sparse, clean, so that there seemed to be an expanse of wood between us, gleaming. I kept my eyes on the oiled grain and waited for Sveva to say something. When she didn't, I turned to her. She too was staring at the desk, her face still, aged by lack of animation, the downward slope of her eyes, the fall of her mouth.

The lawyer continued, "Remember, this is a legal document, Miss Caetani. Please don't think of it as anything other than that."

Sveva began to move again, her brows lifting, mouth open. "What else would I think of it? A love letter?" she said loudly.

"Exactly – that is exactly what it is not. Your mother was trying to ensure your well-being."

"You know nothing about my mother and my well-being." This time, Sveva's voice was quiet, strained.

He looked quickly toward me, then back to her. "Your father's first marriage was never annulled. He was legally married to Duchess Vittoria Colonna."

"That was his first wife!"

"He had one heir with the duchess, a son."

"A son? My father never talked about a son."

"Onorato."

"That was my grandfather."

"Yes, and the name of your father's son, as well. His son died in 1944, the duchess in 1954. In Italy, only they are considered his family – legally, I mean."

With a slight pause between each word, Sveva said, "My father's wife was my mother."

"Legally, no. Neither you nor your mother is documented as a Caetani in Italy – but, even though your mother never became a citizen here, you are a Canadian residing in Canada. Your mother completed documents that absolved her of any legal title as your mother. I tried my best to persuade her to do otherwise, but she was convinced that her religious beliefs nullified her claim to you as a mother."

"A bastard, am I?" Sveva looked from the lawyer to me, back again, brows lowered, eyes hard. "Never mind. The money is gone, isn't it?"

The lawyer looked down briefly at his papers before he looked at me, then Sveva. "There is not the same amount of capital that there once was."

Sveva snorted. "Obviously! How much is there, in simple terms?"

I shifted in my chair, cleared my throat though I had nothing to say.

"In simple terms, I can no longer reveal that to you, Miss Caetani. What was left of your mother's estate has been bequeathed to Monsignor Miles and to Miss Inger-Marie Jüül. They are the only people to whom I can release that information."

"It's all right." My voice came out unnaturally high and slight. I cleared my throat. "I will hide nothing from Sveva."

"I can tell you this. There is not enough to support both of you for long. Miss Jüül, with all due respect, I don't believe you're in a position to supplement your household's income. Miss Caetani, it may be an imperative that you do." Neither of us said anything. "There are also organizations that can help with –"

"Stop! I do not need to hear any more of this! Apparently, it was decided long ago that I not be told these things. I don't know why you are doing so now!" She pushed her chair back with an awful scraping along the wood floor and left the room.

I got up to follow her, said, "I'm sorry," out of habit and immediately felt badly for doing so. I needn't apologize for Sveva – her behaviour was suited to the circumstance, after all. It was me who was peculiar, with so little to say about the dissolution of the Caetani estate, of the life we once had. I suppose I realized the end of that life had begun years before.

I went out of the building onto the main street, looked one direction and then the other – the street so short all the shops could be seen by turning one's head both ways. I saw the courthouse at the crest of the street, the houses that had been built between it and the Caetani home in an area that had once, not long ago, been pastures smattered with pine forest. I felt myself at the valley bottom, there in the middle of Vernon, the place that had been chosen for us. There was nothing else to do but walk back home.

I took a few steps and then Sveva was beside me, her hand in mine for a moment. She gripped it and then let go. I stopped to look at her, her eyes swollen and red, a sloppy smile pulling at her mouth. "So, I am a bastard, Miss Jüül!" She swung her arms out as though presenting herself, then dropped them. "And all this time I've been telling myself to not let the bastards grind me down. I, Miss Jüül, could have been doing the grinding, as it were!"

"I suppose you could have."

She took my hand and we began walking up the hill. "We'll be fine, won't we?"

I was a bit winded by her stride, her legs nearly twice the length of mine, but managed to say, "Of course we will, Sveva. We'll get by, we always have."

"We'll more than get by, my Scandinavian Virgin, mark my words." I did. I marked Sveva's words, my own. We walked up the hill toward our home, sunlight hitting the trees on the rise of the hill, the pale wash of sky over the valley smudged with clouds.

FORTY-EIGHT

Italy, 1915

A man named Mr. Wiinstead picked me up from the port and said my name with a nod but did not meet my eyes. Too tired to feign decorum, I studied his face, pitted with scars, eyelids heavy, skin splotched, spider-veined. He angled his chin and I knew to climb into the carriage. It swayed from side to side as we ascended the narrow dirt path into the mountains, thick with cypress then pine, cut with ravines tumbling green toward the ocean. He said little as we climbed. When we reached the cloister, he took my bags and led me through a series of arched stone walls, some crumbling. We rounded gravel paths lined with pots either empty or sprouting tangles of seemingly wild plants, then reached an inner courtyard where he put my bags down.

Mr. Wiinstead cleared his throat. "You'll be comfortable here, Miss Jüül. God willing, you will find peace." I wondered how he imagined I might find peace after being sent, pregnant, into exile by my married lover. "It can be calming, even rejuvenating."

I'd heard those assurances before, from Carl Marsden on the island, knew not to believe men's beliefs on rejuvenation. It was wartime, after all. Mr. Wiinstead nodded once more, cleared his throat and took two steps backward, still facing me, before he turned and I was left alone, bags at my feet. Girls in long grey dresses, white kerchiefs around their hair, came and motioned for me to follow them. We went in and out of halls, up and down stairs, until we were in a long, narrow room lined with slim wooden cots. The girls set my bags down beside one. One of the girls pointed, her smile a half-twist of her lips.

"Mine?" My voice sounded as fatigued as I felt.

The girl said something in Italian, reached out and put a hand on my shoulder. I was startled by the gesture, flinched slightly. I looked at the bed, so thin, the rope frame showing beyond the edge of the folded blanket. My throat seized as I thought of the night before.

The night before, I'd been with him, Hermann. I was his jewel, a gem cut against his tongue. Afterward, my ankle tucked around his, hand folded between the sinew of his arm and chest, I still thought he might change his mind. That he would realize he could not send me away, that I could not go alone. I knew he believed that if he were to leave his wife and son, he would have to leave everything else – his reputation, his contacts and associates, the business. I still thought that might not matter. His hands in my hair, his hand along my collarbone, my ribs. His hands cupping my buttocks, around my waist and down, inside me, his hands along the length of me, holding my feet. His hands. And so much more. He couldn't take all that away from me; he couldn't empty his hands of me and keep going. Except, my God, of course he could.

There was one girl at the cloister who could also speak English. Clara and I muddled through together in a language that was neither of ours. "I'm not really supposed to be here," I told her. It was one of my first mornings, and I folded clothes to fit into the chest at the end of my cot.

Clara sang out a high laugh. "Of course you're not! None of us are."

"No, but –" I was going to tell her that this was temporary, that the father of the child was coming to get me, but realized then that some of the other women had likely been told the same thing. What made me certain I was different than those I pitied?

"It's all right." Clara ran her hand down my arm and then held my elbow lightly, as though cupping a bird or an egg.

I pulled my arm away from her, shook my head. "It's not." I wasn't like these women, some clearly pregnant, several slim, and all seemingly so young. Here I was both unwed mother and old maid. I didn't belong.

The nuns spoke Italian, French, English, though none but Mr. Wiinstead spoke Danish. Those who could counselled me in English. "We are equal in the eyes of God. All he asks is that we are humble, that we repent."

I had plenty for which to ask forgiveness – relations with a married man first among my misdeeds – but I still felt their words weren't relevant to me, as though appeals for humility and penance were for someone I wasn't. Hermann knew me, truly, even if these women did not. I wrote to him often, as though to remind both him and myself who I was, who he was, who we were to each other. In one letter, I asked if he might be able to come for me before the baby was born. This was folly, I knew. Even though the fighting was against Italy's northern front, soldiers marched through the south and I could hear their boots on the road surrounding the cloister. We'd had drills in which we crawled under our cots, ducked our heads between our arms on the floor, imagined protecting ourselves from falling mortar, though a raid on the southern coast seemed unlikely.

Just as improbable was the chance that Hermann would be able to travel to me during the war. I would wake at night, feel my stomach tighten and tension run through every part of my body, lines of pain twisting around my limbs, burrowing into my head as an ache that would not end. My thoughts brought no comfort – I would birth the baby alone, and then it would be taken away. Mornings, I couldn't eat. I went to the dining hall to drink as much water as I could, then sat at a small desk in the library, pressed the tips of my fingers into my temples and wrote to my H. Almost as often as I sent them, the letters would be returned, or it was Onkel who wrote back, imploring me not to write to his brother. *The censor here is a friend, not one I would trust completely, a master gossip – I suspect that's what got him the post. "Hello, fine friend!" I say to him if he is reading this. Miss Jüül, again, you must not write to Hermann in Cairo! If you have to write, address it to him here. I'll pass on the letters. It's best you not write at all, though I suspect you will keep it up.*

I kept it up. I wrote to Hermann care of his brother. As desperate as my letters were, the responses were always from Onkel. Increasingly, they were marred with the deletions of the censor so that what remained, though intelligible, said very little – nothing of consequence or genuine feeling remained between the black marks. Still, I wrote letter after letter, received censored missives in return, until one arrived with more content visible than usual. *H was pleased to receive your letter*, Onkel wrote. *He remembers your time in Egypt with fondness.* Fondness? *H reminds you that that time is now gone. The war is here now and he knows that we can all be sensible in facing our fate. H appeals to you to be discreet. He knows how good you are, Miss Jüül.*

Of course he knew how good I was. How much more discreet could I be, hidden in a cloister, perched on the rocky coast of southern Italy?

We trust you've received the money from the Danish consulate? 150 lire last month, 150 this month. Please, send word. Two weeks later, after I'd sent more letters, another from Onkel: *Please send word. We have not heard from you and are worried.*

I sent words. I sent so many words. Where did they go? I received so few in response.

One morning, weak light filtered into the room, and the slow, rhythmic breath of my sleeping dormitory mates closed in around me. I was so hot. I peeled the thin cotton sheet and rough wool blanket from me. Stifled by heat, I wanted to be outside in air blown from the sea and sucked into thick trees in the crevices of mountains. I walked across the floor barefoot and left the room. I wanted to be able to go down the stairs, across the courtyard, through the gates. To feel grass under my feet, to lie under a tree. I knew I wouldn't make it. My legs were already so weak, unstable. I went instead to the patio that jutted out from the end of the hallway. There was a glass there, full of water, balanced on the ledge. Or did I imagine it? I reached for it, first grabbed nothing but air, then tried again, felt the smooth cool of glass against my palm. I lifted it to my mouth, but it was empty. I pressed, as though I could draw water from glass, and it splintered in my hand.

I kept clenching and the sensation began as a slice across my palm, then moisture. *Water!* It ran down my hand, over my wrist, dripped onto the patio, and then pain seared through me. The taste of blood in my mouth as I bit down. Heat bearing down through me as my stomach tore with pain that burst between my legs, shattered and ripped out of me, blood on my hands, blood on my legs, blood on my feet. Blood pooling around me. I was so very thirsty. So very, very tired. I lay in warm, lovely sunlight on the patio and dreamed myself into blackness.

I knew in the first moments of waking that the baby was gone. I could feel nothing but an aching absence in the centre of me. I tried to turn my head, to open my mouth, speak. My body rose from the mattress and began to float at the same time as it sank so heavily, its weight pulling it down through the bed frame, the stone floor, until it was stamped in hard-packed earth. I rose again, weightless, into nothing but air, then I was held down by something stuffed, heavy and wet, between my legs. I was still so hot, so unbearably hot. The heat built and built until it shattered, and cold pierced skin and the centre of each aching muscle and organ until my empty body shook with pain so frigid it burned.

Sister Bertha's face was above mine, blurred until it became Sister Anna's, her lips opening and closing, pink and red and white, her teeth, the darkness of her mouth. Clara's was the voice that came out, some of her words her own, in English, others the Italian words of Sister Bertha, and then everyone's voices at once, mounting and merging until there was no one language, no single words or sentences, no answers to the questions I couldn't ask – then they fell away. In the silence, I could feel my body being lifted by several hands, how they pressed the pain back into me, each hand, palm, thumb, finger imprinting aches until they became nothing but air, nothing at all, and I was being carried, as though I had no weight, no body, nothing to me. Nothing but air that I kept rising into, sky throbbing blue, light sharp and insistent. Sun so bright that my eyes couldn't bear it for long, so bright that it burned my sight back into darkness.

When I opened my eyes again, there was a nurse above me. Her cap was tied at the nape of her neck, white fabric down her shoulders like a bride or a nun. She wore a white apron, the red cross level with my eyes as she adjusted my pillow.

"Where am I?"

"Shh."

Shh, shh, shh. And then the prayers. So many voices – in Italian, French, German, English – until there were only two left, Sister Bertha's and Clara's. I opened my eyes again and their faces were clear, in focus, their eyes kind.

"You're in the hospital," Clara said, as though answering the question I'd asked of the nurse earlier – when had that been?

I looked from her face to Sister Bertha's. "Where is my baby?"

Sister Bertha took a step closer to the bed, put her hand on my shoulder. "With God now, child, the best place it can be."

I struggled to move, wanting to sit up, but all I could do was turn my head slightly from side to side. I wanted to yell but scratched a whisper out of my throat. "No, that is not the best place it can be. It should be with me. The baby should be with me."

"Marie –" Clara began.

Sister Bertha spoke over her. "Sleep, child. We're here with you. We are praying for you."

Forty-Nine

I knew there was nothing to me then but passing time. Nothing to me but the weeks the sheets were spotted with blood, nightclothes twisted with sweat, time itself seeping out of me. I'd spent several months balled into myself, my body clenched like a jaw, then slack as a mouth pulled open by sleep. I felt my strength draining away and thought I might cut lines across my skin with broken glass, create brilliant red patterns on the bedding. I knew it was cowardly to think like that. To live, that was the thing that would be difficult. I rolled over and watched a flock of seabirds obscure the sky for a moment, and then nothing but a pale, high blue.

Eventually, I got up, washed and dressed and went into the dining hall. I was silent as I ate with the nuns and the other women who were convalescing. After dinner one night, Mr. Wiinstead approached me. "Miss Jüül, may I have a word?"

"Of course, sir." I stood straight, thought of myself as a marionette, strings holding me, a slight lift of my wrists, feet, the hinges of my hips. I followed him to the hall outside the refectory.

He turned, looked not directly at my face but beside me. "You're doing better now, I can tell."

"Yes, sir, I am."

Not long before, Mr. Wiinstead had invited me into his study, spoken in monotone about how it was only right that we should all suffer as Christ himself suffered, that it was through his empathy of our misery that he could heal us. To be tormented was to be human, wed to our condition. Mr. Wiinstead was no priest and I was no Catholic. I let him speak to me about these things, tell me that the only way to regain my strength would be to give myself to the service of others.

"We've been contacted by Duke Leone Caetani di Sermoneta." I didn't know what this name meant, so I said nothing. "A duke from a very noble Roman family, as you may know. They hold land all over the country." Mr. Wiinstead looked down the hall and took a breath, then held it high in his chest, as though he had something to do with their landholdings. He turned back toward me. "He's requested a meeting with you tomorrow."

"I don't know this man."

He looked directly at me for a moment, brow tight, eyebrow cocked, then looked away. "He's been given your name and your location from someone who does. I have reason to believe he may be coming to offer you employment."

Both the letters and the money orders I'd been receiving had stopped coming. Whether it was the war that had delayed them in the post or something else, I didn't yet know, but I didn't want this duke taking me away. What I wanted was more rest. To be as soft and as pliable as a sheet, tucked away in the cloister until Hermann could come for me so that our lives could continue as they should.

"You are welcome to stay here with us, Miss Jüül." Mr. Wiinstead looked into the refectory, watching the girls clear tables with a detached fascination, as though they were in the distance, animals grazing on a hill. "You're well enough to be of some service. And," he paused, "I've written to you of my intentions." In his office, he had spoken to me of God and philosophy and ways to strengthen the human spirit, but Mr. Wiinstead had made no inappropriate advances. These he saved for letters in which he wrote to me of his great respect for my mind.

"You have, sir." Light dropped from high windows to the tables in jagged rectangles. The girls walked through them as they cleared tables, from shadow to light and back again.

"Have you given my suggestions any thought?"

"I have, sir." What Mr. Wiinstead had proposed wasn't quite marriage, not yet. I was a damaged woman, after all. Both my mind and body tattered. I would need to recover, to gain my strength and then to repent, stitch up the frayed edges of my thoughts. Mr. Wiinstead wanted to give me some time, under his own tutelage and guidance. I didn't tell him that no time would be balm enough for me to consent to marry a greying Danish man and join him as caretaker of a cloister in the Italian countryside.

When I didn't say anything else, he said, "I suppose the duke will be able to offer you more in some respect. Far less in others. Italy has examples enough of how power is at odds with a spiritual life. And with this war . . . I just hope you consider the merit of a simple, healthful life in the service of God."

"Of course. I will." The refectory was nearly cleared. Two girls were still wiping down the tables, cloths in hands, arms sweeping broad arcs across the surfaces, moving toward the middle.

In the library the next morning, Mr. Wiinstead brought the duke into the room. On introduction, I bowed slightly and held out my hand, my arm trembling slightly. My hand had not yet healed properly, had become reinfected more than once at the cloister, and it was bandaged again. The duke was more than a foot taller than me. He turned and nodded once toward Mr. Wiinstead, a signal for him to leave. The duke said, "Please, sit," so I did, on the edge of a straight-backed chair, my hands flat on my knees. He walked the room, looked at the books, pulling some out and turning them over before sliding them back into place, each fitted against the others. Eventually he said, "I understand that you've come from Egypt."

"Yes, sir."

"No need for *sir*." He was still looking at the shelves. "A fascinating country, isn't it?"

"It is."

The duke turned and came toward me, sat in a chair opposite mine. "I've spent a lot of time in that part of the world, so I know it can also be difficult."

He looked at his own hands and I did as well, his fingers long and tapered. "Sometimes, the people could be – I heard it described once as *brutish*." I had said too much, the wrong thing.

The duke folded his hands in his lap, looked directly at me for a moment. "I suppose that people can be brutish anywhere."

"Yes, I suppose they can." It had been unseemly to bring that up. I would find a way to make more appropriate comments.

"You've been told why I'm here?"

I wasn't sure. "I believe so."

"My wife is pregnant. The baby will come soon and she'll need help. I've several people to help us – a governess, a nursemaid – but I'm looking for someone more for her. She's fragile." He looked at me for a moment, then away. "Her health is fragile. She could benefit from a companion, someone to help her through this, to make appointments, that sort of thing."

"Of course." Why had this man come to me?

As though answering, the duke said, "I believe that we knew some of the same people in Cairo."

"Oh?"

"I used to travel there quite a bit on political business – a kind of diplomacy, really. I spent some time at the Danish consulate." I saw light riding the curved rims of wineglasses, felt the warmth of Hermann's hand briefly on the sway of my back as he walked by. Had he given the duke my name? This wasn't right. It was supposed to be Hermann who came for me, or even Onkel at the least, not this stranger, noble though he was.

"You will be able to relocate to Rome?"

We had agreed that I wouldn't leave the cloister. That Hermann would come to me when he could, when the war waned and he knew how he could care for his child. But, as the war blustered on, the letters had stopped coming. The baby was gone and I'd had no way to tell him. I carried nothing, received nothing. Perhaps the duke's nobility enabled him better contact with Egypt. Perhaps he was a kind of messenger and it was understood that I was to go with him.

"Miss Jüül?"

For how long had I been quiet? I held my elbow against my waist, my bandaged hand trembling again. How I wished someone had been able to send me instructions on the answer I was to give. Finally, I said, "Yes, of course."

"We've already quarters set up for you at the villa where my wife is now. She'll like you, I can tell."

"I'm sure I will like her as well," I said, though I was certain of so little.

"You'll be able to come with me today, then?"

"Yes, I will." I had only a few things to pack – clothing and books, no household items.

"I will speak to Mr. Wiinstead. Have them bring your things to the west entrance – I have a car waiting there for us." I wondered who he supposed would be tasked with bringing my things. I asked Clara and a couple of other girls to help me. Before I left, Clara pulled me back, behind an archway. "We'll come visit you, Marie, we will! If, that is, you'll admit us into the home of nobility."

"I'm sure it won't be up to me."

FIFTY

The duke's home, Villa Miraggio, was perched on the highest hill in Rome. Inside the gates of the courtyard, two men appeared and walked off with my trunk as a woman took my arm and began to lead me away. "Mrs. Domitius will get you settled and introduce you to Ofelia." The duke nodded and left, and it was she who led me through the construction, stepping around tools, materials and men with equal efficiency. We took a staircase without a railing and emerged into a part of the villa that was complete, glass on the windows and rugs on the floor, heavy doors hinged to frames. A few more hallways and arches and there was furniture, art hung on walls.

Ofelia was in one of the upper bedrooms, on a chaise near the window, her legs folded and covered in a blanket, belly high and round under her breasts. She turned when I came into the room. "Thank you so much, Mrs. Domitius. That will be fine." The older lady stood beside me near the doorway. Ofelia looked from one of us to the other, her eyes not long on me. "Miss Jüül, is it? Come in, come in!" and, "That will be all, Mrs. Domitius." I walked toward her with a steady gait, as though approaching a dog I'd been assured would not bite. I had no reason to be afraid. Ofelia was looking out the window when she said, "Please, have a seat," and gestured vaguely into the room.

I chose a chair, turned to smile slightly at Mrs. Domitius, who was still standing in the doorway. Once she left and closed the door behind her, Ofelia turned to me. "Silly old hen!" She winked. "She's upset because she thought she would be the only help I would need, apart from those who will be with the baby, of course."

I kept the slight smile on my lips, hands in my lap, perched on the edge of the chair.

Ofelia smoothed the dress over her belly, tucked what I assumed were stray hairs, though none were visible to me, behind her ears. "Thankfully, Leone agreed I should have someone closer to my age. I don't need to be looked after by someone as old as – no, older than! – my dear mother, may God bless her soul." She traced the sign of the cross against her chest and closed her eyes.

I waited for what might happen next and said nothing, not knowing if I was expected to speak.

After a moment, Ofelia opened her eyes and turned to me. Her face was beautiful in its symmetry, colour high on her cheekbones, her mouth full, eyes deep-set, lids heavy. She looked languid, as though she could fall asleep at any moment, and I knew the feeling, the weight of sleep at one's centre that could press outward and pull a body down. "So, you are Miss Jüül."

"Yes." My first word to her, spoken in Italian. I'd learned enough in my time at the cloister to speak quite well, though my accent was thick, hard to identify, I'd been told. "Pleased to meet you, Duchess."

At this, she laughed. "Oh, my! They haven't told you?"

In the household, I had met only the duke and Mrs. Domitius so far, and neither had told me much of anything.

She shifted and spoke to me in French. "I'm afraid the Roman Catholic Church has yet to approve the annulment of my husband's first marriage, so – I know, it's wretched – but I am not quite a duchess, simply a lady."

A mistress, I thought. I answered her in French as well. "Oh, shall I call you that, then: Lady Ofelia?"

She swatted her hand in front of her face. "Goodness, no! Call me Ofelia." She leaned toward me, reached out her hand as though to touch my own before dropping it to her blanketed lap. "You and I are going to be friends." Ofelia leaned back, closed her eyes again and sighed. "The Caetani seniors quite approve, you know."

I didn't know if she was speaking about our new friendship, such as it was, or about anything else, so I listened.

"Well, *approve* may be a strong word. We are in Rome, after all, but the duke's mother and I – we have something. Some kind of understanding," she told me. "I can't explain it. A feeling of kinship, I suppose, even though that sounds trite. Did you know, Duchess Ada once climbed a peak in the French Alps on her own?"

Ofelia had switched back to Italian, and I was doing my best to follow along. The duchess Ada must have been the duke's mother – a mountain climber, apparently. That was surprising.

"Not that I am a mountaineer – my health wouldn't allow it – but I think she appreciates my spirit." Ofelia held her throat, then traced her fingers along her collarbone. "And his father, I imagine he's just glad I'm not a Colonna."

I remained quiet.

"Not even God approves of that marriage, I'm sure!" Ofelia crossed herself and lowered her chin. When she looked up again, she said, "You've hurt yourself." She gestured toward my bandaged hand.

"Yes, but not badly. The dressing will come off soon."

"Well, I know that even small injuries can take some time to heal – just try not to get into any trouble here. This household seems a bit accident-prone!" Ofelia was grinning again, flushed.

I wasn't sure if the words *trouble* and *accident* implied more. I didn't yet know how much was genuine, how much was a lark to Ofelia.

The house girls passed to me pieces of rumour and lore, in quick and sometimes rough Italian, as they oriented me to the partially completed villa. They showed me the kitchen, though I would have little need to be there, they told me. They pointed out the unfinished stairway to the staff quarters, but my own room would be in a different wing, near Ofelia's. As I mapped the parts of the villa that were still under construction, the rooms and the roles of the staff, I collected each bit of gossip, put them together in ways that I could make sense of the family. I learned that Vittoria Colonna was the name of the duke's wife, the daughter of a family as noble as his own whose rivalry with the Caetanis went back as far as each line could be traced – ten or eleven centuries by then. Their marriage had united two of the most powerful families in Rome. "It will never be annulled," one of the girls told me. "The church won't allow it – the pope, personally, will not allow it."

Another girl whispered to me about Vittoria Colonna and her own dalliances – kings and politicians and artists, I couldn't keep track. "It's no wonder, really. I mean we've heard that the duke has had his own affairs – they all do – but it's not so surprising that he'd eventually fall in love with someone else, his own wife more interested in society balls and foreign royalty than in him." These girls, some no more than sixteen or seventeen, thought that they had these tangled relationships figured out. So rarely can anyone other than two people in love know what goes on between them. I tried to take it all lightly. Eventually, I didn't hear much from anyone beyond Ofelia. I supposed I'd proven loyal, that my sympathies lay with her. I tried to capture more slips of gossip, but the rumour mills turned without me and I didn't catch even the bits of chaff they threw off.

In the last weeks of her pregnancy, Ofelia was confined to bedrest, attended to by the Caetani family doctor and a contingent of starchily uniformed nurses who may have been called away from the Italian front to look after her, the duke's mistress. I tried not to form judgment about this. I wasn't certain what was wrong with Ofelia. It seemed that no one was. "Weak heart, poor dear," I heard one of the kitchen women say. "Constant nausea, swollen legs," a house girl told me. Another told me that the baby was in a poor position, though no position seemed ideal carried by a frame as small as Ofelia's. I was more petite than she – I was often mocked for my diminutive stature – but she seemed more fragile.

The baby was born in August, a little over two months after I arrived. Professor Manzonni, the Caetani's elderly family surgeon, was called. I sat in a small room outside Ofelia's quarters as house girls came and went with pots of hot water, cloths and linens. The walls were coated in steam, the air rusted with the smell of blood. After a time, the girls began to emerge with sheets and blankets clotted red, and the younger girls began crying, out of sorrow or fear or melodrama I wasn't sure. I didn't ask any questions. I assumed I would be told what to do; told when I could help. I heard, "loss of fluids," and, "the professor wants the herbalist here." After hours of tension crackling through the villa, the duke was invited into Ofelia's quarters. He emerged cloaked in his own exhaustion but with a cigar in his mouth, his full eyebrows raised, eyes bright. "She's the most beautiful baby girl!" he announced. "Let's ring some bells!"

It was Mrs. Domitius who said, "You know we can't, Your Grace."

"Who says we can't?"

"You know the people will –" she paused. Bells were only rung to celebrate the arrival of the recognized next of kin of nobility. "They will be expecting –"

"I don't care much for expectations or customs, my dear Mrs. Domitius. Now who will show me the way to the bell tower?" It was soon clear that he'd been bluffing; the duke was not going to ring any bells. "I'm going to go tell Mother and Father," he announced to those of us who were in the room. "They will be so excited!"

When he was gone, one of the girls said, "Excited? Imagine. For the illegitimate child of his mistress? And a girl at that." Mrs. Domitius told her to hush and get back to work.

When I first saw Ofelia after the birth, the baby wasn't with her. "She's with the wet nurse. I don't have much strength." She lay flat against the sheets, tapped of colour. There was a bassinet across the room, flounced with layers of eyelet and lace, a satin ribbon bowed at its crown. I wondered if the baby had slept there yet. "She's so beautiful, Miss Jüül." Ofelia's voice was thin, a waver to it. "She looks so much like the duke, it's a bit unnerving, but you'll see, she's just so lovely."

"I'm certain she is." The bedclothes over Ofelia's chest began to darken, and though it had been months by then, my own breasts responded with a hardening and an ache. She was leaking breast milk as another woman fed her baby, yet Ofelia hardly seemed to notice. There was a sheen of moisture across her face and I reached out to touch her skin. Ofelia was so hot that it surprised me. "I will get one of the nurses – perhaps the doctor?" She was already asleep but I kept my hand on her forehead for a moment. I remembered Clara's hand around mine in the hospital, Sisters Bertha and Anna. How they prayed above me; how when I opened my eyes, they told me I was loved. They were so certain. I regretted my own faltering faith. The love of man and God alike seemed fickle, wan. It could fill me one moment, then drain away like blood down my legs, drying.

Fifty-One

Sveva Ersilia Giovenella Maria was a strong, lean baby with a full head of hair and a face so much like her father's already, it was startling. When she cried, she howled, and I wouldn't have been surprised if she was heard for blocks around the villa. Sveva bellowed, balled her little fists, and Ofelia called for her sister, Emerika, to come to the villa. She lived in Florence, where she was married to a Spanish doctor and had her own small son. "They'll be fine for a couple of weeks, my boys, I'm sure."

Emerika slept late each morning, then trailed behind me in nightgowns and robes, her speech a murmured commentary on the machinations of various politicians, theatre actors, artists and Caetani family members. She spoke even of the calibrated worlds of the staff that skittered around all these figures. She seemed to think of me as a confidant. She and the duke adjusted to the other's presence, though neither seemed fond of the other. Emerika was a larger woman than her sister – taller, her curves more insistent in her dresses, her waistline cinched more tightly. One would have thought that, of the two sisters, she had been a singer in a supper club, but that had been Ofelia. Ofelia, with her sallow skin and dark smudges under her eyes, looking more mysterious than sickly then. The smoky curl of her voice making people lean in close to hear. At the end of her sets, she would turn quickly, the layers of her skirts moving like fog across the dim stage, and leave immediately after performing. She refused anyone's company for hours.

It was from Emerika that I learned all this. "It's slightly scandalous, how they met." She lowered her voice. "A dinner club." I wondered if it was a euphemism for something but would not ask. "Not anything untoward about the club or the entertainment, of course," she clarified, as though reading my mind. "Ofelia and I are extremely well-bred." We were in the parlour and Emerika studied herself in a mirror above the fireplace. "She's a better opera singer than chanteuse, to be honest, and that's what our parents would have preferred for her – all those years of voice training. She made an absolutely lovely soubrette but, when our parents died, it was clear that she wouldn't make it past that role." She turned to me. "Our parents would have been mortified, of course."

Of course, I said, but only in my mind.

She smiled, but not with her usual gaiety. "But they're gone now, and while, my God, my sister did not need the money, I feel as though part of her needed to be something beyond the role of a soubrette – to be more seen, somehow. I mean, she truly was something." Her admiration seemed genuine. "You wouldn't know – she was as fragile, as quiet in some ways as she is now, but a slight roll of her wrist, tilt of her chin, and she could have a room enthralled before even singing a note. It's no wonder, the duke."

The wet nurse would bring the baby in to see her, but Ofelia slept for most of each day. While her sister rested, Emerika wanted to visit with me, but I had work to do. I had learned about the schedule of a duke, landowner and parliamentarian, how hours of the day and days of the week were to be slotted up against one another. As with the Brandts, I kept the family's social calendar, made any appointments that were necessary and ensured that baby Sveva was adequately cared for, if not by her mother. When the duke had duties to attend to out of Rome, which was often, it was I who adjusted Ofelia's days to keep her occupied and entertained while she was awake. All I had to do was set up the Victrola with some records in the parlour, set Ofelia up with blankets over her on a chaise, and the sisters would punctuate a couple of hours with the titters, groans and lilts of their conversation, though eventually Ofelia would tire.

"Miss Jüül!" Emerika called to me on one of these evenings. "Honeybee, darling, Jüüly!" Her sister called me by endearments earlier and more often than did Ofelia. "Come, come!" She patted the settee beside her, a signal to sit down, though I remained standing. "Oh, you!" She pulled me down, nearly on her lap.

"Emerika!" said Ofelia. "You leave poor Miss Jüül alone."

"It's all right." I shifted but our hips were still pressed against one another. I tried to sit straight, even stiffly. Though Emerika encouraged me, I knew I was not to lounge around the villa with the sisters.

"So, Moconni." Emerika's mouth twisted into a smirk.

"Mr. Moconni?" I repeated the name of the sisters' estate agent. He'd been by the villa three times since Emerika had arrived, each time with papers for the sisters to sign after he'd explained each one, a process which lasted hours.

"You must know." When I didn't respond, she squeezed my knee and I jumped a bit. "Oh, you. The poor man is besotted!"

I continued to sit as still as I could beside her.

"With you, our Miss Jüül!"

"Well, Emerika –" started Ofelia.

"But it's true!" Emerika shifted on the settee, our hips rubbing against each other, and I battled the impulse to stand, straighten my skirts.

"True or not, I will not have our estate agent make off with the best staff I have."

"And you'd deny her love over being subservient to you, darling sister?"

"I would deny no one love, would I, Miss Jüül?" Ofelia spoke to me as though we held between us many more confidences than we'd shared then.

"We know you don't want to be left to contend with the Caetani family on your own." Emerika stood up, and I sank into the space she'd left behind.

With what was there to contend? Nearly a thousand years of family history. An estranged wife from a rival family, a marriage blessed and now gripped in the fist of the pope. Little did I know then how the currents of dissent in Italian parliament would swell outward, and I hadn't yet heard of the Caetani family curse. Though I carried the heft of my own grief, little seemed to affect us in Miraggio, moving from room to room, the walls being built around us in the villa on the hill.

Emerika continued teasing. "It seems like the duchess Vittoria couldn't cope with being around the Caetanis for any period of time – gallivanting around Europe as she has been for the last twenty years."

"Why do you have to bring up that woman again?" Ofelia threw off her blankets and got up to change the record. When she stood, she looked at me. "Rumour and speculation." Then, to her sister: "Remember that." After a moment, Verdi's *Falstaff* crackled through the room.

Later, when Ofelia was resting, Emerika said, "My sister makes a good show of propriety, doesn't she?"

She did. So much so that I could forget that I was staff to an unconcealed mistress of a duke.

"She's the first of the duke's rumoured mistresses to usurp his wife. I've heard often how desperately the duchess Vittoria wanted to live outside the walls of Palazzo Caetani, to get away from his overbearing family. In twenty years of marriage, the duke wouldn't concede."

I couldn't imagine the duke not yielding; he seemed so pliant, affably so, to Ofelia's will.

"And now, here my sister is, not hidden away or even in dark halls of the palazzo but on top of the hill, the lady of Villa Miraggio, the duke's staff her own." She reached out for me, held my narrow shoulders in the warm cups of her broad hands. I felt like a girl about to be turned out into the world, though Emerika, like her sister, was younger than me. She dropped her hands from their hold to her hips. "You could learn from her, Miss Jüül. I suppose we all can."

I was too old already to learn, though I was still curious. "And so." I paused. "How does she do it, then?"

Emerika crooked an eyebrow and laughed. "How indeed? My little sister had both our parents twisted around her pinky fingers as well, so you'd think I'd know her ways by now. I suppose it's not that she feels that she's better than anyone else, it's that she's never felt less than."

"And she's always been like this?"

"I can't remember her otherwise. At one point, I thought it was because she was the baby of the family. She's always been sickly, our Ofelia, *delicate*. We weren't nobility, but my family had enough to keep her well taken care of. She's used to people doing as she asks – but it's more than that." Emerika was now looking at herself in a mirror, turning her chin from side to side, patting the hair at her temples. A cool regard like a stern mother preparing a daughter for school.

She looked back to me, ring fingers on the tips of her eyebrows as though propping them up, with a small smile, not quite a smirk, but one more of knowledge than joy. She dropped her hands. "I believe that some people are simply born with a sense of entitlement – perhaps we all have this as babies, crying with the indignity of whatever needs are not immediately met. And perhaps some people hold onto that feeling for a lifetime. Who knows? Perhaps more of us should, Miss Jüül."

Eventually, Emerika went home to Florence, and we began to dine with the duke's family at the palazzo more often. Dinner with the Caetanis lasted for hours, often until nearly midnight. One night, as we left, when Ofelia was saying goodbye to Duchess Ada, Marguerite – the American who had married Leone's brother Roffredo – leaned toward my ear as though we were confidants. "The duchess does seem to genuinely like Ofelia." She stood straight to wave at Michelangelo, who raised his hat to us, then bent toward me again. "She's extremely lucky, of course, to be so warmly welcomed."

I remained looking ahead, my expression neutral, I hoped.

"It's unfortunate, it really is, that the child will never carry the Caetani name."

Then I turned to her. "What do you mean?"

"As much as Duchess Ada seems to like Ofelia, and utterly adores her granddaughter, of course, it's still Rome and they are still Catholics. Sveva may grow up as a Caetani, but she'll never carry the name, never be officially recognized as such."

Ofelia had never talked about any of this, nor had the duke, and while it seemed obvious as Margeurite spoke, I hadn't previously thought of whether Sveva would be recognized or not within Roman society. It was as though Rome, for me, was lived entirely between the walls and courtyards of Villa Miraggio and Palazzo Caetani. Ofelia was not a Caetani, so her daughter wouldn't be either. I'd once thought the birth of children and formation of families were inevitable, everyone's right, including my own. I hadn't known it could be more of a privilege and that my own fate would veer, quite doggedly, to the unfortunate.

FIFTY-TWO

When she was well enough, Ofelia was invited to play cards with Duchess Ada at her quarters in the palazzo. While they played, the governess and I trailed Sveva as she toddled from room to room, hall to hall, and kept her hands away from statues, suits of armour, icons and the velvet cloths that hung over paintings. As we scurried after Sveva in the courtyard, a woman and a young man came down one of the stairways, stopped and stared at us. The way the woman watched us made me stop. She stepped toward me slowly and asked, "Who is that little girl?"

I reached for Sveva, who slipped from my hold, giggling, and kept my eyes on the woman the entire time. "She's Duke Leone's daughter."

"I see." Two thin cords appeared along the woman's neck, a flush of colour along her jawline. "You are her governess?" There was an edge to her tone that made me nervous, her words slow and measured as though strained through a tight throat.

"No. I am staff to the family, though."

"You are, are you?" She looked over my head as she said this. Beside her, the young man stood at an odd angle, immaculately dressed, hat pressed low, his hands pulling repeatedly, almost rhythmically, at the cuffs of his suit. He didn't meet my eyes, his gaze darting from side to side and then resting on a point directly above me before his eyes started to swing again.

Sveva and her governess were now gone from the courtyard and I felt uneasy. "Can I help you?"

"I would doubt that." She faced me again, her eyes narrowing to a place above my face. "I don't suppose that my husband, Duke Leone Caetani di Sermoneta, is here?" As she punctuated his name, the woman looked at me, her eyes large and dark against her pink skin.

"No, he's not."

"Well, I will see my mother-in-law, then." She didn't move and I wondered if this was my cue to let Duchess Ada know about her arrival, but the woman turned to the young man. "Come on then, Onorato, let's go see your dear granny." The two walked quickly across the courtyard in the direction of the duchess's wing of the palazzo, the young man's gait awkward and lopsided.

That night, I held Ofelia as she cried, sobs hacking out of her unevenly, an edge to them, ragged with as much anger as sadness. She sat up, pressed her hands over her eyes, covered part of her face. "You should have seen how that woman looked at me, Miss Jüül. You can't even imagine – it wasn't cruelty so much as disregard."

I could imagine. Oh, I could so easily imagine.

"She looked at me as though I was nobody, as though I'd always be nobody, not only to her but to anyone." Yes, I knew how this would feel. "When I told her that Leone was going to do everything – everything! – in his power to have their marriage annulled, she just laughed."

"What was Duchess Ada doing during all of this?"

"Oh, she was trying to help, really. Trying to talk to her, calm her, but then when it seemed like the young man was getting upset, Ada led him out."

"Was that the duke's son?" I'd heard of him from other staff in the villa, never from Ofelia or the duke himself.

Ofelia's hands were on her lap now, lying limp. She slumped when I asked this. "Yes." She straightened up, took a breath and said, "I cannot – cannot! – imagine how Leone ever married her."

"Was it –" I began, not knowing how to continue. "Was it more of a political or familial alliance than . . . ?" *Than love*, I thought, but didn't say the word.

"You would think, wouldn't you? That would be infinitely better, but no, he's told me himself that he was the one who chose to propose – within only a day or two of meeting her. She captured his imagination, or some such fool thing, by riding a bicycle."

"Riding a bicycle?"

"Yes, riding a bicycle. It didn't last long. He realized that she wasn't as carefree as she'd made herself out to be. And his ideals about equal rights and fair unions, she just scoffs at them." I didn't know the details of the duke's ideals, but I was glad that Ofelia did. I heard them speaking late at night, their voices a low thrum through rooms. I heard his teasing tone, her laugh.

"Do you think," I paused, "that she still loves him?"

"Good Lord, no! This has nothing to do with love. It has to do with how she appears in society. Leone cares nothing for all of that – nothing! – but to her it's everything."

"Perhaps she wants to remain married for the boy's sake."

Ofelia wiped the tears from her eyes roughly, left the skin looking pink and raw. "You saw him. He's nineteen or twenty now and – I'll say it – there's something wrong with him. No one has ever been sure what." She paused, and when she began speaking again, her voice was quiet at first. "Leone loves his son – he does, Miss Jüül – but it's been she who keeps him away from Leone and his family for months on end. She who treats Leone like more of a societal ally than a husband."

"That is perhaps not so uncommon?"

"No, I suppose not. I suppose it *is* common." Ofelia lowered her voice, as though uttering a curse or threat. "Imagine people like her realizing that she is, in fact, *common*." She stood up from her bed, patted her hair and then kept her hands on her head as she turned to me. "That era, her era, is ending. Those foolish society balls during which so-called noblemen swap lovers or rear up new ones." She dropped her arms, sighed. "What Leone and I have is different."

I knew so little of that world or its waning days, and I suspected Ofelia's knowledge was based mostly on what she'd heard from the duke and his family. She seemed so certain in her pronouncements, though, and I admired her for that.

FIFTY-THREE

I'd kept up correspondence with some of the sisters and girls from the cloister – flippant, chatty postcards back and forth. It was a surprise, though, when one day the distant ringing of the bell at the entry to the villa was followed by a house girl coming to me to say, "There are sisters here to see you." Sister Bertha and all the *As* – Sister Anna, Sister Adele, Sister Augustina – along with dear Clara, were lined up on the thin street outside the front gate.

"Come in! Come in!" I must have been shouting in my surprise to see them. Clara held my cheeks in both hands, then kissed each twice, three times. The sisters were more subdued in their greetings, but their faces were flushed pink, their eyes bright. They had been to the Vatican and were still intoxicated by it. I led them through the construction into a parlour that was complete, if not quite finished. A place to receive guests who weren't quite nobility. Clara circled the room, looked at the rugs, the large vases – each holding a different floral display – stopped in front of the gilded mirror over the fireplace. She smiled at me in the reflection. "And here you are, living among Roman nobility, yes, our Marie?" she asked, the sisters giggling with the thought. They were like schoolgirls that afternoon.

"Yes, I suppose so." I wanted to be more enthusiastic, grateful, but I suspected I sounded weary.

Sister Adele asked, "The duke, is he really a Muslim?"

I laughed at this. "Hardly! A scholar of the history of Islam. The family is quite Catholic, I assure you." They knew so much, these women cloistered away from the world. I wondered how news travelled to them. I was always one or several steps behind.

"Does this mean you've finally converted?" asked Sister Anna, a beat in her voice.

"Not exactly. But don't worry, there is hope for me yet."

"Oh, we know," said Sister Anna. "Has Mr. Wiinstead been by as well, then?" she asked.

"Oh no, no." I hadn't heard from him since he had arranged my meeting and departure with the duke.

"I'm surprised he hasn't come and whisked you away back to the cloister as his wife, Jüülchen." Sister Augustina blushed pink, as though she was saying something scandalous. "We can't all be married to God."

"I'd rather be married to God than Mr. Wiinstead."

Clara, finished looking around the room, came up beside me and knocked her hip into mine lightly.

"Would you like some tea? Some biscuits? Wine? Tell me and I'll get it for you."

"No, no." Sister Bertha adjusted her habit. "We can't stay long. We just wanted to see you, our Jüülchen. We'll send Mr. Wiinstead to come get you yet – just think, in marrying him, you can have all of us!" I laughed at this, kissed them all in turn.

Before they left, Clara turned to me and said, "There was someone at the cloister to see you, a man."

"Who?" A tight heat rooted in my chest.

"I'm not sure. He'd known you in Egypt."

The heat rose, hit the top of my skull and then spilled down my spine. "Did you tell him where I was?"

"Oh no. We wouldn't do that. I can't speak for Mr. Wiinstead, of course."

After they left, I climbed to my room, lay down, tried to teach myself how to breathe. Of course, I thought of Hermann. I had sent him my new address and told him to write me in return, so I wondered why he would have gone to the cloister. But if not him, who else could it have been? Onkel, most likely, perhaps acting as a messenger again. I searched my mind for what word I was to receive, and why it couldn't find a more direct way to me. I put a hand between my breasts, the other on my stomach. I felt the air rise and leave me, rise and leave. I began to sit up and felt a cramp sear my abdomen, as strong as pleasure had once flared through me with his touch. This wasn't a pleasurable tightening, though, but a scorching fist, twisting. I gripped my stomach and fell on my side, brought my knees to my chest to try to stop the ache. I sobbed with it. I didn't think anyone would hear me, but eventually Ofelia was in the room. "Miss Jüül, Miss Jüül, are you all right? Do you need a doctor?"

"No, no doctor. I'm in some pain, but I'm sure it will pass."

"I can't leave you like this." She knelt beside me, a position in which I'd never seen her. "I'll get you some of what Professor Manzonni gives me, just wait." Ofelia returned with small vials and a spoon and fed me medicine like an infant. I slept easily after that, though I thought I woke once to feel Ofelia behind me, one of her hands wrapped around my waist. That couldn't have been, though. When I woke again, it was the next afternoon and I'd missed most of a day.

FIFTY-FOUR

Increasingly, I heard rows in the halls of Villa Miraggio between the duke and one of his brothers, Gelasio.

Their voices followed me down corridors, through rooms – the sound of his brother's booming voice met with Leone's even responses. "You have no right to lease off – practically give away! – our ancestral land."

"I'm telling you, Gel, if we don't freely lease some of our land it will – I stress, *it will* – be taken from us. You know as well as I that Mussolini is gnawing his way through parliament."

"Is that so? And you know this, you who no longer holds a seat?"

"They will betray everything we hold true about this country. If you don't know this now, you soon will."

"You make pronouncements, grand gestures and – what? We'll give away our land for what? Gestures count for so little, brother. So very little."

At dinner one night at the palazzo, when Gelasio was not there, the duke announced that he would be leaving Italy. His mother put down her silverware and both Roffredo and Michelangelo stopped chewing and looked toward Leone. "You're what?" asked Roffredo.

I remained staring straight ahead, a heat gathering behind my eyes, then willed myself to look at Ofelia across the table. She stared back, her face immobile.

"I can't, in good conscience, remain in this country, more corrupt by the week, rotting from the inside out like a piece of decaying wood."

"A poetic description, certainly, but you're referring to what, exactly?" asked Michelangelo.

"Parliamentarians falling prey to Mussolini's so-called reforms, either agreeing with them or remaining in denial as to how they will change not only parliament but this country."

"You give that man too much credence, Leo," said Roffredo. "He's one of many who are justifiably frustrated at how we were shortchanged at Versailles."

"Exactly, and he's using that to take away more and more rights from not only labour unions but from all of us – which has nothing to do with Versailles and will redress nothing."

Ofelia and I sat still, facing each other, as the conversation moved around us. Neither of us ate, but she moved her hand toward her cutlery and stopped. I could see how she shook before she tucked her hands back onto her lap.

"Things are changing, yes, they always do, but perhaps in not such a dire direction as you seem convinced." Roffredo leaned back in his chair, crossed his arms over his chest. "Why would you think your leaving will make any difference, or any more of a difference than staying? You and Mussolini were on the same footing in parliament – now that you're no longer in government, who says you can't sway more people?"

"Our brother, the socialist prince." Michelangelo took a bite of meat, slid his fork between his teeth. "You think you're the only person who sees this as an evil takeover? You don't think Nitti and the boys can keep Mussolini in line?"

The duke barked out one laugh. "Hardly, Miche. You know Nitti will be out by the end of the year."

"Well, you seem to know a lot more about politics than do I – and a lot more about our bleak future! – so I'll leave that to you, big brother."

The duchess Ada had her fingers on her temples and her eyes closed. "Leone, what do you mean you'll leave Italy?" She opened her eyes and looked at him, her expression almost hopeful. "You know that you're always free to come and go – you all are." She looked around the table at each of her adult children. "They can't change your birthright or your titles."

The duke sighed. "Birthrights and titles mean so little to me, Mother, you know that. I am leaving the country, and not just on a holiday junket. I'm emigrating, as it were – and this may well mean that I forfeit my holdings."

"*Our* holdings," Michelangelo corrected.

"You can keep them, Miche, or try at any rate. And Roffredo, you're next in line for the titles if you want them. It's at the point now that if – when – I leave, there is a possibility I'll essentially be putting myself into exile. For a time, at least."

The duke's mother clutched her neck, her eyes wide. "No, Leone. No, that's not right. Of course you can never be in exile from your home." She looked from family member to family member, nodding as if to confirm this. They avoided looking directly at her.

Finally, Marguerite asked, "Where will you go?"

"America, though I'm not yet entirely certain where, specifically."

"Not yet entirely certain, are you, old boy?" mocked Michelangelo. "You've been turned out of parliament, taken up with your mistress, quite publicly, with no regard to your wife or the church, given away – pardon me, *leased* – ancestral Caetani lands for a pittance, and now you're going to emigrate as some kind of political statement, but to where you're not so certain. And leave the rest of us with the mess you'll leave behind. Good work. More than ten centuries of Caetani legacies felled in a few foolhardy swoops."

"I've felled nothing. The land leased to the villagers at a fair price is a pittance compared to the generations their families have worked it. Why would we, Caetanis, want to hold onto a wealth that is tainted by centuries of corruption by church, government –"

"Leone, Leone," his mother said in almost a whisper from the head of the table. "Enough, darling. We know that your intentions are good. We know, too, that our family is more cut out for libraries, concert halls and mountaintops than government, perhaps."

"You shortchange us, Mother," said Michelangelo. "Just because Leone is giving up on our country doesn't mean the rest of us will."

"I said nothing about giving up." Leone's voice was quiet and steady.

On our drive back to Villa Miraggio, each of us was silent. I assumed that Ofelia would retire with the duke, but when we got into the villa she said, "Miss Jüül will accompany me to my quarters." She looked at neither of us, held her cheek to the duke and he leaned to kiss it. He turned a tense, downward smile toward me, paused as though he was going to say something and then nodded as he left the room.

When we reached her room, I closed the door and Ofelia twisted as she struggled to get out of her dress. "I'll help." I undid each clasp carefully, watched my own hands tremor slightly as I did.

She stepped out of her clothes and perched on the bed, unfastened her stockings. I bent to pick up the dress. "Just leave it there." Ofelia's voice was curt, tired.

I let the dress drop, stood beside it. She threw each stocking, and they arced and fluttered before they crumpled on top of the dress. "Did you know?" I asked.

"That he was thinking of leaving Italy, yes. That he was going to make his grand announcement tonight, no." She collapsed back on the bed, arms held straight out from her sides. "He's been talking up his so-called New World for weeks. I've told him the phrase is already dated."

"You'll go with him, you and Sveva?"

Ofelia made a sputtering noise and sat up. "Miss Jüül, of course I'll go with him! We're family. What did you think we might do?"

"I'm sorry. I just didn't want to assume."

"Why wouldn't you? And I hope you're assuming that you will be coming as well? Because you are. I am not going alone."

"Of course not, you'll have the duke, and Sveva."

"Sveva's a child – and the duke is sometimes as impetuous as one. You're coming with me, Miss Jüül. I can't go without you." Ofelia folded at the waist, head in her hands, and began to cry. I stood where I was for a moment, then took two steps to her side, put my hand on her hair, rubbed her back as she sobbed.

Would I go? I couldn't imagine what I might do if I stayed behind. Hermann had answered none of my letters. I could return to Denmark, a childless spinster, and find work as I always had, but what employers would be better than the Caetanis? Ofelia was desperate to remain in Rome, but it was her home, not mine. I could go anywhere. I wouldn't expect a new beginning, not again. Instead, I would remain with people who treated me well, who held me in their confidence.

Fifty-Five

We left in March 1921, travelling first to London before we sailed from Liverpool on the *Empress of Britain* to Canada. I thought I was accustomed to sea travel by then, but Ofelia, Sveva and I were all sick for the entire journey, though Ofelia had the worst of it. Because we'd not brought a governess with us, it was I who spent much of the day with Sveva. The duke delighted in her but spent much of that trip writing, both correspondence and his academic work, as though in doing so he could both avoid and script the unknown we were sailing into. Ofelia was taking medication for seasickness and slept through the days, barely eating, so that she could attend the dinner and dance each evening. She would wake slowly, ask for some bread, then go through the routine of getting ready calmly, even stoically, as if it was something she had to bear, which I suppose it was. By the time she was ready for the evening, something would shift in Ofelia, as if she'd lit a little flame within herself. Her eyes would gleam, her skin shine with a soft, steady light.

One evening she said, "I know it's expected of me, this ritual – dressing, putting on jewels, presenting myself on the arm of a duke. I'm not saying I don't enjoy it." She lowered her voice to a lilt, "You know I adore the clothes," then continued, "I just know how little it has to do with me. I feel like I can hide in plain sight."

"Do you feel like the duke expects it of you?"

"In some ways, no. I know that in some ways he loves me for what I'm not – I'm not nobility, I don't care much about titles or big society parties. I just want to be with my family. To have a few comforts" – here she stopped and laughed at herself – "Well, a few luxuries, let's be honest! But in some way, of course, Leone expects it. It's all he's ever known, this world."

"I suppose soon enough we'll all know a different world."

"Yes, I suppose we will."

I got Sveva into her party dresses each evening for dinner and held her hand after the meal as we stood to watch her parents dance. Then I took her back to the cabin, tucked her in. "Isn't this an adventure?" we said to each other, over and over. I knew that Sveva's father had said it to her often, as though to instill that this was what it was – not exile, escape or avoidance, but adventure. "Isn't it?"

Sometimes after dinner, the duke would play cards in the men's lounge. On those nights, Ofelia would come to me. She would be sickly and exhausted, so I would help her undress and get ready for bed, as I had her daughter. "Lie beside me, Miss Jüül," she said one night. "Just for a moment. I have a hard time falling asleep alone." And so I did, lay in my evening dress on top of the bedclothes, Ofelia pinned under blankets beside me. We lay without speaking for some time, me listening to her breath, hoping it would deepen and lengthen to indicate sleep so that I could go. Instead, Ofelia whispered, "You've left home before."

"Yes." Over and over I'd left home – my childhood home, my home country, the home that I thought I had with H, so sweet and so small that we held it between us.

"How do you –" she paused. "How do you do it?" I waited for Ofelia to go on, but she didn't.

"Just like this. You pack your things, you board a train or a boat and you go."

"Was there a reason for your leaving?" *Isn't there always a reason for leaving?* I didn't answer and Ofelia kept talking. "I feel like none of our reasons for leaving Italy were my own – or Leone's, really. He pretends that setting off for Canada is some grand adventure, a sport, but really, we had no choice but to leave, it was just a matter of where we would go. Was there a reason you had to leave?"

She still knew so little of me, and this I didn't regret. As much as Ofelia felt increasingly like a friend, I was a paid companion, an employee. I wouldn't let myself be known as I had before. "There are always reasons for choosing to leave any given place, but no, there was nothing forcing me to leave my family farm, or Denmark. There were opportunities. I felt like it was time to go."

Ofelia turned toward me in the bed, and I knew she was looking at me though I couldn't see her eyes – the darkness in the berth was so thick I could barely trace her outline against the bed. "Do you think you'll ever go back?" she asked.

"I'm not sure."

"You know that your home is with us, Miss Jüül." Ofelia touched her hand to my cheek. "With me. We'll make the most of Canada while we're there, won't we? Until we can go back home again." I could hear how her voice faltered, how close she was to sleep.

When she touched me, it was meant as a small gesture, something comforting. While Ofelia was accustomed to being with the duke several nights a week, I wasn't afforded that measure of intimacy. Only she or Sveva touched me in any way that wasn't accidental. Each time they did, a current was set off under my skin with even the briefest touch. *We are meant to be held*, I thought as I got up from Ofelia's bed. She was asleep. I made my way from her berth to my own, lay awake, imagined an ocean of water rocking against the boat but was unable to sleep, so I got up and went out to the deck.

It was a different world than before the war; I was a different woman. This is what I told myself as I watched the bulk and glow of icebergs in black water set against dark sky strewn with stars. They told me all I needed to know of the world. And what was that? We are moving within the gears of some impartial machine, the darkness of our unknowing illuminated by something that lumbers by in the night. Their faint glow rises from under the surface while we are drawn to specks of light in the sky. The distance of stars makes no difference to us. From below, they appear so close together.

FIFTY-SIX

Canada, 1972

Between the duke's death and Ofelia's, we had secluded ourselves in the house on Pleasant Valley Road for twenty-five years. During that time, we each thought of how different our lives could have been. Even those thoughts were fallacy – ones that had sustained us, but delusions nonetheless. We made little fortresses of our former selves, our memories, as we fed ourselves pieces of our sister lives, as sweet and frothy as whipped cream or as bitter as pills broken in two, depending on the day, the moment. And then that moment became the next, and who is to say that what we thought, just then, hadn't split off and become something of its own? I knew now that thoughts became little more than daydreams unless we acted on them, took our chances with the outcomes, as I'd done over and over as a girl and young woman. If I couldn't be that person again, I would try to ensure that Sveva would be.

When Sveva began her schooling at the University of Victoria in 1970, what a pair we made. A fifty-two-year-old freshman and her eighty-five-year-old companion, we confused people. Sveva was often mistaken for a professor, and no one was sure who I was or what I was doing there. Around campus, students lolled and fidgeted, wrapped arms and even legs around each other, snapped gum and strummed on guitars, ukuleles. While most were well groomed, there were students who were more unkempt than the Roma we used to see in Europe. Ripped and threadbare clothing, uncombed and uncut hair, women without a trace of makeup, sometimes without a trace of supporting undergarments, either. Long-haired young men, loose vests floating over naked, skinny chests, smelling as though they gave as little thought to hygiene as they did to common social order. When we saw students barefoot, I thought of Dirk and Anna Soeberg, their tea shop and the salons they'd held in Zealand. This was more than the reckless fray of youth, Sveva told me, it was some sort of social movement – but the smell that came off some of those students! So pungent – *feral*, we would joke together. Ofelia would have been appalled. She found the sight of ordinary Canadians frightful enough.

We lived near the ocean. Sometimes, terrific storms crashed in from the Pacific and Sveva would drive us in her clattering car to watch swells hit the breakwater, arcs of spray fanning out and then falling like crumbling walls. During storms, the road was a mass of cars sitting and watching the show. "It restores my faith in humanity. There is some awe left!" Sveva said as she dashed out of the car. She wasn't even at the water's edge before she was completely soaked. She came running back, laughing as she opened the door. I sat in the passenger seat and looked out through the pouring rain, pretended not to see anything beyond the enormity of it all coming in, hitting the breakwater, and I'd felt then as though nothing had really changed, that it was all repetition, washing up against us again and again. But so much had changed, hadn't it?

In Sveva's final year of studies in 1972, Joan Heriot visited us for Easter. When we had emerged back into society, such as it was in Vernon, a few different social groups in the valley tried to lay claim to us. We knew that for all our oddities and unique needs, we – specifically, Sveva – were a kind of badge of honour to bear as friends. It was the Catholic Women's League that first took us in, but we had so little in common with those ladies, their faith straightforward and clear, their lives prescribed. I wished mine had been as simple, as clearly mapped, yet felt relieved it hadn't been.

We were introduced to members of the Naturalist Club, a group of eccentrics with a perhaps unnatural proclivity for birds. Slightly fanatical, but harmless hobbyists, really. There were several single people in the group, our contemporaries, spinsters and old bachelors. One of these was Joan Heriot, recently retired from her position as a zoology professor in Brighton, England.

"Imagine, MJ." Sveva had taken to calling me by my initials. "She was a fully tenured professor, even though UBC thought it might damage her womanhood to take such an advanced degree in science. She left Canada so she could get her doctorate, taught university and travelled all over the world as a scientist and now! Now, *she* has deigned to be my friend."

"Hardly deigned. You have as much to offer, Sveva."

She swatted at me lightly, then squeezed my shoulder. "You're too good to me, MJ. You always have been." If only she knew how good I was or was not.

Joan arrived on Good Friday, a taxicab dropping her off in front of the house. I was tidying the front room when I saw her get out and carry her airman bag to the stairs. But she didn't come up; I looked out the window to see her sitting on the bottom of the steep concrete steps, legs stretched out in front of her. At a glance, they appeared bare, though I thought she must have been wearing nude-coloured stockings. She was not one of the young larks with whom Sveva took classes. I went to the kitchen to wash and dry my hands. As I came out of the house, I saw that Joan's legs were in fact bare. When she heard me, she pushed herself up straight from her lounged position, then stood. "Oh, Miss Jüül!" she said and leaned into my face to kiss me on each cheek. She sat back down and I stood against the rail while Joan lounged. "How is our Sveva?" she asked, eyes closed, face to the sun.

"She's certainly enjoying her studies. I worry about how much pressure she puts on herself, though. It's a lot for her."

"Of course it is." Joan's voice was quiet, gentle. "I suppose she feels like she's making up for lost time. She'll do well. She's a strong woman."

"She is."

Joan opened her eyes and looked at me. "You don't sound convinced."

"No, no, it's not that." I looked down the street, the boughs of trees arched over its length. "I just wish now that I'd done some things differently."

She watched me as though I might say more. "We all do."

"I kept things from her, Joan. From everyone." There was something more I wanted to say, though I wasn't sure how, when Sveva pulled up, parked the car at an angle over the two lines of paving stones that made the driveway.

Joan propped up on her elbows, laughing, as Sveva opened her door. "Have the good islanders not taken away your licence yet?"

"They have not."

"I could hear you – I could practically feel you – grinding the gears for blocks, Sveva! That poor car."

"Poor car? The car is fine. Poor me having to try to maintain some momentum on these island roads – have you driven them? No thought to ease of travel. They wind round every twisted old oak tree that the road builders could find, I'm afraid."

Joan pushed herself up and leaned to kiss Sveva, who was a step down so she was the same height as Joan. I saw the colour grow along Sveva's neck before she held out her arms. "This is how we do it on campus." She pulled Joan toward her for a hug. "So many hugs – even doled out to old biddies like ourselves!"

The sun was bright and we squinted at each other. "It's glorious," Joan said. "You realize that the valley is in that awful time of year when all the snow has melted, revealing a season's worth of dirt that the sanding trucks left behind. The branches are still bare. Everything is dirt and muck and the prickly beginning of things."

"That sounds good," Sveva said. "*The prickly beginning of things* – like a poem."

Sveva and Joan did an admirable job with our Easter brunch. "We've decided enough with this Julia Child French cooking nonsense, we've gone with classic North American!" announced Sveva and waved her arm over the small table. There was a glossy ham studded with cloves and ringed with pineapple, a spiral of deviled eggs and a trembling dome of lemon Jell-O patterned with bright pink cherries, mandarin crescents and what appeared to be tiny marshmallows. I laughed at the sight of it, unlike anything I would have made.

"Well, perhaps it has a bit of French flair," I said. "It's like a work of art, ladies."

"Exactly!" Sveva looked delighted with the meal, with the two of them, really.

After dinner, when only the Jell-O sculpture remained, gleaming and still, I got up to clear the table.

"Oh no, you sit, Marie," Joan said as she got up. "I'd almost forgotten, I've got some mail for you both." She placed a small stack in front of Sveva, one letter in front of me.

Sveva sifted through hers. "Where are the bills? There must be some bills."

"Svev, darling, I signed off on the last of your bills the day before I left. Except for the banks, you don't owe a thing to anyone in the city of Vernon. Now, tell me that the same can be said of Victoria."

"Miss Jüül's been keeping an eye on my spending, haven't you, MJ?"

I was still looking at the letter in front of me.

Joan asked, "Who is the letter from, Marie?"

"Oh, just an old friend." I knew that both women wanted to ask more.

"Well, come on then, open it!" Sveva said as she scraped her fingernails into the edges of the envelopes in front of her.

I got a knife to slice open mine. It was from Sven Brandt, a short note to say that after more than a decade, he'd finally sold his father's property and when clearing it out he'd found photographs that he thought I would like to keep. I slipped them out of the envelope, stared at a black-and-white portrait of myself. Though it appeared grey in the photograph, I knew the dress I wore, the last Hermann had bought me, was the colour of raspberries. I could remember how lightly the silk fell against my skin. There was a flower tucked behind one of my ears – how whimsical that seemed to me now – and the expression I gave the camera was a slip of a smile. My eyes looked straight into the lens, one eyebrow slightly raised. I looked so confident, so knowing, as though I could anticipate what was going to happen next. How little did I know.

Both women looked toward me, expectant. "So?" Joan asked.

"Yes, so?" Sveva looked at me. "Don't leave us in suspense. Show us what you have there, MJ."

I placed the photos on the table, slid them toward the women.

"This is you?" asked Sveva, picking up one.

Joan held the other. "And who might this be?"

I had hardly looked at the one of Hermann and I together. I would, when I was by myself. "An old friend."

"An old friend?" Sveva raised an eyebrow. "From a time before you were with us? Who? Come on, tell us more."

"Not now, Sveva. I wouldn't even know where to begin."

"Oh, you tease!" She swatted at me and Joan passed me a glittering wedge of Jell-O salad. It looked as though it was lit from within as it came toward me.

How much of my story would I tell them? Not much, I decided, and ran my spoon into the trembling dessert salad, placed a cool slip of gelatin, sweet and tangy, on my tongue.

The women watched me as I ate. When I finished, I said, "That was perfect, ladies. Just as you two are perfect for each other." I looked from Sveva to Joan. "Please, do everything you can to be with the person you feel you can be the most yourself. Be with someone who makes you feel good. Fight for it if you have to, regardless of what other people think."

The women stared at me as though I'd gone mad, and who knows? Perhaps I had. I rose from the table. "I'm going to go for some fresh air now."

Fifty-Seven

Shortly before Ofelia's death, Sven Brandt had let me know he would be passing through Vernon and would like to meet. I had made a list of errands long enough to warrant the time I would take away from the house and arranged to meet him at the hotel across the street from the train station. I arrived first, sat on my own in the restaurant as I hadn't for years. There was a men's group there, Elks or Rotarians perhaps, tables pushed together in the middle of the room, ashtrays set to one side of their plates.

I saw him as soon as he came in, chimes knocking against the door behind him. I was the only woman in the dining room and he looked from table to table until he found me. Sven was a tall, slim man, like his father. As he came toward where I sat, I kept my eyes on him. He looked so much like H – even though Sven was older now than Hermann was the last time I saw him – and yet much like his mother, too. I stood, held out my hand. He took it in both of his and when he smiled, I saw him as a little boy. Our smiles don't change.

"Shall I call you . . . ?" he asked.

I'd a lifetime of being *Miss*. "Oh, Marie is good."

"Marie, then. It's good to see you."

"You as well, Mr. Brandt," I said, his name thick and weighted in my mouth. "My condolences, please –" He stopped me with his hand between us, picked up the menu as though to change the subject.

"Call me Sven."

"You're in Vancouver?"

"Yes."

"With family?" I ventured, as though we were simply friends making small talk.

"No, no more family really. I wrote to you about my father." He looked away, neck craned as though wanting to get the attention of the wait staff. He held one finger up as a call, then turned back to me. "My mother, she died in 1933, in Cairo. I had no siblings, no children, so now all family seems to be gone."

"Oh, I'm so sorry." My words sounded rote, insincere, even to myself. I was calculating dates in my mind, running numbers. Nineteen thirty-three. A year before Leone was diagnosed.

"After my mother's death, father carried on with the business for a while, but something shifted in him – everyone assumed it was the loss of his wife."

"Of course."

"But I knew it wasn't that. He hadn't been happy for some time. A year after my mother died, he immigrated to Canada, put my uncle in charge of the business."

"Onkel?" I couldn't help but grin, just a bit, at the thought of Hermann's brother.

"*Uncle*, that's what I called him, yes. Did you know him as that, as well?"

"That's what everyone called him."

The waitress was there, already pouring coffee into both of our cups, but I lifted my hand, said, "Tea, please."

"Onkel died in '42."

"The war?"

"Not fighting, of course – he was too old by then – but something related to the war. Something to do with our family company and how it was operating in Egypt. They'd received threats before, plenty of them. My father never forgave himself for not convincing Onkel to leave – the business, Egypt, everything."

"What did your father do in Canada?" I tried to keep my voice natural, level, but it went from hoarse to a squeak in a moment. Emotion crackled along my throat. The waitress returned and placed a teacup and saucer in front of me.

"He didn't do much, at first. Joined my wife and me in Vancouver, did some consulting. He bored of that fairly quickly, and with his shares of the business, he didn't really need the money. He bought some property and raised horses in Cranbrook."

Hermann had been in Vancouver; he had been in Cranbrook. He had been here, so close to me. I clutched the sides of my legs under the table.

"I'm sorry," he said. "This is a lot of information at once."

I loosened my hands and looked back up at him. "Oh no, it's not too much."

"He was, in some ways, a difficult man. For me, as his son."

I didn't have anything to offer him, no words. I picked up the teacup, touched the hot liquid to my lips.

"He wasn't happy. I thought I remembered him being happy once, when I was small."

"Yes." I said this involuntarily. I remembered our happiness in Egypt, though Sven hadn't been there then, hadn't been a part of that. Why was he telling me this? He had seemed so familiar to me a few minutes before, though I'd known him so long ago, so briefly. Now he seemed like a stranger. I didn't want him to tell me about his father and his horses and his unhappiness. That had nothing to do with me, with my life.

"This past couple of years, I've been going through his things. I should have finished in the weeks after the funeral, but I lost momentum."

I nodded, tried to sip my tea slowly, naturally.

"I found these." Sven lifted a large manila envelope onto the table. He looked at me as though waiting for me to say something. When I didn't, he told me, "They're your letters." I put my cup in its saucer. I tried to hold my hand steady but I shook so badly that the china rang for a moment before I put my other hand around it. "Yours to him and some copies of his to you."

I could not hide how my hands trembled, so I tucked them back under the table.

"He tried to tell me, before he died. He kept repeating your name – *Marie, Marie, Jewel*. I thought you'd been my nanny and I asked about you.

Oh no, not your nanny, she is the mother to your sibling, he said. I didn't want to hear it. Perhaps you can understand?"

I nodded.

"He said, *I sent her away. Forgive me*, and I didn't know for what he was asking forgiveness – for being with you while married to my mother? For sending the mother of my sibling away? I still don't know."

I was shaking – my entire body, not just my hands.

"What happened to the child?" Sven asked.

I couldn't say anything. Sven reached his hands across the table. "I'm sorry. This must be so hard. If I've got a sibling, though. My parents, they were so distant – with each other and with me. I've been divorced for years, no children. Now my parents are both gone and if there's someone else. Some family –"

I found my voice, though it was quiet, weak. "There isn't." I watched my own hands on my lap. "I went to a cloister in Italy to convalesce, as they called it then. I lost the baby. I never told your father. I went to work with another family and left a forwarding address. I'd hoped he would come. I'd hoped he would –" I finished the thought in my mind: *find me*.

"Oh." Perhaps that outcome had not occurred to him, though I couldn't imagine why not. How little men knew of the lives of women. The group beside us let out hoots of laughter, as though in response to my thought.

I looked at Sven. "It was expected in those days that I would give up the child. The baby would have gone to one of the orders of nuns. It was an honour to have them take a child born of sin on God's behalf." I didn't tell him that I'd already given a child away. That I'd given her to family, not God. His father, Hermann, knew of that child, and he'd accepted that of me, though he never found out what happened to his own. "I don't know if I could have given up your father's child."

"What would have happened if you hadn't?"

"It doesn't matter now."

I'd disappointed Sven, I could tell. He'd come to see me not to tell me that his father had loved me, but to find out where the sibling he'd never known was. He hadn't had enough from his family, but I couldn't give him more. "I'm sorry that I couldn't have told you something else, Sven."

"No, no, that's fine." He looked around the room. The men's group was standing from their meeting, putting on their hats, clapping each other on their backs. "And your husband, he has passed away as well?"

"Oh no, I never had a husband."

"Oh, but –"

"It can't be hard to believe that I never married," I tried to say lightly.

"But, my father. He told me that you were married when he came to see you in Vernon."

"He didn't come to see me."

"He tried. He told me that he had tried to find you in Italy, years before, but was turned away. After my mother died, he tried to find you again – he wrote to everyone he could think of who might be connected to the Caetanis, hoping someone would write back. He tracked down an address – in BC, no less. He came to see you in Vernon."

"He didn't, Sven. I never saw your father again."

"You weren't there. The lady of the house – the duchess? – told him that you'd been there until recently. It was in the mid-thirties, I believe. She said you'd married and had gone on your honeymoon."

"Honeymoon?"

"Yes, I believe that my father must have gone back more than once because the duchess later wrote to my father in Cranbrook. She told him to please not return, that you had moved north with your husband and that she couldn't give him the address. She asked that he not try to contact you again, that it would be best to start your new life and marriage without intrusions from the past."

In 1935, I was in Rochester, Minnesota, caring for Leone. He'd asked me to stay with his family and I had promised him I would while I kept the extent of his illness to myself.

"The only reason I know any of this is because her letter was with my father's things as well." He motioned toward the envelope. "I can leave these with you."

I tried to say something, or even to nod, but I couldn't.

"My father thought that he saw you once, years ago, at the train station in Vernon."

I watched my hands in my lap, turned them over so they were palm up, rubbed the pad of each finger.

"But he couldn't be sure it was you. He saw a man come up and embrace you. He assumed it was your husband."

"He did see me. I saw him as well." My voice was small, tight. I had to force it out of my throat, each word rooted in an ache that, once it reached my mouth, gathered there. I swallowed and swallowed, and I could feel pain leach from my neck to my shoulders to my chest, harden there, a weight in my stomach.

"I'm afraid I've a train to catch soon."

"Of course." I couldn't look at him. "I should be getting home, as well."

His father – Mr. Brandt, Hermann, my sweet H – had lived in BC. Did it matter now that we lived in the same province in Canada for nearly a quarter of a century? That he had tried to find me in 1935, that it must have been him whom I'd seen on the train that day in 1947? It was a different era, far from the one we'd once known together, yet every day I had remembered my Hermann as I had every day before. I thought he was locked in a different time, but he had been here. He had been here and so had I. We had been so close to each other in the world.

Fifty-Eight

While I was tipping back glasses of wine at the Danish consulate in Cairo, playing house with a married man, Leone Caetani was on the front, part of the fourth Italian regiment, fighting along Italy's northern border. His wife, Vittoria Colonna, was waiting for him in a villa on an island on which she and their son, Onorato, were the only residents. She waited until the artist Umberto Boccioni invited himself to join her there. Boccioni painted a portrait of Onorato, the boy that Leone had never accepted even though he was the duke's own son. The artist painted Leone Caetani's wife's portrait. Eventually, the artist stayed and Vittoria's letters to Leone were fewer, revealed less. While I was tipping back glasses of wine, Ofelia was singing in a dinner club in Rome, her dark eyes as haunting as the war, her voice both mournful and stitched with a lilt of hope. When soldiers came home, they went to see her sing.

All this was happening. None of us had met each other yet.

In the last week of 1960, I had circled the house to make sure the drapes were pulled shut against the cold, the doors closed. I'd found Sveva in the parlour in a chair pulled up to the fireplace, the dogs sleeping at her feet. She sat so still, I wasn't sure if she was awake.

"Sveva?"

"Miss Jüül." She didn't turn her head. "Would you like to join me as I stoke the fire with these scraps?"

My eyes had adjusted to the low light and I saw that she held a stack of her sketches in both hands, slightly fanned out like a deck of cards. I moved between her and the fire. "Sveva, no."

"Why not? These are little – nothing – more than kindling. If I were to have any sort of artistic practice, it would need to be more than scribbling sketches on scrap paper. And I'm not going to have any sort of artistic practice, am I, Miss Jüül?"

"Sveva, please." I held my hand out to her. "Whatever art you can manage, you must. I'll store these away in the basement until –" I stopped there. *Until what?* "Your mother is not well. She's asleep more and more. We'll find a way for you to do your art."

"*Do my art?* We will, will we? I recall you burning far more impressive works of mine than these. You didn't seem so concerned with my art then."

"Sveva, I thought –" What had I thought? "I thought this would end sooner. I thought your mother would get better. I didn't intend for this to happen."

"Well, somehow, your lack of intention and my lack of will has allowed this to happen, whatever this is." She turned and looked at me. "I suppose this is our life."

"I suppose it is, for now."

"For now? It has been for years, Marie. It may be a new year for others, but for us? What will change?"

"We can never know how or when things will change."

"Oh, but don't you wish we could?" Sveva tugged at her hair, cut over each shoulder, pulled her head back and exposed her neck, long and pale, unmarked by sun for so long.

"Are you in pain?" I asked Ofelia. Dr. McMurthie had administered her medication less than an hour before, so she was likely numbed.

"I am always in pain. I just want this to end, Marie. I want all of this to end."

"Here, darling." I gave her two painkillers with water, then shook two more into my palm. "And take these to help you sleep." Ofelia gagged a bit and held her throat as she swallowed. I stayed in the room as her breath slowed and waited until I was sure she was asleep.

I let ten minutes pass, fifteen, then I woke her. "Ofelia, darling, it's time for your medication."

She rubbed at her mouth, at her eyes without opening them. "Hmmm?"

"I'm sorry, Ofelia, I know you're asleep, but you need to take these now and then you can fall right back asleep." She opened her eyes for a moment, looked toward me with hooded lids. I moved her so she was more upright on the pillow, opened her mouth and placed two more pills there, tipped water past her lips, held her chin closed. When she'd swallowed those, I added four different pills. I left the bottle of painkillers, the lid screwed off, on the bedside table beside a full glass of water.

I heard Sveva coming up the stairs. I went out of Ofelia's room and closed the door behind me. "She's asleep."

"So will I be soon. No ringing in the new year for this old girl." Sveva spoke with forced cheer, her voiced edged in sarcasm.

"Sleep in your own room tonight, won't you, Sveva? You need a proper night's rest. I'll stay in here." I pointed to the small room beside Ofelia's. "I'll be able to hear if she needs anything."

I kept myself awake until shortly before midnight, then went back into Ofelia's room. Moonlight smattered across her bed; the shadows of trees shook on the blankets. Ofelia's breath was laboured and slow. I woke her as I had before, though it took longer to rouse her this time. Her body folded against mine as I tried to prop her up. I held her like a child over my lap, head cradled against the crook of my arm, placed more pills in her mouth, more water. Again, I held her mouth closed and though she bucked against me, eventually she spasmed and made a muffled yelp as she swallowed. Ofelia reared up and coughed some water onto my lap, but the pills seemed to have gone down. I settled her back onto the pillow, smoothed the hair from her face, folded and straightened the sheet under her chin, along her shoulders.

I held my hand against her forehead for a moment, as though checking a child's temperature, then ran my fingers along her cheekbone, over her nose, cupped her chin. I leaned to kiss her on the forehead. "Goodnight, Ofelia."

Fifty-Nine

Victoria, 1972

I walk down our street, then follow worn narrow paths in the grass through the cemetery to cross the road to the water's edge. The wind roughs up the shore, a ragged, moving hem, and I watch tugboats and tankers move, their slow, measured pace. Emerging from the other side of the peninsula is the ferry that takes people across the strait to America. The steady movement of the boats reminds me that there are lines of travel being cut and sewn all around us.

With me I have the photograph of Hermann and I together. I am not sure what I'll do with it. I run my fingertip along each edge and look at us both. Neither of us looks directly at the camera, our eyes diverted slightly to the left. From under his black hood, the photographer had instructed we do this so we wouldn't be temporarily blinded. For a moment, I can hear the flare of the flash going off, the crackling sound that followed. I slip the photo back into the pocket of my dress.

The ladies are sure to pester me to reveal more when I return. I've told my story, lived with it long enough. I want more for Sveva. Happiness. Love. I could not have it for myself and I've kept it from Sveva for so long. I want to be better to her than I was to her mother. I failed Ofelia. I won't do the same to her daughter. I've done my part. For everything I've kept from Sveva, I have tried to give her more. I want no one to tell her whom she can love, how or when. Her story will continue without me. And mine? It won't really end. Time moves through us as much as we move through it. It shapes us in memories that shift as we try to recall them. I watch as a pulsing flock of gulls obscures the sky then disappears, leaving nothing but a wash of pale, high blue. There is nothing to me but passing time, a faded photograph in my pocket. I've imagined my future and my past until they both seem like so many layered clouds changing shape. What we leave is all we ever had – our love, as bright as the sun and the other stars. This, you can remember. It's no longer my own story but yours. For all we are, and all we will be remembered as, time will keep changing the ending. The sea hurls itself against our puny shore, and I watch children fly their kites, shuddering in the air.

Afterword

Sveva Caetani returned to Vernon in May 1972 and became a secondary school teacher of art, history and social studies. She was admired and loved, a favourite teacher to many students. She died in April 1994 at age seventy-seven. Sveva Caetani bequeathed her home to become an arts and cultural centre and artist residence, now known as the Caetani Cultural Centre, in Vernon, British Columbia.

In 1978, while driving to work, Sveva conceived of a series of paintings that would depict her life story. She spent the next twelve years of her life completing this project. Toward the end of the series, Sveva's sight and physical health were failing, and Joan Heriot was of great help to her in completing her vision. There are fifty-six large paintings in the series, Recapitulation. The Alberta Foundation for the Arts in Edmonton, Alberta, now holds the Recapitulation series in its entirety.

Inger-Marie Jüül died in April 1973 at age eighty-eight. She spent fifty-six years of her life with the Caetani family and never returned to Denmark. The last known contact she had with Mr. Brandt was in letters from 1916. Her personal correspondence and papers were donated, along with the Caetani family's, to the Greater Vernon Museum and Archives. She was laid to rest in Vernon, BC, at the foot of the Caetani family plot in the Pleasant Valley Cemetery on Pleasant Valley Road, a little more than a kilometre from the house in which the three women spent so much of their lives.

Notes and Acknowledgements

Little Fortress is a work of fiction based on the real lives of three women: Inger-Marie Jüül (1886–1973), Ofelia Fabiani (1892–1960) and Sveva Caetani (1917–1994). I am grateful to each of these extraordinary women and have strived to honour the legacy of their remarkable stories.

I grew up a kilometre and a half up the hill from the house where the women secluded themselves on Pleasant Valley Road, walking by it countless times as a child and teen. It wasn't until I was at university that I discovered Heidi Thompson's collection of Sveva Caetani's art and writing, *Recapitulation: A Journey* (Coldstream Press, 1995). Published the year after Sveva passed away, it was my first introduction to her story, and I referred back to it again and again as I wrote this novel.

My major source materials in researching this novel were the personal papers and archives of Miss Jüül and the Caetani family, left to the Greater Vernon Museum and Archives by Sveva Caetani's estate. Thank you to Barbara Bell, Liz Ellison, Jean Manifold and the staff who provided a warm, welcoming space to read through file upon file, box upon box of Caetani archives left in their care. Joanne Georgeson's enthusiasm, in particular, was unflagging as I returned year over year.

Hélène Morgan translated much of Miss Jüül's correspondence and journals from Danish into English for the Greater Vernon Museum and Archives. Had it not been for her, I would not have had access to the stories and thoughts that lay within those papers in Marie's own words. My gratitude to Hélène for volunteering her time and skill in translation, and for meeting with me to talk about her first homeland, Denmark.

Other material that was invaluable to my research was *Caetani di Sermoneta: An Italian Family in Vernon, 1921–1994*, edited by Catherine Harding, with essays by Karen Avery, Melissa Larkin, Sarah Milligan and Carla Yarish (Greater Vernon Museum and Archives/Vernon Public Art Gallery, 2003); and Jim Elderton's film *Sveva: Prisoner of Vernon*. I had fascinating conversations with Daphne Marlatt on our literary projects based on the Caetani archives. Marlatt's own process led to the powerful collection *Reading Sveva* (Talonbooks, 2016).

I spoke with two women who had close friendships with Marie Jüül: Joan Heriot (1911–2012) and Kay Bartholemew (1920–2018). Each shared memories of their time with Sveva and Marie with love, warmth and humour. I feel fortunate to have been able to meet these amazing women and to have been offered a glimpse into their own remarkable lives, as well.

Several people were generous with their time and willingness to share their memories and stories of the Caetani family and the three women: Jude Clarke, Jason Dewinetz, Sharon Lawrence, Christine Pilgrim, Murray Sasges, Andrea Schemel, Peter Shostak, Sue Steinke and Larry Thompson. My sincere thanks to each of them for entrusting their own stories to me. Several other Vernon residents offered anecdotes and observations on the family – I am grateful for every snippet and story shared.

The house on Pleasant Valley Road was left by Sveva to become the Caetani Cultural Centre (www.caetani.org) in Vernon, BC. I wrote an early draft of this novel as writer-in-residence there and have returned several times to write, teach and attend cultural events. Thank you to Susan Brandoli, the staff and the board of directors for respecting Sveva's vision in making her home an artistic and cultural hub in the Okanagan.

Thank you to all who helped me take this research, obsessive interest and years of my life and make it into a book: the BC Arts Council and Canada Council for the Arts for providing vital and appreciated funding for earlier drafts of this novel; Martha Magor Webb, more than a literary agent, an early editorial voice, as well as one of encouragement and persistence; Noelle Allen,

Ashley Hisson and Paul Vermeersch and all those whose editorial, publishing and design acumen and expertise come together to make beautiful books at Wolsak & Wynn and the Buckrider imprint; Emily Dockrill Jones for thoughtful, spot-on copy-editing; and Jen Sookfong Lee, who was the perfect editor for this book – not only are her insight and intellect measured with humour and respect, but she loves these women as much as I do and knew how to guide me to tell their stories in the best way possible.

My first splendid, intrepid readers – Natalie Appleton, Kerry Gilbert and Karen Wall; all the thoughtful, astute readers who followed – Marita Dachsel, Aaron Deans, Jason Dewinetz, Jennica Harper, Lorna Rosnau and Jill Wigmore; Nancy Lee, who went above and beyond and read three different versions of this novel; the spokes on my writing-community wheel who keep me going forward even when I backpedal – Hannah Calder, Michelle Doege, Kristin Froneman and Karen Meyer.

My children, Jonah and Amalia, who cannot remember a time in their lives when I wasn't researching, writing or rewriting this novel, and who keep me going with their humour and love; my parents, Lorne and Lorna Rosnau, who provided not only emotional support but very practical, hands-on child care support, taking the kids for countless hours over the years that I was writing this. As always, every imaginable kind of thanks to Aaron Deans, who has lived with Ofelia, Sveva and Marie for nearly a decade and has never doubted that I would bring their stories into the world in my own way.

I write this from a desk in what was once Ofelia's bedroom in the Caetani Cultural Centre. Late afternoon light streams through the bay windows. Two young deer bound across the front yard of the Caetani property, then walk out the front gate. Pleasant Valley Road is much busier than it was when the women first arrived in Vernon in 1921, and when Sveva and Miss Jüül emerged from seclusion in 1961. Car after car drives by, and the deer watch them, look both ways, then step out onto the sidewalk and walk gracefully away from the house. Some things you just can't make up.

Laisha Rosnau, Vernon, BC, 2019

LAISHA ROSNAU is the author of the bestselling novel *The Sudden Weight of Snow* (McClelland & Stewart) and four critically acclaimed, award-winning collections of poetry. Her work has been nominated for several awards – including the Amazon Canada First Novel Award, the Pat Lowther Memorial Award and the CBC Poetry Prize (three times) – and has won the Dorothy Livesay Award and the Acorn-Plantos Award. Rosnau's work has been published across Canada and in the US, UK and Australia. She teaches at UBC Okanagan's Creative Writing program. Rosnau lives in Coldstream, BC, where she and her family are resident caretakers of Bishop Wild Bird Sanctuary. Visit her website at laisharosnau.com.